Date with a
REGENCY
RAKE

MARGUERITE
KAYE

ANNE
HERRIES

D1337925

MILLS
BOON

Mills & Boon, an imprint of Harlequin (UK) Limited, Eton House, 18-24 Paradise Road, Richmond, Surrey TW9 1SR

DATE WITH A REGENCY RAKE
© Harlequin Enterprises II B.V./S.à.r.l 2013

The Wicked Lord Rasenby © Marguerite Kaye 2009
The Rake's Rebellious Lady © Anne Herries 2008

ISBN: 978 0 263 90283 9

012-0213

Harlequin (UK) policy is to use papers that are natural, renewable and recyclable products and made from wood grown in sustainable forests. The logging and manufacturing processes conform to the legal environmental regulations of the country of origin.

Printed and bound in Spain
by Blackprint CPI, Barcelona

THE WICKED
LORD RASENBY

MARGUERITE KAYE

Born and educated in Scotland, **Marguerite Kaye** originally qualified as a lawyer but chose not to practice—a decision which was a relief both to her and the Scottish legal establishment. While carving out a successful career in IT, she occupied herself with her twin passions of studying history and reading, picking up a first-class honours and a Masters degree along the way.

The course of her life changed dramatically when she found her soul mate. After an idyllic year out, spent travelling round the Mediterranean, Marguerite decided to take the plunge and pursue her life-long ambition to write for a living—a dream she had cherished ever since winning a national poetry competition at the age of nine.

Just like one of her fictional heroines, Marguerite's fantasy has become reality. She has published history and travel articles, as well as short stories, but romances are her passion. Marguerite describes Georgette Heyer and Doris Day as her biggest early influences, and her partner as her inspiration.

The Wicked Lord Rasenby was Marguerite's first novel for Mills & Boon.

For J always. Just love

Prologue

1798—Sussex coast

As the clouds cleared, revealing the moon shining high in the night sky, Kit cursed under his breath. He had counted on the cover of darkness until they safely made landfall. Under the relentless beam of the nearly full moon, the *Sea Wolf* would be in full view as she stole into the remote cove, and that was the last thing he wanted. Surely his luck would hold. After all, it always had until now.

Casting a glance over his shoulder at the two huddled figures on deck, he gestured them to go below. *'Allez, vite'.* Placing a finger over his mouth, indicating silence, he returned his anxious gaze to the shore line. No sign at present of the Revenue cutter, but there was time yet. He knew he was under surveillance.

'All quiet for the moment, John.' Kit's voice was barely a whisper, showing no signs of the tension and mounting excitement he always felt when they neared home with a cargo. He almost *wanted* to be pursued. Faith, at least it made him feel he was alive.

Even as he spoke though, he caught a glimpse of a sail just off to starboard, approaching fast. 'I think they're on to us, John.' Kit felt the rush of excitement in his blood as the *Sea Wolf* wheeled hard. 'We have the wind in our favour, we can still make it.'

John, Kit's captain, and only companion on these night runs, peered anxiously through his spyglass. 'They've spotted us, Master Kit.' Keeping his eyes firmly fixed on the course, John showed no outward sign of worry—Kit would get them out of it if the worst happened and they were boarded. The greatcoat his master wore did nothing to hide the muscular strength of the man underneath, but it wasn't just Kit's height that gave him that air of command. It was the piercing blue-black eyes under those formidable black brows, the thin-lipped determination above that strong jaw that made John fear for any of Kit's foes. He was not a man to cross, that was for sure. Almost, John could pity the cutter's crew. 'They'll know where we're headed.'

Kit laughed softly, viciously. 'Of course they know. But we'll have time to unload before they reach us. I'll go and make sure our French friends are ready.'

The revolution in France was over, and the *Terror*, the mass slaughter of the French aristocracy, which had included King Louis and his queen, Marie Antoinette, was over too. But the *émigrés*, seeking shelter from the new regime, continued to flee to England.

The killing was not yet finished. It would go on, under one banner or another, for years. War was inevitable, and likely to be waged with England again, as anyone who even half-understood the volatile new French state could see. War would signal an end to these trips. But in the meantime, Kit was happy to do what he could to rescue those *émigrés* who made it to the French coast. He took no political sides, but believed one should live and let live.

It took but a brief moment below decks to address the two refugees. The Frenchmen listened with due respect. Kit was well known amongst what was left of the aristocracy as an efficient and courageous rescuer. Well known, also, for taking no payment, accepting no thanks. Addressing the men in flawless, if curt, French, Kit told them to be ready for a quick getaway. The thrill of the chase, the need for speed, the challenge of outwitting the customs men, gave a glow to his hard, handsome countenance.

He was as dismissive of the threat as he was of the men's attempts to thank him. Kit prided himself on doing this job well, down to the last detail. He had promised them safe passage and no one was going to prevent him keeping that promise. In this secret life, Kit allowed himself a sense of honour that his public persona had no part of.

A post-chaise would be waiting to take the *émigrés* to London. They would be off his hands, and it was unlikely that he'd ever see them again. The thrill was in the rescue, that was enough. They would have to sink or swim without him once he had safely landed them in England.

As he had predicted, the wind was in their favour, and the clouds too, played their part, scudding back across the moon to hide the yacht as she closed in on her berth. By the time the customs cutter came close enough to hail them, the *émigrés* were dispatched, with haste and brief adieus, to the waiting chaise. A final reminder from Kit that, should they happen to meet again, under no circumstances were they to acknowledge him, and the Frenchmen were gone. Keeping his smuggling life separate from his life in London was more important to Kit than he cared to admit. As Kit, he could be free. In London, he was somewhat more constrained.

The other cargo, a mere half-dozen kegs of French brandy, was safely stowed in the false floor of the boat house. Kit took his time responding to the hails from the Revenue ship.

'Well, Lieutenant Smith, we meet once more.' His smile was sardonic. He knew he'd won again, and he knew too, that the Riding Officer would make no move to search the *Sea Wolf* now. Lieutenant Smith would need more than a suspicion of smuggling before taking action against the Earl of Rasenby, owner of almost all the land in the surrounding area.

'Another night-fishing expedition, Lord Rasenby?'

'As you see, Lieutenant.' Kit indicated the box that John was unloading. 'May I offer you something to keep out the cold? Or perhaps a share of my catch for your supper?'

Lieutenant Smith bit down a retort. No benefit, he knew, in riling his lordship. It was more than his job was worth. 'Thank you, my lord, but I have a job to do. No doubt we'll meet again one fine night.' Lieutenant Smith consoled himself with the knowledge that at least his informant had been reliable. Next time, mayhap, Lady Luck and the weather would be on his side.

'No doubt.' As he turned to give final instructions to John, the sparkle died from Kit's eyes, and a slight frown marred his handsome countenance. 'Twas always thus. The thrill of the chase made him glad to be alive, but after, he felt drained of energy, listless, and reluctant to return to the tedium of his other life.

It had been close tonight, perhaps too close. It wasn't fair to continue to expose John to such danger, and, if he was honest, the excitement was beginning to pall. Kit had been smuggling for years, for the fun of it—brandy usually, silks sometimes. The human cargo had been a more recent addition, but the smell of war was in the air now, and the scent of change for France in the wind. The need for his services was coming to an end.

Nodding absently to John, and slipping him the usual *douceur*, Kit saddled up his patient horse and headed back across the marshes to his estate. One more run, he promised himself, then he would have to look for distraction elsewhere. One more run, then maybe he would take up his sister Letitia on her offer to find him a suitable bride, and settle down to a life of domesticity.

Lightly touching the sides of the black horse with his heels, Kit laughed out loud. He didn't know which he found funnier. The thought of Letitia's face at being asked to supply a willing bride. Or the thought of the poor, faceless bride, at being asked to wed and bed the most notorious rake of the *ton*.

Chapter One

Two weeks later—London

'You're surely not going out in that attire, Amelia?' The Honourable Clarissa Warrington looked aghast at her younger sister. 'You're positively indecent, I swear I can see through your petticoats.'

Amelia, the younger by six years, and at eighteen in full possession of her glowing beauty, simply laughed. 'Don't be such a frump. It's all the rage, dampening your petticoat a little. You'd know that, Clarrie, if you got out once in a while.'

'I've no wish to go out in the company you keep, Amelia. And if you're not careful, you'll find that you soon get the sort of reputation that goes with dampened underskirts. To say nothing of the fact that you'll likely catch cold, too.'

'Typical Clarrie, ever practical—I never catch cold. Now do stop and fix my hair for me.' Amelia turned the full force of her huge cornflower-blue eyes on her sister and pouted. 'No one does it like you, and it's so important that I look nice tonight.'

With a sigh, Clarissa picked up the brush. She could never stay angry with Amelia for long, even when she felt in the right of it. Amelia was attending yet another party with her friend Chloe and Chloe's mama, Mrs Barrington. Clarissa received the same invitations, but almost always declined. Aside from the cost, she had no wish to spend the night dancing with dull men who bored her to death with their insipid conversation. Or worse, having to join in with the obligatory female bickering and simpering.

Amelia was different. The latest styles and colours, who was likely to marry whom, were to her of the greatest importance. And it was just as well, thought Clarissa wryly, deftly arranging her sister's hair, that she found it all so entrancing. Marriage was the only thing Amelia was good for, really. Clarissa loved her sister, but she was not blind to her limitations. How could she be, after all? Amelia was exactly like their mama.

Marriage was in fact becoming a necessity for Amelia. Not, as their mama hoped, because she would make a fabulous match. With such a miniscule marriage portion, that was unlikely in the extreme. No, marriage was a necessity for Amelia because she had neither the skills nor the inclination to earn her own living. On top of which, Clarissa suspected that Amelia was falling into compromising company. If she was to reach the altar unsullied, a wedding must be arranged sooner rather than later.

'Who are you so desperate to impress tonight then, Amelia?'

Amelia giggled. 'I don't think I should tell you. You're so strait-laced, Clarrie, you'd be sure to run to Mama.'

'That's not fair!' Clarissa carefully threaded a ribbon through Amelia's golden locks. 'I'm not a sneak, and you know it. I wouldn't run to Mama.' No, indeed she wouldn't, she thought sadly. For Mama would be sure to say that Clarrie was a fusspot, and that Amelia knew her own business. In fact Mama, the widowed Lady Maria Warrington, would probably not even have the energy to say that much.

Lady Maria had been disappointed in life from an early age, and constant disappointment had taken its toll. Married to a younger son, then left a penniless widow not long after Amelia's birth, Lady Maria drifted through life with as little effort as possible. Only cards, and the thought of the brilliant match her beautiful younger daughter would one day make, brought any animation to her face. At the slightest sign that any sort of effort would be required from her she wilted, and even on occasions took to fainting fits. Lady Maria had relied on her practical, pragmatic elder daughter for as long as either of them could remember.

Traces of Lady Maria's beauty could still be detected beneath her raddled skin, but the years had not been kind. Amelia took after her, but Clarissa's own deep auburn hair and vivid green eyes came from her father's side of the family. Clarissa barely remembered Papa, and the little she knew came from Aunt Constance, his favourite sister. Questioning Mama simply brought on tears.

Aunt Constance, alone of Papa's family, had never disowned them, and had always taken an interest in Clarissa. It had been Aunt Constance who funded Clarissa's schooling, and encouraged her reading—histories, politics, and even romances. Aunt Constance could not like Mama, and had little success with Amelia, who refused to study anything beyond the pianoforte, but she doted on Clarissa, and was fond of telling her stories of Papa as a child.

A final twist to her sister's coiffure ensured that one golden lock fell artfully over her shoulder. Amelia's thin muslin dress was of palest pink, her little satin evening slippers dyed to match, as was the ribbon in her hair, dressed in the newly fashionable Grecian knot. Perhaps Amelia's figure was a little too full to look its best in the high-waisted style, which still seemed so strange to people of their mother's generation, but Clarissa could see that no gentleman would cavil at being faced with such a lush display of curves.

'There! You look lovely, Amelia.'

'Yes, I do, don't I?'

Amelia preened in the mirror, and Clarissa sighed. Really, her sister was displaying all too much of her ample curves, even if the low *décolleté* was all the rage. 'You don't think that perhaps a fichu…'

The scornful look was answer enough. 'Oh, very well. I hope you won't get goose bumps!' Clarissa tried to introduce a lighter note. There would be no getting anything out of Amelia if she was in the least lecturing. 'At least tell me who your beau is. For you've made such an effort, there must be one.'

'Well, I don't know if I will, Clarrie; you're bound to disapprove.'

The coy look that accompanied this challenge told Clarissa that Amelia was actually bursting to tell. Perversely, she decided not to pursue the matter. 'Of course, Amelia, I respect your confidence.' She turned to leave.

'No, no, I'll tell. Well, a little. Clarrie, you just won't believe it. I think, I'm certain—well, almost certain—that Kit Rasenby is interested. What do you think of that then?'

'Kit Rasenby? Amelia, you don't seriously mean the Earl of Rasenby? Surely you are mistaken?'

'Well, I'm not, actually.' Amelia pouted. 'He *is* interested. At the Carruthers' ball last week he danced with me three times. That's twice more than any other lady. And he sat next to me at tea. And then I met him at the theatre when we went to that boring old play you were so desperate to see. You know, the one with that old woman in it.'

'You mean Mrs Siddons?' Clarissa had been keen to attend the theatre that evening. Lady Macbeth was the part for which Mrs Siddons was most famed. But Lady Maria had had one of her turns, and Clarrie had to stay home to burn feathers under her nose and dab lavender water on her temples. Clarissa was used to self-sacrifice, even though she had long ceased to believe that these 'turns' of her mama's were anything more than habit. But missing the great Mrs Siddons had been a trial.

Amelia had no further interest in Mrs Siddons. 'Yes, well, Rasenby came to our box particularly to see me. And he spoke to no one else. Chloe said he had eyes only for me all night.'

'You mean he was eyeing you from the pit?' Clarissa's tone was dry. Gentlemen did not eye respectable ladies from the pit. The type of ladies eyed from the pit were not likely to be those offered matrimony.

'And then, today,' Amelia continued blithely, 'when he stopped to talk with us in the park, he asked most particularly if I would be at the Jessops' ball tonight. So, of course, I know he has intentions.'

'Amelia, you know what those intentions are likely to be? You do know of the Earl of Rasenby's reputation?'

A toss of golden curls and yet another pout were the response.

'Amelia, I'm serious.' Clarissa might have spurned

most of the invitations she received, but no one could be unaware of the reputation of the Earl of Rasenby. He was a hardened gamester and an incurable womaniser. He was enormously rich and famously handsome, although Clarissa was sceptical about this—in her view, the rich were invariably *good looking*. Lord Rasenby's mistresses were notoriously beautiful and expensive, and, despite endless lures and traps, he remained determinedly unattached. Quite the perfect Gothic villain, now she thought of it.

'For Heaven's sake, Clarrie, do you think I'm stupid? Of course I know of his reputation. Better than you, I expect, since you're such a prude no one would dare tell you the plain truth. But I know he likes me. A lot! I just know!'

Nothing more could be gained from Amelia, and Clarissa went to bed extremely worried. Her sister was both young and naïve, and could all too easily fall victim to the likes of Rasenby. The company Amelia was keeping, never mind her lack of dowry, was likely to ensure that any offer would be strictly dishonourable.

And if Amelia was offered a *carte blanche* by someone as rich as Rasenby, she would take it. Clarissa turned restlessly in her bed. It was so hard to be genteelly poor, she could understand the temptation. To a girl like Amelia, the choice between a brief career swathed in furs and silks and showered in diamonds, or a safe marriage with a no more than adequate income was an all too easy one. But life as Kit Rasenby's mistress would be very short-lived. Amelia's charms were those of novelty and freshness, not likely to entertain so jaded a palate as Rasenby's for long. And who would have Amelia then? There was only one way to go, and that was down. Amelia must marry soon, preferably to someone who would take her firmly in hand. But such a person was likely to be too staid and too poor for Amelia. Even supposing she did meet this paragon, would she even look at him, when dazzled by Rasenby's wealth?

If Amelia was ruined, Clarissa would be ruined by association. Even finding a post as governess, something to which she was daily trying to resign herself, would be difficult. At twenty-four, Clarissa had set her sights on self-sufficiency as the only way to give her some element of the freedom she craved. Aunt Constance's offer of a home was tempting, but Clarissa knew in her heart that it would mean tying herself to another obligation, even assuming Mama was settled with Amelia.

Clarissa had always been the sensible one. Beside her sister's vivaciousness and dazzling looks, which had been apparent from a very early age, she felt plain. Her green eyes and dark auburn curls were no match for Amelia's milkmaid perfection. She had settled compliantly into the role of carer. When Amelia tore her dress, Clarrie stitched it. When Amelia fought with her friends, Clarrie played the peacemaker. And as she grew older, when Amelia wanted to attend parties and make her début, Clarrie scrimped and saved to provide her with the dresses and hats and all the other bits and pieces that she needed.

For years now, Lady Maria's hopes had been pinned on Amelia making a match that would save them from poverty. Having no wish to become a burden on Amelia's future household, and having no desire to find herself a suitable match, Clarissa had started, discreetly, looking around for a genteel position. Surrendering her own chance of matrimony was no sacrifice, for she had never met a man who had caused her heart to flutter. In fact, she had never met a man she had found interesting enough to want to get to know better in any way.

Clarissa's pragmatic front concealed a deep romanticism that the practical side of her despised, but which she was unable to ignore. She longed for passion, love, ardour—despite trying to convince herself that they didn't really exist! She dreamed of someone who would love her for herself, value her for what she was, not for her looks or her lineage—which was good, even if Papa's family did refuse to own them—or even her dowry. Someone to pledge himself to her for always. *Happy ever after* was hardly in vogue though. Clarrie's dreams were out of kilter with the ways of the real world. Marriage vows were taken very lightly these days—once an heir had been delivered—with affection provided by a lover rather than a husband. Clarissa couldn't help but find such attitudes abhorrent, even if it did mean being mocked for her prudishness.

Reconciling these two sides of her nature, the practical and romantic, was difficult. Even when embroiled in reading one of the Gothic romances she adored, Clarissa found herself thinking that her own good sense would be of a lot more use in assisting the hero than the tears and fainting fits of the heroines. But resourcefulness was not a quality valued in a female, real or imaginary, nor was it much sought after in a wife. Since it seemed unlikely, in any event, that she would ever be given the opportunity to play the heroine, Clarissa had resigned herself to becoming a governess, a role which would certainly require all her resourcefulness. On that determined note, she finally fell asleep.

At breakfast the next morning, Amelia was all yawns and coy giggles. 'Oh, Mama, we had such fun, and my new dress was much admired.' This, with a sly look at Clarissa.

Clarissa was in no mood for Amelia's games, having woken this morning resolved to remove her sister from the clutches of the Earl of Rasenby. By force, if necessary. 'I can well imagine that you were admired in that dress, Amelia, for it left little to the imagination.' Her jibe was, however, low enough to avoid being heard by Lady Maria, now deep in this morning's post.

Amelia, predictably, pouted, and ignored her.

'And did your beau turn up, then?'

'Can you doubt it? He can't keep away, I told you. He didn't leave my side all night, and everyone noticed.'

'Amelia, that's not necessarily a good thing. Everyone will be talking about you being so singled out. In fact, it seems to me that by making you so conspicuous, it is less likely that the Earl of Rasenby's intentions are honourable. What can Mrs Barrington have been thinking, to allow it? She cannot be a suitable escort. I must speak to Mama.'

'Clarissa, if you do any such thing, I swear, I will make you pay.' Cornflower-blue eyes bright with intent locked on to emerald-green. 'I don't care what you think of Mrs Barrington, she's all I've got, since you and your precious, snooty Aunt Constance are so determined not to escort me. And our dear mama won't move beyond her drawing room, unless there's a card table to tempt her.'

Seeing her sister's stricken look, Amelia relented. No sense in getting Clarissa all worked up and on her high horse. 'You know I wouldn't do anything silly. Mrs Barrington is perfectly respectable, I promise you. And besides, for the next couple of days, I won't be seeing Rasenby. You're right, it won't do to grant him too much attention, I have to keep him keen.' And in any case, Clarrie didn't need to know that a certain Edward was really a far more attractive companion than Kit Rasenby. Kit Rasenby was rich and powerful, but he didn't cause her heart to flutter the way Edward did. In fact, Amelia was finding herself quite distracted by Edward, whose youthful good looks appealed so much more to her than Rasenby's striking countenance, which could be rather intimidating. Rasenby's wealth was losing a little of its attraction—but she was determined to give it every chance to succeed. Edward would always be there, of that she was already sure.

'Amelia, you must know that the Earl of Rasenby won't offer marriage. His reputation, his feelings about the state of matrimony, they are all against you. And even if he did intend to marry, it wouldn't be to the penniless daughter of a cast-out younger son. It would be to someone with influence and money. Amelia, are you listening at all?'

'Lord, Clarrie, you know nothing.' Abandoning her attempt to soft-soap her sister, Amelia's voice hardened. 'You're right—perhaps Rasenby's intentions aren't marriage.' Well, in fact Amelia knew they weren't, for he had already intimated his offer of a *carte blanche.* She had put him off, unwilling to take so irrevocable a step just yet. 'But he's wild about me, I know. And with a bit of luck, marriage it will be, whether he wants to or nay.'

'What do you mean? What have you done?'

'Why nothing, sister dear, as yet. I don't have to. I merely have to click my fingers and he comes running. And if I click and he runs into a—well, shall we say, compromising situation?—then that's his misfortune. And best for me, too.'

'*Amelia!* The Earl of Rasenby is highly unlikely to fall for that. Why there must have been countless such traps set for him over the years, and never a whiff of him anywhere near wed. Please, I beg of you, stay away from him.'

'Well, I won't. At least, yes, I will, for a couple of days. Just to keep him on tenterhooks.' Amelia slanted another glance at Clarrie's face. Her sister really was such a prude.

'Do you love him? Is that it?' Clarissa was struggling to come to terms with this new, hard Amelia. She had always been determined to have her own way, but she had never before been so openly scheming. If Clarissa had known that her sister was trying desperately to suppress her feelings for Edward Brompton, she would have been less concerned.

'Life isn't one of your romances, you know. Love is such an outmoded emotion when it comes to marriage. I can stomach him well enough to bed him, if that's what you mean. And, of course, his money makes him more attractive than he would be under other circumstances. After all, he's quite old.'

'Old? You talk about him as if he's in his dotage. Why, he can't be more than five and thirty. And if you loved him, his age would mean nothing. Now tell me straight, *do* you love him?'

'Clarrie, I tell you straight, I do not.' Amelia was enjoying shocking her sister. 'Love, I will save for my beaux after we are wed. It's what everyone does. Rasenby will no doubt carry on with his lightskirts, so why should I not do the same? I shall take great pleasure, though, in ousting that supercilious Charlotte du Pres from her position as his mistress. And I suppose I'll need to provide an heir first.' Realising she'd gone a bit too far, Amelia patted Clarrie's hand in a conciliatory way. 'I'm not a little girl any more. I can look after myself. And I know what I'm doing, I promise.' No need to let Clarrie know that the *carte blanche* would still be considered if her other plan failed. One way or another, she'd get her hands on a large part of Rasenby's wealth. But for now, she wanted to think only of the thrill of meeting Edward again. 'Let us find out what Mama has found so distracting that she has paid no heed at all to our conversation.'

Lady Maria was certainly absorbed in her post, one letter in particular holding her attention. There were plenty of others, but they were all bills. Bills that she had no means of paying. Those relating to the house and to Amelia's dresses she would hand over to Clarissa to deal with. But they were insignificant compared to her mounting gambling debts—and of these, Clarissa must be allowed no inkling. She returned again to the note from the owner of the discreet gaming house she had been frequenting of late. The sum that she owed frightened her. The letter was subtly threatening.

'Mama, what is it that you find so interesting in that letter? Clarrie and I have been plotting away, and you haven't even looked up.'

At this, Lady Maria gave a nervous start. 'What? Oh, nothing, nothing. No indeed, nothing for you girls to worry about.' Her slightly protuberant blue eyes blinked out at her daughters. Nervously, she licked her lips, and produced a somewhat ragged smile. 'Now, dears, what is it you were plotting?'

'Silly Mama, only what I would wear to the theatre tonight. For I'm going out with Chloe you know, and her mama, to the new farce. Chloe's brother and that nice Mr Brompton are escorting us.'

'Will they be calling for you here, dearest?' Lady Maria had just remembered a hint from Mrs Barrington, that there were means of paying a lady's debts that she could help—discreetly—with. 'Then I'd like a word with her myself. Just to thank her for her attentions to you, Amelia dear. She's been so good taking you out to parties when my health won't hold up.'

Lady Maria gathered together her post. 'Now, if you'll excuse me, I'm afraid I have one of my heads. Clarrie, do give my regards to your Aunt Constance, I know you'll do all that is right.' And with that, she left for the sanctity of her bedchamber with its carefully drawn blinds, and the ministering of her dear, faithful maid.

'Are you going to see Aunt Constance, then? Rather you than me, I can't abide her sermonising. I'm off for a walk in the park with Chloe.' Looking back at her sister, still seated at the table, Amelia laughed once more. 'Clarrie do stop looking so serious. I know what I'm doing, and that should be enough for you. You should get out more yourself, you know. Even at your age, your looks are more than passable, as long as you don't stand too close to me. I could find you someone suitable.'

'Thank you, Amelia,' Clarissa responded drily, 'but I'm quite content as I am.'

The visit to her aunt only confirmed Clarissa's worst fears. Lady Constance Denby lived semi-retired from society, but this didn't stop her keeping close tabs on the latest *on dits*, and today one of them concerned Amelia.

'Well, my dear, I am sorry to have to tell you that your sister is raising a few eyebrows.'

They were settled in Lady Constance's breakfast room, taking morning coffee. Clarissa loved this room, with its beautifully polished rosewood tables, the cabinets crammed with her aunt's collection of delicate porcelain. The loud ticking of the clock on the mantel, and the scent from the apple wood burning in the hearth were deeply comforting.

Her aunt had been widowed very young—before Clarissa ever remembered an uncle—and, despite numerous offers, had never married again. Her beloved husband had been a rising star in the House of Lords, and Constance had remained faithful to his memory in retaining her widowed status, as well as her avid interest in current affairs. Lady Constance was a beautiful woman, with a little of Clarissa's colouring, although the vivid auburn of her hair had faded now, and was confined beneath her habitual widow's cap. She had been formidable, too, in her brief time as a political hostess, although that, also, had been given up upon the occasion of her husband's death. Having shared something so special, she had told Clarissa once, even for so brief a time, had been enough.

Tact, and a natural reticence, prevented Lady Constance, over the years, from being too critical of Clarissa's mother and sister. She was all too aware of how badly her own family had treated them when James, her dear brother, had died. She found Maria tedious, and Amelia wilful, but she was very fond of Clarissa, and hated not being able to do more for her than provide this sanctuary whenever her niece paid her a call.

And today the talk would be upsetting—but that couldn't be helped. 'I'm not sure if you're aware, but Letitia Marlborough, Kit Rasenby's sister, is one of my friends. A flighty thing before she was married and produced that brood of hers, but still, I've known her for ever, and keep on good terms with her.' Lady Constance waited, but Clarissa had no comment to make.

'Well, Letitia has it on the best of authority that your sister is Kit Rasenby's latest flirt. In fact, she believes he intends to set her up as his mistress.'

Lady Constance sipped her coffee, and considered Clarissa's reaction. No surprise there, only worry. So, there was truth in it. Well, she needed to warn Clarissa in plain language. Amelia was heading for a fall, and Lady Constance could only do her best to ensure that Clarissa was not to be tainted by association. Amelia would go to the bad, she was sure of it. But Clarissa deserved better.

'I take it that this comes as no surprise to you, Clarissa dear? Has Amelia mentioned Lord Rasenby then?'

'She has, Aunt. As a—an admirer.'

Lady Constance gave a bark of laughter at this. 'Is that what she called him? Your sister, my dear, seems determined to take the road to ruin. And if you don't take me up on my offer to come and live here, she'll take you with her.'

'Aunt, please, let us not discuss this again at present. I am overwhelmed at the generosity of your offer, indeed I am. But until Amelia is settled, and my mama with her, I can't desert them.' Green eyes pleaded for sympathy. 'Aunt Constance, you do understand, don't you?'

Clarissa was so very much like her papa when she looked up, that Lady Constance caught her breath for a second. Those huge eyes set in her heart-shaped face were all feminine, but the appeal, and the colouring, they were so like James. If only he had been of a stronger constitution—and a stronger character—then perhaps they wouldn't be in this mess. But to have eloped with Maria, a mere nobody, when he should have made a good match! Well, it was done now, and James long dead. All she could do was protect his child from some of the harshness of the world.

But to do that, she had to save her from her sister and her mama. Lady Constance patted Clarissa's hand reassuringly. She was four and twenty, but had seen so little of the world. 'Of course I understand, my dear, you must know that you will always find a home here, no matter what.'

'Thank you, Aunt Constance, that means a lot to me.'

'But to return to the subject of Amelia, as unfortunately we must, I have to tell you, Clarissa, that I am very concerned.' Lady Constance was brisk now. Straight talking was required, although she was loath to do it. 'The Earl of Rasenby's reputation is extremely bad, you know.'

'I am aware of Lord Rasenby's reputation, ma'am, but surely he cannot be as bad as they say?'

'Child, I know not what you have heard, but believe me, whatever it is, Kit's behaviour is worse. He has been one of the *ton* for nigh on fifteen years, and master of a huge fortune for longer, his papa having unfortunately died when he was still at school. His papa, such a very dreadful man, broke his neck when he was thrown from his horse riding to the hounds. He was a bruising rider by all accounts, but they say he was in his cups at the time. Mind you, there was rarely a day when he was ever anything else. Hardly a role model for his only son. Although, to be fair, Kit seems to be rather more sober and certainly more discriminating than his father. But there is no getting away from it Clarissa, his tastes are still very, very low!'

With pursed lips, Lady Constance poured herself another cup of coffee. 'I will not sully your ears with the details, there is no need for that. But this I will say. It is not just the usual, opera dancers and mistresses. He is wild. Too quick to quarrel and too slow to make up. If you ask me, he has too little to occupy him. I have often thought he could make a most excellent politician.'

Lady Constance paused to sip her coffee, gazing into the fireplace. It was her one regret, not having a son. Not for an instant would she have wished a Kit Rasenby on herself, but a child in the image of her dear husband would have been a precious gift. Still, it had not happened. And here was Clarissa, someone who did need her help and protection. Lady Constance brought her attention firmly back to the matter in hand. 'I beg your pardon, Clarissa, we were talking of Kit Rasenby. Despite all I have said, he is still seen as a good catch by some. Yet he has avoided matrimony until now, and is like to continue to do so. Letitia tells me he is happy for Jeremy, her son, to inherit, and cares naught for the line continuing from him. It is perhaps as well.'

Lady Constance paused, once again assessing the effect on her niece. Clarissa was looking thoughtful rather than shocked.

'Aunt, I am aware of much of what you have told me, although I do truly find it hard to believe that anyone could be all bad.' She held up her hand and gave her aunt a small smile to forestall any intervention. 'I know, you think I'm naïve, but I do like to think there is some good in everyone. However, that is not the point, since I have never met Lord Rasenby.'

Clarissa thought over her next words carefully. 'There is some truth in the rumours, I'm afraid. Amelia has been much in Lord Rasenby's company, and I fear his intentions cannot be honourable, no matter what Amelia may believe. She has no love for him, but I think she is deeply flattered, and is fooling herself into thinking he may offer matrimony. I think that she must come to accept that it cannot be so.'

'My dear Clarissa, you underrate your sister. She is, I have no doubt at all, fully aware that Kit Rasenby can intend only a *carte blanche*. Which she will accept, should no other more honourable offer come her way.

Your sister, whether you want to believe it or not, is avaricious before anything else. There, plain speaking indeed, but you must be made to realise it.'

'Aunt, I know you think no good of Amelia.' Clarissa blinked, trying to quieten the little voice in her head that told her Lady Constance was articulating Clarissa's own fears. Lady Constance had said only what she already knew. 'Perhaps what you say is true. But I am certain that I can prevent her ruining herself with Lord Rasenby. She is a child, she is simply beguiled by his charm and his wealth.'

'You're not thinking of doing something foolish, Clarissa?'

'No, no. No, of course I won't be foolish.' The slight laugh with which she attempted to carry off the denial fell rather flat, and Clarissa bit her lip. She could never lie. She had the makings of a plan which Aunt Constance would certainly call foolish, but she needed to think it through.

'Enough of my imprudent sister, I have to tell you that I am not at all impressed with *Udolpho*.' Clarissa rushed into a dissection of Mrs Radcliffe's novel in an effort to distract her aunt from further enquiries. Lady Constance was, rather to her shame, an avid fan of Mrs Radcliffe, and allowed herself to be diverted into a spirited defence. The two parted on excellent terms.

Mulling over her aunt's words later, however, confirmed Clarissa in her resolution. She must separate Amelia from Lord Rasenby, and that would require desperate action, for Amelia must not know that she was being thwarted. Amelia would accept a *carte blanche* from Lord Rasenby, Clarissa no longer doubted it. And she knew, in her heart, that whatever plan Amelia had to trap him into marriage would fail. Aunt Constance would not have been so blunt with Clarissa had she been less sure. So she had to prevent both Amelia's plot and Lord Rasenby's offer.

A flicker of excitement rippled through her at the thought of taking action. It was as if she was waking from sleep, preparing for the challenge to come. Telling herself that it was the thrill of rescuing her sister, and nothing to do with meeting so notorious a man, Clarissa started to formulate her plan. The first requirement was to meet with Lord Rasenby in order to determine for herself just how much danger Amelia was in. And Clarrie knew just how to effect that meeting.

With a fast-beating heart, she flicked through the pile of invitations on the desk in the morning room. Yes, there it was, discarded at the bottom of the pile. Lady Teasborough was a friend of Aunt Constance, and had no doubt sent the invite at her request. A masked ball. Clarrie would go—incognito, and on her own.

Chapter Two

Kit, Earl of Rasenby, stared down into the limpid blue eyes of yet another eligible young lady, and tried to suppress a yawn as a wave of boredom washed over him. He should never have given in to his sister Letitia's entreaties to escort her to the ball. He had planned a quiet dinner followed by a hand or two of whist at his club, instead of which, here he was at one of the society crushes he so abhorred. With the added, and completely pointless, inconvenience of having to sport a domino and a mask.

Lady Teasborough had thought to introduce a slightly *risqué* element with this masked ball, but Kit was finding it every bit as tedious as any other social event. The heat in the room was overpowering. The candles from the huge chandeliers, the fires lit—unnecessarily, in his view—in the enormous grates at either end of the ballroom, and the crush of too many people in too little space made Kit want to fight his way out into the relatively fresh air of the terrace. He was bored. He had no interest in the latest *crim. con.* story, nor in taking part in the speculation as to who had fathered his hostess's latest brat. If his host—closeted, no doubt, in one of the card rooms—didn't care, why should he? *God, he was bored.* Despite the concealing cloaks and masks, he recognised almost everyone here. Including Miss Pink Domino, being presented to him now by Letitia.

Kit sighed, bowed over Miss Pink Domino's hand, and led her out reluctantly. His enthusiasm for fencing, which he practised regularly with the renowned Harry Angelo at his academy in the Haymarket, lent him an animal grace that singled him out on the dance floor. But his partner was, alas, unable to match him, and it would take a great effort on his part to ensure that they remained in step for the duration of the country dance.

As they worked their way down the set, Kit's mind began to wander. He knew Letitia's game only too well. His elder by some years, his sister had just successfully married off the first of his five nieces, and was once again turning her attentions to his own marital state. It was his own fault for bringing it up earlier—even though it had been in jest. Kit's reputation was too bad for him to be a great catch, of course, as Letitia took pleasure in reminding him. So Louisa Haysham, with whom he was now dancing, fell into the second-best category. *A pretty little thing with an adequate portion who will cause you no trouble.* He could hear Letitia saying it, and he knew exactly what she meant. Louisa Haysham was a nice, inoffensive, malleable female for him to trample on. She'd raise a brood of nice insignificant children for him, and he'd be bored within a week. He was bored now, and he'd been in her company for barely ten minutes.

Over and over again, Kit had assured Letitia that he'd be happy for her son, Jeremy, to inherit his estates. At thirty-five, he was surely entitled to be treated as the confirmed bachelor he knew himself to be. Lord knew, he'd made his views clear to both Letitia and his mother often enough. Matrimony simply had no appeal for him. Rather, matrimony, in the accepted form these days, had no appeal. Fidelity, even if he could find a woman he wanted to be faithful to, seemed not to be valued. And he had seen no evidence, not in his family, nor amongst his friends or acquaintances, that marriage had any rewards other than a string of brats that no one really wanted, and endless recriminations about money. Even his sister, who claimed to be happy, was, he knew, no more than content. Content, Kit was sure, wasn't a big enough reward for the sacrifice of his freedom.

Returning Miss Haysham with a curt bow to her mother, and neatly avoiding catching his sister's eye—he couldn't bear her inevitable interrogation as to whether Miss Insipid Haysham was to his liking—Kit headed instead for the group of gentlemen congregated at the back of the room. His tall figure in a plain black domino and mask was easily recognisable in a crowd that favoured colour and decoration. He was in fact, infamous for refusing to decorate his well-favoured person with any of the fobs, frills and furbelows of the day.

A slight man in a deep scarlet cloak standing on the fringes of the crowd noted Kit's attendance at the ball with some surprise—it was very unlike Rasenby to turn out at these formal affairs. Kit was not aware of the depths of contempt in which Robert, Marquis of Alchester, held him. Brought up as children together, since the estates of their fathers ran parallel, Robert had been forced to play second fiddle to Kit from the start. Kit was the ringleader in all their childish pranks. Kit was the best shot in the area, the handiest with his fists, the most skilled with a sword. And it was Kit who had first call on all the females. To add insult to injury, Kit's estates continued to flourish under his generous steward-ship, whereas Robert's dissolute lifestyle drained every penny from his land, now in sad want of repair. All this bitterness Robert had suppressed over the years, but it was slowly mouldering. And now, he had a card worth playing. It was Robert who had been informing the customs men as to Kit's activities. One day soon, revenge would be his.

Blissfully unaware of this enmity, Kit took a reviving draught of claret, a drink he much preferred to the ice-cold champagne cup being offered to the rest of the guests. Mindful of his resolution to give up smuggling, he mulled over, once more, the notion of matrimony. Letitia had made her point of view perfectly clear when he had raised the subject before dinner. A slight frown marred the perfection of his countenance as he thought over his sister's words from earlier tonight. His handsome features were, in fact, a major bone of contention with Letitia, and had been the trigger for her latest tirade, turning his attempt at light banter into a more serious discussion.

'What would you say, Letitia, if I asked you to finally find me a suitable bride? One who met all my needs, I might add.' He had said this with a wicked grin, delib-erately intending to annoy her.

Letitia sighed. Why should Kit have it all, when she didn't? Of course, she was perfectly happy with her husband, but life wasn't exactly stimulating. So it shouldn't be for Kit, either. That wasn't what matrimony was about.

'For goodness' sake, must you always harp on about your needs. With your looks, I'm sure that sort of thing won't be a problem—ever.' It was positively painful to Letitia that Kit was so very perfectly good looking. 'It's your duty to the family to bestow yourself on one of my sex for reasons of lineage, not for—not for the reasons you're implying.'

'On the contrary, Letitia, I feel it my bounden duty to bestow myself on as many of your sex as I can. And I do my best, you know.' This was said with a rueful smile, for Kit knew that Letitia, despite her perfect breeding, liked to consider herself *risqué*.

'Kit!' She feigned shock, anyway. 'I mean bestow yourself properly. I'm not referring to your mistresses, for Heaven's sake.'

'Tut, tut, Letitia, what can you know of my mistresses?'

'Why, no more nor less than the whole of London society, since you flaunt them so brazenly at every opportunity. Only yesterday I saw you in a carriage in Oxford Street with that shameless hussy Charlotte—harlot, more like—sitting at your side. Draped in the most gorgeous furs, too. No doubt paid for by you.' Letitia couldn't prevent the bitter note of envy entering her voice, thinking back to how stunning Charlotte du Pres had looked. Providing her husband with six children in quick succession had taken a heavy toll on what little looks she herself had once possessed.

'Yes, she really is rather lovely, isn't she? But alas, I fear, becoming rather tedious. Her demands are endless, you know, Letitia, and the rewards less attractive each time. I think that Charlotte is coming to the end of her usefulness.'

'Well, I can't say I'm surprised. She's been with you two months now. Don't you ever find a woman diverting for longer?'

'Alas, no. At least, not yet. And since I've been trying for more years than either of us, sister dear, would care to count, I'm afraid you really must resign yourself to my bachelor state. And incidentally, please don't go breaking your heart over Charlotte, she'll be more than adequately compensated for her loss.'

'Yes, you're very generous in that way, I know. But really, Kit, you're so hugely rich that it means nothing to you. Not, I assure you, that I'm complaining myself, for you've been exceeding good to me and my children over the years, particularly Jeremy, who scarce deserves it. He may be my only son and I love him dearly but it's plain the lad is a wastrel. I just wish you took your duty to marry and produce your own son and heir as seriously.'

'Enough of this. I have no desire to be leg-shackled, it was a jest. I have no wish to be presented to yet another eligible girl who will drive me back into the arms of someone who at least can attend properly to my physical needs. And spare me your blushes, Letty, for you know perfectly well what I mean.'

'No, Kit, I do not. There is no reason why you shouldn't continue to tend to your physical needs, as you put it, outside of the marriage bed. But you must marry for the sake of the family. Jeremy is no fit heir for you. You need the stability of a wife. You need someone to care for you in your old age.'

Kit threw back his head and laughed again, running his fingers through his cropped, glossy black hair. 'For God's sake Letitia, I'm thirty-five, I don't need a nursemaid yet. I'll tell you what, the minute I show the first signs of contracting gout, I'll start looking out for a wife to tend to me.'

'By then, you'll be too old to father children, and it will be too late. Kit, do listen, since you brought the topic up. I know your reputation is bad—and indeed, well deserved—but you're still eligible. I could still find you someone suitable.'

Kit was now deeply regretting raising the subject. 'Letty, enough. You know my views on matrimony, they are not likely to change. There are but two types of women on this earth, and they live in worlds that don't mix. There are those who provide pleasure for a man, and who require payment, and there are those who provide a family—and they require payment in a different way. And I'm happy to pay for the former, if I get something out of it. But why should I pay for a family when I don't want one? Have done.'

Letitia, silenced temporarily by the stern tone of her brother's voice, had done. Reflecting on what he had said, she had to accept the truth of it, for Kit had no experience of any respectable female wanting to give more than she took from him. Starting with their mother—and, she had to admit, herself too. But Letitia wasn't one to give up so easily, either. Her brother must have an heir. He must make some sacrifices. 'Kit, let me see what I can do. I'll see if I can provide you with someone who is at least good to look at.'

'Enough. Let us forgo any further discussion. I must change for this cursed party of yours.'

Shaking his head to banish the memory of that uncomfortable conversation, Kit took another draught of claret, and cast an idle eye over the ballroom. So far, he had danced only with Miss Haysham, but he knew that he'd have to choose at least one other partner soon, or the world would think he had singled the fair Miss Haysham out. And Kit did not want that to happen. Really, the idea of matrimony was ridiculous. Apart from anything else, he had no desire to make his poor wife—whoever she might be—totally miserable. And since he could in no way promise liking, never mind fidelity, miserable she would be, and quickly. Best to focus on this last run with the *Sea Wolf* first, then think to the future after. For now, he needed to find another dance partner.

A brief flash of black domino lined with emerald green caught his eye in the far corner, and roused his attention. It was highly unusual for a female to wear black—in fact, he was the only man to do so tonight. And while he could have sworn he knew everyone here—despite the masks—she was unfamiliar. She was standing by the open window, and for some reason she seemed to be watching him. Her stance was alert, giving the impression of one on the verge of flight. Kit was intrigued. Retrieving two glasses of champagne from a passing waiter, he made his way over to the stranger.

'I fear you are somewhat warm, Miss Black Domino— can I offer you a cooling drink?'

Clarrie gave a start, then tried, rather unsuccessfully, to regain her poise. The black domino, the only other one here, had been pointed out to her as the Earl of Rasenby. He had made the first move. She couldn't believe her luck. Nor could she flee now, as she had been contemplating only a moment before. Fate had decreed that she must go through with her plan.

'Why, thank you, sir. It is rather hot.' He was tall, much taller than Clarrie, and despite the domino she could see he was exceedingly well built. Somehow, she had expected him to be more dandified. But the Earl of Rasenby was obviously of athletic inclination, and favoured a simple elegance that relied on his physique and the quality of his tailoring, rather than decoration. For the first time in her life, Clarrie experienced a strong gust of sheer physical attraction that was both unexpected and unwelcome.

Looking up, she could see little of his features behind the mask, only a pair of piercing dark eyes, looking into hers assessingly. So this was the man who wanted to steal Amelia's virtue. This was the man who intended to sweep her sister—and with her, Clarissa and her mama—into a world of vice and degradation. Well, she could certainly see his appeal. What she needed to find out was just how serious he was in his intentions, before she decided to act. Clarissa still nourished a hope that Amelia had exaggerated—though in the light of Lady Constance's revelations, it was but a faint one.

'Do you not find these masked affairs somewhat tedious, sir? Why, I swear I know everyone here. 'Tis but an excuse to allow those who are so inclined to flirt a little more openly, is it not?'

Clarissa's voice, usually so low and musical, had assumed a slightly breathless quality. The combination of the role she had to play, and the physical awareness of this surprisingly attractive man, were already taking their toll. But she wouldn't fail at the first hurdle, there was too much at stake. Under no illusions about her own attractions, she had studied Amelia closely, and she knew how to flirt—even if she was about to try it out for the first time.

Kit looked down into those vibrant green eyes, surprised at the tone. He could have sworn she was nervous when he first approached her. 'And do you know who I am, Miss Black Domino?' Of course she did, else why flirt so obviously unless she knew her target?

'I will hazard a guess, my lord. You are the Earl of Rasenby, are you not?' Those green eyes looked up into his, a shadow of a doubt clouding them. What if she had been wrong? A flush of embarrassment swept over Clarissa, most of it mercifully hidden by the mask.

'And if I am not, would you be disappointed?'

'Of course I would be disappointed.' Clarrie shook out

her chicken-skin fan with a flourish, partly to hide her eyes, but more practically in an effort to hide her over-heated countenance, and to give her time to pull herself together. 'I'd be very disappointed, since I've heard so much about your lordship, and was counting on meeting you here.'

'Were you, now? And may I ask, are you here at the invitation of Lady Teasborough, or have you taken a chance to come uninvited?' Surely the only explanation was that she was some member of the *demi-monde* with an enterprising turn of mind?

Clarissa, forgetting her part, was indignant at the accusation. 'Of course I was invited, why would I be here otherwise?'

The genuine flash of anger from those green eyes took Kit aback. Despite himself, he felt a faint trace of interest. He didn't believe her for an instant, but any new ploy, after all, was at least a refreshing change. 'I do beg your pardon. It's just that you have the advantage of me. To whom do I have the pleasure of speaking?'

'That is not important for now. And besides...' Clar-rie allowed herself a peep above the fan into those dark blue-black eyes '...it's so much more intriguing, is it not, to save a little something for later?' Nothing Amelia had told her about Kit Rasenby had led her to believe that he was anything more than a rich provider. She hadn't expected him to be quite so like the villains of her favou-rite romances—Clarrie always empathised more with the villain than the hero, although she never liked to ask herself why!

'So, I'm not to know your name, then? Am I to know your purpose in seeking me out?'

'Eventually, of course, my lord. But first, perhaps we should get to know each other a little. Tell me, the lady you were dancing with, what thought you of her charms? Did you not think she danced rather ill?'

'You can do better than that, surely?' He was sardonic. Praising or disparaging one female to another was not a sport that he enjoyed.

Closing her fan with a determined snap, Clarissa decided to go for the direct approach. The Earl was obviously not one for simpering females, and in truth, she didn't do simpering very well. Perhaps if she played things her own way he would take her more seriously. 'I know you not, Lord Rasenby, but you seem to me a man who prefers plain speaking. Mayhap we should dispense with the niceties and progress to my requirements from you?'

'Much better.' His tone remained sceptical, however. 'Now you at least have my attention. Perhaps I should warn you, though, that if it's money you're after, I won't be blackmailed. If you've come on behalf of one of your sisters in debauchery, you'll find scant pickings here.' Ignoring the gasp of indignation from Clarissa, he held his hand up to forestall interruption, and continued in the harsh voice of one used to seeing the worst in everyone. 'I pay my debts direct. And there's no use either, in trying to pretend that it's you I owe—I may have sampled the wares of your like many times, but not enough to confuse me. I'd know you if I'd had you.'

'Well, my lord! Well! Plain speaking indeed.' Clarissa was completely unprepared for this turn in the conversation. He thought her a lightskirt. Well, that's what she'd intended, but she hadn't expected the flush of anger that such an assumption had caused. In fact, the more she thought about it, the angrier she became. The Earl of Rasenby was an arrogant pig, and he deserved to be put down.

Forgetting all about Amelia, Clarrie gave free reign to

her feelings, her temper made worse by the need to continue the conversation, in the middle of the ball as they were, *sotto voce*. 'I am amazed, sir, at your arrogance. And I am sorry, truly sorry, for any of my poor—sisters, as you call them—who would be reduced to pleading with you, for you are obviously a hard case. You tell me you pay your debts direct—well, I can only hope that you do, sir, and that you pay them fully!'

'What on earth do you mean? I pay what is owed and am generous. I have a reputation of being generous. But I won't be blackmailed, so whatever your pathetic plan, abandon it.' Kit was now more angry than intrigued. He had little reputation, and all of it bad, but one thing he had always been proud of was that he compensated—generously—any woman who had provided her services to him. He ensured, too, that there were never any consequences. To his knowledge, he had no natural children. The irony of this—that he, who had the blackest of characters, had the cleanest of stables—contributed to his weariness of the world in which he lived. He was more fastidious in his habits, and more generous in his payments, than most of his peers. It struck him, suddenly, as a poor enough boast.

'Has it never occurred to you that money may not be enough, Lord Rasenby? Has it never occurred to you that some of these poor creatures that you pay off may have feelings? That they may have hoped for more from you than a few jewels and furs?'

At this, Kit laughed. 'It never occurs to me because there are no feelings in this world that cannot be compensated for financially. I should know.' Looking down into those indignant green eyes, Kit felt a twinge of compassion. Perhaps, after all, there was some innocence there? But no, it was sure to be just another act—although a better one than he'd seen for some time. 'I assure you, madam, the type of women I get involved with don't have feelings. Simpering sentimentality appeals to me not. I trade in the more physical side of things, and that, if you don't know already, is always short-lived. So, no, I don't think I owe anything on account there to anyone.'

For some reason, this statement shocked Clarissa more than any other. More than the knowledge that her Aunt Constance had been right in her character assessment. More than Lord Rasenby's outrageously blunt speaking. The man had no feelings at all. She wondered what had forged his deep cynicism. Through the mask, Clarissa's green eyes hinted at tears. 'I'm truly sorry for you, my lord, if you do feel like that.' She touched her hand to his arm in a gesture of sympathy.

Kit shook her off, angry—unreasonably angry—at the gesture. Who was she to question his behaviour, and then to patronise him with her tears and sympathy? 'Don't waste your energy, madam. I fear that whatever it was you had planned to say to me is wasted, too, for we can have nothing in common. Now, I must go and dance with another partner, lest Miss Haysham—the lady in the pink domino, since you were so interested—has her hopes raised.'

'Forgive me, Lord Rasenby, I spoke out of turn, it was not my intention to judge you. But please, do stay and hear me out.' There was desperation in Clarissa's voice as, emerging from her own anger, she realised he was walking away and she had found out next to nothing of his intentions towards Amelia. And she needed to know, in order to decide whether the risk was worth taking.

He turned at the appeal, unwillingly softened by it. There was something genuine about her, despite appearances, that still had him interested. 'I don't make a habit

of ruining innocents, you know. I take only willing partners, who understand the game, and who don't have any
of these more tender feelings you refer to, I assure you.
Come, what is it that you're so determined I should hear,
now that you've finished upbraiding me?'

'Well, actually…' Clarissa sniffed determinedly and
took the plunge. 'Well, I wanted to discuss a similar
proposal with you myself.' She glared at him through her
mask, her expression anything but seductive. In fact, she
was so far away from the flirtatious woman of the world
that she had started out to be, she was questioning her
own sanity. This was most definitely not going the way
she had imagined it from the security of her bedchamber.

Kit stared at her speechlessly. This slim female, a
complete stranger, had sneaked into a society ball and
sought him out. First she had flirted with him, then she
had launched into a tirade at him, had questioned his
generosity and his feelings, to say nothing of upbraiding
his morals—such as they were! And now she was telling
him that she wanted to make him an indecent proposal.
Of a certainty she was unhinged. No matter how attractive the form under the domino and mask—and what he
could see he found extremely attractive, for though she
was slender, she curved most appealingly in all the right
places—it couldn't be worth it.

And now she was glaring at him, as if it was he who
had made the proposal to her. 'I don't think, madam, that
you can have meant what you just said? Surely, you are
not suggesting that you want to become another notch
on my notorious bedpost yourself?'

'I—well, yes, I suppose I am suggesting just that.
But subject to my own conditions, of course.' Clarissa
flushed once more with embarrassment. This was not
going at all to plan. For a start, her proposition was to

have been later, once she'd found out a bit more about what he intended for Amelia, not something she should have blurted out at this first meeting. She hadn't even thought it through properly.

'Ah, your conditions. And what would they be, madam?' He couldn't help but be interested. This was all so very, very unexpected. Kit was glad, for once, that he'd come along to the ball. Mentally, he thanked Letitia—although he didn't expect she'd be too thrilled if she ever found out.

'Well, I'm not going to tell you right now, this is hardly the appropriate place. I thought we could discuss that on another occasion. I was supposed to get to know you a bit first.'

Kit gave a sharp laugh. She was unhinged, but she was amusing. 'Were you now? And who said you were to get to know me first? Who set you up for this, my little intriguer?'

'No one, no one set me up, I'm acting on my own.' The stamp of a little foot and the quick flush betrayed Clarrie again. Her temper, did she but know it, went with the auburn hair, and had been her father's undoing. Normally it was easy to control, but there was something about this man that got under her skin. 'I merely meant, Lord Rasenby, that I wanted to know a little more about you before we have such an intimate discussion. For a start, I wouldn't want to make you any proposal if I'm mistaken as to your current state of attachment.'

'Come now, I feel sure that someone as bold as you are would have done your research. Surely you are perfectly aware of my current state, as you call it?'

'Yes, my lord, I am aware that you have an attachment to Miss du Pres, but I was more concerned with your intentions as to your immediate future. I have heard that you have been paying court to a Miss Warrington?'

'You have been digging, haven't you? And what have you heard about Miss Warrington and my intentions towards her?'

'I have heard that you have been marking her out, my lord. I have heard that she has been the object of your affections for the last few weeks. I have heard that you have even raised expectations of a more honourable kind.'

Kit gave another bark of laughter at this. 'Whatever you have heard, I have nothing honourable in mind when it comes to Amelia Warrington. And I cannot believe that Miss Warrington imagines any such thing either. That girl is a chit who knows only the value of my purse, and aims to dig as deep into it as she can. Can it be that it is she who has set you on to me?' Behind the mask, Kit's eyes narrowed. 'No, she does have a close companion, an insipid, simpering miss, but she bears no resemblance to you. Her name escapes me.'

'Chloe.' Clarissa realised her mistake immediately; the black brows opposite her snapped together with suspicion. 'I believe that's her name. Although I don't really know Miss Warrington personally—at least, not very well.' After today, that at least was true. Amelia was becoming a stranger to her. 'I am merely repeating the latest gossip. And the rumours are that you intend marriage.'

'I assure you, madam, I have no plans to marry. My intentions in that direction are not yet fixed. Miss Warrington is attractive, I'll grant, and more than willing, that I know. I may have a proposal for her, but it would not be honourable.' Kit smiled rakishly. Seeing Clarissa flinch at his words, he narrowed his eyes. 'Did you think her one of those innocent victims you were throwing in my face earlier? Amelia Warrington knows exactly what is on offer, I have made that perfectly clear to her. And if she thinks to hold out on me in the hope of more, then she'll quickly learn the better of it. If I ever deign to marry, it would certainly not be to someone as easy to touch as Miss Warrington.'

Clarissa absorbed this assassination of her sister's character with sadness, but a weary resignation. It was, after all, no more than what her aunt had said earlier. Even, although she hated to admit it, what she was coming to believe herself. But if Amelia could be prevented from making a fatal mistake with the Earl of Rasenby, if she could be prevented from ruining herself now, there would still be time for Clarissa to try, one more time, to establish her more genteelly. She had to secure this chance for her sister, even if it meant risking her own virtue.

'I see. Very well, my lord, then I feel that the way is clear for you and me to discuss terms.'

'You are either very naïve or very stupid. It is for the gentleman, you know, to make terms. And for the lady to accept. You cannot expect me to take you seriously.' Lord Rasenby was by now, against his will, thoroughly interested. It was a trap, he had no doubt about it, but it was a good one, and merited his attention—at least until he discovered what it was.

Clarrie, braced for rejection, was yet determined to prevent it. She had to give her sister a chance of escape. She had to get Lord Rasenby away from her for just a few days, a few weeks, enough to let him cool off, and for Amelia to have her sights pitched at a more achievable and more honourable target.

'I realise that I am being a little unorthodox. But I

thought you would appreciate both directness and a change. You are, as you admitted yourself, a little jaded in your taste. Perhaps a freshness of approach would restore your appetites?' Clarrie smiled in what she hoped was a coy manner, although the effect was ruined somewhat by the pleading in her eyes.

It was the pleading that succeeded. 'I'll give you a chance then, for your boldness, if for nothing else. But you must rise to the challenge, and prove your good faith to me first.'

'How?'

'I'll listen to your proposal in private. Tomorrow, not now. That will give you time to cool your temper, and to make sure that you really want to go through with this.'

'I will be just as determined tomorrow, I know I will. Name the place, Lord Rasenby, and I will be there.' With a toss of her head, and a determined point of her little chin, Clarrie glared into those deep blue eyes. She was anything but propitiating, but she was learning, and quickly, that Kit Rasenby responded badly to anything other than direct dealing.

'Will you? I wonder?' The soft tone sounded just a little threatening. 'I don't take kindly to being deceived, I'll warn you now. I'll have no truck with games and trickery. Come and dine with me tomorrow evening. At my house. On your own.'

'Oh, no, I couldn't. Why, that would be shocking. Oh, no. Can we not meet in the park, or perhaps take a drive? I couldn't dine alone with you.'

'Ah, 'tis as I thought. You are not nearly so bold as you promise. It was pleasant, exchanging views—' his tone was heavily ironic '—but I'm afraid our acquaintance is now at an end. I bid you good evening.'

'No! Wait!' Once again, Clarrie was forced to take a

dramatic—nay, huge—step forward. 'I'll be there. I'll dine with you.'

He was surprised at her agreeing, for it was a mad suggestion, even for him. No one could be under any illusion about a single lady dining alone in a gentleman's house—he had never invited any before now. But he gave no sign of his surprise. 'Very well, until tomorrow evening. I take it you know the address?'

She nodded, mute at her own daring.

'And am I to have a glimpse of the face under the mask before tomorrow? Perhaps even something on account?'

But Clarissa shrank back at this, unable to comply, even for her sister. And she had achieved her objective for tonight, after all. 'Wexford, my name is Wexford. As to my face—tomorrow will be soon enough. Unless, that is, you have more than one masked lady coming to dinner?'

He laughed. Her humour had the desperate touch of the gallows about it, but she was game. 'No, only you. Until then.'

And before he could bid her good night, Clarrie fled, removing her mask with relief, oblivious to Lord Robert Alchester, following discreetly at her back. A small exchange of coins bought him the address the footman had given to the hackney driver.

Back in the ballroom, Kit realised, with a curse, that he would need to find another dance partner.

Chapter Three

On her return from the ball Clarissa went straight upstairs to bed, but the long night brought her little comfort. She dreamt of surrendering to a passionate figure in a black domino, a dream that left her hot, flushed, and far from rested. Sitting up in bed to drink her morning chocolate—her one indulgence before facing the day—she tried to shake off the mists of sleep. Kit Rasenby, she reminded herself, was not a man to whom she should surrender anything, not even in her dreams! But the image of his strong, muscular body, his voice husky and flushed with passion, pressed naked against her own flesh, remained obstinately in her mind.

In person, Kit Rasenby had been completely unexpected. She had not counted on the strong pull of attraction she could feel between them, nor had she counted on him being so plain spoken. Amelia's description had led her to expect a man of the world, that was true, but one like the rest of the *ton.* Instead, Lord Rasenby stood out from the crowd, and his attractions were not those of a primped and perfect macaroni, but of a clean-cut, athletic, very *masculine* man.

Clarissa reminded herself once again not to confuse the outer man with the inner. He only *looked* clean cut and honest. His bitter remark, that all women wanted to be recompensed for their favours one way or another, came from deep within. In many ways, Clarissa could empathise with this. In fact, thinking about her sister, she could understand completely why Lord Rasenby was so very cynical. She fought the urge, growing deep in the recesses of her mind, to prove him wrong. She was not such a woman. She could be his equal. Only by recalling her mission, to save her sister—and her virtue—from his clutches, did she remind herself that her interests in him as a man, a lost cause, or any sort of acquaintance would be of necessity of very short duration. When Kit Rasenby found her out as a deceiver, she had no doubt he would never forgive her.

But she couldn't subdue the wistful thought that during their short time together, she might prove to him that women—or at least one woman—could be different.

Sitting in the small parlour after breakfast, Clarissa attempted to put together the week's menus. Amelia's seemingly endless requests for new dresses, new shoes, and new hats, made economy an absolute necessity, which meant that their meals were very plain fare indeed. Menu-planning was one of Clarissa's most hated tasks. It was not surprising, therefore, that it took a while for Lady Maria's strange behaviour to penetrate her consciousness. Eventually, though, Clarissa became aware that her mama was a little more animated than normal. Instead of occupying her usual position on the *chaise lounge*, she was sitting upright at the little writing desk, frantically scribbling in a notebook.

'Mama, what is it that you are working on? May I help?'

Lady Maria jumped and tried, not very successfully, to assume an air of nonchalance. 'Help? No, no, dear, not at all. I'm just doing some sums, trying to look at our expenses, you know. Amelia needs a new dress, she was saying just yesterday, and her dancing slippers are quite worn away again.'

'Mama, you know that you have no head for figures. Here, let me help you.' Wresting the notebook from Lady Maria's grasp, Clarissa failed to notice her mama's aghast expression. But looking at the vast sums that had been scribbled, in writing that became less legible with each number, she turned to her in dismay.

'What on earth are all these numbers? These are far too large to be household expenses. Mama, what can they be?'

'It's nothing for you to worry about, Clarissa, dear. They're just jottings. Give them back to me.'

Ignoring her mother's desperate attempt to reclaim the notebook, Clarissa continued to look in confusion at the numbers. 'Mama, please tell me what these are. Come, let us sit down and talk comfortably. Where is your tisane, for you look in need of it to me?' As she spoke, Clarissa ushered her mother over on to her habitual seat, and, pulling up a stool, sat down beside her. 'Now, what can be so awful that you can't tell me?'

'They're my gambling debts.' The bald statement was blurted out with relief. Surely, now that she had confessed, thought Lady Maria, Clarrie would fix it. She always did.

But for once her daughter, transfixed with horror, had nothing to say.

'You see, I thought, if I could win, then I could help

with Amelia's gowns,' Lady Maria explained. 'For if she is to save our fortunes through a good marriage then she needs to be tricked out properly—even you would agree, Clarrie. And she says that she's so close to finalising things with Lord Rasenby, I thought I could help. But I kept losing. And then a nice man at the party said he would assist me with my stake money, and I thought, surely I couldn't lose for ever. But I did, Clarrie, I did. And now that nice man is dunning me, and I just don't know what to do.'

'Mama, don't, please don't tell me that you've actually borrowed money to gamble with?'

The abject horror in her voice made Lady Maria defensive. 'What of it? Everyone does it, Mrs Barrington says, and why should I not do so, when I'm bound to win soon.'

'Mrs Barrington? And what, pray, has she to say to this?'

'Well, she first introduced me to the party where I've been playing. And last night, when I had a quiet word with her, she said not to worry, she'd speak to the young man who is dunning me. Except, Clarrie, I can't help but feel I'd rather have you sort things out, you're so very good at it. I'd rather not rely on strangers, even if Mrs Barrington is such a good friend to Amelia, when I know can rely on you. My own *trusty* Clarissa.'

Lady Maria beamed gratefully at her daughter. She felt hugely better, having relieved her conscience and passed the burden, as always, to Clarissa.

But Clarissa was flabbergasted. The sums she owed, if the notebook was accurate, were beyond belief. 'Mama, you have not made any more arrangements for funds with Mrs Barrington, have you?'

'No, no, I promise. I just mentioned it in passing last night, I haven't exactly committed to anything.'

'And this man who is dunning you, when does he expect payment?'

'Well, as to that, I couldn't say. He merely says that he wants something on account soon, if I am to rely on him for further stake money.'

'Mama! You must not, under any circumstances whatsoever, take more money from him. You must stop this gambling at once. You won't win, you know, you will only put us further in debt. Please, I beg you, promise me, Mama, that you will stop.'

'Well, I—well, but do you think you can fix things, Clarrie? For Amelia must have her dress, you know. We can't expect Lord Rasenby to put us in funds until after they are married, once a settlement is agreed. And that is probably at least a month or so hence.'

'There is no question of Amelia marrying Lord Rasenby, absolutely none. We must sort out this mess ourselves, and you must refrain—Mama, you *must*—from further gambling in the meantime.'

'But, Clarrie, Amelia assures me that Lord Rasenby is about to propose. And if he does not, where will we be? No, no, Amelia cannot be wrong. She was born to make a sensational match, and she will.'

'Mama!' Clarissa's temper was rising rapidly beyond her control for the second time in two days. Taking a deep breath, knowing that harsh words would only give Lady Maria one of her turns, she tried once more for calm. 'Believe me, Lord Rasenby's intentions towards Amelia are purely dishonourable, no matter what Amelia may say. I know. Nay, I am certain of it. Amelia must be made to give him up, or she will bring us all to ruin.'

'Well, dear, if you say so,' said Lady Maria dubiously, torn between doubt and an unwillingness to give up her vision of Lord Rasenby as their saviour. 'Perhaps, then, a *carte blanche*—strictly as a temporary measure, you understand—would be a good thing, Clarrie? Then we could see ourselves clear of debt, and after that, Amelia can still make a good marriage. What do you say?'

'What do I say? Am I the only sane person in this family? Aunt Constance was right, we will be ruined.'

'Oh, don't talk to me about your precious Aunt Constance. She is so ridiculously strait-laced as to be positively old-fashioned. And anyway, she's never been short of a penny, so what does she know? You take after that side of the family, Clarissa, I have always said so. Amelia is so much more like me, the darling girl.'

'Thank you, Mama, but I am pleased to take after Aunt Constance, if it means I have some moral fibre! I beg you, please, leave this in my hands. Do nothing further to get us deeper in debt. And get it out of your head that Amelia will receive any proposal from Lord Rasenby, honourable or otherwise.'

Lady Maria was far too used to Clarissa sorting their problems to question her abilities to cope with such huge debts, so she sighed, tucked her scarf around herself more comfortably, and dozed peacefully for the rest of the morning. Clarissa retired to her room with her head spinning to try to make sense of the situation.

Amelia flounced in some time later, disrupting her meditations. 'Why so glum, Clarrie? I hope you're not still fretting over my virtue. It's safe enough—for now at any rate.'

'Did you have a nice night?'

'Yes, I did, thank you very much, and as I promised, saw no trace of Rasenby. Mr Brompton was most attentive, though. I do like him.'

'Do you, Amelia? Enough to marry him?'

'Lord, Clarrie, not that again. I've told you, Edward is a clerk in a lawyer's office, he can hardly keep himself in cravats, never mind marry me. Although, perhaps as a last little fling before I tie myself to Rasenby, he'll do well enough.' Amelia laughed contemptuously at Clarissa's face. 'You're so easy to shock, sister dear. Provided that Rasenby gets no whiff of it, why should I not have Edward first? It's not as if Rasenby would be coming to the marriage bed pure.'

Amelia paused for a moment to reflect. Really, it was too, too vile of Edward to be so poor. And virtuous into the bargain. She was not at all convinced that he would take her to bed unless it was as his wife—even if she paraded naked in front of him! He had found out from Chloe some of Amelia's doings with Rasenby, and had had the temerity to lecture her. He could lecture her all he wanted if he had the funds. But he didn't. Frustrated at the unwonted feelings of tenderness Edward aroused in her, and at the necessity of deceiving him, Amelia turned once more on her sister. 'Yes, I warrant I like Edward enough to marry him. But he has not the means. It's Rasenby or the poor house, and I will not be going to the poor house.'

Clarissa was shocked. She had not realised just how perfidious her sister had become. She was horrified, too, at how she planned to treat Rasenby. Even had she not already resolved to remove Amelia from his grasp, she would have been forced into warning Rasenby about Amelia! 'Perhaps you may find that if this Edward is so much to your taste you may settle for him after all?'

'No, I've told you, Clarissa, my plans for Rasenby are unchanged. A few more days and all will be resolved between us, one way or another.'

'He won't be trapped into marriage, no matter what

your plan.' Clarissa's tone was dry. 'He is far too clever for that. Are you so sure that he is as mad for you as you say?'

'Of course he's mad for me, I'm never wrong about these things.' This with a determined toss of golden curls. 'I have him wrapped around my finger. And there he'll stay, be assured, Clarrie, until he puts a ring on it.'

'That he will never do, I am sure of it. But what of you? How can you contemplate a life of matrimony based on deceit and trickery?'

A scornful laugh was Amelia's reply to this. 'Why do you care? It's not you who's being tricked. He deserves to be played at his own game, it will serve him well.'

'No, he never relies on trickery, he is honest in that sense. Really, he does not deserve such treatment.'

'What are you talking about, Clarissa Warrington? You've never met him—what do you know?'

The suspicion in Amelia's voice reminded Clarissa of the need for secrecy. But it would seem that rather than save Amelia from Lord Rasenby, Clarissa was now intent on saving Lord Rasenby from Amelia. When had come about this switch in loyalty?

'No, I don't know him, except by reputation. But it seems to me that, rake as he is, he deals honestly with his conquests. And he does not deserve to be tricked into matrimony. It is a recipe for disaster. For all, including you, Amelia, don't you see? Dearest, you'd be miserable.'

'Lord, Clarrie, there's no reasoning with you. You like to think you're so practical, but you're the most pathetic romantic, deep down. I won't discuss it further. I merely came in to ask you to come for a walk with me. Edward gets an hour for luncheon, and he said he may take the air in the park, so I thought we might bump into him. Do come, Clarrie, you'd like him.' Amelia's tone was conciliating, but for once Clarissa was not to be won over.

'No, I won't be party to your assignations. It sounds like poor Edward is going to be another man let down by your plotting and scheming. Take Chloe, I'm sure you can persuade her easily enough.'

Amelia flounced out before Clarissa finished her sentence. It wasn't like Clarrie to be obstinate. Well, she'd show her!

Alone, Clarissa resolved on action. She was sure that there was more to Amelia's feelings for Edward, if only money were not the issue. If money, in the form of Rasenby, were removed as a temptation, Amelia would have a chance to see more of Edward. And he sounded like a determined young man; he would surely take the chance himself to secure Amelia. It wasn't much to go on, but it was a start. And if Edward didn't come up to scratch, she could always come clean with Rasenby, tell him her sister's plan. She was not going to stand by and let Amelia trick anyone into marriage. And she was going to do all she could to give her sister a chance at happiness—virtuous happiness.

Only Rasenby stood in the way. And by now, Clarissa had a good enough idea of his character to guess at what would interest him. A challenge, that's what he would like. And a bit of intrigue. She could do it. Clarissa turned her mind towards tonight, ignoring the thrill of anticipation she felt at the contest she was about to invoke. She was excited at seeing a means to save Amelia from herself, that was all. It was nothing at all to do with pitting her wits against such an opponent. Nothing to do with the charms of the opponent either. Certainly not!

Depositing her at the front door of Lord Rasenby's mansion in Grosvenor Square, the jarvey slid Clarissa a calculating look. Single ladies visiting these mansions did not normally travel in hacks. Nor did they arrive after dark, alone and wearing evening dress. Giving up the attempt to square all of these things with his passenger's cultured voice and genteel manner, he shrugged philosophically, and headed off into the night. She might be a toff, but she was up to no good, that was for sure.

As Clarissa tugged the bell and waited nervously at the front door, her thoughts mirrored those of the hackney driver. She felt like a woman of the streets. The look of contempt she received from the butler as he removed her cloak in the spacious hallway confirmed that he too shared this belief.

The hallway smelt of lavender polish, and was warmed by a huge fire burning to the left of the door. The rugs were Turkish, the large clock ticking softly against the panelled wall antique. There was a palpable air of wealth stretching back generations. Clarissa had no money, but there was nothing wrong with her breeding, and she had pride too. A martial flush gathered on her high cheekbones and sparkled in her eyes as she thanked the butler in frigid tones. Clarrie was getting ready to do battle, and she was not about to be put out by a mere servant.

As with the hackney driver, her cultured tones gave the butler a shock, confusing him. Handing her cloak over to the footman, his voice became more propitiating. 'Lord Rasenby is expecting you, madam. I will show you to the parlour, if you'd be kind enough to follow me.'

A quick check in the mirror reassured her—she would do. Amelia's gown of palest blue silk with an overdress of twilled sarsenet was a little too large for Clarissa's more slender frame, and the *décolletage* way too low, showing far more of her creamy white skin than she had ever done before, but none of her own gowns were grand enough— or fashionable enough—to wear. Following Amelia's example, she had dampened the skirt so that it clung to her long slim legs, making the gauzy material almost transparent in the candlelight. Her glossy auburn hair had been cajoled into a Grecian knot, the curls falling over her white shoulder, and her slim arms were covered by long kid gloves. She had forsworn any cosmetics, fearing that she had not a light enough touch, but there was an attractive natural flush across her cheeks.

It was now or never. Head high, Clarrie entered the room and glided gracefully over to Lord Rasenby, hand extended. He was standing with his back to the fireplace, dressed simply but elegantly in an impeccably cut dark-blue coat, his pantaloons of a biscuit hue and glossy Hessians adding a touch of informality. Taking her gloved fingertips, he pressed a whisper of a kiss on the back of her hand, then quite blatantly looked her over.

'Well, Miss—Wexford, I think you said?' A quizzical raised brow told Clarissa he knew perfectly well that she had given an assumed name. 'You've surprised me on two counts.'

'I have, sir?' Clarissa retrieved her hand and, placing it behind her back, retreated a few paces, finding Lord Rasenby's presence somewhat overpowering. The tilt of her chin, did she but know it, was challenging.

'Yes, you have.' So, she was a little on edge, the fake Miss Wexford. Well, he wasn't surprised—it was a brazen enough act to dine with him, and he admired her courage, if not her honesty. 'I wasn't convinced that you'd come, for a start. And, seeing you without the mask for the first time, I'm also surprised at just what perfection you kept hidden from me.'

Clarissa flushed. Tricked out in Amelia's finery, even she had to admit that she looked well enough. But having no great opinion of herself, she was inclined to dismiss his lordship's compliment as flummery. 'Thank you, sir, you are very kind.' A small curtsy of acknowledgement. 'At least I can be sure now that you will listen to my proposal without disgust.'

Kit laughed, finding himself once again confused by this woman. She was beautiful, although not in the common way. Her hair was not a fashionable gold, but burnished copper in the firelight, and the reddish flecks in it hinted at a temper. Those huge emerald eyes were too wide open, a little too perceptive, and had a disconcertingly honest look. Her mouth, with its full bottom lip, was not the cupid's bow that society decreed beauty, but it was, to Kit's eyes, far more sensual. And that chin—it was determined and defiant at the same time. Definitely not a simpering miss, but one with a real spark of fire.

He had been right to make this assignation. He was going to be anything but bored, dealing with the challenging Miss Wexford and her proposition, whatever that turned out to be. Having just this day made the arrangements for his final trip to France on the *Sea Wolf*, Kit was aware that he was in dire need of distraction. It pained him already, knowing this was to be the last of such adventures, and he knew he would miss it sorely. He worried that boredom would turn him to old quarrels and to new depths of depravity. And that thought, too, bored him.

Almost as an afterthought, he had paid off Charlotte du Pres. She didn't know it, but Miss Wexford's timing was excellent—she was just what he needed right now to take his mind off things. 'So, madam, you have no taste for compliments. We shall deal well then, for I favour plain speaking myself.'

Handing her a small glass of Canary wine, Kit ushered Clarrie into a seat by the fire. 'I thought we'd dine here, without the aid of servants. So much more comfortable, if you don't object to helping yourself?' Seating himself opposite her, he watched her take a nervous sip of the wine, and nod her assent. 'I thought, too, that we'd postpone our discussion until after we've eaten. It would be nice to become better acquainted first, don't you agree?'

Clarissa was staring into the flames, wallowing in the all-enveloping warmth, and only nodded, absently, at his words. The room was beautiful, in a restrained way. The furniture was light wood and highly polished, with a marked absence of the rococo gilt and ormolu currently so à la mode. With a sensuality she didn't even know she possessed, Clarrie snuggled deeper into the chair, and stretched, her white skin picking up a glow from the flickering flames, the red tints in her hair alive with colour. A small smile curled up at the edges of her mouth, and she sighed, deeply.

'Perhaps, you would prefer I left you to the comfort of the fire, and your own company?' Kit had been at first beguiled, then disconcerted, at her behaviour. He was not used to being ignored. He was a little piqued, and more than a little aroused. She was like a sensuous cat, stretching luxuriatingly in front of him.

The sharpness of his tone recalled Clarissa to her situation. She sat up abruptly, spilling a little of her wine on to Amelia's dress. 'I am so sorry. It's the heat, it's a little overpowering.' She rubbed at the dress with her handkerchief, but was succeeding only in making it worse.

'Here, let me.' Lord Rasenby bent over her, his own large handkerchief of white linen in his hand. 'There, that's better. Now, if you can force yourself to stay awake for a while, we'd better dine, I think.'

His touch, light as it was, made her shiver, and she drew back abruptly. 'Thank you.'

Kit eyed her quizzically. She was as nervous as a kitten under that veneer of calm. More and more, he was intrigued. But he would let her set the pace. For now, he was content to watch—and be entertained.

Over dinner, of which Clarissa partook little, confining herself to the duck and peas, she set out to charm. She had a fair idea by now of Kit Rasenby's preconceptions of her sex, and rather than make the expected idle small talk, conversed instead on the politics of the day. Her conversation was informed, thanks to her Aunt Constance's tutelage, and she was not frightened of expressing an opinion.

'I can't help but feel that things in France are not as settled as they claim. It seems to me that there will be another war, do you not agree? And then, perhaps all the *émigrés* presently here in England will become our enemies?'

'Yes, war seems to be inevitable. As to the *émigrés* I have no views at all. Some will turn, some—those who have found a home here—will not. 'Tis human nature to follow the easiest path.'

'That is a sadly cynical point of view, my lord. Do you grant no room, in human nature, for loyalty to a cause? Must everyone be so selfish?'

'Do not tell me you are a do-gooder, for you are far too pretty. You are obviously an intelligent woman, and unaccountably well informed, but believe me when I tell you that the French are no different than anyone else. People do what is easiest and most lucrative for them, naught more.'

'Well…' Clarissa pursed her lips and frowned '…I think that we will simply have to differ on the subject. For I choose to believe there is some good in everyone that is not simply self-interest!'

The challenge was accompanied again by that tilt of
the chin, and a flash from those green eyes. She looked
so sure of herself that Kit almost laughed. He contented
himself with an inward smile, however, and merely
offered her a dish of cream. She helped herself with
relish, blissfully unaware of her naïvety.

'You sound like the heroine in one of those dreadful
novels my sister raves about,' Kit said. 'Virtuous despite
the overwhelming odds. How would you cope, I wonder,
locked up in a castle like *Udolpho*, faced with the vile
Signor Montoni?'

'So you've read it, then, *Udolpho*, although you
despise it? I'd like to think I'd have a bit more presence
of mind, and would escape. And I don't believe in blind
virtue, just that there's more to people than self-interest.'
Temporarily distracted, Clarrie wondered whether to
continue this line of conversation, but quickly abandoned
the idea. Ruefully, she realised that a discussion of virtue
didn't really fit with her proposition for his lordship. 'We
were talking of the French. Do you know anything of
them, personally, Lord Rasenby—the *émigrés*, I mean?
I have often thought that they must have such romantic
tales to tell of escape. Far more exciting than Mrs Radcliffe's novel.'

'On the contrary, it's not at all romantic. They escape
with no wealth, often only the possessions they can carry.
And they have to rely on the goodwill of friends and
relatives in order to survive when they land abroad. To
see it as romantic is to persist in holding an uninformed
point of view.'

'And yet, I cannot help but do so. I would so much
like to see for myself what such rescues involve.'

'I think you wouldn't find it such fun if you were
present. Have you eaten sufficient? I think it's time we

talked terms, as you called it last evening.' Kit's tone brooked no argument.

'Yes. Yes, you are right.' Now it came to the bit, Clarissa was more than a little apprehensive. She knew what she had to say, but she wasn't convinced it would work. And if it did, she was worried it might work too well—for this man would want more than talk. How to go through with her plan and keep her own virtue intact? Especially when, it seemed, she was becoming less inclined to do so. Kit Rasenby was not just attractive, he was *interesting*. Becoming better acquainted was proving no hardship at all.

Taking a deep breath, Clarrie launched into her proposition with no thought for preliminaries, determined on seeing it through before her courage failed her—or her common sense intervened. 'I think, my lord, that it would be no exaggeration to say that you are rather bored with your life? Well, I wish to offer you a temporary diversion.'

'Bored? Well, that's one way of putting it, yes. I think you should realise there's not much you can offer that I haven't tried, one way or another, though. You are no doubt aware, madam, of my very dreadful reputation when it comes to your sex? After all, we touched on it last night.'

'Yes, and if you don't mind me saying so, I think that you're rather maligned by society, my lord.'

A cynical smile twisted Kit's lips, as he looked down into her honest-seeming emerald eyes. Was she truly naïve, this woman, or was she just an excellent actress? 'You know, if you hope to redeem me in some way, there's no point. I am, according to my mother and sister, long past redemption.'

'Oh, no, no one is *ever* past redemption. I can't help

but think, Lord Rasenby, that you cling rather too much to your reputation. You seem to actually enjoy being an outcast. By your own admission, you do have principles, although you keep them well hidden. You deal far more honestly than some, but you don't like people to see that, do you? You like to be the bad Lord Rasenby. And I can quite see why that would be convenient.'

'Pray do give me the benefit of your insight, then— why would my being bad be convenient?'

'Why, it means people expect less of you, of course. They can't rely on you, and therefore they won't be likely to turn to you when they need help, will they?' Clarissa held up her hand, as Kit tried to interrupt, too taken up with her line of argument to let him. 'I know what you're going to say, you told me yourself, that people do rely on you—for money. I'm sure that your mama and your sister and your mistresses all get plenty of that from you. But that's easy. What you don't give is anything of yourself.'

'I'm not sure I follow. Is bleeding me dry not enough of myself to give?' There was bitterness in the words. Kit was so wealthy that it would take more than his mama and Charlotte du Pres to ruin him, but they certainly tried. Paying Charlotte off had cost him a fortune and a diamond bracelet to boot, and his mother was hinting at new hangings for the Dower House. To say nothing of his nephew Jeremy and his regularly accumulated bad debts.

'You understand me perfectly well, my lord.' Clarissa's voice was terse. She hated deliberate avoidance, and Lord Rasenby was no fool. 'You substitute money for everything, and then you don't like it when you get nothing back.' Seeing his brow crease, she realised that she'd gone too far again. Lord Rasenby might like plain speaking, but he didn't like home truths. Clarrie cursed her blunt tongue, it was always getting her into trouble. And it wouldn't get her anywhere with this man.

Biting her lip, but failing to look totally contrite, she apologised. 'I beg your pardon. I get carried away sometimes, and speak without thinking. Let us talk of more congenial matters.' She smiled cajolingly up at him.

'Yes, but you're not truly sorry at all, are you—it's just that you've realised you've angered me.' With an effort, Kit dismissed the idea that she'd managed to see through him with ease—and that she'd echoed, almost to the word, his own thoughts. It was just luck. He wasn't so transparent. He was more than ever sure she was playing some sort of game, but it was a deep, and therefore challenging, one.

'Come clean, Miss Wexford. For a start, I know that's not your real name. What can I call you? If we are to talk openly, I would like *some* element of truth in our conversation.'

'Very well, you can call me Clarissa. Since we are to be informal.'

'So we are to be informal, Clarissa? The name suits you. And will you call me Kit?'

'Kit. It too suits you.' The humour was reflected in her eyes as she echoed his words. 'I think, since our relationship is to be both informal and of short duration, that we can manage on such intimate terms. It's not as if there will be any witnesses.'

'You intrigue me. I take it, then, that you do not aspire to Charlotte du Pres's position?'

A flash of anger was quickly disguised. 'No, I want no such relationship with you. Nor do I want any financial recompense, nor any presents nor anything at all of that sort. Let us be clear on that now, Lord—Kit, please.' She reached out, touched his arm lightly with the tips of her fingers, then quickly withdrew. Even such a tiny touch sent tingles up and down her skin.

'I can see you are serious. You are not someone who lies easily, are you? Whatever your game, you have honest eyes,' Kit said wryly. 'So, no presents. Well, it will be a refreshing change, certainly. But you are happy for Charlotte's position to remain unchallenged?' Kit had already decided she didn't need to know that Charlotte was already history.

His question gave Clarissa pause. If he got rid of Charlotte du Pres, then it created a vacancy, and it was likely he'd offer it to Amelia. It had been no part of her plan to comment on his current mistress, but perhaps, now that the opportunity had arisen, it was worth while?

'Are you contemplating a replacement? I thought you said last night that the rumours concerning Miss Warrington had no substance?'

'I said she would not be my wife. I have no need of a wife, when I can take my pleasures outside the marriage bed. From what I have seen of matrimony, there are few pleasures to be had there. Daily, the scandal sheets give us another tale of adultery and bastard children. And behind it, heartbreak for someone—the children, at the very least. Matrimony does not require affection. I have no wish to sample the insipid and dutiful caresses of a virgin wife. There is naught to substitute for experience. But you already know my feelings on this subject. I'm more interested in why you bring Amelia Warrington into the conversation again. Has she put you up to this?'

'No, no, I assure you she has not.' At least that was the truth. In fact, if Amelia found out, she would never forgive her. 'But I am a little acquainted with her, and I cannot feel she would make you a very good mistress. She wants to be your wife—she is hardly likely to be happy settling for less. No, on consideration, I think Charlotte du Pres is much more suited to your needs.'

Kit smiled, humour lurking deep in his midnight-blue eyes. Looking into them, laughing complicitly, Clarrie was suddenly breathless. His mouth, which he normally held in a firm, hard line, had softened, and there was a slight growth of stubble on his jaw. She had a sudden urge to run her hand along it, to feel the contrast between the roughness there and the smooth contours of his lips. Clarrie felt her mouth go dry at the thought, and licked her own lips nervously. She had never felt such blatant attraction emanating from a man.

Reminding herself that it was exactly this attraction he traded on, she looked away. 'I didn't come here to give you advice about your mistresses, but you did ask. I am aware that this is not really a conversation we should be having.'

Kit laughed out loud at this. 'My dear Clarissa, you shouldn't even be here, let alone discussing such intimate matters with me. But that hasn't stopped you. However, I think you're right about Amelia Warrington, I think she is likely to be rather too demanding. And virgins, you know, can be so unsatisfying. I prefer my women to know what pleasures a man.'

'Oh! Well—well, I think then you can quite safely dismiss Amelia Warrington.'

'You seem sure of her. She won't be a virgin for long, you know. It may not be me, but she will be plucked soon. And likely not by a husband. She aims high.'

'Is she really so bad? She is young, you know, but not—not calculating.'

'You don't know her at all well if you think so. She is a pretty and very ambitious young woman. Though in my experience, she has the kind of looks that fade quickly.

Any man can see that he has no need to offer marriage to have her. It's just a question of how high she'll sell herself. I'm not personally convinced it's a price worth paying.' Looking at Clarissa, he was surprised to see the hurt on her face. He possessed himself of her hand. 'It's the way of the world. She will take me not because she likes me better, but because I have more money. You are wasting your energies, concerning yourself with such a one. She will go her own way, and no friend will stop her.'

Looking into Kit's eyes, such a piercing, deep, dark blue colour, and for once showing such genuine concern, Clarissa acknowledged that he spoke the truth. But Amelia was her sister. She couldn't give up on her, it wasn't yet too late. And if nothing else, she could make sure that Amelia didn't throw herself away on this man.

With a sigh, and a renewed determination to get her proposition finally out of the way this evening, Clarrie smiled up at Kit. 'We've wasted enough time discussing other women. I've no aspirations to replace them in your affections. What I want from you is temporary.'

'You're frank, at least. Tell me then, precisely what is it you want me for—temporarily.'

'I will, then. But you must hear me out without interruptions, for it is vital that I make the terms as clear as possible—do you understand?'

His lips twitched as he repressed a smile, but Kit simply nodded his assent and sat back to watch her. This was proving to be worth every minute. Not once this evening had he been bored.

'I said I did not want to replace Miss du Pres, or anyone else—any of your opera singers or bits of fancy or whatever term you prefer.' Clarissa looked up, flushing. 'You're laughing at me?'

'No, no, I promise. I am merely impressed at your opinion of my prowess. Just how many of these bits of fancy am I supposed to be maintaining at one time? I am but a man, you know.'

A small gurgle of laughter escaped Clarrie. Shocking as this conversation was, it was more shockingly fun. 'Well, you told me yourself that your reputation is very bad, so I naturally assumed that you would place quantity over quality.'

At this, Kit gave an amused chuckle. 'No, I assure you, Clarissa, you are mistaken. I very much prefer quality, it's just that it is so difficult to come by. However, I am interrupting you once again. Please do continue, this is most—most—intriguing.'

'Well, I'm glad to hear you say that you would prefer quality, because that's what I'm offering. I'm four-and-twenty, and it is way past time I was married. But marriage, as you've said yourself, is a lifetime commitment to boredom, and for a lady, especially, promises no real pleasure.' A deep blush was stealing over Clarissa's cheeks, but she was determined to get this over with, no matter how embarrassing it all was. 'However, married I must be, and soon, or I will be too old.'

Looking up, Clarissa saw unease writ large on Kit's handsome face. She hastened to reassure him. 'Fear not, I have no matrimonial expectations of you. I am under no illusions there, and must aim rather lower, for I have neither dowry nor traditional beauty. I have someone in mind, you know, but the problem is that he is just a little staid and more than a little old.' Ruthlessly thrusting her neighbour Bingley Smythington into the role to give her lies some authenticity, Clarrie shuddered effectively. Bingley had clammy hands, and such a bumptious manner, as well as being nearer fifty than forty, that she had no qualms about using him so ill. 'So I thought, while I resigned myself to a life of propriety, that I might indulge myself first, and have one little adventure.'

Clarrie stopped talking, and looked at Kit, trying to assess his reaction to her words, but he merely raised an eyebrow, indicating that she should continue. She had thought through this approach so carefully, knowing she had to come up with something that would surprise him, that she forgot her modesty in her determination to make him agree.

'So, you see, that is why our relationship would have to be kept very private. And of short duration. I must on no account be publicly compromised. And I picked you because you said you had no qualms, you see, about seducing virgins, provided that they were willing. And I *am* willing, provided that it's fun. And of course, I know it will be—fun, that is—since your reputation as a ladies' man must mean—well, you know what I mean.' Clarrie paused, flushed at the path her thoughts had taken. Of course it would be pleasurable, sharing herself with this man, she had no doubt at all on that score. But she wasn't actually going to go that far, she had to remind herself. So really, she had to stop thinking about it.

With a shake of her curls to dispel the images she had conjured up, Clarrie returned to her proposition, finding that Kit was watching her with an amused, and slightly bewildered, look upon his face. 'I must insist that you promise to abandon—for just a little while—your pursuit of any other females. Indeed, I must make it a condition of your acceptance that you do so. What I want first and foremost is for you to surprise me. I want an adventure, not just a liaison.'

Once again, she held her hand up to stop him speaking. This was the tricky bit. 'I know you said that lack of experience was not something you relished. And I can't pretend that I have the skills of the likes of Charlotte du Pres. But I'm willing to learn, and I'm sure you won't find me bashful or—or unsatisfying, if you're willing to take a chance.'

She sat back, amazed at her own temerity. She had said it. She had been as blunt as she could be, and as clear about her terms. Surely he wouldn't resist the challenge? This evening had shown to her, if nothing else, that he was ripe for a change, and surely she had offered just that?

'Let me get this straight—for I have to tell you that I've never heard anything like it in my life.' Kit ran a distracted hand through his hair. He didn't believe her, but he was tempted, just to see how far she'd go. The claim of virginal innocence, he dismissed immediately. No virgin discussed such things so openly. It was a mere ploy to whet his appetite. And it was working. Virgin or no virgin, he wanted her.

'I have to forgo all other women for the duration of our acquaintance. I must see you only in secret. And you want nothing from me other than this—no recompense, only my silence?'

'Yes.'

'Further, you wish what you call an adventure in my company. I take it you mean something other than the adventure of sharing our bodies?'

She was blushing furiously now, and managed only a slight nod. Really, she was an excellent actress.

'And you cannot be more specific as to the nature of this?'

'No. That is your payment, you see. You arrange something out of the ordinary, something illicit, something thrilling, something I can remember when I'm old. And something too that you will enjoy, of course. As a prelude. I thought that you'd relish the challenge, that it would help, for a while, to ease your boredom. I thought—well, I thought we could have some fun together.'

'Fun? Good God, I don't think I've ever had fun with a woman. I'm not even sure I would know what you mean by it.'

He was looking at her assessingly now, and Clarissa desperately wanted him not to turn her down flat. The whole idea of an adventure was just a delaying tactic. The longer he took to organise something, the more time she had to separate Amelia from him. And until he could arrange whatever he was going to arrange, Clarrie was free from any threat to her virtue. She also needed time to think over what she had done—for she really had no idea yet how she was to manage to pull this off.

'Perhaps it would be best if I were to leave now, and we can discuss this further once you have reflected?'

'You're right, I need time to think. I'll meet you in Hyde Park tomorrow at four.'

'No, no,' Clarrie said agitatedly, 'that is the fashionable hour. We will be seen. I will meet you at the gates of Green Park—no one goes there at that time.'

'Very well.' Kit stood and raised a hand to help her out of her seat. Taking her by surprise, he pulled her close, one arm around her slim waist, cool on her skin through the thin fabric of her dress, the other tilting her chin upwards. 'No women other than you? You ask a lot of me. I think a sample of the merchandise would be appropriate, don't you agree? Just to prove you are worth the sacrifice. I warn you, my fair Clarissa, I won't be cheated, and I won't let you go back on your bargain. You do realise that?'

Clarrie licked her full bottom lip nervously, but made no move to escape. The sensation of his hand on her body was sending shivers up her spine. She had never been so close to a man before, and had no idea that it could be so very exciting. 'A kiss to seal a bargain, then,' she whispered.

Kit laughed, low and aroused. 'You are sealing a bargain with the devil.' His lips brushed hers, smooth and cool at first, a featherlight touch at the corners of her mouth. He ran his tongue over her full bottom lip. She smelled of roses and vanilla, she tasted sweet and hot. Her breath was warm, her breathing shallow.

Clarrie sighed at his touch, leaning closer in to the hard wall of Kit's chest, inviting him to deepen the contact. She could feel the heat from his body building a slow fire somewhere deep inside her. Experimentally, she let the tip of her tongue run over Kit's lower lip, mimicking his actions, feeling him groan in response. His lips took possession of her mouth fully, one hand on the sensitive nape of her neck, holding her carefully close, the other at her waist.

Clarrie surrendered to temptation and let an instinct she didn't know she possessed take over. Tongues met in a kiss that took them both by surprise. In an instant, Clarrie moved from warm tingles to searing heat. Kit's lips were soft and hard at the same time. He was kissing and licking her mouth in a way that left her weak with wanting. His tongue flicked to the sensitive corners of her lips, then back to tangle with hers. He licked along the length of her lower lip, then his mouth fastened fully on hers again.

She wanted more. She ran her hand over the nape of his neck and up into the short cropped hair on his head, relishing the rough feel of it, contrasting it with the soft, hard, smooth feel of his mouth on hers. Her nipples hardened as she pressed into his chest, rubbing against him, relishing the small shivers and the pleasure-pain feeling that the contact gave her, even through their clothes.

Kit groaned softly, and pulled back. His breathing slowed. He eyed her through heavy lids, careful not let her see how much she had aroused him. All her pretence of virginity must be at an end. This woman knew exactly what she was doing. 'Enough. That is definitely enough for now, I think. You have proved yourself entirely, madam.'

Clarrie, still trying in vain to control her overwhelming and totally unexpected response to his kiss, could do no more than blink up at him, confused. 'I—I—I'll get better in time, sir.'

'A word of warning. I will play these games only so far. You can abandon, once and for all, this pretence of innocent virginity, for the passion in your kisses prove you to be far from innocent.' Looking down at her, he was taken aback to see a sheen of tears glazing her speaking emerald eyes.

'Rest assured, your lack of innocence does your case no harm. Had you really been the virgin you claim to be, I would have hesitated. I need now have no scruples, and can consider your proposition with a clear conscience. The footman will call a hack for you. Good night.'

With a slight bow, he turned away from her, ringing the bell for the servant. Clarissa stumbled out to the waiting hack, her mind a swirl of abject confusion and unexpected hurt.

So distressed was she that she failed to notice the figure turning the corner into the street. Lord Robert Alchester, returning home early of necessity since his pockets were to let, from the tables of the hell in

St James's currently favoured with his patronage, was most intrigued. Well, well, the woman from last night, if he was not mistaken, and emerging alone from Kit Rasenby's town house. This development was worth keeping an eye on.

Chapter Four

Clarissa rose heavy eyed the next morning, having slept only fitfully, haunted by the memory of Kit Rasenby's kisses and her own shocking response. What was it about the man that made her act so out of character? Needing to clear her head, she eschewed her usual morning chocolate and settled instead for a brisk, invigorating walk around the park. This fever her body had succumbed to was but a passing fancy, surely. Triggered, like as not, by the novel experience of being kissed for the first time, and nothing more. It was not that Kit was irresistible at all. It was just that she had never had such contact with a man before. He was a novelty, that was all.

Entering the little breakfast parlour an hour later, she was grateful to find that both her mama and her sister were as yet abed. Resolutely putting all thoughts of Kit to one side, Clarissa partook of coffee and warm rolls, finally able to mull over the events of the previous night with something approaching her usual rational calm.

Kit's ruthless assassination of her sister's character

she acknowledged to be sadly all too accurate. There could be no doubt that Amelia would accept whatever Kit Rasenby offered, proper or improper. What would count with Amelia would be the recompense in purely financial terms. And the higher the terms, the less Amelia would concern herself with the loss of her virtue. Kit Rasenby was right. Amelia would be *plucked*—she shuddered at the awfulness of the term and all it implied. If not by him, then certainly by some other opportunist with a large and generous purse and a taste for virgin flesh.

Ruefully, Clarissa realised she would not wish Amelia as a wife on Kit Rasenby even had he any such intentions. It would be the road to misery for them both. Not, she cautioned herself, because she had any feelings for Kit herself, mind you. No, it was merely that she was sure they would bring only unhappiness to each other. And even a rake, after all, deserved more from matrimony. No, Amelia and Kit must not—*would not*—marry.

Amelia herself put an end to these musings, storming into the breakfast parlour in a state of high dudgeon, bright flags of anger flying in her cheeks. She was not yet dressed, and though she had discarded her nightcap, her hair was hanging loose, and the muslin wrapper she wore over her chemise was only loosely tied.

'Clarrie, there you are. I've been looking for you everywhere—where have you been? I've had the most dreadful night, I've hardly had a wink of sleep.' Throwing herself into a chair, failing to notice that her sister looked singularly tired from her own restless night, Amelia's mouth puckered in temper that boded a storm of tears in the near future. Reaching for a roll from the basket, she discarded it again petulantly. 'These are cold. And I expect the coffee is, too! I want fresh. Where is that dratted maid, she's never here when I need her?

Honestly, Clarrie, is it too much to ask that we employ servants who can actually fulfil their duties? I swear that woman hates me. How I detest being poor!'

Pulling the bell to summon fresh coffee, Clarissa eyed her sister with an impending sense of gloom. The last thing she needed was one of Amelia's tantrums, which were not only exhausting, but all-consuming. And unstoppable. There was no point in trying to do anything other than let them run their course, so she simply sat back and waited.

'Don't look at me like I'm some tiresome child to be indulged. I won't be ignored! Oh, Clarrie, you don't know—how can you know?—how truly dreadful it is to be me. Sometimes I almost wish I wasn't so beautiful. If I was merely pretty, like you, then it wouldn't be so bad.'

Clarissa, inured to such casual insults, continued quietly with her breakfast. Amelia slumped into her seat, causing her to hope that a full-blown tantrum was to be avoided, but this was dashed when, with a long drawn-out 'Ohhhhhh' of frustration, her sister rose abruptly, pushing her chair over, and started pacing in front of the fireplace. With a sigh, Clarissa gave Amelia her full attention.

'Come Amelia, what ails you? Won't you sit down and tell me?' She patted the chair invitingly, but Amelia continued to pace.

'I tell you, Clarrie, I am positively sick to my teeth of my life. Look at me!' Pausing to inspect herself in the mirror above the meagre fire burning in the grate, Amelia looked temporarily gratified at what she saw. Really, she was simply beautiful, even with her hair uncurled and her nightwear in disarray. But that was just the problem. 'I mean, I'm lovely. I'm not being vain, Clarrie, I can see it myself. And everyone says so—Mama, you, Chloe, *everyone*. I can't be this beautiful if it's not for a purpose, can I? I *must* be meant to marry well, I don't want to be an ape-leader like you.' Her breathing quick and shallow, Amelia paced, determinedly nursing her anger. 'It's my destiny, a good marriage. The end to all of my problems.'

Wryly Clarissa noted that Amelia concerned herself only with her own fate. No thought, as usual, for Mama. But then, when did Amelia ever think of anyone but herself? Last night Clarissa had accused Kit of escaping all responsibility by using his money to pay people off, everyone from his mother to his mistress. Sometimes she wished she had the means to do the same thing. Kit's wealth would do a lot to ease the many responsibilities she carried on her slim shoulders. Her mother's debts. A dowry for Amelia. Even enough to put adequate coals on the fire, or something other than rabbit and onions on the table for dinner.

Amelia unwittingly echoed her thoughts. 'I need money. I was born for luxury. I can't go on like this, I just can't. I'm fed up with wearing the same old clothes all the time, and never having nice jewellery. I'm eighteen, for goodness' sake, I'm practically on the shelf. I mean, look at you, Clarrie—what have you got in front of you except life as an old maid, or a governess, or married to some ancient old fossil and having to spend your days changing his gout bandages? I've got to get out of here. I've got to get married. *I've just got to!*'

Giving her temper full reign, Amelia's voice rose shrilly. Her face became unattractively red and tears flowed rather unbecomingly down her cheeks. A bout of crying was one of the few things that drew attention away from her charms. For a few moments, there was silence in the parlour, interrupted only by hearty sobbing.

Amelia cried with a passion, her shoulders heaving, her face hidden in her arms, as she sprawled once more on a seat at the table.

Eventually the tears turned to hiccups and she looked up, a sorry sight, hair tangled and lying damp on her cheeks, eyes puffed and red, to continue her lamentations. 'And if I'm to marry without a dowry, then it stands to reason that I'll have to resort to some *underhand behaviour*, as some people have called it. It stands to reason that I'll have to be *less than honest* in my dealings, as some may accuse me. It's just that fate needs a helping hand sometimes. And if *some people* can't see that, well, that's their problem, not mine. And what's more, if that's the way *some people* think, well…then they'll find that I'll refuse to see them again. Not ever! *Then* they'll be sorry.' The sobbing resumed, but more quietly now. The storm had almost worn itself out.

Smiling inwardly, Clarissa realised they had finally come to the crux of the matter, the real reason for Amelia's tears. Amelia's plans for tricking Kit into marriage had obviously been in part revealed to Edward last night. And Mr Brompton, bless him for the honest man he must be, had obviously severely upbraided Amelia. The fact that Amelia had listened sufficiently to be able to quote his reservations back word for word this morning was evidence enough of her affections being engaged, would she just admit it. With satisfaction, Clarissa realised that Amelia was, rather astonishingly, falling in love with this sober and righteous young man.

Trying to persuade Amelia that Edward and his reservations should be paid heed was, however, beyond Clarissa's capabilities for the present. With resolution borne of experience, Clarissa decided to sit back and let Amelia cry herself out, inwardly calmer herself now in the knowledge that she was right to pursue a course of separating her sister from Kit Rasenby. And hopeful too that Edward had played a part in putting at least some obstacles in the way of Amelia's plot to trick Kit.

But it took the rest of the morning and well into the early afternoon for Amelia's tears to run dry. Only then did she allow Clarissa to dose her with hartshorn and water, tuck her up in a darkened room, and leave her to sleep off the damage done to her complexion.

Which left Clarissa with little time to continue her own reflections before having to ready herself for her assignation with Kit in the park. He would say yes, he *had* to say yes. And if he turned her down—well, that simply wasn't an option. She told herself, with more bravado than conviction, that she would persuade him—somehow—to come round to her way of thinking.

Had she been aware of just how Kit had spent his extremely busy morning, Clarissa would have been more than a little perturbed. As it was, she set out for the Green Park by hack, looking smart in a pale green merino walking dress and matching spencer, a gift from her aunt. Her feet were clad in boots of Morocco leather, and a reticule of her own design dangled from her wrist. A treasured pair of kid gloves and a simple poke hat completed the outfit. Clarissa was content with her appearance, and happy that she looked her best. She carried no muff, it was a luxury she could not afford, but the day was none too cold, and she was not anticipating being in the carriage for long.

With a heart fluttering with anticipation, despite having given herself a stern talking to on the subject of attractive rakes, their kissing abilities, and the need to avoid all such intimate contact in the future—somehow or other—Clarissa paid off the hack, and stepped lightly through the park gates.

Lord Rasenby was waiting in a high-perch phaeton to which two glossy, perfectly matched chestnuts were poled. They were restless, contained with some effort by the small tiger at their heads, and Clarissa looked up at their master, carelessly lounging in the seat of the vehicle, impossibly high off the ground, with some trepidation.

'Don't be alarmed, I assure you I have them well under control. Any rake worth his salt, you know, is an expert at mastering even the freshest of fillies.' The sardonic look that always accompanied any mocking reference to his reputation was tempered by a slight smile. 'It's not so high as it looks, just place your foot on the step and I'll help you up.' Leaning over to take her hand, Kit pulled Clarrie easily into the carriage and briskly tucked a rug over her knees. His touch was cool and impersonal, but she flushed slightly all the same. With a curt nod of dismissal to the tiger, he jerked sharply on the reins, and the chestnuts set off at a brisk trot.

The few moments it took to get the horses under control allowed Clarissa to rein in her own feelings at the proximity of this man. His thigh brushed hers through the rug, for the seat was narrow. She could not but be aware of that hard, muscled body which his caped greatcoat did nothing to hide. He was every bit as overpowering as she remembered. Every bit as attractive. *And every bit as dangerous,* she chided herself. Think only of what you have to achieve, and make sure you do it with regard to your own safety, Clarissa Warrington.

'I congratulate you for your punctuality, Clarissa, it's not a trait common to your sex.'

His words startled her from her thoughts, and she replied with unthinking asperity. 'As I believe I have been at pains to point out to you, sir, I am not inclined to be taken for the common herd. I pride myself on being punctual.'

'And frank, too. You could not be accused of reticence.'

She laughed. 'Yes, that too. I'm sorry, I didn't mean to be rude. It's just that—well, I hate being judged. I know you'll think me foolish, but you've no idea how irritating it is when people assume you are just the same as every other young lady. I try not to be so predictable.'

'You do me a disservice, madam. I sympathise with your frustration and assure you I understand only too well both your feelings and your reaction. But are you not being a little hypocritical, for did you not so judge me—as a rake—when first we met, in exactly the same way?'

'Yes, I did, and it was wrong of me. Although I have to say that you've been at great pains to confirm me in my assumptions, have you not?' A glance at him showed, from the lips firmly suppressed, that she had hit home. 'And when I did point out that you were hiding behind your reputation, you were not best pleased.' Another glance showed that he was not best pleased again. Oh dear, her unfortunate tongue—when would she learn to guard it? 'I'm sorry. I fear I have offended you once more. And I so meant not to—offend you, I mean. I meant to be more *propitiating.*'

A crack of laughter made her look up, an answering sparkle in her own eyes.

'You think that's funny. I know what you're thinking.'

'I doubt it. Pray tell me.'

'That my behaviour is hardly conducive to achieving my goal. Getting you to agree to my proposition, that is. And I do most abjectly apologise, for contrary to what

I may have said, and even with the benefit of a night's reflection, I *do* want you to agree.'

'Actually, I was thinking that you're the most unpredictable woman I've ever had dealings with. And I was thinking that I would very much like to kiss you again. So you see, my fair Clarissa, you're not as able to read my mind as you think you are.' A smile, warmer than before, softened the words.

'Oh.' A blush stole across Clarrie's pale cheeks, for his words roused such pictures in her head as she had been trying to suppress since last night.

As she looked up at him, her eyes wide, her soft mouth trembling slightly, Kit was surprised at the sharp gust of desire that ripped through him. The combination of honesty—or the appearance of it, in any case—and the undercurrent of passion, the fiery nature that must surely accompany those auburn locks, was captivating. Once again he reminded himself that he was no doubt being embroiled in a plot of her making. Once again he decided that whatever it was, it was a small price to pay for the use of the exceedingly comely body being offered to him.

Raising a dark winged eyebrow in query, he smiled. 'Oh? Is that all you have to say? You are not normally so succinct.'

'No. That is…well, Lord Rasenby—Kit, I mean, there must be no kissing yet, for we have not sealed our bargain. We were to discuss it further, were we not? Then, in case you need reminding, there was to be payment in advance on your part, in terms of our adventure, before any more such—intimate contact.' Ignoring the blush that heated her face despite the cold wind, Clarissa tried to pull the conversation back on track. 'So, there will be no more talk of kissing at the moment, if you don't mind. We have other things to discuss.'

'You would concede then that our kissing last night was exceptionally pleasurable?' He was enjoying the act in front of him, she was squirming in seeming embarrassment. Really, the woman should be on the stage.

'As I told you last night also, sir, having no other kisses with which to compare yours, I cannot say whether it was *exceptional*, or merely mundane.' The sparkle in her eyes and the challenging tilt of her chin belied the put-down. Clarrie could not help it, she enjoyed sparring with this man. She ignored the added *frisson* of awareness that such very *risqué* subject matter aroused, deciding that since no one else could possibly overhear them, she had naught to be ashamed of.

And she was rewarded for her barbed witticism with another burst of laughter. '*Touché*, Clarissa. But your kisses gave you away last night. Your claims to virginity are both false and unnecessary. So once again I will remind you to cast off that part of your repertoire. Your passion and your experience are what I desire. And what I shall have. For, having considered your terms, I have decided to accept your offer.'

His capitulation was so unexpected and so sudden that his determined disbelief in her innocence was cast momentarily from her mind. Clarissa was betrayed into a small crow of delight. She would do it. She would keep him away from Amelia. Edward would have his chance. *And she would spend some more time in his company. His exclusive company.* Ignoring this inward voice—for it was of no relevance, she told herself—Clarissa tried, rather belatedly, for composure. 'Thank you, Kit. I look forward to our adventure, when you've had sufficient time to arrange it.'

Kit merely smiled and gave his attention to the horses, relaxing his grip slightly on the reins to give them their heads. 'Since our business is concluded for the moment, then, let us relax and enjoy the ride.'

The phaeton was built for speed, and responded so smoothly that it was quite some time before Clarissa, deep in her own thoughts, became aware of their change from sedate trot to swift gallop. Even longer before she became aware that they had left the confines of the park, and even the traffic of the city, and were now traversing open countryside. How long had they been travelling thus? 'I'm afraid we must turn back, sir, I'm expected at home. I hadn't realised you intended more than a drive around the park. I'm not dressed for a longer journey.'

'Not far now, my horses need some exercise. Be patient, and enjoy the scenery.'

Suddenly Clarissa became aware of how foolish her behaviour must seem, alone in an open carriage with a notorious rake. Fleeting thoughts of abduction passed through her mind, to be dismissed summarily. She was being foolish. Kit had no need to take her by force when she had already offered herself so freely. After all, he did not know that she had no intention of fulfilling her promise. And while he was a rake, he was surely no villain. No, her imagination was simply overwrought, what with lack of sleep and too many lurid novels. Clarissa tried to relax and follow Kit's advice to enjoy their surroundings, but it was a relief none the less when, a short time later, the carriage slowed to a halt as they approached a whitewashed and thatched inn set prettily by a bridge over a lazily flowing river.

The small seed of doubt as to his intentions died. They would partake of some refreshment here and he would return her safely home. He had merely wished to try the paces of his horses, that was all. Well, they had certainly had a good run. How long had they been on the road? She was chilled. The horses being released from the traces by two uniformed ostlers were steaming with sweat. She had no timepiece, but Clarissa was starting to worry, from the darkening sky, about returning home in time for dinner.

'My lord, I—'

'Inside, Clarissa, where there is a fire. Come along, you're cold. I must see to my team first, then we may talk more freely.' An imperious hand in the small of her back propelled her forward, and she went with him, more reluctant with each step.

'I had no idea we had been driving for so long. We must turn around quickly, my lord, for my mama will be expecting me.'

A curt nod was his only response. He would brook no discussion in front of the servants. But *what*, exactly, was in need of discussion? Surely they were just waiting on fresh horses? That was it, of course. Fresh horses. And some warming coffee while they were poled up. With a lighter step, Clarissa preceded Lord Rasenby through the door of the inn, and towards the reassuring warmth of the fire in a small private parlour.

'I won't be long.' A stiff bow, and she was suddenly alone.

But as she stripped off her gloves to heat her chilled hands at the blaze of the fire, Clarissa was beset by doubts. He hadn't needed to command the parlour. What was it the innkeeper had said when he had welcomed them at the door? *Everything is ready, just as you requested, my lord.* Well, perhaps he had decided in advance that they would take a drive. No harm in that, was there? And he was obviously well known to the proprietors, so it wasn't as if he was concerned about his identity becoming known. So the growing fear Clarissa was trying to subdue, that she was being abducted, was ridiculous, wasn't it?

Of course it was. And here to prove it was the landlady herself, bustling in with a pot of hot steaming coffee and a large jug of foaming ale. She busied herself, putting another log on the fire and fussily adjusting one of the porcelain ornaments on the large mantel. No sign at all of anything untoward.

'Will that be all, madam? Lord Rasenby said to tell you to take your coffee while it's hot, he is just making sure his horses are stabled properly. If you require anything else, just ring the bell to summon me.' At Clarissa's nod, she bobbed a curtsy and left.

There, seeing to the horses, the woman had said. Making sure the fresh pair were ready for a quick departure. She would be home, if not before dusk, at least before full dark. With a sigh of relief, Clarissa snuggled down on to the settle before the fire, and poured her coffee. The warmth of the flames after the cold outside lulled her body into comfort and her mind into a calmer acceptance of her situation.

It was not until she was pouring her second cup from the pot that she realised Kit had been gone an overlong time. And the doubts awakened again, with renewed force. Nervously, she stood and peered out of the window into the growing gloom. Judging from the light, it must be near six of the clock. They had driven nigh on an hour and a half. It would be well after dinner before she was back. What on earth was he thinking? And where on earth was he? As her worries grew, so Clarissa's temper also rose.

The object of her ire finally walked back into the room, bringing with him a blast of cold air and the faint smell of the stables. 'Ah. I see you are a little warmer. An open carriage for such an extended period at this time of year is not ideal. I apologise.'

'Had I known you intended such a long drive, sir, I would have cautioned you against it. As I have told you twice now, I am expected at home.'

'Yes, and I heard you the first time. I am not dim-witted, Clarissa, I do understand simple English.'

His bland tone provoked rather than calmed her. 'Then you will understand the simple fact that we must leave at once and return to London, sir.' This, through gritted teeth. 'I would not wish to be at odds with you, but we seem to have rather different interpretations of the phrase *a short drive in the park.*'

He smiled at this sally, but she received no other response. Kit seemed more intent on the refreshing draught of ale he had poured himself, and the warmth of the fire. His very indifference made her throw caution to the winds. Clarissa stamped her foot in a fair imitation of her sister that very morning, had she been inclined to notice. It did not occur to her, however, so intent was she on gaining Kit's attention. She really needed to get back home.

'If you will not rouse yourself from your beer, then I will just have to commandeer a carriage myself.' She had nowhere near sufficient funds in her purse to do so, but she tried not to think about that obstacle for the moment. Clarissa moved purposefully to the looking glass above the fire in order to adjust the strings of her bonnet.

He moved like a cat. One second he was lolling in a hard wooden chair, drinking from a brimming tankard, the next he was on his feet, standing all too close, his presence dominating her slim form, his face not angry exactly but stern. Forbidding. The full extent of her predicament struck Clarissa forcibly. No one knew where she was or who she was with. She had little money. And this man, this impossibly attractive, intimidating, over-poweringly strong man, was in full command of the situation. Nervously, Clarissa licked her dry lips, and decided to try a different tack.

'You are teasing me, Kit, I know you are. But really, the joke has gone too far. I must go home now. We have agreed terms. You are happy with my proposal, you said so yourself. You'll be wanting your dinner soon. And surely your horses will be rested by now. You will no doubt wish to have a think about our adventure too, to spend some time planning it. So we should go now, and make arrangements to meet in a few days. Should we not?' Her voice faltered, seeing no change on his face, no response at her attempt to lighten the mood. 'Kit?'

He was looking down at her, scrutinising her closely. There was confusion and fear lurking in her wide-open green eyes. He knew perfectly well what she was think-ing, for he had fully intended to frighten her just a little, to let her know that whatever her game was, she wasn't going to have it all her own way. But he had been unpre-pared for this feeling of pity, tenderness even, that her fear invoked. With difficulty, Kit resisted the sudden urge to reassure her, to soothe her anxiety. He reminded himself that she was an excellent actress. All the talk of Mama, the show of bravado, even the slight tremble of that full, sensuous bottom lip. Really, Mrs Siddons could not have acted better than this wench. She had no need of tenderness.

Grasping her small determined chin, he moved closer, feeling her light breath on his hand, inhaling that alluring combination of roses and vanilla. His thumb stroked the corner of her mouth, and ran over her full bottom lip. She was staring up at him, those huge green eyes pleading, the lashes so dark and long that she must employ some artifice, no matter how natural they looked. He could drown in those eyes. For a timeless moment they stood thus, Clarissa silently pleading, Kit coolly assessing, implacable.

'Kit, please take me home.' Her words were spoken softly, a gentle request, for somehow she was no longer frightened.

'I'm not planning to abduct you Clarissa, although I know you fear that is my intention. I have no need to take you by force. Anything we do together, you'll do willingly or not at all. I would not have it any other way, and you know it.' As he spoke, Kit pulled Clarissa to him, holding her with one hand lightly by the waist. 'You can leave directly, only say the word. Ask me again, I'll take you home and we can forget everything. Our adventure. Our kisses. The union of our bodies will be consigned for ever to our imaginations. It will be as if we had never met. We can forgo it all, Clarissa, if you tell me that is what you truly desire.'

The closeness of their bodies invoked memories of last night. His words were a whisper on her face. His mouth, his tempting, cool, hot mouth, was inches away. His thumb continued its slow, languorous caress as he spoke, the line of her jaw, back to her mouth, over the planes of her cheek. Brushing gently. Soothing her. Distracting her. Hypnotising her. But the clasp on her waist remained light. She could leave now, she believed him. Instead of turning away, Clarrie moved forwards, drawn closer as if mesmerised, casting aside all doubts and reservations, any sense of the danger of her situation, in the need to taste him once more.

Her tongue flicked over the tip of Kit's thumb. And

flicked over it again, her teeth just grazing the skin, before she closed her lips around it and sucked with a slow, sensuous and purely instinctive movement. She sucked harder, drawing the length of his finger into her mouth, closing her eyes to delight all the more in the sensations it was arousing all over her body. She moaned slightly as his finger was withdrawn, only to purr with satisfaction when it was replaced by the lips she craved.

Opening her mouth to receive his kiss, Clarrie gave a mewl of frustration as Kit's lips moved slowly, deliberately, delicately, when she wanted hard, hot, fast. Reaching up to pull his head down more firmly, relishing the rough graze of his chin on her tender skin, Clarrie drew tight against his hard, aroused body, and stopped thinking. Their kiss deepened, rocketing her body temperature, causing the flames that had flickered somewhere in her belly to strengthen and focus lower down. She could feel the male hardness of him between her thighs through the delicate wool of her walking dress, and tilted slightly to press herself against him.

The action was too much for Kit's self-control. Suddenly she was free, a cold distance between them, the room silent save for their ragged breathing. The flame of passion was replaced by a deep blush of shame.

Clarrie looked up to find Kit's eyes on her, that sardonic, devilish look of his accentuated by his slightly raised brow, the half-smile on his mouth. 'Well? Are you going to persist in your demands to be taken back to your mama? Have you decided, after all, that to deal with so notorious a rake as me is just a mite too dangerous? Speak now, Clarissa, or for ever hold your peace. Is it to be safe home? Or is it to be onwards into the unknown with me? Think carefully, for if you choose onwards, my bold Clarissa, *your adventure begins this very day.*'

Chapter Five

What on earth had she done? Clarrie wondered. Broken all her resolutions, and some she hadn't even thought she'd need to make, for a start. Betrayed by her own body, tricked by her own desires, she had placed herself in a position of real peril. She had thrown herself—quite literally—at this man, when only moments before she had been terrified of abduction, and protesting her innocence. Clarissa turned to look bleakly out of the window. How stupid her plans had been. How poorly she understood her own true nature. A few hours in his company, and here she was launching herself at Kit like one possessed. If she persisted in such brazen behaviour, he would tire of her far too quickly and return to his pursuit of Amelia, and then she'd have sacrificed herself for nothing.

Leaning her hot cheeks against the cool of the glass, Clarissa realised that her scathing denunciations of romantic heroines had been naïve in the extreme. Here she was with a notorious rake, and succumbing to his charms—nay, hurling herself wholeheartedly at them—

with nary a thought for the consequences. Stupid, stupid Clarissa!

As if that wasn't enough, she had walked with eyes wide open into this impossible situation. A situation, she was forced to acknowledge, of her own making. She had asked for an adventure. It was natural to assume that adventures involved surprise, and foolish of her to suppose that one so impetuous as Kit would do anything other than rise immediately to her challenge.

What on earth was she going to do? Return home and forget her plan? Clarissa had no doubt that Kit would take her back if she wished. He might be a rake, but he was an honest one, she was sure of it. He said he would not abduct her against her will and she believed him. But to return home was to put an end to everything. She would have failed in her attempts to save Amelia. And she would never see Kit again. Never. At the thought, a huge chasm seemed to open at her feet. Never share a joke with him. Never test her wit against his. Never see that smile, so rarely given, of genuine amusement, which lit up his face, changing him from devilish to absurdly, overwhelmingly handsome. Never taste his lips on hers. Never feel his hard body pressed against hers.

Reminding herself that she had no intention of succumbing to more intimate advances did not prevent Clarrie from craving more of the forbidden fruit she had already tasted. Surely a few more kisses would be no compromise? Surely a few more hours, a few more days in his company, would satisfy her, and suffice to save her sister? Suffice to subdue this fire. Surely a better acquaintance with Kit would cure her of this irrational infatuation? A surfeit of his presence would ensure she saw him in a more rational light, and would have the happy consequence of doing Amelia good too.

Lost in her thoughts, Clarissa stared unseeingly out of the window. Kit watched, judging it best to give her this time to adjust her thinking, refusing to attempt further persuasion. She would come, of that he was certain. She would accede to his terms. He had neither the desire nor the need for an abduction. She would come. He was sure of it.

Checking his watch, he tugged the bell by the fireplace, summoning the landlady. 'We will dine in twenty minutes. You'll oblige me by bringing some writing materials immediately, and some brandy too.' The woman curtsied and left.

'Dine?' The words startled Clarissa from her musings.

'Yes. I know it's early, but we have a long journey ahead of us. If you're not hungry now, you should be. And I'm ravenous.'

'But we can't be much more than an hour from town. I'd rather wait if you don't mind, Kit.'

'We're not going back to London. I had credited you with more wit than that, Clarissa. You demanded an adventure, but you also demanded secrecy you may recall. You may not be particularly well known in town, but I am. How can we conduct any sort of private liaison with the eyes of the world upon us?'

'Yes, I suppose—that is, I had not thought…'

'You had not thought? I find that difficult to believe. Well, you can think now. We are not going back to London unless it is to abandon all. And if we are to continue, we must dine. So Clarissa, for the last time, do you wish to continue?' He was growing weary of her prevaricating. Had she not been so very tempting, he would have readied them both for the journey home with no regrets. But he was finding her inordinately tempting.

And he wanted, more than he realised, for their liaison to continue. 'Well?'

It was *yes*. It had to be *yes*, she knew that. But some instinct for self-preservation made her stall. 'What about Mama? I can't just disappear. She'll be beside herself with worry.' Actually, Mama would probably indulge in a fit of the vapours, then simply assume Clarissa had forgotten to inform her of a visit to Aunt Constance, but that was neither here nor there.

'You can write her a note. You forget, I am already familiar with your ability to deceive. How else did you manage to escape your mama's tender care for two evenings in a row, and on your own? I am sure you can think of something to allay her fears.'

'Yes, but why the need for haste? I don't understand, Kit, why could you not have informed me in advance of your arrangements, then I could have been prepared, packed a bag, told Mama some tale. Surely there was no need for such a rush?'

'Where would be the adventure then? You wanted a surprise, something memorable—you were most specific. Isn't the unexpected part of the thrill?' Kit had been sitting by the fire, watching her from a distance, but now he moved to stand beside her at the window. His voice became huskier as he looked at the small, defiant, and strangely alluring woman at his side. 'The kisses you bestowed so willingly a few moments ago, my lovely Clarissa, simply confirmed what I already knew. I wish to have the preliminaries of our liaison over as soon as possible in order to enjoy the fruits of my labour more quickly. Your charms, as I am sure you are perfectly well aware, are considerable, and I wish to wait no longer than necessary to sample them more fully. I was persuaded by our kiss last night you know, although your reminder was very pleasant—I thank you.' A brief, ironic bow accompanied this last remark.

'I'm sorry, I hadn't meant to—I don't know what came over me.'

'No? Well, whatever it was, I'm grateful. But it might be best to save it until a more convenient time. You won't have to wait long, Clarissa, never fear. Nor will there be any gainsaying me when it happens. Once I have fulfilled my part of the bargain, I won't let you renege on yours.'

The glint in his eye was uncompromising. She had known it from the start, he was not a man to cross. Yet she had tried to ensnare him. He had pulled the ground from beneath her feet, but still she fought to recover it, as a general rallies his troops even at the eleventh hour. 'You are premature, my lord. I won't go back on my promise, but I must remind you that you have an obligation to fulfil first. My adventure, lest you need reminding.'

'Strangely, Clarissa, I need no reminding at all. Your adventure has already started. Had you not realised?'

'I had not mere abduction in mind, and well you know it. I particularly remember, for 'twas but last night, that we said it should be fun. Lest it has escaped your notice, this is not fun for me, and I am not enjoying myself. So you must try harder, sir, or you will have failed.'

'This is no mere abduction madam, I assure you. No matter what you may think of my morals, or lack of them, I pride myself on my finesse, as you will find out when the time comes for me to bed you. No, this is but the preliminary to the fun you are so intent on receiving.'

He was angry, frustrated at her refusal to give an inch, unused to being cross-questioned. It made him all the more determined that she would comply. With an effort, Kit bit down on his temper, deciding wisely that an explanation would be more likely to result in cooperation. 'We drive tonight to the coast, and thence we board my yacht, the *Sea Wolf.* You seemed so interested in the plight of the French refugees that it seemed only fair to allow you to experience first hand the kind of daring rescue mission required to deliver them from the fate that surely awaits them. It is an illicit undertaking which I confess I am intimately familiar with.'

'Why, Kit, I had no idea you were involved in such work when we discussed it last night. How exciting. And how very noble of you.'

'Don't be deluded, Clarissa, there is naught noble in my motives. 'Tis a sport to me, is all, but I hope it will be an exciting adventure for you. Especially since we'll be clapped in gaol if we're caught. I trust you will find the experience *fun* enough. Now, you may write your note to your concerned mama to ensure you are not looked for. Then we must dine and be on our way.'

Silencing the words of protest forming on her lips with a swift, brutal kiss, Kit grasped Clarissa's chin and looked straight into her troubled eyes. 'I will brook no further discussion. Write your note and we shall dine. The innkeeper's wife is famed for her table, we would not wish to disappoint her.' A smile curled his sensuous mouth, but did not reach his eyes. 'And you will need sustenance, my dear, if you are to make the most of your adventure.'

Clarissa vouchsafed no answer, but she sat obediently to write her note, consigning her worries about the future to the back of her mind. Her adventure was indeed about to begin. She might as well make the most of it, now that she was committed.

As Kit had promised, the landlady's cooking was a delight, but the neat's-tongue, the platter of delicate sole and the side-dish of artichokes sautéed in butter might as well have been cooked in ashes, for all Clarissa could taste. Conversation was desultory, both Kit and Clarissa being distracted by their own reflections.

Despite his earlier threats, Kit had no wish for an unwilling companion, and no taste for a resistant lover. Watchfully, he poured himself another glass of the excellent claret and waited for Clarissa to come to terms with the situation. She had been bested and she was not happy to have been forced to relinquish the reins, but she was yet determined on her course. She would go along with his scheme, he knew that, yet her real intentions were still unclear.

She was a puzzle, this beautiful woman before him, and one he wished to unravel. Her claims to virtue and the preposterous tale she spun him last night about wishing to enjoy herself before settling to the boredom of matrimony, Kit dismissed out of hand. She was no innocent, that was for sure. And if perchance there was some unsuspecting dotard waiting in the wings to wed her, he was sure she would continue in her scheming, wanton ways, whether she was married or no. Her plotting would come to light in the end, and he would deal with it then. For the present, he resolved simply to enjoy himself as much as possible.

Rather to his own surprise, Kit found himself reconciled to postponing their physical union for the present, content enough as he was with Clarissa's company. She was challenging. Her habit of speaking without thinking, of never saying quite what he expected, even her frankness, all were a refreshing change. And she seemed to understand him too—her attack on his rakish reputation had so nearly reflected his own cynical view of himself as to make him wonder if she could somehow eavesdrop on his very thoughts.

To be plain, he wanted to know more of her. Once they were bedded, he doubted not, he would become bored. Putting Clarissa from him when their kiss got so out of hand, when she had rubbed so sinuously against the throbbing evidence of his desire as to almost overset him, had not been easy. But passion was enhanced by anticipation, so postponement there would be—for a day or so, at least. Pouring the last of the claret into his glass, Kit looked up to find Clarissa's green eyes fixed on him with resolution. 'Speak, fair Clarissa, I can see you are pregnant with words. I am, as they say, all ears.'

This was said with a lurking smile that she found reassuring, as he had intended. She was in no danger for the present. Returning the smile tremulously, Clarissa pushed aside her plate. 'I take it, sir, that there is no point in my wasting time trying to persuade you to delay this undertaking?'

A shake of the head was her reply. Well, she had resigned herself to this. She knew she had taken a risk when setting out on this whole preposterous journey, and she had been foolish enough to ignore the warnings her Aunt Constance had delivered as to the perfidious nature of the man before her. Beguiled by his physical attractions, drawn on by her desire to know him better, Clarissa had fashioned her own fate. And now she would pay for it. But at least if Kit was aboard a boat sailing for France, he would not be in London waving his plentiful purse under her sister's nose.

And, oh, she so much wanted to go! There, she had admitted it to her deepest soul. The Earl of Rasenby understood her desire for adventure very well. He could not, in fact, have selected a more enticing trip. To sail out to sea on his yacht, to be part of a rescue mission, perhaps to be chased by the customs men—it was so much like a romance she could not resist. And she would not, simply would not, behave like a simpering miss when faced with the challenge. If she must go—*and she must, she must*—then she would go with flags flying and battle colours held proudly aloft. Kit would not intimidate her. On the contrary, she would make sure to enjoy every minute of it.

Kit watched in amusement, reading Clarissa's face fairly accurately, surprised and more than a little impressed at her courage in the face of adversity. He had thwarted her, but she would not submit easily to his will. 'Well? Your eyes give your thoughts expression, but really I would rather have them spoke plain, lest there be any misunderstandings between us. Are you ready to commit to our adventure, Clarissa?'

An answering smile, tinged with something—fear? Again, he repressed the urge to reassure. She did not need it. He would play along with her only so far.

'Yes. You give me no choice, Kit, but I will not pretend to go unwillingly when you are offering something that interests me so much. In fact, I'm already looking forward to it. How long shall we be gone?'

The question, almost casual, did not fool him. The lady was already planning her escape. 'One night only, if the winds are with us—and they usually are. Two at most, I believe. Had you something of longer duration in mind?'

'No, no, not at all.' Short enough a time, but surely sufficient for things between Amelia and Edward to flower? Resolving to put Amelia and Edward and everything else aside for now, and to extract the most from the situation which would surely be the adventure of a lifetime, Clarissa gave Kit a direct and steady look. 'You could not have picked anything more exciting for me, you know. I was not in jest last night when I told you that I find the idea of rescuing these poor *émigrés* completely enthralling. Since reading Mrs Wollstonecraft's account of the revolution, their plight has moved me. I've never been to sea before, though—I hope I'm not taken poorly.'

He made no comment on her reference to the infamous and now dead Mrs Wollstonecraft, being unsurprised at her sympathies with that lady, but stored the information up with which to annoy her later. He enjoyed pitting his wits against Clarissa, so rare it was to find a woman with a brain worth testing. Sea sickness, however, had not occurred to him as a possible issue. Immediately it was brushed aside. 'I am very sure, Clarissa, that if you decide not to be sick, then you will not be. I imagine there are few things—or people—you cannot subdue to your wishes.'

'What a strange thing to say. If you knew more of me, you'd realise just how constrained and burdened with other people's wishes my own life has been. I am not used to indulging myself, you know.'

'Well, if I am your chosen indulgence then I am flattered. But be aware, Clarissa, that I am not an indulgence to be abused. Once and for all, I remind you of your promise. When we go forward from this inn, you are not just committed to a trip to France. You will pay for it with that delectable body of yours. And you will not pretend that the payment will be anything other than desired by us both. Are we understood?'

The urge to tell the truth passed fleetingly across her mind, followed quickly by the urge to admit that she would be delighted to pay with her body. Both urges were suppressed. There could be no question of it, and she would deal with denying him later. But the lie that her tremulous agreement required sat heavy on her conscience.

Kit noticed, but ignored it. Time was against them. Checking his pocket watch, he rang the bell and demanded the bill. Clarissa, clad once more in her less than adequate spencer and gloves, was ushered out through the passageway and into a closed carriage. A hot brick was placed at her feet, and a fur rug tucked around her legs.

'I will ride alongside. There are not usually highwaymen on this stretch of road, but I prefer not to take the chance. Try to sleep for a while, we have a journey of some hours ahead of us.'

'Kit?'

'Yes?' The terse voice was intimidating. He was impatient to be off.

'I trust you.'

'What am I to take from that?'

'To keep me safe. To share the experience with me—properly, I mean, don't just bury me below decks. To leave me unmolested for the while. I trust you.'

'Then you are a fool. Rakes, my purported innocent, are never to be trusted. But I will allow you to be right, just this once. You may trust me thus far. But no more.'

'Yes, but you will keep me safe. For now.'

Leaning back into the warmth of the carriage, Clarissa was unaware of the anger she had aroused in Kit. And confusion. The urge to tell her he would keep her safe always had been unaccountably strong. Once more, Kit's instincts warred with his mind, as he told himself she was merely a very clever actress playing him like a professional. 'For now', however, was the only reply he vouchsafed.

The door of the chaise was banged shut. The ostlers let go of the horses, and the carriage leapt forward into the dark of the falling night, the tall man astride his powerful black stallion riding alongside. Clarissa was left to her own reflections, but the long day and her lack of sleep the previous night took their toll. Exhausted, the gentle rocking motion of the carriage soothed her and, to her surprise, Clarissa drifted into a sound sleep.

The carriage was stationary when she woke, and she could smell the salty tang of the sea air. Rubbing her eyes and casting off the rug, she descended to a scene of ordered but frenetic activity. They were at a small quayside. The boathouse, doors open and an oil lamp blazing inside, was waiting to shelter their carriage. There was a stable at the back for the horses, but no other sign of buildings, and the track they had come ran through deserted marshland.

On the quay she could see Kit, wrapped in an enormous black greatcoat, barking out orders to two men, one on the deck of the sleek yacht, and one beside him on the jetty. It was a cloudless night, and the stars were bright, much brighter than they ever were in London, where lights dimmed them to a soft glow. Here in the middle of nowhere they glared like so many burning braziers lighting up the heavens.

Shivering in the cold wind, Clarissa picked her way carefully down the jetty, avoiding the coils of rope and boxes of supplies stacked ready to be taken on board. Calling out a final instruction to the man on deck, Kit came towards her smiling, his eyes shining with anticipation as he trod with cat-like grace on the boards. He was obviously in his element here.

'Take care not to trip on those nets. When we're not

out on these night runs, John and I—that's my captain, on the deck there—take the *Sea Wolf* out on fishing expeditions. You'd be surprised at what we catch. And, of course, fishing provides an excellent cover, should we meet a customs cutter. Are you rested?'

Shivering now, for the cold was biting, Clarrie looked up into Kit's face, her own eyes reflecting his gleaming anticipation. 'Yes, thank you, I slept almost the whole journey. Please, will you show me around? And tell me everything? I want to make the most of this trip, for it's unlikely I'll ever get the chance of another. Tell me about your yacht.'

Laying a small gloved hand on his arm and making to urge him forward, she was treated to one of Kit's rare, genuine smiles. 'Very well. But wait here for a moment. You are ill equipped for the cold; I have a cloak in the boat house.' Returning quickly, he fastened the enveloping wool around her throat. 'There, that should keep out the chill, although you must take great care not to trip on it, especially when we're on board. I would hate to lose you to the sea!'

Laughing as the wind whipped her hair from under her bonnet, she snuggled the soft folds around her and turned back towards the gangway. 'Since I can't swim I would be lost indeed, and you would lose out on your payment. Even I am not such a prize as to risk a wetting in a rescue attempt.'

'I'm beginning to think that you're more of a prize than I realised. But rest assured I wouldn't get wet myself. I would send John in. Or more likely I'd pull you back with the boat hook I use to haul less alluring catch on board.'

'Well, I'm flattered indeed to be held more attractive than a fish, my lord,' Clarrie said with a grin, but her words were lost in the sudden gust of wind that swept in from the sea.

'Tide's on the turn, Master Kit,' John said, 'we'd best be going.'

The *Sea Wolf*, riding high against the jetty, was straining at the ropes that held her. The constraining hawsers creaked. John was looking anxiously at Kit, keen to be away. He had a bad feeling about this trip, and it wasn't just because of the close call with customs a few weeks ago. Someone was informing on them, he knew that. Bringing a woman on board, obviously one of Master Kit's flighty pieces, was a new departure, and one he could well have done without. He didn't hold with women on board unless absolutely necessary. They got in the way, to say nothing of bringing bad luck.

Standing at the foot of the gangway, Clarissa was shaken by a sudden attack of nerves, unable to move, one hand on the rail, but both feet still firmly on shore. Boarding this ship was madness. What was she thinking? The wind ripped across the bay, making the yacht pull, anxious to get away now that the anchor was up. The riggings creaked and moaned, and the gangway shifted, to Clarissa's eyes, treacherously.

'Last-minute qualms, brave Clarissa?' Kit's words were mocking.

The taunt was sufficient to urge her to action. With a defiant toss of her head and a silent prayer, Clarissa put first one foot, then the other on to the slippery walkway, and boarded the *Sea Wolf*. Feeling none too steady, for the deck rocked and swayed even though they were still berthed, she stood still for a moment, trying to find her balance. Aside from a curt nod, Captain John ignored her, making his resentment at her presence clear.

Carefully clutching the cloak around her, and taking

care to avoid the plethora of ropes, boxes, and goodness knows what else that made the deck an obstacle course, Clarrie found her way to stand by Kit at the wheel. A distracted smile was all she received, for they were in the process of putting to sea. John was casting off, making the ropes safe, loosing the sails, and in an instant the yacht responded to her freedom and leapt towards the open sea, riding the waves effortlessly.

As they left the cove behind, tacking to catch the wind, the waves rose higher, the spray soaking their faces, the *Sea Wolf* tilting up, then down, in a rhythmic, lulling motion that filled Clarrie with a wild joy. Lifting her face to the wind, she looked up at the stars with a strange, exhilarated expression on her face. This was what freedom must feel like. Freedom from all the trammels of her mundane life. Freedom from her mama, from Amelia, even from her staid Aunt Constance. Freedom from her past and her depressing future. There was only here and now. This man. This open sea. These stars.

A gust of wind blowing directly over the starboard side jolted the yacht, and would have knocked her over but for an iron grip on her arm. Looking up to thank Kit, Clarissa caught an unguarded expression of pure, unadulterated lust on his face and blinked at the sheer force of it. She blinked again and it was gone, replaced by his usual sardonic expression.

'You should go below. The crossing is likely to be fast but vicious, and I have to give my full attention to the *Sea Wolf*—I have not the time to be constantly making sure that you are safe.' Nor the time to be constantly distracted by the wild joy on the beautiful face beside him, if truth were to be told.

Deflated by his cold words, Clarissa turned to hide the hurt on her face. She had expected to stay above decks in order to see and experience everything to the limit. Being confined below was not her idea of an adventure. But she was too sensible to argue, for she could quite see that the stormy conditions were likely to be taxing. Quelling an instinctive protest at the command, therefore, she bit her lip and turned obediently towards the stairs.

Her obvious disappointment was too much for Kit to bear. He felt like an ogre stealing sweets from a babe. He had been watching her face more closely than she had realised, gratified to see the look of unadulterated pleasure that suffused it when the yacht set sail. Gratified and aroused to perceive his own feeling of joy at the freedom of the open sea reflected there. And disturbed, too, for it was not an emotion he had expected to share with a woman. And now she was thwarted yet uncomplaining.

'Clarissa.'

She turned at his call, a hopeful smile curling her full mouth, her skin bright with the sting of salt, her curls entrancingly dishevelled around her heart-shaped face. 'Kit?'

'Once we are settled in to the journey, I'll hand over to John, and you can come back up on deck, then, if that is what you wish.'

She clapped her hands with excitement, leaving him in no doubt.

'Contain yourself. If the weather worsens, you must stay below. Now go, before I change my mind.' He turned from her as she made her way gingerly below decks, before he could call her back regardless of the danger. Having Clarissa by his side at the wheel felt just a bit too right for his own comfort. Some space between them was a sounder idea.

The spartan cabin was built on practical rather than luxurious lines, with few fixtures other than the bunks that doubled as seating. Not a place for seduction, that was for sure. In fact, Clarrie thought with wry humour, as the yacht rolled with the waves, they would like as not end up on the floor, even had they managed to cram two bodies on to the narrow bunk. Still, having nothing else to occupy her mind for the while, she gave some time over to imagining how such adversities could be got over. She had just concluded that with determination two people could overcome such difficulties as a narrow mattress on a heaving yacht, when the door opened and Kit entered, bringing with him a cold gust of air.

Blushingly thankful he was not privy to her thoughts, Clarissa stood rather hurriedly, her foot catching in an uneven board, and fell unceremoniously on to the opposite bunk. Lying sprawled there, presenting Kit with her deliciously rounded posterior, Clarrie managed a soft laugh at the indignity of the situation. Her attempts to scramble to her feet were hampered by the continued rocking of the boat, and her sense of humour finally got the better of her. She succumbed to laughter, and lay for a few moments helpless, face down on the bunk.

'Kit, help me up, for goodness' sake. Now I know you're no gentleman, standing there and watching me.' Another abortive attempt had her on all fours on the bunk.

'You present such a very attractive picture that I'm loath to move, Clarissa. Your position may be uncomfortable, but I should tell you that it displays your curves very well.' Extremely well, in truth. His body was reacting rather vigorously to the display. Had it not been for the circumstances…

Restraining an urge to lift her dress above the bottom so pertly presented and thrust himself into her sweetness there and then, Kit reminded himself that John was above decks, and they were in the middle of the English Channel in a storm. That there was a cargo awaiting them in Normandy. That there was likely to be an excise cutter waiting for them on their return. That Clarissa was a perfidious, scheming actress. That… None of it worked.

Like an automaton, he moved towards the tempting bundle sprawled in front of him and grasped her by the waist, pulling her rear into his hard body, noting her laughter change to a surprised gasp, and then a soft, accepting moan. Clarrie wriggled slightly against him, causing him to throb almost uncontrollably. His hands tightened on her waist to pull her close, and his breathing quickened, coming in harsh gasps in the confines of the cabin. Steadying his knees against the base of the bunk, he allowed one hand to trace the line from her tiny waist along the curve of her spine, and to cup one soft buttock through the wool of her dress, aware, from the soft panting of her breath, that she was as aroused as he. Bracing himself more securely, Kit moved to the hem of her dress, preparing to lift it up over her in order to grant him the access he craved. He met with no resistance.

The sea saved her. A violent movement that sent them both sprawling, as John called urgently for help. Kit was gone at once, leaving Clarrie alone again. Alone with her feelings—of despair at her easy submission, of anger at herself for her lack of resistance. But most of all, the one that really scared her, a feeling of deep frustration at the unconsummated act. Clarrie could fool herself no longer. When Kit decided to take her, there would be no question but that she would submit. No matter what the consequences.

Chapter Six

The tossing of the ship had become less violent, or perhaps she had simply accustomed herself to it. In any case, to stay below and nurse her feelings of frustration would, Clarrie decided, be as fruitless as it was a waste of the precious time she had on board the *Sea Wolf*. She prepared to brave the upper decks and to pretend that nothing of note had happened below.

The yacht was holding a steady course in the face of the wind. Kit had the wheel, idly maintaining conversation with John, whose talk was of the future, his plans for life once this last mission was completed.

'I'll not be sorry, Master Kit, I tell thee true. It's old bones I've got now, too old to be chasing after them Frenchies and running away from the excise men. I've enough set aside to buy my own smack and do a bit of legal fishing for a change. Won't net me a fortune, but it'll keep us well enough, I reckon. I've my eye on a little beauty I spotted for sale down Romney Marsh way, fore-and-aft rigged like the *Sea Wolf*, but smaller, just big enough for me and a lad to handle. And Sal, she'll be glad to have me home at night regular again.'

'How is the lovely Sal, your good lady wife? The last time we met, she threatened me with a rolling pin for getting you into mischief.'

A gruff laugh greeted this remark. 'Aye, you know her ways, Master Kit, she means no harm, just frets for my safety is all. She's never liked me going off on jaunts like this, but she's not one as would ever complain neither. A good woman, Sal, she knows her place. And she deserves some peace of mind, after all these years. She's earned it.'

'You both have, John. I really envy you, the way you've got your life all mapped out. I have no idea what I'll do without these trips. My sister wants me to marry, but lord, what a dreadful husband I'd make. I'm afraid I'm destined to be the devil's own, one way or another. I'll miss these trips more than I can say.'

'Aye, well, Master Kit, like as not summat'll turn up, you'll see. I'm a great believer in fate, myself.' With this laconic reply, John turned his attention seawards, scanning the horizon for signs of sail, leaving Kit free to pursue his thoughts.

As if summoned by them, Clarissa appeared head first, ascending the cabin steps gingerly, struggling to contain the cloak that whistled around her in the wind. She had abandoned her hat, and her bright auburn tresses whipped around her face, temporarily obstructing her view. Tottering, she grabbed the rail and righted herself before smiling and offering a tentative greeting. 'I thought I'd take you up on the offer of a tour. That is, if you are not otherwise occupied.'

A terse nod from John, who took over the wheel, gave Kit no option but to accede to her request. 'We're about an hour away from landfall, we've made excellent time. I'll be happy to show you round—she's small but beautiful, my *Sea Wolf*—and then you can stay on deck as we berth.'

The technicalities were lost on her, but she listened with intelligent interest as Kit explained everything from the rigging to the sleek lines of the yacht, comparing it favourably, and with obvious pride, to the slower, clinker-built cutters still used by the Revenue. Pointing out the key navigational stars high above them, he talked a little of his early sailing days, his fishing trips with John when he was no more than a child, sailing his first skiff and learning the hard way about the tides and vagaries of the coast line. That Kit loved the *Sea Wolf* and was an expert sailor, Clarrie had no doubt. That she too could learn to love sailing, she had no doubt either. At his side, with his tuition, she was sure she would quickly become adept.

Standing at the guard rail, watching the yacht cut cleanly through the waves and the coast of Normandy looming into view in the distance, Clarissa felt a rush of freedom like champagne fizzing through her blood. At home, so far away as it now seemed, freedom had meant her sister married, her mother comfortably settled and herself earning a living as a governess. Such a vision seemed merely a new set of fetters compared to this. How had she ever imagined that life at the beck and call of an employer would be any different to life at the beck and call of her family?

No point in thinking about such things now though, no point in spoiling this moment. Turning to Kit, standing so close she could feel the heat of his body even through the thickness of their clothing, Clarissa asked about the people waiting for them on the French shore.

'We can never be certain that they'll be there when

we arrive,' he explained. 'There are so many things that can go wrong. On occasion we've had to wait—usually a few hours, but once it was a whole day and night. We went ashore, but John did not take to the French cooking!' Kit laughed at the memory of John's face when presented with a huge piece of beef, the blood pooling beside it on the plate. 'Tonight, we're to pick up a man and his daughter. Their name is Renaud. Madame Renaud is dead by the guillotine, and Monsieur Renaud and his daughter have been in hiding on a country estate in Burgundy. He is a classical scholar; of her I know naught more than that she is young and unwed. Needless to say, they are rich no more. They are alive, that is the main thing. Or they were when last I heard a few days ago,' he added bitterly. 'To come out of hiding and journey north to the ports is hazardous even after all these years. There are informants everywhere.'

'They cannot have been in hiding all this time, surely? It is almost ten years since the revolution.'

'Aye, ten bloody years. But remember, the *Terror* grew slowly at first. The wholesale slaughter only really started when Louis was beheaded, four years after they revolted. For many, especially those of the lesser nobility such as this family, it seemed possible to keep their heads down—if you'll forgive the gallows humour—and survive the killing. Monsieur Renaud, whom you will meet tonight, God willing, is not himself of high rank, but his wife was the younger daughter of a duke. The blue blood was hers. And so, in the end, it was she who sealed the fate of the whole family. 'Tis certain they would not have been spared had they been found.'

'But is it not safe enough now in France under the Directorate? Are they not more tolerant? Surely it's becoming possible to start again in their own country, rather than to take such a drastic step as these people make tonight?'

'For some, yes, perhaps you're right. But for others, those who have lived the life of privilege, to accustom themselves to the new regime seems unnecessary, when in England they can bear their titles proudly once more.'

'With no money, how can that mean so much? Money is by far more important than a title, as I should know, Lord Rasenby.'

'And what, Clarissa, do you know of such things?'

She shrugged. 'My own father was titled, my widowed mother still bears his name. It means naught, for he was cast off and poverty-stricken just the same. At times, I would happily swap my birth right for the wealth of a merchant family—at least that way I wouldn't have to worry about avoiding the coal seller at quarter time.' An embarrassed laugh concluded this admission. She had not meant to say anything so revealing, being merely caught up in the need to understand more of the situation in France. But looking into those piercing eyes above her, Clarissa realised Kit had missed none of what she had said.

'So you claim to be of noble birth? And may I be allowed to ask what this family name is, for I know— have known all along, of course—that the name you gave me is false.'

'No, there's nothing to be gained for either of us in that. Rest assured, my real name is Clarissa. That should suffice, for the duration of our brief acquaintance.' Smiling nervously, for she had no wish to continue this turn in the conversation, Clarissa resolutely faced away from that all too penetrating look, back towards the approaching land. 'You were telling me about Monsieur Renaud.

If he has no title and his poor wife is dead, I still don't understand the need for him to leave France.'

Thrusting aside the urge to probe into Clarissa's background—for like as not it would only lead to more lies—Kit focused instead on the Normandy coastline, anxious to catch the first glimpse of their destination, a tiny fishing village, where a beacon to guide them would be lit if all was safe. 'The likes of Renaud leave because the future is still so uncertain. True, he has no title, but he has a daughter to protect. And he has the sense, as anyone who has studied the situation can see, to realise that this regime is every bit as volatile as the last. There will be war soon, do not doubt it. In England he'll be sleeping with the enemy, but at least there is less chance there of invasion, more chance of a respite from bloodshed. France has not come to the end of its sufferings, mark my words. For all these reasons, and others, too, these trips on the *Sea Wolf* are, however, coming to an end. I must find some other occupation to sate my appetite for danger.'

The bleakness in his voice betrayed his true feelings. Giving up this life was hard for him. Having tasted the thrill of it for herself, Clarissa was not surprised. Laying a hand on his arm in an attempt to convey her empathy, her words were yet hesitant. 'I can see that you'll miss this life. But you must take comfort in the good you have done, the lives you have saved. All these *émigrés*, they must be so grateful. I expect, when you meet them in London, as you must often do afterwards, you are something of a hero to them.'

'You are much mistaken, Clarissa, to set me up for a hero.' The habitual cynical drawl had returned. 'I don't rescue these people for any more noble motives than a desire for adventure spiced with danger. I care naught

for their fate. I take no sides in their politics. Their country can gnaw at its own entrails until it has consumed
itself in the process for all I care. Do not attribute to me
any heroic virtues, for you will find yourself far from
the truth. These people are just cargo, like the silks and
brandies we will carry tonight alongside Monsieur and
Mademoiselle Renaud. And as to recognition from those
I rescue? Never. They are under strict instructions not to
acknowledge me once they leave the *Sea Wolf*. I am not,
nor never will be, a hero.'

'You may choose to deny it. Indeed, to do so is in your
character for you are overly fond of your raking, care-
naught reputation, Lord Rasenby, as I have pointed out
to you several times now.' His determined cynicism was
having a rousing effect on Clarrie. She would not allow
him to be so harsh on himself. He was not a complete
villain, no matter how much he played the part.

'I notice that I become Lord Rasenby and not Kit when
you are lecturing me, madam. I do not take to it kindly
either, for you have not the right to lecture. No one has
that right but myself. And believe me, no one could be
harder on me than myself either. But to no avail. I am
destined for the devil. You would learn, if you chose to
spend more time in my company, that I can neither be
reformed, nor am in wont of it.'

'No, you're not in need of reform, because you're not
anything like as black as you paint yourself. You are not
stupid, you told me so yourself. Well, neither am I! You
would not have continued with these trips, which put John
as much as yourself in danger, had you not felt they were
worthwhile—and I don't mean for the brandy. These rescues mean something to you, would you but admit it, if
only to your own heart. To these people at least, you are

a hero, I doubt it not. The only need you have of reform is to think as well of yourself as you are entitled.'

'You persist in this belief at your peril, foolish Clarissa, but be warned. Such determinedly positive appraisals of my character will not change it one jot. Nor will you, by applying such soft soap, beguile me into releasing you from your promise. Now let us have an end to this conversation, for we have important work to attend to. Look straight ahead and slightly to starboard—there is our beacon. We are expected. You may watch, but you must keep silent and take care not to get in the way.'

With that he was gone, joining John at the wheel and leaving Clarissa to her reflections. Anger at his abrupt dismissal and pity for the contempt in which he held himself were foremost in her mind. But there was, too, a growing desire to be the one to bring him to a sense of his own worth. Not to reform him, that phrase he so despised, but to raise his sadly low esteem. *She* believed in him, and she could prove it to him, too, if only the situation was different.

But to wish things were different was to wish their whole adventure away. Increasingly all Clarissa wanted was for their time together to go on—and on. The thought of an ending to it was a thought she thrust firmly from her mind. A future without Kit Rasenby was not a future she wished to contemplate just yet.

John dropped the sails, and the ship glided smoothly into calmer, shallower waters, navigating by a beacon lit at the end of the harbour wall. Watching Kit's face as he guided the yacht through the treacherous rocks that guarded the bay, Clarissa realised how truly handsome he was when his countenance was not marred by his habitual cynical frown. Kit's eyes sparkled with anticipation as he steered the difficult course confidently. The gleam of excitement was contagious, stirring her own heart with a longing to be at his side, to face the danger with him. Here was a Kit released from the constraints of his London life. Here was the real Kit, the bold rescuer, not the dissolute rake. Like a shooting star brightening the cold, crisp night sky, Clarissa saw the truth. Here was her Kit. The Kit she had begun to love.

Breathless with the realisation, she clutched the rails, trying not to allow the elation that the admission brought reflect in her face. For just a moment, the thrill of finding herself truly in love was all-encompassing. She was soaring upwards towards the stars, the brilliance of the flame inside her outshining even the brightest of lights in the night sky.

But her spirits plummeted back down to earth all too quickly. That man standing so proudly at the helm of his yacht felt more for the ship shifting beneath them than he could ever feel for any woman, especially not the deceiver he believed Clarissa to be. He wanted her body, nothing more, a wish that would no doubt prove both fleeting and quickly sated.

Even Clarissa's dauntless spirit was downtrodden by such a thought. For a moment she stared blankly ahead at the approaching shore. But long experience of coping in the face of adversity stood her now in good stead, and, ever the optimist, she resolved to enjoy the present, and to let the future take care of itself. It was enough for now to be here with Kit, sharing this experience. Enough to know that he desired her body, at least. With resolution renewed, Clarissa turned to the scene before her, determined to extract the last ounce of enjoyment from it. Enough to last her a lifetime.

They had reached the bay and were dropping anchor, the tide being too low for the yacht to pull alongside the jetty. The night was still, the wind almost gone, the only sound the gentle splashing of the oars from the small boat that was making its way towards them, two passengers huddled together in the bow. John was lowering a rope ladder over the side, and as the small dinghy neared, called a greeting in rough French to the oarsman, obviously a familiar face.

Responding to Kit's nod, Clarissa moved to stand alongside him at the wheel, which he held steady with one hand, his other outstretched towards her. 'Well? Are you enjoying yourself, fair Clarissa?'

'Oh, yes, how can you think otherwise? It's perfect.'

All enmity was gone from him, caught up as he was in the thrill of the rescue, the constant awareness of danger, the unaccustomed warmth of sharing the experience with this feisty, self-assured female at his side. One minute passionate wanton, next as curious as a child, and next again launching into a defence of his character like a lioness guarding her cubs. Nary a trace of fear at their situation, never a hint of a tear, not a single recrimination had he heard from her, only staunch fortitude and sparkling enjoyment. It was a potent mixture.

Clarissa was watching the small boat and its precious cargo tie up alongside. She was right, of course, these people *were* precious. Transporting *émigrés* to the safety of England's shores was of deeper import to him than he cared to admit even to himself. Her hand remained tucked in his own as she watched, and she nestled close, the length of her body safe against him.

'They look so frightened huddled down there,' she said softly. 'How much they must have been through to get here. It's a humbling thought, but they must know they are safe, now you are here.'

She looked up at him with such trust that he could not

restrain himself. Bending down, Kit kissed her softly on her lips. A gentle kiss without the heat of passion, a kiss one would give to a child, designed to—what? He wanted to keep her safe, not to betray the trust he saw writ in her eyes. She persisted in seeing him as a saviour. Fleetingly, he wished it could be so.

He was bewitched. She needed to be saved from nothing except her own wiles, and whatever this scheme was she had embroiled him in. Hardening his heart, Kit stepped briskly away. 'Wait here. They'll need help coming aboard, and John will need help with the rest of the cargo too.'

Left alone to watch, Clarissa could only admire the sleek process of loading from the tiny dinghy tied loosely to the *Sea Wolf*'s side. The men worked in silence, broken only by hushed instructions from Kit to John and the French oarsman, as Monsieur Renaud and his daughter were guided with care up the ladder and on to the deck. Several casks of brandy, boxes of tea, and bales of fabric—silk, she assumed—followed, handled by Kit and John effortlessly and with a practice born of familiarity. The cargo was stowed in a small compartment reached via a trap door on deck, which was hidden beneath some fishing nets. The *émigrés* were ushered to the cabin below. The dinghy cast off back to shore, the oarsman having received a generous *douceur* for his troubles. John and Kit were preparing to up anchor and away.

Clarissa watched all of this with fascination, taking in every detail while at the same time trying to reconcile Kit's strange behaviour. He believed her to be a fraud, and did not trust her, that much was obvious. Nor did he believe her story—and who could blame him, for it was indeed flimsy. Yet he had gone along with her proposition, none the less, for reasons she could not fathom. He was bored, true. And he found her amusing, that was also true. And tempting. That, too, Clarissa knew to be true, although she found it harder to believe, so many real beauties had he had, and no doubt would continue to have. Yet he told her she was beautiful, and she believed him, for he did not lie.

Well, the novelty would no doubt wear off, but it was flattering all the same. Still, none of this explained why he went along with her scheme. He wanted her, but he trusted her not. He seemed, as when he kissed her just now, to be fighting against more tender feelings, but each time he pulled her close he pushed her away all the harder. He believed her to be false, and she had herself conspired to ensure that he would do so.

There was nothing to be done. The situation was of her own creation and she would have to accept the consequences. It had been no part of her plan to fall in love, but she could not regret it, even if Kit would never know how she felt.

The rocking beneath her feet told her they had turned back out to sea. Sure enough, the sails were set and the land was falling away behind them. *Monsieur* and his daughter were below decks. Clarissa decided the best way to assist was to provide what comfort she could to the French family on the long journey ahead. They would be chilled, and no doubt hungry. She could do something about that. She slipped away from the rail and was below decks before Kit had even noticed she had gone.

Monsieur and Mademoiselle Renaud were huddled together on one of the narrow bunks, fatigue etched on their wan faces. Mademoiselle was young, fifteen or sixteen, and bid fair to being a beauty, but at the moment all Clarissa saw was a girl at the end of her tether and in need of comfort. Pinning a bright smile to her face, and summoning up her schoolroom French, she set about providing it.

Warm blankets were retrieved from a locker beneath the bunk, and the supply box Kit had tucked into a corner was opened, revealing a ham, cheese, bread and wine. The *émigrés* fell on the food with obvious relish, and were considerably cheered by the time they had made a good repast. The sea was smoother for the return journey, and fortunately neither of the new passengers was subject to sickness. Clarissa poured herself a glass of burgundy and settled down to conversation with the father and daughter, keen to find out their story for herself. Keen also to discover their opinion of their rescuer without Kit himself being privy to it.

It was as sad, sordid and harrowing a tale as she had ever heard. Yet *Monsieur* emerged from it with a quiet dignity, a respect for life and a trust in humankind despite all his experience. He had no wish to dwell on the details of the past, the worst of times, when his wife was held in captivity, the only certainty that of her death by the blade. He focused instead on the goodness of the people who kept his daughter safe in the country while he pleaded in vain with the authorities in Paris. Of their kindness in providing him with a roof over his head, food, even some work tutoring the village children. And the generosity of the people who offered him a new home in England.

Monsieur spoke perfect English. 'Over the years before the revolution, my studies led to friendship with some eminent professors at Oxford university. It is these very good friends who offered sanctuary to myself and Lisette, my daughter, as soon as we got word out that we were alive.'

'So, you've been planning your escape for some time then, *monsieur*?'

'Yes, for more than a year now. My wife, Lisette's *maman*, was killed by the guillotine three years ago. Until she died, we had hoped to survive in France, to simply wait until this madness, this *terreur*, was ended. But when my dear wife was executed—murdered...'

'Papa, we must think of the future now, it is what *maman* would want.' Lisette's gentle voice, full of compassion, roused her papa from his maudlin thoughts.

'You are right, *ma petite*.' Monsieur Renaud heaved a sigh, and, fortified with another draught of wine, resumed his story. 'We heard of the English *monsieur* and his rescues through another of my countrymen, but it proved difficult and time-consuming to make contact and the necessary arrangements. Easy to understand, given the need for secrecy and the danger to all concerned. But now, thank God, we are finally here.'

'The expense must have been a big problem for you?'

'Oh, no, *mais non, madame*, there was no cost. *Monsieur* never takes a fee for his rescues, nor even a gift— and he has been offered many. Not once, in many, many attempts, has he been caught. Not one passenger has he failed, even when he had to wait in France, at great danger to himself. He is a hero.'

Clarissa smiled, wishing just for a moment that Kit was present to hear himself being described in the very terms he had denied so vehemently only hours before. She had been right about him, but it was reassuring to have it confirmed.

'Yes, I believe he is a hero, *monsieur*, would he but admit it.'

'We are not even permitted to know his name, *madame*.' Lisette joined in the conversation now, her pretty face animated, the only traces of the frightened little girl who had boarded the yacht showing in the lines of exhaustion. 'He is known as the *Loup de Mer*, the name of this yacht, and I think it suits him, *non*? He is just like a wolf, is he not, so dangerous, and so brave. But you, *madame*, you must know him well to be here on the boat with us. Tell me, is he of noble birth, as they say he is?'

Clarissa blushed, for Lisette was obviously curious as to her relationship with Kit, even if she was too polite to ask. 'I think, *mademoiselle*, that if he wished his name to be known he would tell you. It is not for me to give away his secrets.'

'Well spoken, my dear, my secrets are nobody's property but mine.'

Kit entered the tiny cabin with his usual cat-like grace, making the room suddenly seem much smaller. The cynical smile was firmly in place, the slight frown drawing his black brows together demonstrating clearly that he had overheard enough of the conversation to know Clarissa had been asking questions.

'My aunt always told me that listeners hear only ill of themselves, you know. You are fortunate you didn't arrive any earlier.'

'Ah, so you have an aunt, as well as a mother. Quite a little family gathering there will be awaiting you on your return from your trip. And what, pray, would I have overheard that would have been so unwelcome to my ears?'

'Why, sir, only what I told you myself, and to your face. You are a hero. And it came this time not from my lips, but from those of Monsieur Renaud here.'

'And, oh, *monsieur*, it is true. To us you are a hero, *je vous promis*.' The worshipful tone of Lisette's voice could not be ignored, but instead of taking umbrage with her, Kit laughed.

'*Merci du compliment, mademoiselle*. But I didn't come here to discuss my character, I came to remind you of your promises to me. We will be in England soon. A chaise awaits you, to take you to London and thence to Oxford. Once you are disembarked, you must not discuss this journey, nor may you tell any of your friends still in France how you came to contact me. From tonight, the *Loup de Mer* is no more. You have the honour of being my last passengers. And after tonight, even if we meet in the street, you must not recognise me. Is that understood?'

'But why? *Monsieur*, I do not understand why?'

'Lisette!' Monsieur Renaud laid a constraining hand on his daughter's shoulder. '*Tais-toi*. I speak for both of us, *monsieur*, when I say that it shall be as you demand. But I beg you, if you should ever be in need of a friend yourself, to consider me your eternally grateful servant.'

'Thank you, *monsieur*.' Only Clarissa realised that the curt tone hid Kit's own pleasure at the compliment. 'Now, I will bid you adieu. I will be busy on deck until we disembark. I am sure that *madame* here will look after you well. She is adept at it, I can vouch.' A brief nod and a smile, and he was gone.

Clarissa settled Lisette down to sleep on the narrow bunk, letting her head rest on her own lap, soothing her into slumber by stroking her hair as she had done with Amelia countless times. After a while, Monsieur Renaud slept too, more fitfully, uncomfortably upright on the bunk opposite, and Clarissa sat watching over them, her own mind too tired to grapple with the travails that lay ahead when they arrived back in port.

Finally she too dozed off. She woke briefly to see Kit

hovering over her, tucking a blanket round her, but he put a finger to his mouth and left as silently as he had arrived, so she smiled faintly, and turned to a troubled sleep once more.

When Clarissa next opened her eyes, the porthole revealed a choppy iron-grey sea rising to meet the pale dawn sky. It was morn, though she had no idea what o'clock. Even with a poor wind, they must be near home. Gently, so as not to disturb Lisette, still soundly asleep on her lap, Clarissa rose and stretched, stiff and sore from lying on the rough planks that passed for a bed. Her eyes felt gritty from the briny salt of the sea-spray, and she was ravenously hungry. She had not eaten since the inn, which seemed like long ago now, though it was only yesterday. But breakfast would have to wait until they landed, and she had a suspicion that once they were safely ashore, breakfast would be the last thing on her mind.

The yacht was slowing, but she could see nothing from the porthole to tell her their position. Steadying herself to go above decks, she was stilled by the sound of strange voices, and waited, suddenly alert to danger. The cabin door opened abruptly and John appeared, his face creased in worry.

'Master says to stay down there, and make no sound. There's a cutter coming alongside, they mustn't find you.'

'A cutter? Do you mean a customs ship?'

'Aye. They've been tipped off, must've been, as they were lying in wait for us. I warned the master after the last time that someone was informing on us. And this time they want to board. They must be certain sure of their information.'

'But can't you prevent them boarding?'

'Master Kit'll try, lady, but they do seem mighty determined this time. And Master Kit, happen he's riled that Lieutenant Smith once too often. The lad's got summat to prove.'

Looking desperately round the tiny cabin, Clarissa realised there was nowhere for them to hide. The brandy casks were in the hidden compartment on deck, but no Riding Officer worth his salt would fail to discover the hiding place if he was permitted a thorough search. Looking anxiously at the still peacefully sleeping *émigrés*, Clarissa knew that if the customs men found the brandy they would almost certainly want to search the cabin too, where, unknown to them, a much more valuable cargo was stored. They must be prevented from searching or the game was up for them all. And if Kit couldn't stop them, she thought, a plan forming in her mind, well, then she would have to.

Something of her thoughts must have shown on her face, for John was entreating her to remain in the cabin and stay quiet. 'Do as Master Kit commands and don't even think of doing anything silly or you'll get us all hanged.' With this, he closed the cabin door firmly on Clarissa's face and returned above decks.

'I must command you to allow us to escort you into port, Lord Rasenby. We have a warrant to search the *Sea Wolf*.' Lieutenant Smith stood stiffly on the deck, his dinghy tied alongside in the calm waters of the channel, his cutter swaying a few yards off and behind the yacht.

'This obsession with my night-fishing trips is becoming tedious, Lieutenant. I thought you would have better things to do with your valuable time.'

'You have been less fortunate than usual, my lord, from what I can see?'

'I don't take your meaning.' Kit's temper, usually so

cool under pressure, was frayed. Never before had they been unable to outrun the customs men, and he cursed the ill luck which had seen the wind drop suddenly. The thought of the Renauds and Clarissa hidden below decks made him nervous, more nervous than the thought of the cargo concealed in the secret locker. He had no clear idea of the law regarding the *émigrés*, but he had a very clear idea indeed of what would happen to his reputation if this story got out.

'My meaning, my lord, is simple. Where is your catch?'

Cursing volubly under his breath, Kit turned helplessly to John, who shrugged in consternation. They had caught no fish.

'As you say, I was unlucky last night, Lieutenant. Come now, we both know this is foolish. I am in need of my bed, as I'm sure you are of yours. Nothing can be gained from searching us, for there is nothing to be found.'

'Perhaps your catch is below decks, my lord?'

'Devil take you, Lieutenant, what are you implying?'

'You know very well, Lord Rasenby. You are carrying contraband and this time nothing will prevent me from discovering it.'

'I'm afraid you're going to be disappointed all the same, Lieutenant.' Clarrie's husky tones, as she stepped boldly on to deck, startled the men into silence. John, standing behind Kit, looked on slack-jawed.

'Lord, Kit, I thought we'd never get back to England. I've missed you, darling, it's no fun below decks on my own.' Laying a proprietorial arm on Kit's, Clarrie pouted. Her hair was loosened to curl freely down her back, and her dress unbuttoned sufficiently to add to her air of abandon. There could be no mistaking that she had this moment arisen from a night of passion.

Lieutenant Smith's jaw dropped in imitation of John's at this lush display, but Kit, quick to take advantage, merely pressed Clarissa's hand in acknowledgment of the ruse, and smiled tauntingly at the Riding Officer. 'My cargo, Lieutenant Smith, as you see.' Taking Clarissa's hand in his, he raised it to his mouth and planted a lingering kiss on her palm. 'Good morning, my love. I'm afraid this gentleman was rather intent on searching your quarters.'

'Oh, please, Lieutenant, let me preserve some modicum of dignity. The cabin is—how can I put it delicately—a little untidy.' There could be no mistaking her meaning. Lieutenant Smith blushed as scarlet as his uniform.

'You can see now, Lieutenant, why I had no time for fishing last night. I was rather more agreeably occupied with this particular little piece of bait.' A rather unnecessary pat on her bottom made Clarrie start.

'Please, Kit, not in front of the gentleman. You can see he's embarrassed.' Indeed, the Lieutenant was playing with the collar of his coat as if suddenly finding it too tight. 'I'm so sorry, Lieutenant—as you can see, I'm having a little difficulty in taming his lordship here. What he needs is his bed.' This accompanied by a wink, which made even Kit raise an eyebrow.

'I—well, I—yes. Excuse me, Lord Rasenby, it would seem that once again I was misinformed. Please accept my apologies, ma'am, for disturbing you—I mean, for disturbing your...'

'My rest, I think you mean,' Clarrie said with a saucy smile.

'Yes. Your rest, ma'am. Of course.'

'Lieutenant?'

'My lord?'

'A word, if you please, before you go. I would ask you to keep this encounter to yourself for all of our sakes. The lady, you understand, belongs to another, and it would grieve him greatly should he find out about this night's fishing trip.'

Realisation dawned in the officer's eyes, and they widened at the temerity of the man standing shameless in front of him. Lord Rasenby's reputation was well known to those hereabouts, of course, but never before had Lieutenant Smith been faced with such blatant evidence of his raking. And she so young and pretty too! Nodding wisely in an attempt to pass off the encounter as he was sure a man of the world would do, Lieutenant Smith thrust the proffered note away in confusion. 'My discretion does not need to be bought, Lord Rasenby. I am a man of honour. You can accept my word that I will not discuss this encounter.'

Kit's brows rose in surprise. 'You are a credit to your uniform, sir, and I honour you for it. And in return, I'll tell you something to your advantage.'

'Sir?'

'It will perhaps relieve you to know that my night-fishing trips are at an end. You may wish to share that knowledge with the Marquis of Alchester, your informant.' Raising his hand to forestall the confused denial, Kit continued. 'I have been aware for some time that he has been keeping you apprised of my movements. Rest assured, I will be taking the matter up with Alchester personally. But for now, I trust, you take my meaning? The *Sea Wolf* will not be going fishing again.'

'I thank you, sir. I take your meaning well. Now I must bid you good morning." A blushing nod to Clarissa, and the lieutenant was gone, over the side to the waiting dinghy, and back to his cutter.

He was barely back on board before Clarrie turned, exultant and bursting with excitement, towards Kit. 'Oh, Kit, I can't tell you, my heart was thumping fit to burst. Just for a moment there I thought he—'

Kit cut short her excited torrent of words with an imperious wave of his hand. 'You were told to remain below. Can I not trust you to follow even the simplest of instructions? I would have found a way to deal with Lieutenant Smith. John, make haste for the quay. We are long overdue. Clarissa, go below and make sure the Renauds are prepared to disembark.'

Curtly dismissed, Clarissa stumbled below, blinking back the tears. Kit turned to take the wheel, confused at his own sudden temper.

'Don't you think you're being a mite hard on the girl, my lord?' John asked gravely. 'She got us out of a pretty pickle there and no mistake.'

'I know, John, I know. Your point is well made.' She had saved them all from a perilous situation with her quick thinking, cool head and bravery. So why, then, was he so angry with her?

Chapter Seven

'Can you finish up here on your own, John? This way, Clarissa, we have unfinished business to attend to.' Kit, his expression impassive, ushered Clarissa towards the awaiting chaise. His tightly reigned temper had been in evidence ever since the *Sea Wolf* docked. Monsieur and Mademoiselle Renaud were disembarked and dispatched in a separate post chaise with uncommon haste, allowing Clarissa time for only the briefest of farewells. John was kept busy amid a flurry of barked orders from Kit, unloading the remaining cargo, securing the yacht, and then finally the boathouse.

Aside from pointing Clarissa towards the chaise, Kit had said nothing to her. Deducing correctly that she was the source of his anger, although having no clue as to how she might have provoked it, Clarrie felt her own temper starting to rise, fuelled by a sense of injustice. She wheeled to confront him.

'What have I done to incur your displeasure this time, my lord? At least have the decency to tell me to my face. I thought you would be impressed by my actions when we were boarded by the Revenue. My motives were of the purest, I did it only to protect all of us—you, me, John and the Renauds. Would you have me in the wrong for that, would you have me apologise for trying to save you? For it worked, didn't it?' She added proudly, 'The look on poor Lieutenant Smith's face was priceless!'

'Yes, it worked. But you were lucky and, more to the point, extremely reckless, for things might easily have gone awry after your impulsive behaviour. This is not merely a game, some sport for your entertainment, Clarissa. Innocent people's lives are at stake. Lives that you put at risk.'

'I thought you cared naught for these people yourself. Did you not make me a pretty speech that it was all sport to you and you were indifferent to their fate?'

'Well, I care for John, at any rate,' was his lame response. Confound the woman, Kit thought, looking distinctly uncomfortable now. First she knows my thoughts, and now she seems able to look into my very soul and read what lies hidden within.

Clarissa pressed on, warming to the task, recognising that for once she held the upper hand. 'As usual, my lord, you would be better served aiming your words at a more deserving target—yourself! Putting innocent lives at risk for sport and pleasure! For shame, sir, is that not exactly the fate you intended for Amelia Warrington?'

'Her again,' Kit exploded. 'What is your obsession with that girl? As I've said before, I pride myself on amply rewarding those with whom I play such games.'

'Indeed you do, Lord Rasenby. But have you ever considered that what you proudly call generosity is, in fact, conscience and guilt?'

Kit stepped towards Clarissa, grasping her by both elbows, looming over her threateningly. 'That may be so, Clarissa, but we are embroiled in a game of our own, remember. One we both chose to play willingly and in which neither of us could be called innocent. A game that is about to resume.'

Giving her no time to reply, Kit nodded farewell to John, ushered Clarissa into the chaise, and mounted his own horse. Almost before the door was fastened shut, the chaise started forward. They were journeying back to London, that much seemed certain. But how was she to forestall Kit to give her plan more time to succeed with regards to Amelia and Edward, while keeping her virtue intact? Kit would be expecting payment soon, that was plain. So much had happened in the last twenty-four hours, Clarissa could not find it in her to care at this moment. Mentally and physically exhausted, she fell into a deep dreamless sleep.

She awoke to the heat of a fire and the rattle of a tea tray. Sleepily she sat up rubbing her eyes, to discover that she was no longer in the coach, but on a sofa in a small parlour. The curtains were drawn, giving no indication of the time of day. For a minute in her confusion Clarissa imagined she was back home. But as she gradually took stock of her surroundings, noticing the tasteful, opulent furnishings, the paintings and ornate tapestries that adorned the walls and the huge roaring fire with its impressive over-mantel, she realised this was not her own humble home but somewhere much grander, redolent of money and privilege. Clarissa also became aware that she was not alone. Kit was studying her quietly from the comfort of the generously upholstered leather armchair opposite.

'Where am I? What is this place?'

'This is my home, Clarissa—or the one closest to

the coast, in any event. Thornwood Manor to be exact, although, if you wish, you may call it *Castle Udolpho*.' Kit closed the book he had been reading while she was asleep. 'I have been familiarising myself with Mrs Radcliffe's novel, of which you seem so fond. Naturally I wish to ensure that I live up to the villainous Signor Montoni. Bringing you back to my lair while you slept seemed rather appropriate.' His smile was twisted, every bit the unrepentant rake.

Clarissa felt a small curl of trepidation clutch the pit of her stomach. But to show it, she knew, would be to surrender. Challenge, and if she could manage it, a cool approach to quell his ardour would be the most likely weapons to succeed. She yawned and sat up properly on the sofa, pushing the cashmere shawl that had covered her to one side. 'Lord, Kit, you take me too seriously, I fear. Mrs Radcliffe's novels are much too dramatic for me—'tis my aunt, really, who has a liking of them. Perhaps you should abduct her instead.'

'Very good, Clarissa, but I know you better than you think. This latest act does not fool me, nor will it put me off. I was happy to play the wicked Montoni, but I think, do not you, that the wicked Lord Rasenby will suffice just as well?' The smile that accompanied this remark was bleak, curling his sculpted mouth only slightly, but he made no attempt to move, seeming content with talk for the present.

'I know you well enough by now, Kit, to know that you are not, nor never shall be, the wicked Lord Rasenby. I presume you brought me here that we may partake of refreshment before the journey back to London. A sound idea, I am badly in need of a wash and some sustenance.' Watching him cautiously from under her lashes, Clarissa was not encouraged. Kit was showing no signs of relaxing.

'Several times now, Clarissa, I have warned you to ignore my reputation at your peril. You persist in doing so, but that is your look out. Do I need to remind you that we struck a bargain? A bargain with the devil it may be, but one that you must see through, none the less.'

Licking her dry lips nervously, Clarissa forced herself to relax against the cushions, feigning an indifference she was far from feeling. He had no intention of letting her go, and would insist on their union here in this house, and soon. For all she knew they were alone, although common sense told her there must be servants around somewhere. But servants in Lord Rasenby's employ were not likely to come to her rescue.

Rising to make the tea, Clarissa noted with relief that at least her hand did not betray her as she carefully measured out the delicate bohea from the wooden chest and poured the hot water from the little copper kettle into the delicate Chinese porcelain pot. Handing Kit a dish and settling gratefully to sip on her own, Clarissa frantically reviewed her options. They numbered two in total, and she was not confident of the likely success of either. She could stall, persuade Kit to postpone their union until some later point, and then somehow manage never to see him again. Or she could simply tell him the truth, and beg him to release her from her promise.

Actually, there was a third choice. She could submit. The thought brought a flush to her cheeks. To experience true passion just this once. To succumb to Kit's love-making. To bring this flame lit by Kit's kisses to a fire. To know real fulfilment. Oh God, it was tempting. Clarrie shivered at the thought.

But it was a fantasy. Impossible. For she knew that

one taste of Kit would leave her desperate for more. One slip and she would be wholly in his power, incapable of refusing him aught. Kit would use her and discard her, of this Clarissa was certain. She had to refuse him at any cost, no matter how much her body begged her to say yes to him.

Postponement, then, is what she would aim for. Taking another sip of the beautifully scented tea, Clarissa tried to relax. 'Do you think the Renauds will be safe, now? *Monsieur* told me a little of their troubles. Despite all he has been through, he seemed to me a kind man. He looks for good in everyone, even his enemies. I am not sure I could be so forgiving.'

'No? You surprise me, I thought that seeing good in people, despite ample evidence to the contrary, was something you took pride in doing yourself. Your determination to cast me in a positive light, for instance?'

She was nervous, Kit realised, looking for a way out, that much was obvious. Like a cat toying with a mouse, he decided to humour her. The outcome was inevitable— why not enjoy seeing her writhe in his clutches?

'That's different,' Clarissa replied. 'I merely pointed out to you that you have good qualities as well as bad. That is not at all the same thing as believing in goodness when faced with true evil, as Monsieur Renaud must surely have been. Were it my husband locked in a prison, condemned to death for no reason other than his birth, I would not be so forgiving.'

'Would you not? And what, fair Clarissa, would you do?'

'I have no idea. It would depend on the circumstances, I suppose. But if I found harm had been done to the man I loved, I would seek revenge.'

'I'd like to see it. I had no idea you could use a sword. Or would you choose pistols at dawn?'

'Of course not, I did not mean a duel. I meant—oh, you are infuriating! You take nothing seriously, there is no point in this discussion.' Petulantly, Clarissa placed her tea dish on the side table. So much for trying to involve him in conversation. All he seemed to do was aggravate her.

She took a calming breath and tried again. 'This is a lovely room. Is it a large house—Thornwood Manor, I think you called it?'

Only the slight twitch of his sculpted mouth betrayed Kit's amusement at this latest sally. 'Not large by the standards of my other properties—a mere cottage, some would say—with only ten bedrooms, and really quite small grounds.'

'And do you stay here often?'

'Not as often as I'd like. I spent my youth here. Nowadays I come when I want to sail, or to escape the tedium of London for a spell.'

'Oh.' The silence grew as Clarissa searched her mind desperately for another topic.

'You could always ask me about the weather.'

Looking up at this taunting remark, she could not help but smile, acknowledging the hit. 'Oh, no, for I feel I have not yet exhausted the possibilities of asking about your other residences first. The weather is far down the list. I'd be surprised if we reached that topic before we returned to London.'

'We are not returning to London for a while yet; you really must resign yourself to that fact. We are staying here, Clarissa, in the solitude of this ten-bedroom house with its small but beautiful park, until I have received my payment from you. To return to London without it would, I very much fear, be to give you the chance to disappear while still in my debt. And I have no intention of allowing that. You should not play if you cannot pay. Every gambler knows that.'

Would that her mama had followed that advice, Clarissa thought bitterly. But Mama and her debts seemed so far away. And unless she could escape from Kit, and soon, Clarissa was not sure she would ever be able to face them again.

'I can't stay here, it's not practical. I have nothing with me but what I stand in. No clothes, not even a toothbrush. No, no, Lord Rasenby—Kit—I must beg of you to return to London. I *will* pay you, but not here.' She was frightened, but it was tinged with a strange excitement. She did not fear hurt. He was making her suffer to tease her, perhaps even frighten her a little bit. But he would let her go, surely? He would not really make good his threat to keep her here against her will?

'A toothbrush I can supply you with. As to clothes— what need will we have of those? You need no adorning other than the glow of love-making. Lying naked in my arms, I have no doubt you will look your most beautiful.'

'Oh!' The thought was shocking, but the picture it conjured up, crystal clear in its detail, was more shocking still. A flush stole across Clarissa's pale cheeks at the idea of Kit naked beside her, his hard masculine body starkly contrasting with her own feminine curves. She felt a slow burning heat suffuse her. A rhythmic pulse picked up an insistent beat deep within that refused to be dispelled. Shaking her head in an effort to clear the fog clouding her brain, Clarissa looked up to find Kit watching her knowingly, perfectly well aware of the direction he had given her mind.

'Well, Clarissa? Have you any other objections? If so,

I would prefer that you raise them now, for pleasant as I find it to talk with you, there are other more—pressing—things we must do together. I find I am growing impatient with waiting, and wish to conclude our bargain.' Kit rose and crossed the room to stand before her. 'Come, Clarissa, enough of your excuses. You have a promise to fulfil.'

'I can't, I...'

'You would do well to co-operate, you know. I have no wish for an unwilling partner.' His words were spoken low, but the threat and the iron will behind them were unmistakable. Kit was annoyed at this show of reluctance, and could not understand it. She had never intended to pay at the start, that much was certain. But she wanted him now, he could not have mistaken her response to him. So why this pretence of reluctance? Surely she could not be planning to trap him into a commitment?

The thought gave Kit sudden pause, for it had never occurred to him that this could be her purpose. That she had some secret scheme he doubted not, as he doubted not that this maidenly modesty of hers was a ploy. But that the plot could have been a honey trap! No, he could not believe it. 'Come, Clarissa, it is time. I know not why you are feigning reluctance, you were eager enough in the cabin last night. You know full well this will be no ravishment, nor seduction even. Better to show good grace in defeat. You will enjoy yourself with me, I promise.' This time his smile was wolfish.

Taking his hand reluctantly, Clarissa stood. She was trembling, a combination of fear and anticipation mixed with desire making her unsteady on her feet. She stumbled, clutching Kit's arm to steady herself, and found herself drawn close when she would have made to pull away. 'No, no, I can't, I—'

'Oh, I think you'll find that you can.' His arms were around her, pulling her tight to his chest. His breath was on her face, and his lips captured hers in a sweet, tempting kiss before she had time to reply.

It was a kiss that promised of delights to come. A prelude, an appetiser of a kiss, softening her lips, forcing her mouth gently open, making her sigh softly as she melted.

Anchoring Clarissa to him with a hand placed firmly in the small of her back, Kit carefully stroked the soft curls on her forehead with the other, soothing, caressing away her resistance. His mouth left her lips to nibble gently on her ear lobe, and then to whisper light kisses on her brows, her eyelids, down to the swan-like line of her neck, licking the tender hollow of her shoulder.

It was a kiss that threatened to be her undoing. Clarissa unfurled like a spring flower in the bright March sunlight, slowly turning to the heat of the sun after the long cold winter. The defences she had thought so strong melted under this slow, sensual assault. As Kit slowly licked his way back up the white column of her throat to find her mouth once more, Clarissa sighed again, more deeply this time, surrendering to the inevitable. His tongue swept slowly along her lower lip, now pulsing with response, and she opened her mouth in anticipation of his onslaught.

To her surprise, it didn't come. Kit pulled back, just enough to look into her face, but the break awoke her to the extreme danger of her situation. Once more, fear battled with desire. Once more, she tried to pull together the tattered shreds of her resolution.

'No, you don't, Clarissa.' The arm around her waist tightened, preventing her from moving away.

'Let me go!'

'No. I didn't stop in order to resume this tedious pretence of reluctance on your part. In fact, quite the opposite. I want you willing. I know you are willing, and you know it too. I have no wish to force you, but I think we both know I won't have to. Admit it, damn you!'

'No. I won't. Let me go.'

'Don't make me lose my temper. I am fast approaching the end of my tether with you, I warn you. Now, admit that you are willing, for the love of God, woman, for in case it had escaped your notice, I am more than a little in need of satisfaction.'

Indeed, she could hardly be unaware of his arousal, pressed so close as she was against him. Clarissa shifted slightly, trying to move away from him, but succeeded only in rubbing herself more intimately against him, causing him to wince.

'If you don't stop struggling like that, we will not make it to the bedroom.' Kit's tone was urgent, his voice husky with passion, but his eyes were hard, dark pools of determination.

Clarissa knew she could not fight such a man with subterfuge any longer. If she was to escape from here with her virtue—what was left of it—she must confess all. 'Kit, please let me go. There is something I must tell you.'

'I thought I had made it singularly clear that the time for talk is over, Clarissa. I am not interested in words at present, I am more concerned with the other things our mouths can do. I need one word only from you, and that is yes. Just say it, Clarrie,' Kit said urgently, 'say yes.'

'No! I won't. Let me go.' Her voice betrayed her desperation as she twisted in his grip. 'Kit, you've got to listen to me. If you don't you'll regret it, I promise.'

'The only thing I'll regret is that I stopped when I did. I am tired of your tricks. I want to hear no more of your lies. Your kisses tell me clear enough that your answer is yes.'

Clarissa's struggles became more determined. She felt the flounce on her petticoat rip as Kit held her effortlessly tight. One long curl escaped its pins, and she shook it impatiently from her face. Her heart was beating so fast she felt it must escape the confines of her rib cage, and she could no longer hide the apprehension in her eyes. 'No! I am not who you think I am. I am not here for the reasons you believe. Kit, please, you must listen to me. Please!'

The single tear, the first he had seen her shed, was so surprising that he released her abruptly. Thrusting her back on to the sofa in confusion, Kit watched as she wiped it away. Even in extremes, it would seem, Clarissa was not a female to fall back on the traditional ploy of waterworks. Striding to the side table, he unlocked the tantalus and poured brandy into two glasses, downing his in one swift gulp before taking the other glass to Clarissa. 'Here, take this.'

She pushed it away, still intent on regaining some measure of control over the panic that was engulfing her. 'I don't want that. There is no need to get me drunk, my lord, it will not make my consent any more forthcoming.'

'I have no intention of making you drunk, damn it! You are upset. The brandy will calm you. And before you even think about it, no, it is not laced with any drug. I am not, after all, such a villain as Signor Montoni. Now drink up.'

The fiery liquid made her gasp, but it did help calm

her. Trying rather ineffectually to push her hair back into its pins, Clarissa looked up to see that Kit was watching her, a grim look on his face. 'I must look a fright.' Her voice was shaky.

His hand reached out to grasp hers, his fingers wound round the curl, and tightened, just enough for her to sense the threat. Despite the concern he had shown, he had not softened towards her. Idly twisting her curl round and around those long, shapely fingers, Kit watched Clarissa, his eyes like cold chips of flint, a slight frown between his dark brows, giving her no hint of his thoughts.

She shivered. She had badly miscalculated; he would not be swayed from his purpose. Her only hope was in making him listen to the truth before his temper took control. If she was going to speak, now was her only chance.

Clarissa took a deep breath. 'Kit? I know you're angry, but, please, won't you listen, just for a moment?' Forcing herself to look up into his face, she was taken aback at the bleakness there. His eyes were expressionless, his mouth a hard, grim line. His breathing was harsh and he trembled with a mixture of barely suppressed anger and frustrated desire. The urge to reach up, to place a small, soft hand against those grim lines on his brow, to try to smooth them away with her thumb, was irresistible.

Kit closed his eyes at the touch, but almost immediately swatted her hand away and sat back from her, as if the contact gave him pain. 'Another of your tricks, Clarissa, pity? I have no need of that. If anyone is to be pitied, it is you.'

The frown deepened, the brows drawn together to meet in the middle, giving him a satanic look that made her retreat, truly afraid for the first time. Noting her reaction, Kit gave a harsh laugh. 'Yes, now you see before you the real wicked Lord Rasenby. Just as I see before me the real, treacherous Clarissa. I have but one advantage over you, my sweet. At least I played fair.'

'What do you mean?'

'I never pretended to be other than what I am. Whereas you… Well, I still don't know what your game is, but I no longer care. I knew you lied when you sought me out. I knew you lied about your reasons for wanting this little *adventure* as you called it. But I thought—hoped—had come to expect, in any case, that you would play fair, that at least your more intimate dealings with me would be honest. It seems I was mistaken, and you are simply a better actress than I thought.'

Kit ran a hand through his thick black hair and shook his head in an effort to clear his brain. He was exhausted, had barely slept for almost two days. Against his will, he had begun to like this woman in front of him, to honour her for her courage and her quick wits. He enjoyed her company, but that made her treachery all the harder to come to terms with. Subtly but surely over these last few days, this woman had got under his skin, and he thought she felt the same. Now there could be no doubt that it had all been an act. This determined blowing of hot and cold, even the meagre tears, all were mere trickery, designed to make him take pity and to let her go. But he would not!

No longer caring about the means, Kit was determined that the end should be as she had promised. He would have her, and she would admit that she was willing, would admit that she wanted him as he wanted her. He had to have her, his blood would not be cooled without her. Then, thank God, it would be over. She would be out of his system, and he could go back to his life—whatever that turned out to be.

Kit stood to pour himself another measure of brandy. Looking over as he drained his glass, he saw she was crying, silent tears, which she was frantically trying to mop with her sleeve. Her shoulders were hunched, and her breathing uneven, and she looked so forlorn, with her crumpled dress and her hair in disarray, that he had to quell the urge to go over, to wrap her in his arms, and tell her no harm would come to her. Hardening his heart, reminding himself it was just another of her games, he returned instead to the armchair opposite, and waited for her to gain some control over herself.

A loud sniff and a final surreptitious wipe of her nose informed him that she was ready to speak.

'I'm sorry,' Clarissa muttered, 'I don't usually cry.'

'No, and you wasted your effort, you know. Your tears move me as little as your protestations of maidenly modesty. Both are false.'

'You're quite wrong, Kit, but I can see that it will do me no good to protest.' She had ruined everything with her lies, she could see that. What little trust there had been between them was spoilt. What tiny, faint fantasy she had clung on to for some kind of future happiness was an impossible dream. 'I need to tell you the truth—will you listen?'

'The truth? That will be a novelty.' The harsh, cynical laugh, almost a snarl, with no trace of humour, proved she had lost him for ever. 'I'll listen, but it will make no difference. By the end of tonight, you will be mine. By the end of tomorrow, you will be gone and we can both say good riddance. I wish to get the whole thing over with, for this game begins to bore me—sooner than I had thought. So, please, tell me your tale and then let us talk no more.'

The words sounded a death knell to her hopes, faint as

they had been. The only thing now was to try, at least, to extract his promise to leave Amelia alone. With a deep breath, she began. 'My name is Clarissa Warrington. I am Amelia Warrington's sister.'

With many pauses, stumbling over the words, and all the time waiting in vain for a reaction, any reaction, from Kit, silent and brooding in the chair, Clarissa told her story. Making little of her own trials, she still gave away enough to paint Kit a sorry picture of her circumstances. 'I just feel that if Amelia had the chance to meet an honourable man who would be a calming influence on her, she would marry and could be happy. There is someone, a good man who loves her, and I am sure his feelings are reciprocated. But she has been so spoilt, and she is so beautiful, that the kinds of riches you can offer make it difficult for her to choose the honourable path.'

Lacing her hands together as she concentrated on putting Amelia in the kindest light, Clarissa frowned. 'She's not a bad person, she's just weak. So I thought if I removed temptation from her, it would give Edward a chance.' Realising just how foolish this plan sounded, now that she told it aloud for the first time, made her shoulders sag with despair. What a fool she had been!

Kit echoed her thoughts. 'Well, if that really was your plan, I can only say that you must have windmills in your head. For God's sake, Clarissa, do you really believe for a moment that my absence will make any difference at all? Merely, it means that Amelia will look for a replacement, and I can assure you that it will not be this worthy Edward, unless he has miraculously come into a fortune over the last couple of days.'

'I know, it sounds so stupid now.' Looking back, Clarissa was hard put to understand her own behaviour. To have believed that Kit's mere absence would make a difference was ludicrous, not just stupid. With hindsight, of course, it was clear to her that her proposal to Kit had not been to save her sister, but to save Kit. Worse, she realised now, she had wanted Kit for herself from the first moment she had met him at the masked ball.

'But you are not stupid, Clarissa. In fact, you are a very intelligent, well-informed young woman. I find it difficult to believe that you came up with this madcap idea merely to save your sister from an indecent proposal. And despite what you have said, I cannot believe either that you thought Amelia to be so very innocent. She is a scheming wretch, and you know it.'

His words, so nearly reflecting her own thoughts, caught her unawares. Looking over at her, Kit saw a slightly hunted expression flit across her face. 'I'm right then, Clarissa. The story you have told is not so simple, is it?'

'I don't know what you mean. I've told you the truth, I wanted to save Amelia. There is nothing more.' Terrified that Kit had some inkling of her feelings, Clarissa sought desperately for something to say that would assuage his curiosity—anything but the real truth, the truth that was only just becoming apparent to Clarissa. She had thrown herself in Kit's path from the start, not for her sister's sake, but for her own. He must never find out.

'Look at you. The lies are writ large across your face. What twist have you left out of your sorry story?'

'I—well, if you must know, I—the truth is, my lord, that I discovered from my sister that she planned to trap you.'

'Trap me? In what way, trap me?'

'Into marriage, my lord. She knew, you see, that you intended only a—a dishonourable proposal, but she was sure that she could persuade you into matrimony but some underhand means.'

'What means, exactly?'

'I don't know, I swear I don't. I only know that she had some plan, something that was to take place over the next few days, and she was certain that you would fall for it. I—I could not condone it, I had to stop it. Marriage should not be based on deceit and lies. I tried to reason with Amelia, I tried to find out what she was planning, but she merely laughed at me.'

'And knowing your sister so well as you say you do, did you really think she had the brains to carry off such a scheme? Did you think for one single minute that I would fall for anything that trollop had up her sleeve? You vastly overrate your sister if you do. I don't believe you.'

The temper on which Kit had been keeping such a tight rein was leased suddenly and wholly unexpectedly. 'Do you think I'm so stupid? That a simpering girl with cotton wool for a brain, so obviously determined to sell herself to the highest bidder, would find a way to coerce me into marriage? *Well, do you?*'

Without waiting for an answer, the words coming in a cold, harsh voice, Kit continued, all the while towering over her, his face a mask of white anger. 'No, I don't think for one second that is what you thought my fair, deceitful Clarissa. You are more like your sister than you admit. Though your plan was not quite so crude, was it? Not quite so obvious, but with the same intention.'

'I don't understand, I—'

'Don't bother to deny it, I am sick of your lies. You knew perfectly well Amelia could not succeed with me. But you thought *you* could, didn't you? Well, *didn't you*?'

'No! No, oh no. Kit, no, I wouldn't, I—'

'Oh, spare me the injured innocent, madam, it cuts no ice. I see it all clearly now. It was you who were planning to seduce me all along. Not to save your precious sister, oh, no, this was no sacrificial seduction. No wonder you were so desperate to get back to London. You had never any intention of fulfilling your promise to me, but you had every intention of blackmailing me, did you not? No doubt your so-respectable aunt, or more likely your poor frail mama, was to be brought into play. A sad and sorry tale of abduction, perhaps? Yes, that would be it. A night away in my company, and then you return home, your mama cries rape, and you await my proposals. Not bad, as far as these sorts of things go, but it wouldn't have worked, Clarissa. I've told you many times, I'm every bit as bad as my reputation. Mama could have published your tale of woe in a scandal sheet for the *ton* to read and it would have provoked no reaction from me.'

Silenced by this onslaught, Clarissa sat, motionless and appalled at what she had done. Kit fell silent too, gazing unseeing into the fire, trying to come to terms with his own anger, which seemed out of all proportion to Clarissa's crime. After all, he had known her to be deceitful from the first. Eventually, the black humour of the situation got the better of his temper. The scheme had at least the spark of originality he had come to expect from Clarissa. Placing himself at her side, Kit took hold of her cold hand. 'Let us have done with all pretence. Admit I have discovered your plans, then we can kiss and make up.'

Snatching her hand away, Clarissa moved as far from Kit as the sofa would allow. She did not trust herself to stand. 'I admit nothing other than the truth. I wanted to protect Amelia from her own foolish self. And I wanted to save you from being tricked into marriage. I had no intentions, none whatever, I assure you most vehemently, of tricking you into any sort of proposal for myself. I meant it, Kit, I promise you, I do most truly believe that no relationship, marriage or otherwise, can be built on deceit. As to my mama's involvement—well, all I can say is that if you knew my mama, you would know her incapable of any sort of plotting.'

'Ah, I assume that Amelia takes after her then?'

A subdued giggle gave him his answer. Clarissa's sense of humour did not fail her, even in the midst of such emotional trauma. 'I'm afraid so. Mama is rather—well, suffice to say that I am the practical one.'

'The only one with any brains, you mean. It is time you put them to use. Admit that you have failed. Come clean with me, and we will call it quits.'

'You mean I can go?'

'No, I mean I will not be angry with you any more. I will save my energy for more enjoyable emotions. I still expect you to come to my bed. You can't seriously have expected me to change my mind?'

'But I never intended, I never meant—I mean, I didn't think it would come to this. I can't—please don't ask me to, please, Kit.'

Her green eyes were for the second time in a short period drowned in tears, but she would not look away, nor shed them willingly. Beseechingly, Clarissa looked up at him, silently begging for mercy. But she could see no signs of softening in the harsh mask of his face.

'Your tears won't sway me, so dry your eyes. You've tried every trick in the book over the past few days, and this sight affects me no more than any of the others, save I am in awe at the breadth of your talents. And before you try the virtuous maiden on me once more, may I remind you that your kisses have given you away several times. You are no more a maiden than your sister.'

Gently pulling Clarissa to him, Kit produced a large square of linen from his pocket, and applied himself to wiping her eyes. She lay compliant under his ministrations, almost drained of resistance, unable to think of any way out of this mesh she had woven.

'There. Your plans have gone awry, but that is no reason to prevent us enjoying each other's company.' His hand tilted her chin towards him, and he looked close into her captive eyes. 'No more tears. No more lies. Tonight you will fulfil your part of the bargain, and tomorrow you will go home. We will enjoy our coupling, you know we will. If our kisses are an indication, then it will be more than enjoyable, for we are extremely compatible, and I have tasted enough of you to know that you have been well schooled in the arts of pleasing a man.'

'I can't, Kit, please don't make me.'

'I won't make you. I won't have to. You will come to my bed of your own accord. You know you will.'

'No! Once and for all, you are mistaken in me. I have no such experience. If you take me, it will ruin me. Please, my lord, I beg of you, let me go.'

The hand on her chin tightened as his eyes darkened with anger, and something else. Dark desire, selfish need, frustrated passion—all the pent-up emotions Clarissa had roused, then dampened, then set on fire, then quelled, then blown once more into life until they burned as an inferno. Without warning, without thought, with only base, urgent need, Kit surrendered all restraint. Pushing Clarissa back on the sofa, trapping her under the hard length of his body, his mouth descended on hers in a revengeful, possessive kiss.

She struggled, her hands beating ineffectually on his

chest, his shoulders, his arms. The kiss went relentlessly on, his lips hard, his tongue seeking, controlling, his body taut, pushing against hers, demanding a response. And surely, as surely as a drug injected straight into her veins, mixing with her blood, he was having an effect. She fought, but more weakly. Her mouth softened, compliant under his, if not yet responding to his demands. Her body arched into his, relishing the feel of pulsating muscle, hard bone, rough skin, all the evidence of his overwhelming masculinity against her wholly feminine softness. With every second his mastery of her became more complete.

Sensing the change in her, Kit's kisses became more sensuous, his tongue more teasing, his hands stroking her into submission rather than holding her to ransom. Clarissa sighed, her own hands ceasing their fluttering against his back, to drop boneless by her sides. She was drowning, lost, swirling deep into the eddy of their mutual desire. The fingers of her right hand trailed on the floor beside the sofa, feeling the soft pile of the Turkish rug beneath them, the texture of the wool rough against her skin like the growth of Kit's beard on her face.

The strings of her reticule caught in her hand. It must have been under the sofa. Her reticule. She clung to the last desperate shreds of her weakening resistance and pulled the strings open, groping inside as Kit continued his assault on her mouth, as her own mouth started to co-operate, poised on the verge of making her own demands. A kerchief. Her purse. A small mirror. And something else, heavy, cold and sharp.

Summoning a last strand of resolution, Clarissa extracted the small, jewelled dagger from the reticule. Calling on all her strength, she clutched it tight to the hilt and brought her hand up, the deadly blade glinting in the firelight. At the same time she placed her other hand on Kit's chest and pushed with all her might, struggling free from under him. Taken by surprise, he rolled over onto the floor with Clarissa landing on top of him. Without thinking, she reached out to break her fall. The dagger slipped from her grip, glanced off the large brass button on Kit's coat, and plunged into his arm.

Chapter Eight

'Kit! Oh, my God, Kit! I've killed you.'

'Don't be ridiculous, Clarissa. You've barely scratched me.'

'Oh, you're not dead. Thank you, God. Are you sure?'

'Have you any idea how ludicrous a question that is? Do you think it's my ghost talking? You do not kill a man by sticking a knife into his arm. It's hardly even bleeding.'

'Let me see. No, no, don't stand. Sit there. No wait, take off your coat so I can bind it. No, wait, perhaps I should call a doctor? Or get you some brandy?'

'Stop! Sit down, take a deep breath and for the Lord's sake just be quiet for a minute and let me have a look at this grievous wound you have inflicted on me.'

'But, Kit, I think you should—'

'Clarissa, if you don't just shut up for a few seconds, I swear I will be forced to murder you with that toy of yours. Where in damnation is the thing, anyway?'

Reluctantly Clarissa sat, only to stand again instantly as the point of the dagger jabbed her thigh. 'Ouch! Here, I think.'

'Give me that. Serves you right.' Kit grabbed the dagger from her hands, inspecting it with raised brows. Not a toy after all. Had it not been for his coat, she could well have injured him, seriously, if not fatally. Reluctantly, he was impressed. He had to give her top marks for originality, if nothing else—no one had ever managed to knife him before, though he was sure there were many who would have taken pleasure in it.

'It was my father's. It's one of the few things of his that haven't been sold off. I had it in my reticule. I'm sorry, truly sorry, I didn't mean to hurt you.'

Kit raised his brows questioningly, a gleam of humour lurking in his dark eyes. 'I find that difficult to believe, and I'm not sure a jury would take your side too readily. If you did not mean to hurt me, why did you try to stab me?'

'I didn't! I mean, yes, I did have the knife in my hand, but my intent was only to threaten you. I slipped, it was an accident. I just thought you would take me more seriously—I just thought—oh, I don't know what I thought. I'm sorry.'

'Well, it's certainly a drastic measure to take to escape my advances. I had no idea that you found me so unattractive.'

'I don't.'

This time the denial was a whisper so soft he was not sure he had heard it. And even as he took it in, she had reverted to her concern over his injury.

'Does it hurt? I think I should take a look, even if it is just a scratch. It will need to be dressed, you'll probably need a sling.'

The hopefulness in her tone was unmistakable. So, despite everything he had said, all that had passed between them in the last few hours, Clarissa was still determined to escape. Well, she could for now, for he was in no fit state for love-making at present, in need of some time to cool his temper, if nothing else. Some rest was what they both needed. 'Very well, do your worst.' With difficulty, Kit shrugged obligingly out of his tight-fitting coat, ruefully surveying the damage the knife had done to the expensive fabric.

The wound was small and bleeding sluggishly, situated in the fleshy part of his left arm. At his behest Clarissa rang the bell, and to her astonishment it was answered in a remarkably quick time by a liveried servant. The man betrayed no sign of surprise at the sight of his master, wounded and half-undressed on the sofa, in the company of a somewhat dishevelled and tearful young woman. Her request for fresh linen, hot water and basilicum powder were received as if she had ordered tea and biscuits.

'Are your servants used to seeing such sights?'

'Hardly. I have never been wounded before nor am I accustomed to bringing my mistresses here. That is two firsts for you.'

'I am not your mistress.'

'No, but you will be soon.'

'No, I won't. I can't. *You* can't, that's what I mean. Your arm, it will be in a sling, so you won't be able to—well, you won't want to—I mean, you won't be up to—'

'I think you'd better stop there, don't you?' His grin was tinged with wicked humour, but his voice showed signs of fatigue. Stifling a yawn, he smiled wanly. 'I think you're safe for the moment. You may bind my arm, then we could both do with some sleep—alone. When you are rested, you may command the servants to draw you a bath. We will dine together later. No—' he raised his hand as she tried to speak '—do not, I beg of you, argue with me further. We are not returning to London tonight. Apart from anything else, your over-eager attempt to defend yourself has ensured that I am not fit to travel. And before you ask, no, you cannot go on your own. Now, once and for all, accept your fate and let us have an end to this futile discussion.'

And for once Clarissa judged it best to take his advice. She vouchsafed no reply.

The servant returned, placing a bowl of water on the table in front of her, the bandages, lint and powder to the side. His countenance, and the nod he gave to her as he did so, showed no trace of disrespect towards her. 'Will that be all, my lord?'

'Yes, thank you, Robert. Wait. Tell Mrs Hatchings that we'll dine at seven. And warn the kitchen that Miss— er—Warrington here, will be requiring a bath later. Oh, and before all that, get the housekeeper to prepare the red room for Miss Warrington as soon as possible.' Turning to Clarissa, he held his arm out in resignation. 'I hope you know what you're doing. I wouldn't put it beyond you to make it worse for your own devious purposes.'

Ignoring the gasp of indignation aroused by this remark, Kit leaned back and closed his eyes.

He awoke to find himself alone. His arm had been efficiently bandaged and mercifully left without a sling. The room was dark, the fire a heap of glowing embers. He must have been asleep for some time. Rising, Kit rang the bell, demanding hot water for his own bath, issuing a series of brisk, clear instructions for the morrow as he strode across the hallway and up the wide stair-case. Refreshed by his sleep, a quiver of desire arrowed through him as he thought of Clarissa asleep in the room adjoining his own. He tried to remember the last time he had felt such a rush of anticipation, and couldn't. He must needs make the most of it, for tomorrow she would be gone and out of his life for good.

Clarissa had slept soundly in the huge four-poster bed, oblivious of her surroundings, save for the comfort of the feather mattress, the warmth at her feet from the warming pan, the crisp Holland sheets and the reassuring weight of the soft, luxurious quilt of eiderdown which had been fashioned to match the bed hangings. She awoke, feeling refreshed. The room was large, lit by a brightly burning fire in the gleaming grate. The curtained bed faced an enormous picture window, which must look direct to the sea over the marshes, for she had been aware of the soothing murmuring as she slept. Aside from the usual chests, there was a pretty lacquered writing desk in one corner, and an array of delicate Oriental porcelain on the mantel. The rich Turkish rugs were warm under her feet, and by her bedside there was a beautiful array of flowers.

The overall effect was of comfort, and of excellent taste. Despite his wealth, Kit was not an ostentatious man. His extravagances were all for public consummation—the horses, the mistresses, the gaming. In private he was obviously much more restrained.

Her thoughts were interrupted by a gentle tap on the door, preceding the entrance of a maidservant. 'If you please, ma'am, it's close on six o'clock. Would you like to bathe now?' At Clarissa's nod, a flurry of activity saw a large copper hip bath placed before the fire and filled with bucket after bucket of steaming water. Several screens placed strategically ensured that no draughts would intrude. Towels were placed on a rail to heat, and rose oil added to the water to give the final touch of complete comfort.

Clarissa had never bathed in such opulence, and luxuriated in the heat and steam, allowing it to ease her tense muscles. She emerged in a rosy glow, feeling much better. Her underclothes had been miraculously laundered, and the creases in her dress ironed out. There was a supply of brushes and combs on the dressing table, allowing her to tame her unruly curls into a simple but fresh style. Checking her *toilette* in the glass, she was pleased with the result. A nod, a deep breath, and she was ready to be shown downstairs, ready to face Kit, though how to deal with him, she had no idea. Trusting to her instincts and her sense of self-preservation, trusting also that Kit would have had time to reconsider his actions in the light of her story and his injured arm, Clarissa followed the maidservant with her head held high and a sparkle in her eyes.

She was shown into a small dining room on the first floor. It was brightly lit and, as she had come to expect, showed impeccable, if restrained, taste. The table was set for two, the white damask cloth laid with gleaming silver cutlery and delicate Spode. On the walls, the paintings were more modern than those in the parlour and on the staircase, obviously Kit's own purchases rather than those of his ancestors. Clarissa recognised a small seascape very much in the style of Mr Turner, whose work she had seen and admired earlier that year in the Royal Academy. There were others, portraits and landscapes that were unfamiliar to her, but all unmistakably of the new, naturalist school.

Kit was standing by the fire, resplendent in a dark, tightly fitting cutaway coat, tan pantaloons replacing his buckskins. His cravat was intricately tied and adorned with a small diamond pin, his black hair brushed forward. He appeared to be in good humour, but Clarissa noted immediately the smile was his satanic one, his lips curled in that mocking way she knew so well.

'I trust my servants looked after you? You found everything sufficient to your needs?'

'Even a toothbrush, thank you. I feel much better.'

'You look much better too. Quite charming, in fact.'

'And you, my lord? How is your arm? I notice you have decided against a sling?'

'Yes, I'm sorry to disappoint you, but really I had no need of it. Now, I expect you are hungry. I know I am.' As he spoke, Kit pulled out a chair for her, at right angles to his own at the head of the table. Almost immediately, the door opened and dinner was served.

The food was delicious. There were stewed oysters, woodcock roasted on the spit, a broiled turbot, and side dishes of artichokes, a delicate soup, and braised chicory. A Rhenish cream and a fruit jelly followed. Both Clarissa and Kit ate with appetite, warmed by the excellent burgundy, confining conversation to general subjects. In the relaxed atmosphere, they discovered anew a delight in each other's company, and shared opinions on many things, from a hearty dislike of Mr Pitt who, they both believed, had been in office much too long, and a liking for the plays of Mr Shakespeare.

Clarissa asked Kit more about his childhood in Thornwood Manor, and in turn shared some of her memories. The days when her father had been alive, his habit of turning up, after an absence of days, with presents, full of laughter, brushing aside her mama's remonstrations to hug them both, swinging Clarrie high over his head. 'Now, of course, I realise he must have been on a gambling spree. He would bet on almost anything, and I suspect that he won less often than he lost. The times he came back with his pockets to let, drunk and in a foul temper, pushing me aside rather than picking me up and throwing me into the air—well, there were more of those.'

Clarissa paused, deep in the memories of those past childhood days. Papa, in his evening clothes even though it was always morning when he returned, his breath stale, his wig askew, pushing aside a small Clarissa, anxiously tugging for attention at the skirt of his coat. Mama, so pretty and so young, pulling at his other side, tugging his sleeve, demanding to know where he had been. Papa intent on his bed, swatting at them both, calling for a servant, demanding to know why breakfast was not on the table for him. Mama handing Clarissa over to the servant, pulling her father up the stairs, her father shouting, waving his hands in the air, but allowing himself to be pulled.

Looking up to find Kit watching her closely, Clarissa blinked, and smiled. 'I haven't thought of these things in years. I'm sorry, I didn't mean to give the conversation such a depressing turn.'

He shrugged. 'So, dear papa was a gambler. I take it that explains the poverty?'

'Yes, he left us with nothing. And by the time he died, you know, he had been cast off completely by his family. They did nothing for Mama, she was left almost penniless. Except my aunt. It was she who provided for my schooling. She would have done the same for Amelia, had she wanted it—but Amelia, I'm sorry to say, was inclined to frivolity from an early age.'

'Leaving you to be the dependable one?'

'Yes, I suppose so.' She was surprised at his perception.

'Well, from what you've said, you could hardly have relied on your mother.'

She laughed at that. 'No, you're right. Mama's idea of economy is to buy only the best, most expensive wax candles because they burn more slowly than tallow. Or to place another order with a merchant when the bills come in on quarter day, rather than to pay what we owe.'

'My own experience of parents isn't so far from your own, despite the differences in our financial circumstances.'

'I find that difficult to believe.'

'My father was a gambler too, prone to disappear for days on end. We all learned to dread seeing him on settling day, and Newmarket was worse—he never seemed to win. As to my mother, she is just as air-headed as yours in her turn. Her latest idea of saving money is to buy new curtains for every room in the house at once, on the assumption that the bigger order will get her a bigger discount. The only difference is that my father added womanising to his vices, and my mother can well afford to indulge her extravagances, having my purse to turn to when her own runs dry.'

The deep cynicism in his voice betrayed his feelings. Like Clarissa, Kit was the provider. She suspected that like her, too, the role was not one that garnered much by way of thanks or loving appreciation. Looking at him, she realised he was as surprised at the comparison as she. Knowing him well though, she thought the better of dwelling on it, merely reaching over to squeeze his hand, before turning to a less personal subject.

The meal was a success. After the covers were removed, they left the table to sit opposite each other in the cosy downstairs parlour, Kit sipping contemplatively on a brandy, Clarissa merely watching, relishing his presence, desperate to make the moment last for ever, yet knowing that she must bring it to a close.

'I think I should retire. Thank you for a most pleasant evening. I take it we start early for London in the morning?'

Placing his glass to one side, Kit raised an eyebrow in surprise, having expected another show of resistance. 'Very well. I'll join you when I've finished my brandy.'

'Join me?'

'In your bedchamber, of course. Or if you prefer, we can use mine?'

'Yours?'

'If you prefer.'

'But I thought...'

'What, my fair Clarissa, did you think?'

'I thought that you had—had—I thought you realised—now you know I was telling the truth—I thought you realised I cannot go through with this. I thought you had accepted my reasons, understood my reasons. I thought that...'

'That I would forgo payment?'

'Yes.'

'Did I say so?'

'No, but...'

'But you thought I would let you off anyway, after your touching tale of rescuing your sister? And just to make sure, your touching revelations about your papa and mama over dinner to arouse my sympathy.'

'No, that's not true. You make it sound as if I had planned to tell you those things. I've never talked to anyone about those things before, I was just—I thought we were becoming friends.'

'Friends!' The astonishment in his voice was genuine. 'Don't be ridiculous. There can be no friendship between men and women. What we were doing, Clarissa, was simply foreplay. Mental stimulation, a prelude to physical stimulation. We are not, nor ever will be, friends. Tonight we will be lovers. After tomorrow we will be strangers. And for now, we will stop talking, lest we lose the benefits of all this mental foreplay and I remember what a lying, scheming, double-crossing wretch you are.'

'Please, Kit, I beg you this one last time, won't you believe me? I am not the woman you insist on thinking me. I'm simply a foolish sister whose plan to save her sibling from ruin has gone awry. I have done you no real harm. We've enjoyed each other's company when we've not been at odds. I give you my word that I will never attempt to blackmail you, nor even to recognise you, should we meet again. Please, let me go.'

Almost, he did. Despite her lies, despite her scheming, she was right. He had enjoyed her company, more than he could have believed. He found her challenging, brave, surprising. Friendship was not the word—it was *affinity*. In many ways, they were kindred spirits. The thought gave him pause, Clarissa's fate hanging in the balance, the scales tipping slightly, very slightly in her favour for the first time.

But then he remembered the rest, and the scales swung heavily against her finally and for ever. She had lied to him from the first. Despite all her protestations, he believed her intention was entrapment. All the evidence was against her. But most of all, it was her body that had betrayed her. Her kisses, those kisses, which roused in him a passion more intense than any he had felt before. The way she knew just where to touch, how to hold, to caress, to stroke. The depth of her arousal when they kissed matching his own. None of this came from inexperience. These were not the actions of a virgin. And tonight he would have them all, her full repertoire. Nothing would stop him.

The decision was there in his eyes for her to interpret, as clearly as if it had been writ. There would be no last-minute reprieve. He would show no mercy. Wordlessly, Clarissa turned and left the room.

Alone in her bedchamber, she sat by the fire and thought deep. She was curiously calm, resigned to her fate, certain that there was nothing more she could do to fight it. She had gambled, and she would pay the price with the loss of her virtue. Now that the decision had been taken out of her hands, she felt something almost akin to relief that she would not have to resist him further.

Raising her cold fingers to the flames, Clarissa sighed. There was no point in fooling herself. A large part of her was glad this was happening. She had fought and lost. To the victor would come the spoils. Kit would have her body. But she would also have his.

Stop fooling yourself, Clarrie, you want this as much as he does. It was true. She had always tried to be ruthlessly honest with herself. She would not have chosen this fate, but since it had chosen her she would take everything from it that she could. She would relish tonight. It was like to be her only experience of passion, for she knew she was designed to love like this only once in her lifetime. There would never be another to replace Kit in her affections. So, she would have Kit in the flesh tonight, and she would have the memories of it to savour for the remainder of her years.

A shiver ran through her body at the thought, which had nothing to do with the cold. With a defiant toss of her curls, Clarrie rose to prepare. She would not present herself as a sacrifice. She would not let Kit think this was a seduction. She would do her best to meet him on his own terms, as an equal in passion, if not in experience.

The vision that met Kit when he opened the door some fifteen minutes later made him pause on the threshold in amazement. Clarrie stood by the fire, her back to the flames. Dressed only in her chemise, her arms and neck were bare, her breasts gleaming white and taut against the restraining lace. The full glory of her bright auburn hair tumbled in curls down her back, the only additional colour her soft lips and her bright emerald eyes. Quite literally, she took his breath away.

'Won't you come in, my lord?' Clarrie extended a welcoming hand, her voice husky. Only the rapid rising and falling of her breasts gave away her excitement. Her stance, her commanding invitation, the direct look from those intelligent eyes, showed her to be a woman secure in her own attractions, sure of herself, and equally sure of the man she was waiting for. It was an intoxicating mix.

Walking slowly over to take the outstretched hand, Kit pressed a long, lingering kiss in the palm. His tongue caressed the pad of her thumb, and he licked the tip of each finger in turn, causing tiny ripples of feeling to run down Clarrie's arm. Kit pressed his lips to the thin skin on her wrist, his tongue on her pulse, which fluttered like a bird against a cage, betraying her excitement. But still Clarrie stood, unmoving, content to let him take the initiative, resisting the urge to run the fingers of her other hand through the crisp dark hair on the tender nape of his neck as he bent over her arm.

Kit worked his way to the skin on the inside of her elbow, his tongue circling hot erotic circles, stirring that pulse deep within her to throbbing, insistent life. She could restrain herself no longer. With a sigh that expelled all final doubts, all cares of the future, allowed for no thoughts other than this moment, this man, these feelings, Clarrie surrendered. 'Kit, kiss me. Please.'

The words were whispered, but they were enough. She had submitted. Admitted to her own desire. With a harsh moan, Kit swept Clarrie into his arms, pulling her close against him, enveloping her yielding mouth, kissing her with a deep, encompassing intensity that threatened to consume them. He was on fire, but the flames licked at them both.

Wrapping her arms around his neck, pulling his head closer, his mouth harder against her own, Clarrie matched move for move, passion with passion. She arched against him, feeling the lean length of his body against hers through the thin cotton of her chemise, but it still wasn't close enough. She wanted flesh on flesh. His tongue entered her mouth, thrusting, a foretaste of the more intimate thrusting to come, and his hands roamed over her back, through her silken hair, spanned her waist, clutched at the soft, round flesh of her bottom, pulling her tighter, closer, all the time kissing her harder, more insistently.

Breathing heavily, Kit pulled back. 'Clarrie, slow down, for God's sake.' Grasping her hands and holding them in a clasp in front of her, Kit looked into the flushed face before him. Never had he felt so aroused. Never had his passion been matched like this. She was fighting him every step, demanding as much from him as he was demanding from her. She was not submitting to him, he was not extracting payment—she was giving it. But he wanted to savour every second. And he had waited too long for this to be over quickly.

Shrugging out of his dressing gown, clothed only

in his shirt and pantaloons, Kit picked Clarrie up in his arms and deposited her on the bed, where she lay sprawled, her hair streaming out in a fan of colour on the pillows, a tempting, wanton picture that he could happily dive into and drown. Struggling to remove the rest of his clothes, he watched her, as she watched him, her eyes roaming his body as he revealed it to her, drinking in the hard, muscular flesh of his torso, the black, crisp hair that curled over his chest, arrowing down to the line of his breeches. Widening when he removed the rest of his clothes to stand naked in front of her, gasping slightly as she took in the full extent of his proud, erect manhood, but refusing to look away.

The hot feel of his tongue sucking on her toe, flicking on the tender skin of her ankle, moving slowly up to circle the back of her knee, was more erotic than she could have imagined. She moaned, and tried to find purchase on the soft feather mattress to raise herself up to return the contact more freely.

'No. Relax. Enjoy it. Let me pleasure you, I want to.' Kit pushed her gently back, and she was like jelly, unable to resist. He undid the fastenings of her undergarments, and removed them. His fingers gently caressed her soft, perfectly rounded bottom, the thumbs running tantalisingly down the insides of her thighs as he pulled her clothing free.

The throbbing within her centred, focused between her legs. Clarrie moaned low in her throat and twisted restlessly on the sheet, her body making demands she had no idea it possessed.

Still Kit forced himself to go slowly, drinking in the beauty of the body revealed before him. The long, shapely legs, the delicate ankles, the gentle arch of her feet. He ran his fingers over each part, familiarising himself with the curves, the delicate bones, taking note of which touch made her shiver, anticipating the moment when those legs would be wrapped around him, the muscles flexed, holding him close. Yet he was content to wait, postpone the ecstasy.

He moved onto the bed beside her. Spreading her legs to allow him to kneel between them, he pulled Clarrie slightly upright to remove her chemise, to free the rest of that delectable body for his ministrations. Lifting her arms above her head, he pulled the last piece of fabric between them free, taking in the high, full breasts, thrust upwards by her raised arms, the dark nipples proud evidence of her desire. He licked each one slowly, lazily, then sucked on them, running his tongue across the valley of her breasts to alternate between them, pinching one between his fingers as he tended the other with his mouth. When they were pebble hard, he allowed himself the brief pleasure of pulling her naked body close against his.

Clarrie moaned his name, her breathing rapid and shallow, her lids heavy on eyes dark with a passion reflecting his own. Mindlessly she wrapped her arms around his neck. Sinuously she rubbed herself against his skin, her nipples responding to the abrasion of the dark crisp curls of hair on his chest, warm, hot, wet, with desire as she felt the hard silkiness of his erection against the soft skin of her belly. Their kiss was swift and hard, their skin hot, heating, the need for fulfilment becoming almost unbearable.

Clarrie reached round to pull Kit more fully against her, grasping his firm muscled buttocks, pushing against him, into him, revelling in the contrast of all this male hardness against all her feminine softness. But she wanted more. She wanted—she wanted—oh!

She was on her back, splayed out before him, thrust away from him, but before she could object his mouth was there, right at the very centre of her desire, and she lost all ability to think. His tongue circled, lapped, licked. His fingers dipped, stroked, flicked, plunged slowly, tortuously slowly, making her pant, lifting her ever higher to a place she had never been, didn't know existed. She felt swollen with desire, soaked with desire, bursting with desire, and still Kit's tongue and fingers drove her on, questing, taking her to dizzying heights higher, higher until at last, with one long, slow, pulsing caress, she plunged down, down, swirling headlong, rushing towards the depths, then soaring high through a stunning climax that jerked her up from the bed.

He could contain himself no longer. Raising himself over Clarrie's hot, wet, body, Kit thrust into her depths with one hard stroke, feeling her heat clenching around him. And meeting an unexpected resistance.

My God, she hadn't lied. He couldn't believe it. Looking down into her face, the question on his lips, he felt her move beneath him, her head shaking from side to side in denial.

'No, no, don't stop. Please.' She reached up her arms to pull his head down, fastened her mouth on his, and thrust upwards underneath him, urging him on. Suddenly the resistance was gone.

He had no option but to respond. Shifting to take his weight on his elbows, Kit moved gently inside her, slowly, praying that he could withstand the ripples of pleasure which each tiny movement gave him.

'Kit, Kit,' Clarrie whispered his name, a whisper of pleasure, not pain. 'Please.'

He needed no more urging, and as she wrapped her legs around him, the movement opening her up inside, all worries about hurting her, all conscience at taking her virginity, were quelled, lost, forgotten, in the urge only to thrust harder, deeper, longer, responding to the moans of encouragement, feeling her muscles tighten against him, feeling the responding ripples of her own climax as he finally reached his own, pouring himself, hot, endlessly, possessively, deep into her molten core.

Chapter Nine

They lay enfolded in each other's arms without speaking, basking in the warm, rosy afterglow of their tumultuous love-making. With nothing to compare it to, Clarrie knew only that it had been everything she had ever dreamed, all she had ever desired it might be, and more. She had not thought she was capable of giving way to such an intensity of emotion, had no idea she could abandon all restraint without a trace of modesty, had not believed that instinct could lead her so surely down the path to fulfilment. As her body slowed to a steady thrum of satisfaction she smiled, completely content in this moment, certain only that she didn't want to move, that she wanted to feel the heavy, rough, solid weight of Kit holding her safe, possessively like this for ever.

For some time Kit was also beyond thought, caught up in the wholly new experience, for him, of feeling such profound passion, unable to believe the intensity of what had just passed between them. His sated body curled possessively round the fragile, wanton, deliciously beautiful woman beneath him, giving in to the instinct to protect, hold on, prolong the perfect intimacy of the moment.

Clarrie sighed and opened her eyes to look into the face of her beloved. So strong and starkly handsome. So passionate and giving. How had she come to feel so much for this wonderful, complex enigma of a man, in just a few short days? She had no idea, and no intention of questioning anything for the remainder of the night. She had only this one time and she intended to savour it.

When Kit kissed her tenderly, his mouth framing the question uppermost in his mind, Clarrie reached out to sooth his brow, whispering, 'Shh, this is no time for words' in his ear. Turning to him in a deliberate echo of his own confident and dominant possession of her body, she pushed him back on to the sheets and began a slow, sensuous exploration of her own with her tongue. She might not have the experience of his other mistresses, but she knew enough by now to be certain that the same things which gave her pleasure would pleasure Kit, so she set out to prove it. And she was right. He was lying back, his eyes clenched shut, the question forgotten, and she could see quite clearly that he was enjoying what she was doing—very much. So she carried on, down, and further down, until she knew he could think of nothing, nothing in the world, save her ministrations.

Kit awoke to bright sunlight streaming through the gap in the heavy curtains, and blinked. Rubbing a hand over his forehead, shaking his hair from his eyes, he stretched luxuriously, wondering idly why the slight ache in his muscles felt so good. Opening his eyes properly, he realised he wasn't in his own bedchamber, but the adjoining one. Then it all came flooding back to him, a vivid montage of tangled limbs and blissful love-making.

'Clarrie?' There was no response. The other side of the bed felt cold, though there was an indent on the pillow where her head had been. The bruise on his shoulder where she had bitten him showed her tiny teeth marks. His lips felt rough, tender, and the bed was in complete disarray. She was no figment of his imagination. That night of passion—exquisite, never-before-experienced passion—was no dream. So where was she?

Kit sat up, examining the room properly. His clothes had been picked up and folded neatly on a chair, but of Clarissa's attire there was no sign. Perhaps she had gone for a walk? Kit got out of bed and donned his dressing gown, striding through the connecting door to ring the bell and summon his valet. He was being foolish, he knew he was, but he couldn't help the feeling of panic rising inside him.

The blank look on Fanshaw's face only added to his concern. 'The young lady, my lord? But she left for London early this morning.'

'Are you sure? I gave very specific orders to the stables yesterday. My coach was to be ready at noon. I can't believe they would leave without checking any change of plan with me first.'

'Oh, she didn't go in your coach my lord, naturally,' the valet said reassuringly. 'No, no. No need to worry about that.'

'Damn the coach, man. I am not worried about my coach. In case it had escaped your notice, I am more concerned for the lady. If she didn't go in the coach, how does she intend to get to London. Walk?' Actually, Kit realised ruefully, he wouldn't put that past her.

Fanshaw, with all the consummate professionalism of his calling, remained impassive, one eyebrow raised quizzically skyward the only sign that he was somewhat taken aback by his master's agitated behaviour. He had been Kit's valet for a number of years, and had never seen him anything other than pleased to be rid of whatever female was currently gracing his bed. Come to think of it, mind you, he could not recall Lord Rasenby ever having allowed a female to stay in his bed overnight before. Preferred to stable them in their own quarters.

Kit was pacing the room anxiously, trying to work out what Clarissa had done. 'Did anyone see her leave?'

'I shall make enquiries of the staff immediately, my lord. It was very early, but perhaps one of the maids knows something. Will you require your shaving water now?'

'Just go and find out where she is, will you? No, wait. I need to get dressed, so bring the water. But make enquiries first.'

Fanshaw left, returning a short time later with a steaming jug of water and a letter on a silver salver. 'It seems the young lady left a short time after seven, my lord. She asked for the nearest inn, and young Jem, the stable hand, took it upon himself to drop her off at the Green Man, since he was on his way out to fetch some sacks of horse feed. I believe the mail coach passes through at about nine; no doubt she obtained a seat on that. Although Jem, of course, did not wait to wave her off.' Fanshaw permitted himself a small smile at this witticism, but, seeing Kit to be in no mood for joking, quickly suppressed it. 'She left this for you, my lord.' He proffered the salver.

'For God's sake, could you not have said that in the first place? Go away, I will shave myself, and I'll call if I need you.'

Dismissed, Fanshaw left the room with slow, dignified

grace. Kit, ripping the wafer from the letter, was already
intent on the contents and did not look up.

Dear Kit, it started prosaically enough, *I have decided
to return to London immediately. Having fulfilled my
part of our bargain, our adventure is concluded, and
we must never see each other again.* Exactly as he had
specified it should be. Kit sat down abruptly, a feeling
of emptiness sweeping over him. Last night had changed
everything for him. For Clarissa to leave without any
forwarding address, with no goodbye even, giving him
no chance to suggest—whatever it was he was thinking
of suggesting—beggared belief. *Bereft*: that is what he
felt. And very, very lonely.

Kit returned to the letter. It was brief enough and to
the purpose, giving him no clue as to her feelings. She
thanked him for her adventure and assured him of her
discretion. *I will not seek you out, for there can be no
relationship of any nature between us in the future.* Even
had he wanted her as his mistress, the message was quite
unmistakable. She would not accept. The plea beseeching him to refrain from renewing his pursuit of Amelia
was, after the events of last night, rather unnecessary,
but it was the final words that really hurt. *I want you to
know that you took nothing from me that I did not want
to give, and give freely. We had a bargain and I agreed
to the terms. You have nothing to feel guilty about, nor
to blame yourself for.* The words pierced his conscience
more deeply than any recriminations could have done.
You have nothing to feel guilty about! God Almighty,
what had he done?

The reality of the situation was as clear as the bright
light of day streaming through the window. Clarissa
was a virgin—or she had been until last night. She had
told him she was untouched, had in fact told him so

repeatedly from the first, but he had ignored her, refusing to believe what did not suit his purposes. He had not stopped when he realised the truth. And even afterwards, lying sated on top of her, he had not tried—not very hard, anyway—to apologise, even to find out if he had hurt her.

Worse. There had been little respite from their ardour the whole night long. Carried away with lust, he had given no thought, after her gentle *don't*, to calling a halt or soothing her hurt.

Kit clutched his head in his hands, clenching his eyes shut in an effort to rid himself of the visions his mocking conscience was running through his mind. He groaned in despair. What kind of man was he? He had seduced an innocent girl, and now she was gone from him, ruined but refusing even to blame him, dismissing him from her life and taking all the responsibility for the consequences on her own slim shoulders.

Thinking of those possible consequences, Kit groaned again. Who would she turn to if, in addition to taking her virtue, he had left her with child? He had been careless, had given the matter no thought last night. So unlike him, but then in all his dealings with Clarissa he was unlike himself.

A child. Kit tried to picture what the product of their union would look like. A girl, he decided, with her mother's eyes and his own colouring. What a temper she would have. How much he would love her. She would wrap him around her little finger.

Enough, damn it! Reminding himself that he had no desire for children, legitimate or natural, Kit dismissed the vision of his imaginary daughter, ruthlessly brushing aside the pang it caused him, and returned to the problem in hand.

What in the devil's name was he going to do? Go after her? And offer her what exactly? he asked his reflection as he shaved. A *carte blanche*? Money, recompense? She was likely to throw it back in his face, and who could blame her. Tying his cravat in a simple knot, paying it so little attention that Fanshaw would have tutted disapprovingly had he witnessed it, Kit decided he must return to London and seek Clarissa out. He ignored the tight feeling around his heart as he considered the possibility that she meant what she said, and would never see him again. He would find her, if only to ensure she knew she could rely on him if ever she was in need.

A breakfast of ham and eggs washed down with a tankard of ale brewed from his own hops did nothing to lighten Kit's mood nor break his thoughts of last night. Their love-making had been beyond anything in his previous—plentiful—experience. Clarissa matched him step by step in everything, her own desires seeming as strong as his. She had come to him readily enough in the end. It had been no ravishment, he had not taken her against her will, had not forced himself on her. The passion between them was real. No, he could not doubt her consent.

But he could not deny to himself that he had ensured Clarissa had no option but to consent. That was the nub of it. Kit's conscience, which had lain dormant for the vast part of his thirty-five years, was making up for lost time now. He might not have seduced her, but he had made sure she couldn't say no.

As soon as the coach was ready Kit set out impatiently on the journey to London, aware of a growing need just to see Clarissa. He missed her in truth, even after such a few short hours' absence. They had spent almost three days constantly in each other's company, and he had come to depend on her being there—if not indefinitely, then at least for some time to come. To be without her made him feel as if some part of him he'd never known he'd had was missing.

You took nothing from me that I did not want to give, and give freely. The words ran in circles round his head, but he was no nearer to a course of action than when he had first read them. Clarissa could not have made him feel more guilty had she accused him to his face.

This thought gave Kit pause. Could the letter be a very clever ruse? Not a salve to his conscience, but a deliberate twist of the knife to ensure that he came after her? True enough, she had come to him a virgin, but did innocence of all other crimes follow automatically? Had she given him the prize of her virtue hoping for recompense in the form of marriage? Had he been duped after all?

Kit stopped at an inn *en route* to London for a change of horses. It took but a moment to swallow a cup of hot, strong coffee before he re-entered his chaise, anxious to be on his way. When he arrived later that afternoon at his house in Grosvenor Square, he was no closer to finding any answers to the questions dogging his thoughts.

Clarissa's journey had been slow and tedious. She reached London not much in advance of Kit. She had not had sufficient money to purchase a seat on the mail coach at the Green Man, and had been forced instead to buy a ticket on the stage. For much of the journey she was squashed between a large fat woman on a visit to her sister who, she informed Clarissa proudly, was expecting her eighth child, and a prim, elderly vicar, who clutched his bible as if afraid it would be wrested from him, and who smelled unmistakably of strong spirits. Emerging shaken and nauseous, she thought how apt was the term *rattler* for such public conveyances, realising in retrospect just how well sprung had been Kit's own equipage in contrast.

Completing the journey in a hired cab exhausted her meagre funds. As the hack turned into the familiar street and she caught the first welcoming glimpse of home, Clarissa emitted a long, low sigh of relief. The last three days had been tumultuous ones, by turn thrilling and terrifying. She felt as if her whole world had been shaken to its foundations and turned on its axis. She had a splitting headache and craved only the restful sanctuary of her own bedroom, to safely return to the welcome predictability of her life where no more dramas lay in wait for her.

Clarissa stripped off her gloves and was about to mount the stairs to her chamber when Lady Maria's trembling voice called to her from the small parlour. 'Clarissa? Is that you back at last? Oh, thank the Lord.'

Turning, Clarissa noted with surprise that her mother was actually standing in the doorway, her lace cap askew, obviously just arisen from her couch in order to greet her. 'Mama, dearest. Did you miss me so much?' Stooping to press a light kiss on her mother's soft cheek, Clarissa noticed traces of tears. 'Mama, what's wrong? What has upset you? Come into the parlour and tell me what's amiss.'

'Oh, Clarrie! I have been so stupid. And I am so sorry, but I simply did not know what to do, and you were not here to advise me.' A sob stopped Lady Maria from further speech, and her tears flowed afresh. Clarissa sighed wearily, placed an arm around her mother's shoulder and guided her towards the sofa. All thoughts of her own problems were effectively driven from her head.

It took a little effort to stop the flow of Lady Maria's tears, and even more patience still to extract the cause of them from the garbled, inarticulate story recounted to her, accompanied as it was by sobs, apologies for being so silly, and countless accusations of villainy against some unknown figure who preyed on poor widow women. 'Oh, Clarissa, I knew you would have advised me against it. I am sorry for being so foolish, but you were not here—what was I to do? With Amelia clamouring for a new dress, and that money-grabbing *modiste* Madame Clothilde refusing to provide it until we paid at least part of her last bill, I was at my wits' end. I even tried to reach you at Constance's, but your aunt refused to tell me where you were.'

'You spoke to Aunt Constance?' That Mama would do such a thing had not occurred to Clarissa when she had written the note from the inn to explain her absence. She had said that her aunt had need of her and explained no further, sure that Mama would not enquire.

'Yes, I did, for you left me no choice. I needed to talk to you, and your note said you were staying with her. But Constance just said you were engaged on some errand and could not be disturbed and could she help instead. As if I would let myself be beholden to *her*. Nor would she understand—what knows that woman of the trials of being poor? So you see I had no one to turn to, and, oh, Clarissa, I wish you had not needed to be away at such an inopportune time for me.'

Overcome by sobs once more, Lady Maria searched fruitlessly for her handkerchief amongst the plethora of shawls and wraps that lay strewn over the sofa on which they were seated. Clarissa wondered fleetingly why her aunt had not given her away. No doubt she had not wanted to alarm Mama, but she would demand answers from Clarissa, and she was not a woman who could be lied to. Dreadful as this prospect was, however, Mama's needs were rather more pressing.

Pouring a few drops of sal volatile into a glass, Clarissa helped Lady Maria to sit back and waited on the calming effect of the medication to take effect. 'There, dearest, that's better. Now tell me what happened after you spoke to Aunt Constance?'

'Well, I know I promised you I wouldn't borrow any more money, but I felt so bad leaving my problems to you, and then Mrs Barrington—you know, Chloe's mama—said that she would fix it for me to borrow just a little more from the same nice man as before—the one who was dunning me. And I thought, you see, that my luck at the tables was simply bound to turn on account of it's been so very bad until now. So I borrowed just enough for one more night at the tables, and I planned to use my winnings to pay it straight back and pay Madame Clothilde too, and then be able to buy Amelia her dress. It would have worked, I know it would have worked, if only I had not played faro, which is not my game as you know. Mrs Barrington said it would be a quicker way to win a bigger sum. But, oh, she was very wrong. And if I had but ignored her and stuck to my usual game of ombre we would not be in this situation. But I did, and there we have it. And really, it is all your fault for not being here to stop me, Clarrie dear. Now we are in such a fix, for soon this gentleman—though really he cannot be a gentleman to be treating me like this—will be dunning me for payment and if I cannot pay I cannot imagine what we will do and it is such a mess. But you will fix it, won't you, Clarrie?'

Clarissa's head whirled at the attempt to sort out the salient points from this tangled tale. 'Let me understand this, Mama. You borrowed more money from the man who was already dunning you after I told you, and you promised, not to?'

'Yes, but it was all perfectly above board, for I signed a document when he gave me the money. Then this morning I received a letter from a different gentleman saying he had acquired my debt from the first gentleman and I do not understand it all, for I have no head for business.'

'Mama, may I see the letter? And the one you signed?'

'Oh, Clarrie, dearest Clarrie, do you think you'll be able to make things right?' Lady Maria said, clasping her hands.

'I have no idea until I have sight of the letters. Does Amelia know about any of this?'

'No, no, how could I burden the poor child with my worries when she is so taken up with her own plans.'

That her mama had no qualms about burdening Clarissa with her worries did not surprise her elder daughter. With a worried frown, she read through the two documents Mama had retrieved from the desk. The first, the original loan, to be paid back at a rate of interest that made her brows rise in consternation, was signed by a Mr Dalton. This must be Mrs Barrington's friend—a loan shark, no doubt. No doubt either that Mrs Barrington had been paid a healthy retainer for putting the business his way. Clarissa would have words with Mrs Barrington later. She looked forward to that.

The second letter was from a lawyer acting on behalf of an unnamed client. The paper was heavy and expensive, the letter brief and to the point. The unnamed client had acquired Lady Maria's debt by unspecified methods. The letter informed Clarissa's mama that she had a new creditor and confirmed that for the present the agreed interest rate would stand, but the schedule of repayment had been reduced, so that the full amount became due not within six, but three months. Should this be unacceptable to Lady Maria, the writer would be pleased to put any alternative proposal to his client, but felt it prudent to advise her that an extension of the loan period was unlikely to be granted.

A cold fear clutched at Clarissa as she re-read the epistle. Whoever the creditor turned out to be, Lady Maria could expect no sympathy from him. The plain fact was that they were now in debt to the tune of thousands of guineas to a complete stranger who was likely to be ruthless in extracting payment. They had no security. They had nothing left to sell, no means of raising the capital, never mind the outrageous amount of interest that was growing almost by the hour. Mama would be clapped in irons and taken to the Fleet prison. It did not bear thinking of. Reminding herself that panic never did anyone any good, Clarissa folded the letters carefully and tucked them into her reticule.

'Well, dearest? Can it be fixed?' Lady Maria's voice was tremulous, her words pleading.

'I need to think about it, Mama. For now, the best thing you can do is to put it from your mind and try for some rest. You look exhausted.'

'Oh, Clarrie, it's so good to have you back. You will make all well now, I know you will. I missed you, child. Tell me you won't go off to live with Constance when I have sore need of you here.'

'I won't go and stay with Aunt Constance, Mama, you may put that thought out of your mind. Now, why don't you try to rest for a while? Here, let me tuck this shawl around you. There, that's better, is it not? Best to say nothing to Amelia about all of this, we don't want her worried.'

'Oh, no, no, Clarrie, I won't say a thing. Except—what about her new dress?'

'I'm afraid that will have to wait,' Clarissa said drily. 'It is hardly a priority in the grand scheme of things.'

'Oh, but it might prove to be so, Clarrie. Only think, if she gets a new dress and Lord Rasenby sees her in it, he will like as not be so taken with her that he will propose, and then all of our troubles will be at an end. You would not want to spoil that for the want of a new dress now, would you dear?'

'Mama, I beg of you, you must put all thoughts of Amelia marrying Lord Rasenby out of your head. It is simply not going to happen.'

'But, Clarrie, Amelia assures me he is on the very brink of asking. She has seen him the last two nights at balls, and he has been most pressing.'

'She saw Lord Rasenby last night?'

'Yes, and the night before. He was most attentive, apparently, and would not leave her alone. Begged three whole dances and would not take her nay. So you see Clarissa, she simply *must* have a new dress.'

The only thing Clarissa saw clearly was that Amelia had been lying to their mama. Well, she would not get off so lightly when Clarissa spoke to her, that was for sure. 'Leave Amelia to me, Mama, think no more of it. But you must promise me one thing.'

'Anything, dearest, for you always know best, and I feel so much happier now. When you came in I was quite sunk in despair, what with the letter, and Amelia's dress, and the cook demanding to know what was for dinner. I am very glad you are home; we don't get by nearly so well without you.'

'Well, Mama, and I am glad to be home too. But you must give me your solemn promise that you will not play cards with Mrs Barrington or any of her cronies again. And you must on no account, under any circumstances, borrow any more money.'

'No, dearest, I won't, I promise.' Thus unburdened of all her cares, oblivious to the turmoil she had stirred up in her daughter's mind, Lady Maria composed herself for sleep.

Rest was not a luxury Clarissa could afford, much as she was in need of it. Thrusting thoughts of her mother's debts to one side for the time being, she went in search of her sister. She did not have to look far. Amelia was waiting in her bedchamber, a vision in pale green printed calico.

'I was sure I heard you come in. Mama has been in a tizzy about something, I've barely been able to get a word of sense out of her. I thought I should have to give her a James's powder to calm her, she was so upset, and you know I can't be doing with quacking her. I trust you've calmed her down?'

Amelia's breathtakingly selfish attitude made Clarissa grit her teeth in order to keep a clamp on her temper. She needed to find out what her sister had been up to. Upsetting her would only make her defensive, much as she yearned to give Amelia a sound slap about the cheeks. 'Mama is sleeping now,' she said merely, sitting down at her dressing table to remove the pins from her hair. Her head was thumping.

'You look tired, Clarrie. Did Aunt Constance have you run ragged? When Mama tried to get her to send you back, she was quite rude. She told Mama that it was time she stood on her own two feet and stopped relying on you to resolve every petty domestic crisis. Mama was really quite upset.'

'She's not such an ogre, you know, our aunt. She just

has different ideas from Mama, but we shouldn't forget that she is the only one of Papa's family who stands by us.'

'Much good it does us. It's all very well for you, she likes you, and you can talk for hours to her about boring politics and books and things. It's different for me. I'm too pretty, for one thing, and she's always so nit-picky, I really can't abide it. You should do this, Amelia, or think about that, Amelia, or consider this, Amelia. What she really means is that I should be more like you. Well, I'm not like you.'

A sharp pang of guilt shot through Clarissa as she thought bitterly of her behaviour over the past three days. 'Maybe we are more alike than you realise,' she said ironically. 'Anyway, never mind Aunt Constance or Mama for the moment. Sit down and tell me about you. Have you seen much of Edward?'

'Too much! He has become almost as tedious as Aunt Constance, prosing on and on about what I may do, and what I may not do. I'm fed up with Edward.' With a flounce Amelia sat down on Clarissa's bed, her rosebud mouth in a pout, and burst into sudden loud sobs. 'Oh, Clarrie, I'm so unhappy. You can have no idea.'

Clarissa eyed her in astonishment. 'Calm down, Amelia, try not to talk until you are more composed. Let me get you a glass of water.' Much to her relief, Amelia's sobs quieted. She sat up, the threatened tantrum averted. 'Now, tell me what's bothering you. You'll feel better when you've got it out in the open.'

'It's Edward. He's—he's—he wants to marry me.'

Clarissa struggled to contain the mixture of relief and euphoria that swept over her at this much-hoped-for development. 'Well now, that's surely something to be very happy about.'

'No, it's not, Clarissa, for he has no money and no prospects, only his stupid job, and I won't marry him and live without money, I *can't*. He says that if we are happy it shouldn't matter. He says that I don't need new gowns and balls and parties and—and such, if I have him. He says that if we have each other, I won't notice our modest means. But Clarrie, he's *wrong*. I *need* money, but I don't want to lose Edward, so I need to find a way to have both. But every time I suggest what seems to me a perfectly simple solution, he threatens to leave me and never see me again.'

With a sinking heart, Clarissa posed the question. 'And what is your simple solution, Amelia, that Edward is so set against?'

'Well, it's obvious. I'll accept Lord Rasenby's *carte blanche*, then he'll be obliged to buy me lots of dresses and jewellery and a carriage and maybe even set me up in my own establishment. I'll save every penny of the allowance he gives me, and then I can marry Edward.'

Even for Amelia, this was breathtaking. Clarissa could find nothing to say, and sat staring at her sister in open-mouthed amazement.

'Why are you looking like that? You look like Edward did. I thought you'd be pleased.'

'Pleased?'

'Yes, for I have quite given up my plan to trap Lord Rasenby into marriage, you know.'

The smug satisfaction in Amelia's voice was too much. Clarissa was tired and heartsore. Instead of the sanctuary of her own room, she had been greeted with her mother's gambling debts and impending imprisonment. And now her sister was gaily recounting a plan to become the mistress of one man in order that she might marry another.

That the man she intended to extract payment from was the man Clarissa was in love with was the final straw.

'You thought I'd be pleased to hear that you're proposing to sell yourself to Lord Rasenby in order to fund marriage to Edward?'

'Well, I thought at least you'd be pleased that I'd given up my idea of tricking Kit Rasenby to the altar. And pleased to find that you're right—I do love Edward after all. And I want to marry him.'

'But you're still willing to let another man take you to bed?'

'Well, but it might not come to that.' Amelia's pout was back, her posture defensive.

'You expect to persuade Lord Rasenby to take you as his mistress, to fork out a fantastic sum on kitting you out in style, setting you up in a house, and not expect anything in return?'

'Well, I thought I could string him along for a while without having to—you know, without actually letting it come to that. There are ways, Clarissa, of keeping a man in suspense, without—'

'Do tell me, Amelia, what are these ways, exactly?'

Taken aback at the martial light in her sister's eyes, and unused to having her bluff called quite so directly, Amelia faltered. 'Well, I don't know exactly, but I'm sure I could—at least I… You know, I don't think we should be discussing this, Clarissa, Mama would be shocked.'

'And you think it would shock her less if you told her what you intended? Don't be ridiculous. You clearly haven't thought this through, you've just got carried away with wanting to have your own way as usual. And so long as you get your own way, you don't care who pays for it, whether it's Edward, or Kit Rasenby, or Mama or me! You're a selfish, stupid, inconsiderate little girl, and you don't deserve Edward. In fact, if I were him I'd wash my hands of you. All I can think is that he must be so madly in love with you as to be beyond reason himself, for you are nothing more than a—a—trollop! Kit certainly deserves to be protected from the likes of you.'

Amelia watched her normally placid sister's outburst in astonishment. Clarrie didn't seem at all concerned about poor Amelia. Didn't seem to want to help her, hadn't even put her first, as she always usually did. Had seemed more worried about Edward, in fact, not to mention Lord Rasenby. And—but that was it! 'Why are you suddenly so concerned with protecting Kit Rasenby?'

'I don't know what you mean,' Clarissa replied defensively. 'I don't want anyone hurt by your stupid behaviour. I'm just as worried about poor Edward.'

'No, you're not. And now I come to think of it, I haven't seen Kit Rasenby for a few days. No one knows where he's been.'

'Yes, but that's not what you told Mama, is it? You told her you'd been dancing with Kit—Lord Rasenby—at two different parties.'

Amelia waved her hand dismissively. 'Well, what did you expect, I had to find an excuse for seeing Edward, and I didn't want Mama to worry. And anyway, that's not important right now. What I want to know is where was Lord Rasenby—or Kit, as you now seem to be calling him—over the last few days? The same few days, dearest sister, when you were also absent? I think there's something you're not telling me, isn't there?'

Clarissa could not think of a reply, and only shook her head in silent rebuttal.

'Goodness, I'm right, aren't I?' Amelia said gleefully.

'There *is* something you're not telling me. Look at you, you're all red. You can't lie to me, Clarissa, what's going on?'

'Nothing! Nothing's *going on*, as you put it. I'm tired. I need to be on my own. Let's leave this discussion until later.'

'No, you don't, Clarissa Warrington. I know you, you're going to lie in here on your own and make up some clever story to tell me later. I'm not going to leave you on your own. Whatever was going on between Kit Rasenby and you, I'm going to find out right now, so you might as well tell me and get it over with.'

Amelia's eyes sparkled at the confusion on Clarissa's face. She had never seen her normally unflappable sister so distressed. Leaping from the bed, all trace of her own upset vanished, she pulled Clarissa towards a chair and pushed her into it. 'Talk, Clarrie. I won't leave until you do.'

'I—Amelia, if I do, you must promise not to say a word to anyone?'

'Yes, yes, just go on.'

'Very well. But no matter what you think of my behaviour, you must believe me, I meant it only for the best.'

'Clarrie, will you just tell me what on earth you've been up to?'

Thus was Clarissa persuaded to provide an openmouthed and increasingly incredulous Amelia with a highly censored version of the events of the last three days.

Chapter Ten

Once Amelia had fully recovered from the shock of discovering her sister capable of such wantonly reckless behaviour, she predictably took Clarissa's interventions on her behalf sorely amiss. 'You spiteful cat, you couldn't bear to see me happy, could you? You've gone and spoiled everything, ruined my only chance of ever being rich. How could you? What am I to do now?'

'But, Amelia don't you see, I did it for you, I saved you.'

'*Saved me!* Saved me for what, pray tell? For a life with Edward in a horrible little cottage with a dozen brats running round my feet? I'd rather go on the streets!'

'*Amelia!* How can you talk so? You don't know what you're saying.' Taking a deep breath, almost relieved to have the confession over with, Clarissa tried to turn her full attention on her sister. 'My actions have come as a shock to you, I can understand that. But when you've had time to reflect, you'll see it's for the best. You love Edward, for goodness' sake, and now there is no real obstacle in the way of your marriage.'

Unfortunately for her peace of mind, this phrase served only to remind Clarissa of the many and insurmountable obstacles she herself had placed in the path of her own, never-to-happen marriage. It took an effort to focus on the problem in hand. 'You cannot seriously think that wealth is so important, Amelia? It's not as if Edward will have no money at all—in fact, you'll probably find that as a married lady you'll have at least as much to spend as you do at present.'

'But I don't have *anything* to spend at present. I'm sick of eating the poorest cuts of meat. I'm tired of having to make do with only three or four pairs of evening gloves, and living in terror of getting stains on them. I'm fed up having to beg and plead for every new dress I need. And if I have to fashion one more hat from the trimmings of an old one, I'll scream.'

Clarissa smiled in what she hoped was a winning and reassuring manner. 'But when you're married, you won't need so many clothes, for you won't be going to so many parties and the like, will you?'

'Oh, Clarrie, don't you understand? That's exactly the point! If I marry Edward, we'll be cooped up together in our hovel because we won't be able to afford to go out. I do love him, but I'm neither stupid nor entirely blind to my own character. How long do you think I could endure such a life? How long before I get bored and start to blame poor Edward for it? How long before I start to look for entertainment elsewhere, no matter how dear he is to me?'

Taken aback by Amelia's unexpected insight, Clarissa could only shake her head sadly.

'And as for Edward,' her sister continued despairingly, 'well, it wouldn't exactly be a bed of roses for him either. I'd be sure to make his life a misery with my constant nagging about our lack of money. He'd soon get tired of coming home to ruined dinners and a disgruntled wife. I have no idea about cooking, I've never placed an order at a butcher or a grocer, I don't even know which coals to burn or anything at all about running a house. Don't you see, Clarissa, it would be a disaster?'

Clarissa did see, but she wasn't about to give up so easily. 'Surely Edward has some prospects?'

'He works hard and he seems to be well respected by his employer, but without backing he has little prospect of rapid advancement. Mr Fortescue said that there's a good opportunity coming up soon for a partnership, but without money to assist him, the post will go elsewhere.'

'Mr Fortescue?'

'He's a partner in Edward's firm, Fortescue and Browne. Their offices are in the city—Lombard Street, I think. They're a very prestigious law firm, Edward says, with any number of clients from the *ton*.'

Fortescue and Browne. That had been the heading on the letter Mama received this morning, now safely tucked away in Clarissa's reticule. And Edward worked for them. An idea began to form in Clarissa's mind. Perhaps Edward could be persuaded to find out the name of the man who held Mama's debt? It wouldn't be ideal, having to involve a stranger—well, almost a stranger—in their affairs. Edward might prove reluctant to compromise his position too, but since he clearly loved and intended to marry Amelia, surely these were not insurmountable obstacles. What she would do when she had the information she had no idea, but at least it was a step forward.

'Amelia, do you think you could give Edward a note from me when you see him next?'

Amelia looked suspiciously at her elder sister. After

her recent revelations, who knew what subterfuge she was capable of? 'Why? A note about what?'

'I need some advice about a trifling legal matter on Mama's behalf, and he may be able to help, that's all. Nothing for you to be worried about, I promise. Well, will you do it for me?'

'I suppose so, I'm seeing him later this evening. Although we had such a disagreeable conversation last night, he may have already decided that he doesn't love me after all.' Amelia's lip trembled. 'Oh, Clarrie, I do love him. I must marry him, for I can't marry anyone else. And now you've spoiled it all. If you hadn't gone off with Lord Rasenby, I could have accepted his *carte blanche*, and maybe by as early as next month I could have been Mrs Edward Brompton. And now you've ruined any chance of that. Oh, I do hate you.'

'Don't be silly. I'm sure things may still work out for the best, if only you will have patience.'

'And pray, what difference will patience make?' Amelia demanded with a stamp of her foot. 'I need money! Kit Rasenby has plenty of it, and he's famed as a generous provider into the bargain. Now I'll be forced to accept an offer from someone else, who like as not won't be as rich or as generous. So I'll have to stay with them for longer, and then Edward might not wait for me. Oh, why did you have to meddle in my affairs?'

Once more Clarissa could think of nothing to say. In truth, from Amelia's point of view, she could see that she had ruined things. It was clear that her dream of Amelia and Edward disappearing into a future of unclouded marital bliss without the funds to provide Amelia with a decent life-style was just that, a ridiculous fantasy. Now she faced the prospect of a future with Mama in prison, Amelia on the streets, and herself a ruined relic teaching someone else's children their letters. Always assuming she hadn't already conceived a child of her own—then she really would be ruined. That thought she refused to give house room, having more than enough worries without it!

'You're very quiet all of a sudden, Clarrie. What are you thinking?' Amelia had regained control of her temper. Having mentally reviewed Clarissa's tale, she was beginning to sense some glaring gaps in her sister's story. As an accomplished liar herself, she prided herself on having a finely tuned nose for such things, and there were some aspects of the story that just didn't quite add up. 'Remind me again, Clarrie, just exactly how you left things with Kit Rasenby.'

'As I said, he told me he had no intention of getting married and that he had been aware of your plot to entrap him all along,' Clarissa replied. 'He also agreed not to offer you a *carte blanche* since you are in love with someone else.' It was close enough to the truth, and all Amelia needed to know.

'And how did you persuade him, in the end? You must have had to work exceeding hard at it, for you were away nigh on three days.'

'Yes, but I explained that to you. He was not happy at first with my interfering, and insisted that I accompany him to France. While we were on board the *Sea Wolf*, there was little time for discussion.'

'So you didn't really get a chance to persuade him until you returned and spent the night at Thornwood Manor?'

'Yes, that's right. Then when I talked to him properly over dinner, he finally saw sense.' Repeating the story only served to make it seem even more flimsy and unlikely. Clarissa tried to change the subject. 'There's

no point in going over it again. I'm tired. You're upset.
Come, let's leave matters until tomorrow.'

'No, let's discuss it now, sister dear, while it's still
fresh in your mind,' Amelia said remorselessly. 'You
admit you were alone with Kit Rasenby for three days?'

'Not alone, precisely. There were servants and the
émigrés and—'

'But you spent last night alone with him, did you not?
And then he gave in to your demands without asking for
any sort of recompense? Nothing at all, no payment of
any sort?'

Amelia's use of the term payment made Clarissa
flush deeply, a fact her sister spotted immediately. 'He
did want something in return, didn't he? And knowing
Kit Rasenby, I bet I know exactly what it was. I've said
before, you're really quite pretty, Clarissa, although you
pale beside me, of course. Did he kiss you?'

A blush and a shake of the head were not convincing
denials but they were all Clarissa could muster.

'He did kiss you. Well, well, Clarrie. Tell me, did you
find it to your liking?'

Again, a blush, deeper this time. 'Amelia, please, I—'

Amelia continued relentlessly. 'But what you were
asking was really quite a big favour. Giving me up when
he was really very taken with me was no small demand,
Clarrie, was it? So a kiss probably wouldn't have suf-
ficed. What else did you give in return for saving me,
my virtuous sister? It must have been more than a few
kisses?'

'Amelia, you must not ask. Suffice to say it was not—
it was not—well, it was not Kit's fault in the end, but
mine.'

'Not Kit's fault in the end? Lord, Clarissa, you make
no sense. Why would you—good God!' Realisation

dawned on Amelia just as Clarissa covered her face with her hands and burst into tears. For a few seconds, Amelia was too astonished at the sight of her sister crying to take in the full extent of her confession—but only for a few seconds.

'He bedded you! Clarissa Warrington, I can't believe it. Goodness, my holier-than-thou sister deflowered by the most notorious rake in town. Well, well, well!'

Speechless at the full import of what she had learned, Amelia sat down and stared at her sister in a completely new light. A thousand questions came to mind, but for the present she was simply fascinated by the fact that Clarissa had experience of something she hadn't. A malicious smile marring her beautiful face, Amelia pulled her chair closer. 'Come then, Clarrie, you must tell me all. Was it as nice as they say? Did he give you pleasure? Was he gentle? Did it hurt? Did *he* enjoy it?'

'Amelia, I have no intention of discussing this with you, so you can stop your questions right now. It's a private matter between Kit and myself.'

Head tilted to one side, Amelia looked closely at Clarissa's flushed face. She was deeply embarrassed at the revelations, of that there was no doubt. But there was something else. She was different in some way. Despite being so tired, she looked prettier than before. And sort of—glowing. Realising that nothing was to be gained by threats, Amelia tried a different tack. 'Clarrie, even if you won't talk about it, won't you at least tell me—since I'm going to get married soon—did you enjoy the act?'

'Oh yes. It was wonderful.' The blush, and the look of sublime fulfillment, took Amelia aback. The final flaw in the story became clear. 'You're in love with him, aren't you? It's the only explanation. Poor Clarrie, to fall for a rake. It's true, isn't it?'

Clarissa's silence was answer enough.

'I knew it! In fact, now I come to think of it, you've probably been in love with him from the start. You just used me as an excuse, you wanted him for yourself all along. Well, am I right?'

'No, no,' Clarissa said hurriedly. 'I had no such intention, you must believe me. I wanted to save you. My only aim was to buy you some time so that you would realise the depth of your true feelings for Edward. I had no other thought.'

'Rubbish, I don't believe you. In any event, you are in love with him now, aren't you?'

'I—I—oh, what does it matter, for nothing can become of it, Amelia. He cares naught for me and I must live with that, and what I have done. But he won't be making you an offer now, and no matter what you feel at present, I'm still glad of that outcome, at least. We'll find a way for you to marry Edward, if only you will have some patience and a little faith. Kit Rasenby has no place in either of our lives. I don't want to talk about him, or this, or anything any more. I have the most awful headache. Please, Amelia, I need to be alone.'

Clarissa got abruptly to her feet, grabbed Amelia by the hand, and shunted her unceremoniously out of the room with a final reminder, on pain of death, not to breathe a word to anyone. Locking the door, she threw herself dejectedly on the bed and sobbed as though her heart was breaking. And indeed, indeed, it felt as if it was.

Dinner that evening in the Warrington residence was a very subdued affair, each of the three ladies being preoccupied with their own thoughts. Lady Maria fretted over her gambling debts. Clarissa was trying very hard—and failing—not to think about Kit. She dared not imagine how he had reacted to her sudden flight. She wondered where he was, what he was doing, who he was with. The stab of jealousy at the endless possibilities such speculation led to felt like a physical pain.

The truth, if she but knew it, was that across London Kit was enduring a similarly miserable dinner with his sister and her husband, absorbed in almost identical thoughts.

And Amelia? Had her sister been privy to the plots she was hatching as she chewed her way indifferently through her Hogg's pudding, she would have thrown up her hands in horror.

After dinner, Clarissa wrote a note to Edward, beseeching him, for Amelia's sake, to find out the name of her mama's creditor if he could do so without compromising himself. She sealed it and gave it to Amelia with strict instructions to pass it straight on without reading it herself. Needless to say, the strictures merely served to arouse her sister's already inflamed curiosity further. Amelia opened the letter as soon as she was out of the house.

When Clarissa finally retreated to the sanctuary of her bedchamber she could scarcely believe she had been home for less than a day. The rescue mission to France and the events at Thornwood House seemed like a lifetime ago, and yet only this very morning she had been lying in another bed encircled by Kit's strong arms, his warm muscular body pressed against her own receptive flesh. Clarissa tried desperately to conjure the sensations of that moment, the feel of Kit's skin, the scent of his body, but she was exhausted. Frustrated and lonely, she drifted into a troubled sleep.

* * *

The next morning, while Clarissa slept unusually late into the morning, her sister and mama sat together in Lady Maria's bedchamber, discussing Amelia's latest scheme to solve all their troubles. Having broken the seal of Clarissa's letter to Edward, Amelia had made sense enough of it to realise her mama was in dire need of an enormous sum of money. Since she was still determined to find the means of laying her hands on an equivalent sum for her own purposes, she had formulated a plan that would resolve both issues in one fell swoop.

Deciding that the need to enlist Mama's help in solving their monetary difficulties was of much more import than keeping Clarissa's confidences, Amelia had no hesitation in disclosing all. 'Mama, I'm afraid I must tell you something shocking.' Her version of Clarissa's story was brief and to the point.

Lady Maria was deeply shocked. 'Are you saying that your sister, my daughter—our Clarrie—was *compromised* by Lord Rasenby,' she uttered shakily.

Amelia impatiently handed her the vinaigrette she had had the foresight to bring along. 'Yes, Mama, but please don't go off into one of your swoons at the moment, for I need you to pay attention.'

Taking a sniff strong enough to make her recoil, Lady Maria blinked owlishly. 'No, no, Amelia, your sister was with Constance, her letter said so.'

'Mama! For the last time, I tell you she was not. She was with Rasenby. He abducted her and took her to France on his yacht. Then he took her back to his house. And he ravished her!'

It took burnt feathers and a tisane to revive Lady Maria from her swoon, and when she came to, Amelia had to repeat the entire story. 'So you see, Mama, he seduced her. And now she is in love with him. Do you not think that he should pay for such a dastardly crime?'

'Pay? What payment can there be to recompense my poor girl for the loss of her innocence?' demanded Lady Maria, frantically tugging at the strings of her cap, which had become entangled in the chicken-skin gloves she wore to keep her hands soft. 'The monster! There is nothing too bad for such a man. Nothing! If I were not a poor widow woman, with no one to defend me, he would not have taken such an advantage.'

'Yes, yes, Mama, indeed he is very wicked. But never mind all that, I have an excellent idea. Lord Rasenby shall pay, but not with his blood. He shall give us something much more useful. Money!'

'Well, to be sure dear, that would be much more useful, but why would he?'

'We shall threaten him, of course. And demand recompense for the loss of my sister's virtue. Then you can pay your gambling debts and I can marry Edward.'

'How do you know about my gambling debts? And who is Edward?'

'Edward. I *have* mentioned him to you, Mama. I'm in love with him.'

'In love with Edward,' Lady Maria exclaimed, momentarily distracted. 'But you barely know the man. Don't be foolish, Amelia, my head is spinning as it is.'

'Well, you might as well get used to it, for I'm marrying him, no matter what you say. Once I lay my hands on enough funds to do so, that is. Let us not discuss Edward just now, we have much more pressing matters to see to. We must write a letter to Lord Rasenby. And we must on no account tell Clarissa any of this, for she would be sure to try to stop us.'

'No, no, dear. Clarrie knows how important it is to

settle my debts, though I wish she had not told you about them—she said she would not.'

'No, Mama, she must know nothing, for she will put an end to it all, and then we won't get any money, and she will be ruined, and you will be in prison or the poor house, and I won't be able to marry Edward and—so you see, you must promise.'

'Well, when you put it that way…' Lady Maria remained doubtful, but she was a woman used to being told what to do, and was no match for Amelia in this determined mood.

The letter was duly written and dispatched within the hour. When Clarissa finally emerged from her room dressed for walking, Lady Maria and Amelia were huddled innocently together over a pattern book in the parlour. Calling a subdued good morning, Clarissa left the house for a brisk walk around the park. Her head was still aching.

Kit had also taken to the fresh air to clear his head. One minute he was missing Clarissa desperately and castigating himself with having taken her innocence. The next minute he was sure his suspicions had been right all along, and congratulating himself on having been rid of the baggage. The next again, he was trying to persuade himself that to take Clarissa as his mistress would be a compromise well worth attempting, even if it did mean humbling his pride a little. At least he would have her delectable body at his disposal long enough to sate this consuming passion, which was overthrowing the normal order of his mind.

On his return, the arrival of Lady Maria's letter put an end to the torture. Kit did not recognise the hand, and the name signed at the end was unfamiliar. Skimming through the note with difficulty, for Lady Maria's writing was spidery and had a tendency to slope dramatically at an angle on the page, Clarissa's name leapt out at him. Kit repaired to his favourite chair in the large, oak-panelled library and read through the epistle carefully. By the end of it his temper was as white hot as the flame in a blacksmith's forge—Clarissa's duplicity was the bellows which fanned it.

He had been right from the first. She was a scheming wretch. She had not lied when she reassured him she would not be getting in touch. Had not lied when she said she would not blame him for taking her innocence. *Oh, no, she had not lied.* Clarissa had done none of these things. She got her mother to do her dirty work instead!

My God, it was beyond the pale. Screwing the letter into a tiny ball, Kit hurled it into the grate. That it missed and lay intact on the hearth added fuel to his anger. How could he have been so duped? He had been so close to believing her. So racked with guilt for most of the last twenty-four hours. So afraid that Clarissa was hurt, upset, sobbing her heart out somewhere, alone and facing an uncertain future. And all the time, the plotting, scheming doxy was waiting to launch her attack on him. He was beginning to wonder if it was possible somehow that she had faked her innocence in the first place. For a woman who could lie so very convincingly, pretending virginity would be simple enough trickery. She was a witch, and she had come so close to bewitching him that he was overcome with rage at how gullible he had been.

Kit groaned. He prided himself on being up to snuff. He was so sure he knew every trick in the book. Yet here was a variation on the very oldest trick, and he had almost fallen for it, hook, line and sinker. Almost convinced himself that he cared. Almost decided to seek her out, to offer her his protection. Almost believed he had true feelings for her. My God, he had almost come to believe that they might have a future together, one based on—damn it, one based on genuine affection!

Almost, but not quite. And certainly not now. Revenge would be his. Nothing would prevent him from putting Clarissa at his mercy. He would see to it that her suffering was slow and drawn out, preferably something that would ensure that she and that entrancing, delightful body of hers were at his disposal night and day. Until he tired of her, that is. Until his desire for her was sated and his need for her exorcised.

It was a relief to Kit to be able to think ill of Clarissa, having spent the last twenty-four hours thinking so ill of himself. He was well and truly vindicated. She spoke the truth in that damned letter of hers. He had taken nothing she had not freely given! And no doubt had freely given to any number of others in the past, too. He did not relish the idea of Clarissa in any other arms than his own, however. She was a doxy, but she should be his doxy, and his alone!

Bitterly, Kit tried to repress the feelings that, despite all Clarissa's perfidy, were determinedly calling to his conscience in her favour. She had courage and integrity. She was witty and intelligent. Surely there was some mistake in all this? Alas, the facts combined with this dastardly letter did not lie. And yet he still wanted her.

There can be nothing without trust, nothing worth while based on deceit. Clarissa's own words mocked him. Her face, those expressive green eyes, that slumberous, quirky smile. The voluptuous curves of her body. She haunted him, filling his mind, leaving little room for aught else. There was no escaping the hurt and disappointment that were his overriding emotions as the full depths of her betrayal sank in.

Kit retrieved the letter from the hearth and unravelled it. Lady Maria demanded *suitable recompense* for the loss of her daughter's innocence. There was no indication of how much this sum would be, but he had no doubt that it would be enormous. After some garbled threats and recriminations over Kit's *cruel and callous treatment* of her *pure and innocent child*, Lady Maria's epistle launched, confusingly, into a catalogue of Clarissa's charms. Clarissa was *very fair*—Amelia had baulked at *beautiful*—her brain *above ordinary*, her wit *very clever*. She could manage a house efficiently, was well versed in *books and the like*, and was generally considered to be an asset that any gentleman would relish the opportunity to *have at his side*.

Kit wondered idly if Clarissa herself had been privy to compiling this list of accomplishments. He doubted it. He wished he could have watched her face if she had. How she would laugh. Her eyes would sparkle, that kissable little top lip of hers would quirk up at the corner, and that delicious gurgle of hers, like a brook in full flow, would escape, as she read her way down the eulogy. She would look up at him, a brow raised in question, and ask if he thought her merely *very fair*, knowing full well he thought her the most beautiful woman he had ever seen. Had he not told her so during their night of passion? Had he not shown her so as he worshipped her body? And she would smile, content.

Damn it! He had to stop this. Returning to the letter, the point of Lady Maria's eulogy became clear. Not only did she revile Kit and demand compensation for the taking of her child's innocence, she was offering to assist him in persuading that same innocent child to become his mistress. One thing Clarissa had not lied about—her mother was singularly lacking any trace of intelligence. Clarissa might be at the root of this plot, but of a certainty she had no part in this bird's nest of a letter.

He would not demean himself by writing back to the mother, Kit decided. His dealings would be with Clarissa, and Clarissa alone. He would be happy to cross swords with her again. She would very soon realise she had underestimated him as an adversary. She might have outwitted him, but retribution was nigh. He was looking forward to it.

Kit's reply on hot-pressed paper was brief and to the point. He was pleased to have received *your mother's charming blackmail letter sent on your behalf*, but he preferred, in matters of business, to deal with the *puppet master and not the puppet*. Unless Clarissa would correspond with him direct, all contact between them *of any nature* would be at an end. He congratulated her on her *effortless and skilled deceit*. Kit would not be threatened, nor would he negotiate. He would be happy to make her an offer of a nature *suitable and appropriate to her station*, and he anticipated to *compensate her more than adequately for her services*.

With grim humour Kit pictured Clarissa's response to these well-turned and carefully considered phrases. She would not misunderstand him. *He was hers, etc.*, the letter ended, and was signed with a flourish. A last-minute postscript assured her that he took issue with her mother's rather harsh description of her in her *bill of fare* and that he considered her not just *very fair* but *quite beautiful*. Satisfied, he sent a footman off to deliver the letter by hand.

It was too late in the day to expect a response. Kit

poured himself a brandy, trying to ignore the flat depression that threatened to overtake him at the thought of Clarissa's betrayal. Some male company, cards, and a good deal more brandy were what he needed right now. He set off for White's in St James's Street at a cracking pace, and passed the following hours losing such a satisfactorily enormous sum as would have met the demands of Lady Maria and Amelia more than sufficiently. He also became systematically and resolutely drunk.

Chapter Eleven

Kit awoke the following morning with a splitting headache as his valet drew back the heavy curtains with a
flourish. The weak morning sunlight struck the bed,
making Kit squint wearily at the unwelcome intrusion.
With difficulty he resisted the urge to burrow back under
the pillows.

'The young lady is waiting to see you, my lord.' Fanshaw spoke in hushed tones. 'She has been here some time,
but I was reluctant to disturb your rest since you returned
in such—er—obviously high spirits last evening.'

Kit tried to sit up, but groaned at the effect the sudden
movement had on his already delicate constitution. He
ran a hand through his tousled hair, looking puzzled.
'What young lady? What o'clock is it? This is no time
for morning callers—get rid of her, whoever she is, for
pity's sake.'

'It's the young lady from Thornwood Manor, my lord,
the one who left so precipitously the other day. I thought,
since you were so animated by her departure, that you
would wish to see her.'

'Clarissa is here?' Kit could not stop the quiver of anticipation at the thought of seeing her again. 'How long has she been waiting? What does she want? Never mind, never mind. Make sure she is looked after, and have Hodges inform her that I'll join her in fifteen minutes—no, better make that twenty. Come on man, what are you waiting for?'

'Twenty minutes, my lord? But you are not shaved. I have not laid out your dress. I require an hour at least to make you presentable. Please, my lord, I beg of you—'

'Fanshaw, shut up and do as you are told. And bring me a draught of porter before you bring my shaving water, I have sore need of a hair of the dog that so savagely bit me.'

Clarissa was pacing the floor of the small withdrawing room anxiously, becoming less and less confident as time went on. Kit's letter had come as a complete shock, and in those first numbing moments after reading and re-reading it in disbelief, she had thought it must be some sort of monstrous practical joke. Reality quickly set in, however, as she realised, with growing dismay, that there could only be one possible explanation for this extraordinary turn of events, and that the answer, unfortunately, lay very close to home. Her confrontation with Mama and Amelia had been far from pleasant.

Tears there had been aplenty. And drumming of heels—Amelia—and lamenting on the trials of life imprisonment—Mama. Remonstrations and threats alternated with an attempt to paint a picture of the bright and comfortable future that awaited all three of them, would Clarissa but comply with their plan and take Kit for a protector. Throughout, Clarissa remained intractable and implacable, determined to ensure that their interference ended once and for all. A threat to tell Edward the whole sorry tale put a stop to Amelia's resistance. And from there, it was not much to persuade Mama to keep quiet and reassure her that all would be well without Kit Rasenby's help.

Clarissa had then spent a torrid night haunted by what Kit must think of her, for her mama and sister had unwittingly ensured that she appeared every bit the scheming wench he had accused her of being. There was nothing she could write in return that he would believe. Nothing she could say in a letter to make amends for the one he had received from Mama. She must see him in the flesh and apologise, try to convince him that she had naught to do with the letter. But it would be the most difficult thing she had ever had to do, and she dreaded it.

She dressed for the task with care in a walking dress of palest blue wool and a three-quarter pelisse of dark blue merino. The hack deposited her at Grosvenor Square just before noon, but it was now nearly one and she had been waiting for almost an hour, having been informed, rather snootily, she thought, that his lordship was currently indisposed. Resisting all the butler's attempts to persuade her to return at another time more convenient to his lordship, eventually the determined tilt to Clarissa's chin and the mulish look in her green eyes had gained her the interview. Taking another turn around the room, unable to sit still, she wondered if he would keep her waiting for ever.

Finally, the door opened. In the time it took him to become presentable, the effects of last night's brandy had added to Kit's already-worn temper. He surveyed her coldly.

Clarissa's heart leapt at the sight of him, so tall, so handsome, so *exactly* right. But the frown was firmly in place, the dark brows almost meeting, the eyes almost black, unforgiving pools, glittering as brightly as his polished Hessian boots. His mouth was fixed in a firm line, not even a trace of the normal mocking smile.

'So much, then, Clarissa, for your promise never to see me again.' Kit closed the door behind him and walked slowly into the room, not once taking his eyes from her face.

As he approached she could see faint lines of tiredness, and had to put her hands firmly behind her back in order to prevent them from reaching up to sooth away the harsh frown on his brow. 'Good morning, my lord. I beg your pardon for intruding, I assure you I had no intention of breaking my promise not to see you again. I came merely to clear up the grave misunderstanding that has arisen between us from my mother's misguided letter. A letter whose contents I knew nothing of, and condemn with all my heart.'

More denials. He was not in the mood for her games. 'For God's sake, woman, have done with your lies.' The ice-cold voice was gone, replaced by a hot rage that made her tremble. 'I don't think I've heard one word of truth from those treacherous lips of yours since we met. You have schemed and plotted your way into my life. You have bewitched me with that body of yours. And when you've found yourself bested, instead of giving in and admitting defeat, you simply twist and turn until you find another way to gain your devious ends.'

Kit paced around the room, breathing deeply in an effort to control the rage that was consuming him. A rage that was fuelled by the sight of Clarrie standing in front of him looking so vulnerable. Those big green eyes were gazing up at him full of hurt. That full bottom lip was clenched between her little white teeth to stop her from crying. He would not, *would absolutely not* be taken in by her wiles again.

'I thought you understood enough of me, after the days we spent in each other's company, to see that plain dealing would get you what you wanted. I thought there was enough truth between us for you to realise that an honest request direct from you—not through the medium of your mama—would have gained my attention. I thought you would at least grant me that.'

Fleetingly, the hurt her behaviour had caused showed on Kit's face, but the mask was back in place before Clarissa could be sure. She could find no words at present, could only watch in dismay the results of her own reckless actions, of Amelia's and Mama's idiotic attempts at blackmail. The damage was well and truly done. With each word Kit uttered, she felt her heart shrivel and grow colder, felt herself retreating a little more into that dark place deep inside where she would have to learn to live.

'Well I was wrong, obviously,' Kit continued. 'You have played me for a fool, Clarissa, but you have mistaken your man. Now, if you've said your piece you can go, and this will indeed be the last of our acquaintance. No, wait,' he added urgently as she turned to obey him. '"Let us kiss and part," Clarrie, we should end on a more pleasant note. You must realise by now that you will "…get no more of me."'

For the first time that morning he smiled, that lopsided, harsh, malicious, mocking smile which made her go weak at the knees with desire.

'"And I am glad, glad with all my heart, that thus so cleanly I myself free."' Clarrie recited the next line of the poem bleakly. 'Oh, Kit, don't let it end like this. Won't you believe me? I'd do anything to have you believe me.' Clarissa laid a beseeching hand on the cloth of his dark blue coat, her eyes wide with unshed tears as she looked up at him.

'Anything, Clarrie? But what is there left that you have not already given me?' Kit lifted the hand from his arm and held it, trapped and fluttering between his own, like a small bird.

I would give you my heart, Kit, if you would but take it. But the words could not, would not, ever be uttered. Instead, a watery smile and a shake of the head were all she could summon. She turned to go, overcome with weariness and despair, realising how useless it would be to try to persuade him of her honesty after all that had transpired. But he held tight to her hand, perversely refusing to let her leave.

'Surely, Clarissa, you don't want to go without extracting something from me? All that effort, all that work to charm me. All the trickery you employed to entice me. Surely you want some form of return for such a very time-consuming investment?'

Clarissa's face was burning with shame and embarrassment, but she was as cold inside as if sculpted of ice. His scorn at her behaviour, his callous dismissal of all the passion they had shared, were clear evidence of how little it had all meant to him. He had taken her to bed once, and obviously had no desire to do so again. As for the rest? Well, he would never trust her, never believe her. What future could they possibly ever have? Best that she walk away now with some shred of dignity and spend the rest of her life trying to forget him.

Clarissa blinked away a tear and tugged her hand free. 'I want nothing from you, my lord, except perhaps your forgiveness. Since that is unlikely to be forthcoming, I can only apologise once more for any pain I have caused you, and assure you that you will not see me again. I bid you good morning.' A small curtsy, a last look into that beloved face, and Clarissa made for the door.

She had the handle in her hand when he reached her. Grasping her by the shoulders, Kit turned her round to face him and, ruthlessly pushing her bonnet back, kissed her. A hard, long, vengeful kiss, his lips devouring hers, his tongue seeking entry to her mouth, determined not to be gainsaid.

'No, Clarrie, don't go. Not yet. I've missed you.'

The words were growled low, drawn unwillingly from him, but they were enough. Clarrie melted into his arms, throwing her own around him, clutching desperately at him to pull herself into his hard, achingly familiar body, feeling as if she was coming home. 'Kit.' She opened her mouth, her soft lips giving against his hard demands, the fire of passion igniting instantly as the tip of his tongue touched hers, the heat starting low down in her belly and rising quickly to engulf her as Kit's kisses became passionate, hungry, commanding.

His hands roamed restlessly over her body, frustrated by the thick wool of her clothing. Her cloak was cast off, her bonnet hung down her back by its ribbons, but it wasn't enough. Kit licked the corners of her mouth, then traced a pattern of kisses down her neck, pulling at the fichu of her gown to reveal the white mounds of her breasts underneath. He kissed the valley between them, and circled her nipples with his thumbs through her clothing, the cotton of her chemise causing a delicious friction that added to the sensation of pleasure.

Casting off her gloves, Clarrie pulled him closer in, pulling his lips to hers once more, meeting his demands with her own, threatening to overpower his control with her passion. It was this, Kit thought hazily, this matching of needs and wants, that was at the root of his obsession.

A woman who was his equal in desires, who challenged and commanded and was unafraid of expressing her own needs—this is what made Clarrie so very necessary to him.

Necessary? The word startled Kit back to reality. Forcing himself to let her go, slowly unfastening his lips from hers, he shook his head in disbelief. So near she had been to leaving. So quickly had passion overtaken them. Looking at her, flushed and dishevelled, her green eyes dark with desire, he knew that what she was feeling, for now at least, was no pretence. She wanted him every bit as much as he wanted her.

He could not let her go. The stark truth stared Kit in the face. He could not let her go. Not until he was over her. Not until he could face a future without her. No matter what kind of scheming trollop she was, she needed to be *his* until he had cured himself of this strange addiction. He could not contemplate any alternative.

Taken up with the attempt to put her clothing into some sort of order and to control her breathing, Clarissa noticed none of the thoughts flitting over Kit's face. *I've missed you.* That was all it had taken from him to destroy her resolution, to turn her into this strange, wild, Clarrie she didn't recognise. A Clarrie with no control over her passions. A Clarrie with no thought other than the fulfilment of those passions. A Clarrie so far from the upright, staid, practical Clarissa that she seemed like quite another person.

I've missed you. Did she imagine it? Did it matter, when ultimately it would make no difference between them? He wanted her body, that was all. He would take her and use her and dispose of her, and she would be left with an empty shell. Nothing had changed. Dejectedly, she retied her bonnet, thrusting the curls that had escaped their pins under the brim any old how, afraid to see the evidence of their passion should she look in the mirror. She had to get out of here before she made an even bigger fool of herself.

A vice-like grip on her arm made any move impossible, however. 'You're not going anywhere until we've talked.'

'We have nothing more to say to each other. I must go; Mama does not know where I am.'

'I suspect your mama knows exactly where you are right now, my dear, and moreover heartily approves.'

'You have her wrong, Kit. She is merely a foolish woman in desperate need of funds. She did not really intend to bribe you, nor to sell me.'

'No? I'm afraid it is you who are mistaken. But I'm already bored with discussing your sainted mama. I am much more interested in what happens next between us.'

'Nothing. Nothing more can happen, Kit, you know that as well as I.'

'Don't insult me. We have unfinished business between us. As well it were settled now while we are alone.'

'I don't understand.'

'Come, Clarissa, don't pretend. We are extremely compatible. You must admit that, for you are obviously experienced. I have not met such a passion in a woman before. Together, we are well matched.'

The burning flush that covered her face was a mixture of anger and disappointment. To discuss what they had shared seemed so wrong. To denigrate what for Clarrie had been love-making, into something that was mere bodily pleasure, made her furious. And for him to deny, despite the evidence, that he had been her first, her only lover, was the final straw. 'You do me a grievous disservice, my lord. If your intention is to hurt me, then let me assure you that you have been more than successful. I have not your lordship's experience in such matters, despite what you think of me. And I find it distasteful to discuss our love-making—' she could not bring herself to give it another name '—in such cold terms. I was an innocent until two nights ago, you know it yourself, though you choose to deny it. I gave you my body in payment, as I promised—I am no longer in debt to you, nor you to me. I am pleased that our union was not distasteful to you, but it is over. Now let me go.'

Completely taken aback at her anger, Kit's grip on her arm did not relax. The tiny voice deep inside him that had been on Clarissa's side from the start, supporting her claims, telling him to trust her, gained volume. One truth he would allow her. He knew she had been innocent, had been mad or desperate to think otherwise. But still, he could not reconcile this fact with his experience. She might have been unpractised, but she had definitely been tutored. Innocence was not, after all, the same as virtue.

It did not matter. None of it mattered. Allowing himself to accept that he had been the first, the only lover she had ever had, gave Kit a glow of satisfaction, making him realise how necessary it was that he continued to be so. She was, must be, exclusively his. 'Clarrie, we can deal better than this. I'm sorry for disbelieving you, I'm not thinking straight. I beg your pardon. Please, let us sit down and talk properly.'

'There's nothing to talk about, Kit. Please let me go.' But she allowed herself to be led over to a sofa, and sat down nevertheless.

Kit sat down beside her. 'There, that's more like it. I awoke with such a headache,' he said apologetically, 'I was a trifle foxed, a touch too much brandy last night, for which I must blame your mama and her letter. I confess I am not at my best, and my temper is ragged as a consequence. But I am feeling better by the minute.'

'Really, Kit, blaming my mama for your headache is a trifle unfair.'

Clarissa looked up, the tilt of her determined little chin, the challenging lift of her brow, so exactly as he remembered that for a moment he forgot all that had gone before and laughed, his rare, genuine laugh. 'Fair enough, I must accept some of the blame. You allow me no quarter, do you, Clarissa fair?'

'Nor you I, my lord and in that we are certainly well matched.'

'Clarissa, I want you to listen to me, and not to interrupt.' Seizing her hand, Kit gazed into her eyes, urging her compliance. He would do it, he had to ask her, he didn't care what damage it did to his ego. What use was it to have his pride intact when what he really wanted was right here in front of him? He could nurse his injured pride at length when his more pressing needs had been satisfied. 'Please, listen. I don't want an answer now, I want you to think carefully about it.'

'Very well. But I think you should know that—'

'Clarissa, be quiet.'

This time his smile lit up his eyes, making him so incredibly handsome that Clarissa gulped in an effort not to lean over and kiss him once more.

'We started out our liaison, both of us, under false pretences. No matter your real motives, whether to rescue your sister or to entrap me for yourself, you lied to me from the start. And I was not so honest with you either, for I led you on, knowing full well that you were scheming, yet so bored with my life that I chose to indulge you in your pretence.'

A brief silence greeted this, as both reviewed the last few days, acknowledging the truth. Neither could claim to be blameless.

'Yet much good has flowed from such inauspicious beginnings, Clarissa,' Kit continued, 'you must see that now. I have never met a woman whose courage I have so admired. You took everything I threw at you and coped without tears or tantrums. You showed such a lust for life on board the *Sea Wolf*, such an empathy towards Monsieur and Mademoiselle Renaud. I came to honour your judgement, to enjoy testing your intelligence. In short, despite your scheming, I enjoy your company, Clarissa, in a way I have never liked the company of any woman before.'

Her heart was beating faster with every word, for she could not quite believe what Kit was saying to her. She dared not speak, dared not hope, merely gestured for him to continue.

'The consummation of our relationship was—well, I will not cause you to blush further. Let me just say that it was all I had hoped and beyond all my previous experience. I want more of it, I cannot think straight until I have more of it. I think we will deal well together. What do you say, Clarrie. Is it yes?'

She could not quite believe it. He had proposed. He had not mentioned love but it was there surely, clearly implied. 'Are you sure it's what you want, Kit?'

'I never offer anything unless I'm completely sure.'

'Oh Kit, yes, yes, yes.' Clarrie threw her arms around him, almost knocking him flat back on the sofa, her body lying on top of his, pressing against him with abandon. Their kiss was slow and languorous. Tasting, renewing, hot, yet restrained. Clarrie pressed tiny kisses onto Kit's eyes, his cheeks, his ears, kissed her way across his mouth, licking the tender skin inside his lips, and licked back again. She ran her fingers through his locks, feeling the fine silk of his hair run through them, contrasting with the crisp dark hair on his nape—the feeling awakening a vivid memory of the crisp curls on his chest.

Kit made to sit up, but she pushed him back down, arching into his arousal, rubbing herself against him, the friction of their bodies and their clothes sending shivers of raw desire through her. Cautiously, she rubbed herself against him again, cat-like, sinuously, testing his control, revelling in the feeling of power this ability to arouse him gave her. All thought of restraint left her as she heard his groan of surrender and wild Clarrie took over from staid Clarissa, heedless of their surroundings, intent only on giving pleasure and receiving it in return.

She kissed him again, a hard, passionate kiss, holding his face in her hands, refusing to let him move from underneath her. Clumsily at first, but with growing confidence, she fumbled for the fastenings of his breeches and released him from their constraints. His arousal was a hard silken length in her hand, hers to hold, to caress, to rub, to tease, and she did all of this, all the time watching Kit's face, flushed like her own with passion, his eyes closed, his breathing heavy. *She* was causing this, *she* was doing this to him—he was hers. A thrill of possession ran through her, causing her hands to tighten, threatening to upset the delicate balance of control. Just in time, she released him, twisting away to stand upright.

Clarissa quickly disposed of her own undergarments, discarded the fichu at her neck, and untied the strings of her chemise. Kit needed no encouragement, but sat up, pulling her back down astride him, freeing her breasts with urgent hands, enveloping first one, then the other, nipple with his soft mouth, sweeping circles on each with his clever, tantalising, teasing tongue. Clarrie panted, wet with desire, and pulled her dress up around her waist. Bracing herself with her hands on the back of the sofa behind Kit's neck, she began, slowly, delicately, to draw him inside her, slowly to engulf his hard length with her own silken heat. Kit's hands held her waist to guide her, support her, but she needed no encouragement. She held them both still for a heart-stopping instant, her muscles clenched around him, then moved, tilted up, then slowly down, twisting herself against him to heighten her own pleasure, feeling him pulse inside her. Slowly, resolutely resisting the urge to quicken the pace, she repeated the motion, rising up and thrusting down, hearing Kit's gasping, growled pleasure in her ear, feeling his grip on her waist tighten, feeling her own climax climbing to its peak with each downwards motion, until suddenly she was soaring, released, flying in ecstasy. As she lost herself in the feeling, Kit's grasp became demanding, and she instinctively thrust more urgently, hard and fast, relishing the feeling of still being in control even as she floated in the afterglow of her climax, moaning as Kit's own climax came in a final powerful thrust that pulsed through her, ripples of pleasure ebbing out from a whirlpool of passion.

They lay limp and panting, a tangle of clothing around hot, damp, satisfied bodies. Clarrie raised her head from where it rested in the nook between Kit's neck and shoulder to look into his eyes, still dark with passion behind hooded lids. A crooked, exhausted smile met her own slightly trembling, slightly questioning look. Holding her tight against him, their bodies still joined, Kit reached up to curl a bright auburn lock around his finger. Pressing a slow, sated kiss to her mouth, he finally moved to separate them, brushing her skirts down, adjusting his breeches, holding out her undergarments to her with a rueful smile.

Retreating behind a small screen by the fire to compose herself, Clarissa felt a hot flush of embarrassment. What had come over her? She could not blame Kit this time for becoming carried away, it had been all her own doing. What if the servants had come in? She doubted she would even have noticed.

'I think we had better confine such activity to our bedchamber when we are married, do not you, Kit?' Clarissa emerged from the screen, tying her fichu into place, and saw the smile on his face freeze at her words.

'Married? Whatever gave you that idea?'

'Why, you did. You proposed to me—and I said yes.' Her confidence faltered. Looking back on the conversation, she realised that he had not specifically mentioned marriage at all.

'You are mistaken, Clarissa. My proposal was of a nature much more appropriate to our relationship, as I believe I indicated it would be in my letter.'

'But I thought you had changed your mind. You said you couldn't do without me. You said you missed me. You said you wanted me.'

'All true—for the present, at least. But none of those words imply marriage, my dear. You don't bring me up to scratch so easily.'

Clarissa slumped down in an armchair, her legs too weak to support her. He was right. She had been so carried away just being with him, with his avowal of need, of desire, she had not questioned the nature of the proposal. In a small voice she determined once and for all to clarify the situation. 'You were not offering marriage?'

Kit's raised brow and mocking smile were the only answer, but they were sufficient.

'What, then? I don't understand.'

'A temporary but exclusive liaison.'

'You mean I would be yours and only yours?' *He had that already, and for ever, if he were but interested.*

'Yes, but I would be yours too, exclusively, for the duration. I have never offered a woman that before, Clarrie, you should be honoured.'

'Yes? Well, then, thank you, my lord, I must be honoured if you say I should be.'

She glanced up at him, hurt and confusion writ large on her face, causing that nagging voice in his head to speak in her support. His instinct to hold her close, to promise never to leave her, was quelled with extreme difficulty. Defiantly, he reminded himself that she would do anything to have her way, to trap him, even into marriage. He would not be a victim. He would take her, he had to have her, but on his own terms, and those terms alone, no matter how urgently he wished it could be otherwise.

'Come now, Clarrie, there's no point in tears. We have something out of the common way together. Let us make the most of it while it lasts. For it will end, as these things always do, so it's best to make arrangements now, to make that ending as painless as possible. Then we can enjoy to the full the precious time we have together. I am a generous protector. You will find you want for nothing, I promise. And when we part, as part we must, you will be more than adequately recompensed. I think that is a bargain neither of us can carp at.'

She continued to look up at him, the hurt reflected deep in her emerald eyes, but the tears were held defi-

antly in check. Reminding himself that she was an astonishingly good actress, Kit leaned over to pull her to her
feet, pressing a swift, gentle kiss on her yielding lips.

'I asked you to think carefully about my proposal,
you may remember. Don't say no, Clarrie, it would be a
mistake. Go home and think about what we have. Think
about the alternatives. Then give me a yes that you will
honour. I'll meet you tomorrow, when you've had time to
reflect. But bear this in mind. Though I offer you something I have never offered before, I will not offer more,
nor will I offer it twice. If you say no, it will be final, and
we will see no more of each other. And much as I wish
and hope that will not be so, I won't be blackmailed, nor
held to ransom. This is my final offer, Clarissa, so think
carefully before you turn it down.'

Shaking her head, Clarissa could still find no words,
silenced as she was by the deep hurt inside her, the determination not to show Kit how much she cared. Submis-
sively, she stood while he re-tied her bonnet and draped
her cloak around her. Wordlessly, she allowed him to
kiss her cheek, permitting herself only one brief, final
embrace before she left without looking back, and the
door to Grosvenor Square closed firmly behind her for
ever.

A small boy in dark green livery stepped aside into a
doorway as Clarissa exited the house and hailed a hack.
When the carriage pulled away, the boy launched himself
on to the back of it, unbeknownst to either the jarvey or
his passenger. As the hack pulled up to deposit Clarissa
at her home, the boy leapt off and hid round the corner,
taking careful note of her address. With a satisfied whistle, he waited to make sure she went through the door,
before running off to inform his master of his findings.

* * *

Robert, Marquis of Alchester, was partaking of a late luncheon in the sunny breakfast parlour when his servant returned. Lowering the *Morning Post*, to listen carefully to the boy as he recounted his morning's observations, he smiled with satisfaction. The coin he handed over was larger than the lad had anticipated, and the boy bowed low, thanking his master with assurances of his continued service, and a rather gappy, cocky smile. Alchester dismissed him with an imperious wave, and returned to the table.

The address the boy had given him was the same as the one he had received from his lawyer. Lady Maria Warrington's gambling debts had been acquired almost by accident, payment from another of Mrs Barrington's innocent victims in the gambling hell to which she had introduced Lady Maria. Alchester had not made the connection with Kit Rasenby until last night, when Kit, in his cups, had let slip Clarissa's name after a deal too much of White's brandy.

Robert Alchester had waited a long time for revenge. For years, he had watched as Kit's reputation as a rake increased as surely as the richness of his lands, as abundantly as his wealth. Robert looked on in bitter resentment as Kit flourished, as his callous treatment of women was rewarded with devotion, as his reckless gaming was rewarded with winnings beyond anything Robert could dream of. The *Sea Wolf* had seemed to offer the first chink in Rasenby's armour, but he had somehow escaped from the excise men. As Kit's lucky star continued in the ascent, so Robert Alchester's plummeted. He was known to be in debt, reduced to extorting money from acquired gambling debts such as Lady Maria's in order to keep his many voracious creditors at bay. And as the vultures circled closer, so the ladies moved further away.

Now surely the tide was turning his way. The innocent Miss Clarissa Warrington would prove to be Rasenby's Achilles' heel and Robert Alchester's salvation. Rasenby would be crushed once and for all. The Marquis of Alchester cut himself another slice of bloody beef. He was suddenly ravenous.

Chapter Twelve

Clarissa returned home for the second day in a row in desperate need of the solace of her bedchamber. She wearily opened the door, feeling that everything which could possibly go wrong with her life already had. For the second time in two days she was summoned urgently into the parlour before she even had time to remove her hat. This time, the voice belonged not to Lady Maria, but to Aunt Constance. Her heart sank. This was an encounter she had been dreading and could well do without.

'Child, what on earth have you been up to?' Aunt Constance got to her feet as Clarissa entered the room. Dressed neatly as ever, in a plain but elegant dress of brown silk with matching ribbons in her cap, she was clearly upset. A frown darkened her pale countenance as she anxiously assessed her niece. 'Come and let me look at you properly. I have asked your mother to afford us some privacy. Your mama has already given me some muddled story about your escapades, but I confess I would much rather have it direct from you. Why don't you sit down and tell your aunt exactly what's been happening, there's a good girl.'

The gentle voice and the obvious note of concern in her voice, when she was entitled to anger, were quite oversetting. Clarissa cast herself into her aunt's arms and gave way to another unaccustomed fit of tears.

Lady Constance held her close, patting her back and whispering soothing platitudes while patiently letting her have her cry. When Clarissa finally looked up, gulping down the last of her sobs, Lady Constance handed her a fine linen handkerchief, but continued in her silence, concern for her normally placid niece having the upper hand over curiosity.

Eventually Clarissa sat up properly, and with a sigh turned to her aunt, her face resolute. 'I don't know exactly what Mama will have told you, for it was Amelia who broke my confidence and told a version of the tale to her. I have yet not apprised Mama of the true facts myself. I'm afraid I put you in a difficult position, forcing you to lie to Mama, and no doubt making you worry about my whereabouts. I am so sorry, Aunt Constance, but you must believe me when I say that I did it only because I thought it for the best.'

'Silly child, of course I realise that. I am only sorry that you felt the need to act without first consulting me. I thought you trusted me, Clarissa. I thought you knew you could always turn to me if you were in need of help.'

'Indeed, dearest Aunt Constance, I thought of it, I assure you. Only, knowing what you think of Amelia, I was not sure you would *want* to help. And so I did such a stupid thing, and now we are all reaping the consequences of it, myself as much as Mama and Amelia. And, oh, Aunt Constance, if ever any of this gets out, I will have brought such shame and disgrace to your good name, too, as you truly don't deserve.'

'Clarissa, my dear, I cannot believe you would ever deliberately do anything to shame me, you must not be worrying your head about that. Whatever has happened, I'm sure that if we put our heads together we can fix it. But first you must tell me exactly what has transpired, for I could get no sense out of your mama, and Amelia would only say I must talk to you, and that you had ruined her life.'

'Well, that's true enough, Aunt, I think I have. And mine too, for I am ruined, and it is all my own fault.'

'Ruined? Do not tell me, Clarissa, that your mother spoke the truth? Is it—no, I cannot believe it. She told me you had been seduced. Please tell me that she is mistaken.'

'No, I wasn't seduced.'

Aunt Constance clapped her hands together in relief. 'I knew it, I knew that muddle-headed mother of yours must have managed to get the story amiss.'

'No, you don't understand. I was not seduced, but I am no longer innocent. I was not coerced, nor was I ravished. I was—I was compliant. It's not Kit's fault, no matter what Mama says, but I am ruined none the less. Oh, Aunt Constance, the truly wicked thing is, I cannot bring myself to regret it.'

Her aunt struggled to absorb the import of Clarissa's words. 'My dear, please tell me you are not deluded into thinking you are in love with this man?'

'Oh, but I am, I am, I am. I cannot help it, I can't, I love him so much, and I have made such a mull of it, and now there is no future for it. But still, I cannot regret it. You will hate me for it, but I won't lie to you, Aunt. I do love him.'

Slowly, determinedly, Lady Constance extracted the round tale, her face becoming grimmer with each admission from her niece. Of Amelia and Lady Maria's part in the whole thing Clarissa made little, but Lady Constance heard enough to make up her own mind. Heard enough to have a pretty clear picture of Lady Maria's stupidity and Amelia's selfishness.

At the end, she held Clarissa close, assuring her that all would be well, that she was on her side and would never think ill of her. Inside she was cold and furious, already planning the best way of raining retribution down on Kit Rasenby's arrogant, selfish head. His sister, Lady Marlborough, was long overdue a visit. Lady Constance would start there. If nothing else came out of this, Kit Rasenby's conscience would certainly take a battering from which it would never recover.

Allowing her niece no hint of these thoughts, Lady Constance turned to practicalities. The letter from Fortescue and Brown detailing Lady Maria's debts was pursued with a deep frown, and Amelia was summoned. 'I understand that you opened your sister's letter to Edward Brompton, Amelia. I trust that you are aware that you should not have done so? To pry into another's private correspondence is the kind of behaviour one would expect from servants.'

Amelia, who had never been able to stand up to Aunt Constance, hung her head in shame.

'Well, have you nothing to say?'

'I'm sorry, Aunt Constance, I only did it to help Clarissa out.'

'And in what way did you imagine you would be helping her, Amelia?'

'I just thought if I knew why she was writing to Edward, I might be able to give her some advice.'

'That is a ridiculous lie, and you know it. I can only hope that this Edward fellow was as shocked as I to find his correspondence tampered with.'

Amelia blushed at the memory of Edward's reaction. He had indeed lectured her, and it had quite spoiled the evening.

'Well, I can see from your face that Edward does have some sense then. And did he also have a reply for Clarissa's query?'

'No, not immediately, Aunt. He said he would look into the matter, and would give Clarissa the information she wanted if he could do so without any breach of confidence.'

'Hmm. Obviously a much more sensible young man than you deserve. I am told you love each other and wish to marry, but his meagre prospects are a barrier. In that case I would like to meet this young man. You may inform him that he can call on me tomorrow at eleven. If I am happy with him, I will see what I can do. Despite what you think, Amelia, I have no desire to see you unhappy, and every wish to see you happily settled, even if you scarcely deserve it. If there is anything I can do to further Edward's position, I will look into it—if, and only if, I have your promise that you will interfere no further in your sister's concerns.'

'But, Aunt, what about—'

Lady Constance continued inexorably. 'I will hear no more from you on any subject, Amelia. You will leave Clarissa alone and refrain from any discussion at all of the events that have taken place over the last three days. If I hear that you have made any attempt to open negotiations of any sort with any gentleman other than Edward Brompton, I will disown you. Am I absolutely clear?'

'Yes, Aunt Constance.'

'You may leave us now.' Lady Constance waved an imperious hand. Amelia left with relief, casting a backwards sympathetic glance at her sister, looking extremely subdued on the sofa.

'I must go now, Clarissa,' Lady Constance said, drawing on her gloves. 'I have a lot to do, and a lot to think about. You must get some rest, child, and try not to worry for the present. We must wait and see if there are any other consequences of your liaison with Lord Rasenby, and pray for your sake that there are not. In the meantime, you must naturally have no further contact with him. As to your mother's debts, you may trust me to investigate the matter fully. It may be possible to negotiate repayment on easier terms, I will know more when I have spoken to this Edward person and learned who your mother's creditor is.'

'Aunt, I'm so sorry that you've been put through all this. I hadn't meant you to become involved. I've made such a mess and caused you all this worry when I thought I could deal with it myself.'

'Clarissa, once and for all I assure you, dear child, that my only regret is that you didn't feel you could turn to me in the first place. Perhaps this could have been avoided if you had.' Seeing Clarissa's lip tremble, Lady Constance hastened to hug her reassuringly. 'There, you are a good child, you deserve better than this. Now try to put all of this out of your head, you really must get some rest. This whole episode has been traumatic for you, more than you realise yourself at present. But time, you know, is a great healer. One final thing before I go. I want your assurance that you have told me everything. I would rather know the worst if there is aught else.'

Of Kit's latest proposal and their meeting this morning, Clarissa had not spoken, and she found that she could not bring herself to now. So she shook her head in denial, hugging her aunt close, promising to retire at once to her bed and to worry no more.

Lady Constance left in her waiting town coach, already planning her next steps with something akin to relish. It was nice to feel she could be of use. She was looking forward to getting one over on Lord Rasenby. He would find she was no mean adversary.

Deciding to act immediately, while her anger still fuelled her thoughts, Lady Constance directed her coachman to take her to Lady Letitia Marlborough's house. She was fortunate enough to find Kit's sister at home alone. The interview gave her some satisfaction, providing, as it did, a relief for her pent-up emotions. When Lady Constance departed she left her old friend shocked, upset, and in a state of high dudgeon. Lady Constance had every expectation that all this pent-up ire would soon be raining down on Kit Rasenby.

It was late in the day and she was tired but reasonably satisfied with her efforts. Her only regret was that she would not be present to witness the confrontation between Letitia and Kit.

Having spent the remainder of the evening, despite her promise to her aunt, ruminating on events, Clarissa went to bed clear in her own mind that there was only one possible answer to Kit's proposal. She loved him, that much was beyond dispute. His offer was therefore tempting from a purely selfish point of view, scarcely impossible as it was to contemplate life without him. Tempting too since she could, if she chose, conveniently assuage her guilt by convincing herself she was making a selfless sacrifice to secure Mama's and Amelia's future. But it was wrong and she knew it. She could be nobody's mistress, it was marriage or nothing, and even then, only if she was truly loved. Since Kit was offering neither marriage nor true love, it could not be.

Clarissa realised that there was something else even more important. Kit cared for her more than he knew, or would admit, but eventually he would grow tired of her and bring their liaison to a conclusion. Knowing that the ending was coming, inevitably, surely, on some yet-to-be-decided date, would be intolerable to Clarissa. No, she could not settle for anything less than perfect. She knew in her heart what she must do. It was precisely because she loved him so deeply that she must turn him down.

A night's rest saw Clarissa full of renewed determination. She arose early, but her note to Kit, brief as it was, took her some time and many sheets of paper before the final version was ready to be delivered. Clarissa thanked him *profusely* for his *very generous offer*, was most flattered by it, but found that, alas, she must *in all conscience, refuse it.* She reminded him of his promise to make her no other offers, and assured him that she had no regrets. While their time together had been *enlightening and for the most part enjoyable*, it was time to end it. She trusted Kit would respect her wishes and cease all communications between them. There was no need to reply to this letter. Clarissa wished him well.

Refusing steadfastly to give in to the tears that seemed to be taking over her life these days, Clarissa next turned her attentions to the future. Aunt Constance seemed confident that something could be done about Mama's debts, and perhaps even Amelia's marriage, if Edward came up to scratch, but she could do nothing for a ruined niece. Forcing herself to face up to harsh reality, hoping that it would eventually dull the pain in her heart that threatened to overcome her with each thought of Kit, Clarissa turned her mind to obtaining a position. It would not be easy, but a governess or lady's companion she must be. With a heavy heart she pursued the advertisements in the *Tatler*.

Kit slept soundly, confident that the morrow would bring Clarissa's consent to his proposition. Waking at his usual time he smiled, embracing the day with a sense of pleasurable anticipation that surprised him, until he traced the feeling of well-being to Clarrie, and thoughts of what today would bring. He looked forward to spending his money on her, looked forward to looking after her—for the present, in any case. They could travel, she would like that, and he could teach her to sail. They would spend some time at Thornwood. She would not like to mix with the *ton* as his mistress, and he did not in any case wish to share her.

With irritation, he dismissed the voice in his head that asked him just how long he expected their liaison to last, his record to date of a mere two months being hardly sufficient for these plans. There was no need to put a timescale to it, no need to think of life after Clarissa. She was different. Two months—that was paltry.

The familiar writing on the letter proffered by his valet caused Kit's heart to skip a beat. Assuring himself that she was merely writing to confirm their arrangement to meet later, Kit opened the short note and quickly scanned the contents, anger warring with disbelief and enormous disappointment. What was her game? Surely she did not think she could up the stakes now?

Swearing softly, he became aware that Fanshaw was hovering by the bed. 'Well?'

'I am sorry to have to tell you that Lady Marlborough awaits your lordship's pleasure. She apologises for calling at such an early hour, but says that the matter is of such import it will not wait. Hodges has placed her in the breakfast parlour, my lord.'

'God damn it, what the hell does she want? Did she say what it was about?'

'No, my lord, when Hodges inquired further she merely repeated that the matter was urgent.'

'No doubt that brat of a nephew of mine has been trying out his blasted gaming system again. Oh, very well, then, tell her I'll be down as soon as I can.'

'And the letter, my lord—is there a reply?'

'No, there is not. And you can take your interfering nose out of my business and get on with shaving me.'

'Yes, my lord.' With injured innocence, Fanshaw traipsed to the dressing room to gather together the necessary component's of Kit's riding dress. There was definitely something afoot with the master, and if Fanshaw knew anything about it, it had to do with that young woman from Thornwood Manor. He'd give a lot to see the letter, but it was already locked away safely in Kit's writing table.

'Well, Letty, what is so urgent that you must needs call before breakfast? It's not like you to be up so betimes.' Kit strode into the breakfast parlour an hour later, planting a brief kiss on his sister's cheek before pouring himself a draught of ale. 'Have you eaten? Did Hodges bring you coffee?'

'I am in no mood for sustenance, Kit, and neither will you be when you've heard what I've got to say. I have a very busy day ahead of me, I can scarcely afford the time for this matter, you know. I am engaged to take the girls to see the illuminations at Vauxhall tonight, and I have a host of errands to attend to before then.'

'Well, make it quick then, Letitia,' Kit said, 'I have pressing business to see to myself. Has Jeremy been out on the tiles again? How much is it this time?'

'It is nothing to do with Jeremy. You may say what you want of my son, Kit, but at least he is not a seducer of innocent virgins!'

Kit grinned distractedly. 'No? Well, he's young yet, I suppose there's still time. So what is this pressing matter then?'

Kit sat down at the table, addressing himself to a plate of ham, his thoughts on what he should do in reply to Clarissa's letter, only half-aware of his sister fuming silently beside him.

'It is you, Kit. You really have gone too far this time. I am appalled, absolutely appalled at what I hear. You have placed me in a dreadful position; I have never been so embarrassed. And poor Constance—well, needless to say she is up in arms at your behaviour.'

Kit's attention finally secured, Letty sat back in satisfaction, watching her brother carefully putting his knife down on his plate before speaking. His voice was measured, but she knew that look of old. He was angry. 'Who is this Constance that I have so unwittingly offended?'

'Lady Constance Denby. You must have heard me mention her, Kit, she's one of my oldest friends.'

'I remember her vaguely now—a widow, isn't she? Her husband was that rare thing, an honest politician. What of her?'

'She called on me yesterday. You are obviously not aware that she has a niece. Two nieces, to be precise.'

'And,' Kit said cautiously, 'what of them?'

'I am led to believe you've had dealings with both

of them recently. Amelia, Constance informs me, you intended to offer a *carte blanche*, but were induced to change your mind. Not content with trying to ruin one who, Constance admits, was at least colluding in her own downfall, you then proceeded to ravish the other, Clarissa—a complete innocent—who is now apparently heartbroken in love with you.'

'Clarissa Warrington is Constance Denby's niece?'

'Yes, and not just her niece, but very much her aunt's favourite. Constance thinks highly of her, paid for her schooling, had hoped to have Clarissa as her companion. But she is unwilling to abandon her mother and sister even though, from what I can gather, they live in rather straitened circumstances. Honestly, Kit,' Letitia said exasperatedly, 'the girl is respectable through and through; it's not like you to make such a mistake.'

'I had no idea she was so well connected, Letty, nor such an innocent, I promise you.'

'So I informed Constance must be the case. A rake you are, Kit, and no mistake, but I know that seducing innocents is not in your usual line.'

Kit smiled grimly. 'Thank you for the tribute, sister.'

Letty's face softened. 'I am not going to deny, brother, that you have *some* good points. I am particularly grateful for the unwavering support you provide to my poor weak, foolish Jeremy, you know I am. But really, Kit, you have gone too far this time. What possessed you?'

'God, Letty, I'm sore pressed to understand that myself.' Kit shook his head in an effort to assemble his thoughts. Clarissa, it would seem, had been telling him the truth all along, and was every bit the innocent she claimed to be. He could not for the moment reconcile this with his own knowledge of her. If she was the person her aunt claimed, why had she behaved so recklessly?

It would certainly explain her letter this morning—she would never accept a *carte blanche* from him.

'Is it true that you abducted her and took her to France on the *Sea Wolf*?' Letitia enquired incredulously. 'I told Constance that part must be a lie, for no woman has ever been on board that yacht of yours, even me!'

'Letty, you'd be sick before we left harbour, as well you know. That part is true, actually, although she came willingly—or so I believed.' Kit ran his hand distractedly through his hair, causing one lock to fall forward into his eyes. He brushed it away angrily. What had he done?

His conscience, dormant since yesterday, launched itself with renewed vigour, castigating him so thoroughly that his voice, when he recovered enough to speak, was clipped and grim. 'I thought she was lying. She protested her innocence, but I chose not to believe her. I wanted to take her with me, you see, I was—I don't know, Letty, I was bored, she was different, I was enjoying myself. She must have been terrified, though she gave no outward sign of it. I didn't realise what I was doing to her.'

'Well, according to Constance, there was precious little you *didn't* do to her.' Letty's reply was tart, the stinging dressing down she had borne from her friend still fresh in her ears.

Kit looked up at the sharp words, seeing the hurt on his sister's face. 'I'm sorry that you have been embroiled in this. I take it that Lady Constance vented her spleen on you in my absence?'

'It was awful! Constance has an extremely sharp tongue—I did not at all relish being on the receiving end of it, I assure you. But that is nothing to what you must have put that girl through, Kit. Why, it is a very ravishment, for goodness' sake.'

'No, no, it's not that simple, I assure you, Letty. But

never mind that, did Lady Constance say how she does, my poor Clarissa?'

'Much you care.'

Seeing Kit wince, Letitia softened. At least he wasn't wholly indifferent to the damage he had done. 'Clarissa apparently knew nothing of her aunt's visit to me. She is upset and hurt, but she is obviously a girl of some strength and backbone, I must say, for Constance told me she would hear nothing against you, and despite all the evidence, insisted that she had consented to everything. She makes no accusations against you and wants merely to forget the whole episode. And that, let me tell you, Kit, is far more than you deserve.'

Some vestige of self-preservation made him cling to the idea that he had been the victim of a plot. That somehow, despite the overwhelming evidence to the contrary, he had not behaved completely abominably. 'Why did Lady Constance seek you out? She must have known you would come straight to me.'

'Naturally, I assume that was her intention. Sometimes, Kit, you can be quite dim-witted.' It was not often that Letitia felt superior to her brother, and it had to be admitted that in spite of the circumstances she was enjoying it for now. 'Regardless of her niece's wishes to the contrary, Constance felt that you should understand the extent of your—perfidy, she called it. It's obvious, Kit, she wants you to suffer.'

'So she wasn't asking you to intervene in any way?'

'Intervene? In what way? Oh, you mean with you?' A trill of laughter greeted this idea. 'Quite the contrary, Kit. She was immensely relieved Clarissa wanted no more to do with you, for the last thing on earth she would wish on her niece was marriage with a rake like yourself.'

'Are you sure she said that? This was definitely no

plot to entrap me in some way?' The voice in Kit's head that had always been Clarissa's supporter scented the winning post, with just this one obstacle to clear.

Letty stared at her brother open-mouthed. 'You actually think that Lady Constance Denby would plot with her niece to trap you into marriage? You have windmills in the head, Kit, I declare.' Letitia continued in full sail. 'Do you have any idea, my dear brother, just how very respectable that family are? I mean, I know the mother and the other daughter are plainly not the brightest buttons in the box, but the family pedigree is impeccable, and Constance is probably better connected than you or I. No, Kit, there is no plot. Face it, the poor deluded girl must be in love with you, there can be no other explanation.'

'She never said a word of her feelings towards me.' *Not a word, but what about her actions?* The seed of doubt Letitia had planted in his mind was taking firm root. What else explained Clarissa's behaviour? The way she had accepted him yesterday with hardly a moment to consider when she thought he was offering marriage? Could it have been love and not avarice? His past experiences made him assume the worst of everyone. But, then, did not Clarissa turn all those things on their head? 'Letty, are you sure you are right? I find it hard to believe Clarissa would keep such a thing from me.'

'Do you? Well, perhaps this chit understands you better than you think. How would you have reacted had she declared her love for you in the circumstances? Would you have believed her?'

No, of course he wouldn't have. He would have thought it yet another ploy. Yet it was the one thing, the only thing that made sense of her behaviour. Despite the shock of Letitia's revelations, following hot on the heels as they did of Clarissa's letter refusing his *carte blanche*, Kit began to feel a sense of rising excitement.

But Letitia had not finished with him yet. 'You have done a very stupid thing, Kit. I can only pray you have not left the girl with child—although, to give you credit that is not, to my knowledge, something you make a habit of. The best thing for everyone involved in this dreadful affair is to forget it ever happened. And as for you Kit, I recommend you repent for the first time in your life, and look to the future. Put the girl out of your mind. Constance is the best person to deal with her. She will find her a position as a governess or some such thing, and we can all get on with our lives. But let this be a lesson to you.'

Letitia rose to go, well satisfied with the visit. Her brother was looking thoughtful, his initial anger long since dissipated. Well and good—perhaps now was the time to give his mind something else to think about. 'You know, Louisa Haysham is not yet betrothed. I've mentioned before, she would make a biddable bride for you. It's time you settled and mended your ways, Kit. Think about it.'

Kit had been thinking hard on his sister's words. His conclusions, only just now reached, were not likely to make Letitia happy. In truth, he found them quite shocking himself. How could he have been so blind? It was as if a fog had been lifted from his mind, allowing him to see with frightening clarity. Now that the situation was for the first time crystal clear, he was determined on a rash course that made him feel quite light-headed. He stood to usher his sister towards the door. 'Put Louisa Haysham from your mind, I am not interested in her. The woman I am going to marry is a fiery, feisty, green-eyed temptress who goes by the name of Clarrie.'

'Clarrie?' Looking at him, Letitia saw a strange light in his eyes, a small smile quirked at the corner of his mouth. 'Kit, you're not going to do anything foolish, are you? I'm sorry I spoke so harshly, even if you did deserve it. You are not all bad, you know. Sometimes I think you act the part because you enjoy it.'

'Do you, Letty? You are not the first to tell me so, strangely. Clarrie said something similar almost the first time she met me.'

'Kit, listen to me. That will not do, you know, Constance will not hear of it. Kit, tell me you're not going to... Oh, if I had known you would do this, I would not have come.'

'But I am very glad you did come, for you have put it all in perspective for me. You were right, Clarissa would not have behaved the way she did unless she loved me. I was just too stupid to see it. Thank you, and say thank you to Lady Constance, although I intend to do that myself when everything is settled.'

'Oh, Kit, please don't do it. She'll not have you. Kit, you can't marry a ruined girl—think of your good name.'

'Letty, you have assured me all too many times that I don't have a good name to think of, and you are right. I am thinking only of Clarissa's good name. She is not ruined, we merely anticipated our vows, and that is hardly an uncommon thing. And if I find that one word of this story escapes, I will know who to blame, I warn you. Do not be the cause of an estrangement between us.'

'But I don't understand. Why are you doing this? You don't have to marry her.'

'Oh, but, Letty, I do. Don't you see? I love her. There, I've said it! Don't look so astonished. No, do, because it is quite the most astonishing and extraordinary thing ever to happen to me. Now you must pick your chin up from the floor and go, for I have important things to attend to.'

Finding herself deposited in the hallway, a frankly flabbergasted Letitia had no option but to leave, which she did reluctantly, directing her coachman to drive to the Royal Exchange where she intended to purchase several unnecessary pairs of kid evening gloves. The afternoon would be more profitably spent in indulging an unwonted fit of the vapours.

Before Letitia had even mounted the steps of her barouche, Kit had already ordered his carriage and bounded up the stairs calling for his valet. Fifteen minutes later he was negotiating the streets with care, perched high on the seat of his phaeton. He felt he was seeing the world with a clarity of vision never before granted to him. Clarissa, the embodiment of all his desires, who overturned everything he believed in, was in love with him. It seemed so obvious now—how could he have deluded himself so? Challenging, brave, lovely Clarissa. His other half.

For he could deny it no longer, he was every bit as much in love with her. Had been in love with her for who knows how long, but was too stupid to recognise it. Calling it lust, desire, bewitchment, refusing to recognise that this need to see her, be with her, was anything other than love. He had been too afraid to admit it, but he was afraid no longer. If only it wasn't too late. If she would only forgive him.

Impatiently, Kit urged his horses forward to overtake a cumbersome gig loaded high with bales of hay. Recklessly he took a corner at breakneck speed, narrowly missing a crossing sweeper standing idly in the middle of the road, barely noticing the string of expletives that trailed in the air behind him. A mere half-hour after saying goodbye to Letitia, Kit pulled up in front of the Warrington household.

A maid in a mobbed cap showed him in to a small parlour where a faded woman much resembling Amelia was waiting. 'Lady Maria, I presume. Lord Rasenby, at your service, ma'am. I am come to see Clarissa, if I may.'

'I am surprised at your temerity, my lord. I cannot believe that you have the nerve to intrude on our privacy like this. Vile seducer.' With this, Lady Maria sank back on to the sofa, clutching a small vial to her nose, and dissolved into wild sobs.

The noise brought the maid back. Kit watched, appalled and intrigued, for he had never seen such a determined display of distress. Forgetting that Lady Maria had quite legitimate grounds for being upset, he stood to one side as first, feathers were burnt under her nose, then her wrists were chaffed, a cordial was poured, and when this had no effect, the bell was rung. Lady Maria continued to sob, and still Kit stood, becoming bored and more than a little anxious as time passed and Clarissa did not appear.

The door opened and finally Clarissa entered the room. Seeing Kit, she stopped abruptly and blushed a deep, fiery red. Her voice, however, was cold. 'I have no idea what you are doing here, Lord Rasenby, but as you can see you have upset Mama greatly. Please go, and let me tend to my mother.'

'My God, Clarissa, how do you stand it? I'm extremely glad that you take after your father's side of the family. Is she always this operatic?'

She couldn't help it; she smiled reluctantly. 'No, no, not always quite this bad. Please leave, I beg you, Kit. I wrote you a letter, which you have obviously not yet received. When you have read it you'll understand that you have no need to visit me again.'

'I've already seen the letter, Clarissa. That's not why I am here.'

She looked up at this, temporarily arresting her ministrations. Lady Maria lay quieter, but still incoherent, on the sofa at her side. 'If you've read it, you'll know that you have no need, nor any right to be here.' Clarissa turned back to her mama, after some time succeeding in making her comfortable enough to summon the maid to take over.

Lady Maria sat up. 'Clarissa! Do not, I beseech you, sit alone with that—that monster!'

Clarissa walked purposefully towards the door. 'It's all right, Mama, Lord Rasenby is just leaving.'

Kit followed her out into the hall, but when she made to open the door to show him out, placed a restraining hand on her arm. 'Clarrie, I must speak with you. Is there a room where we may be private?'

'I have nothing further to say, Kit. All is at an end, I said so clearly in my letter. And you promised, Kit, you were quite specific, in fact, that you would make no more offers if I turned you down. My answer is no, and it is final. Now please, let me alone.' She was pale where she had been flushed earlier, determined not to break down, nor to show him how much this was costing her.

'Please, allow me just a few moments. It's very important, Clarissa. Please? I promise not to touch you. I want only to talk.'

'Can I trust you?'

'Please, Clarrie.'

It was the edge of desperation in his voice that swayed her. Without another word she directed him into a small, dark room at the back of the house where she was wont to do the household accounts. She closed the door behind them, but stood with her back to it, as if poised for flight. 'I'm listening, but you must be swift. It's cold in here, and I must go back to tend to Mama.'

Having never in his life thought to make a proposal of marriage, Kit had not considered how to phrase it. He therefore plunged into words without any of the finesse he prided himself on when making a proposal of a less permanent nature. 'I'm sorry. I was wrong. I didn't listen to you. I didn't believe you. I've made a big mistake, thinking all the time that you were lying to me when you spoke the truth about yourself. I got it wrong, and now I want to make it right between us.'

'I've told you, Kit, you have nothing to apologise for. I consented to everything we did together. You neither abducted nor seduced me. And in any case, both are beside the point. I won't become your mistress. I won't spend every day wondering if it's going to be our last together. I won't go to sleep at night wondering if you will decide you've had enough of me on the morrow. I can't live like that, Kit, I won't do it. Now, if that is all, I must go and see Mama.'

'Clarrie. I'm not asking you to be my mistress.' As she turned to open the door, Kit grabbed her wrists, only to drop them as Clarissa stared haughtily at him.

'You said you wouldn't touch me.'

He flushed and loosed his hold. 'I'm sorry. Don't go. God, I'm making such a mess of this. Clarissa, I'm trying to ask you to marry me.'

'Don't be silly, Kit, it's the last thing you want, and there's really no need.'

'There's every need. I want you. I don't want you to go off and be a governess somewhere.'

'How did you know that was my plan?'

'What? I don't know. My sister may have mentioned it this morning, I don't know. Does it matter, for God's sake?'

'What has your sister to do with all of this?'

Too late, Kit remembered that Clarissa knew nothing of Lady Constance's visit to Letitia. Too late, he realised just how Clarissa would interpret his proposal in the light of this knowledge. Foolishly, for almost the first time in his life allowing his emotions to get in the way of his logic, Kit tried to brush aside the facts. 'My sister has nothing to do with this. I just—she called on me this morning.'

'Why? Why should your sister take an interest in my affairs? She knows nothing of me. What is going on, Kit?'

'Your aunt and my sister are good friends,' Kit blurted out. 'Your aunt confided some of our affairs to my sister. My sister was mightily displeased with my behaviour. She came this morning to inform me of such.'

'My aunt is acquainted with your sister? Yes, now I remember, she mentioned it; I had forgotten. But I swore my aunt to secrecy. I thought Aunt Constance of all people would have wanted to keep the whole thing as quiet as possible. This is dreadful.'

'Clarissa, your aunt quite naturally wanted to make me, through the medium of my sister, feel a little of the guilt I sorely deserve for the grievous hurt I inflicted on you. She is angry at me on your behalf, and wants me to suffer. Do not blame her for that.'

'But I told her it was not your fault. I told her I did nothing I didn't want to. I told her to keep it to herself.' Clarissa left the doorway to take a quick turn about the room, her brain in a turmoil. 'And what has any of this to do with you asking me to marry you? You were certainly

not of that inclination yesterday, as I know only too well.
Tell me, Kit, what has changed your mind today?'

'Yesterday I was not myself. I didn't see things as
clearly. I want you more than anything in the world, I
see that now. I know you want me.'

'You said yourself, Kit, that passion fades.'

'I was wrong, Clarrie. What exists between us, I've
never felt that before, never.'

'Well, but that doesn't mean you'll feel the same
thing in a month, a year, ten years hence, does it? And
your track record, you know, is not in your favour—two
months, I believe, is the longest period you have ever
managed to remain faithful.' She felt as though the pain
would prevent her speaking, but she was determined to
finish things while she retained some dignity. So easy it
would be to give in. But so painful it would be to watch
Kit spend his life regretting.

'You're different, Clarrie,' Kit said desperately. '*I'm*
different now, you've changed me. And I know the truth
about you. I'm so sorry I didn't believe you.'

'That's just it, Kit, you didn't believe me yesterday,
you wouldn't believe me today, or tomorrow either. It's
your sister you believe, your sister who enlightened you,
and it is due to your sister that you are here now. In fact,
were it not for your sister, you would still be at home, and
no thought of marriage would have crossed your mind.'

'No, that's not it—well, not precisely. I would have
realised, sooner or later, Clarrie. Surely the only thing
that matters is that I have come to my senses now?' Kit
could see her retreating inside herself with every word,
and felt helpless to stop it. This was all going horribly
wrong. 'Clarissa, I want you to marry me. I've never
offered that to anyone before, I've never wanted to. But

I want to offer it to you now. Say yes, say you will be my wife.'

'You asked me to say yes yesterday, and I did. But I was sadly mistaken, wasn't I? I don't think I'll make the same mistake again, Kit. Thank you for the honour, but I'm afraid I can't accept.' Clarissa blinked back the tears as she spoke, biting her lip to stop the words *yes, yes, yes* come screaming out. He did not love her. He was driven to propose by guilt, coerced by her aunt and his sister. She didn't want him on those terms. In the end, wife or mistress, she'd still wake up every morning with that same feeling of impending gloom, wondering when he would tire of her. She would not let him grow to hate her.

'But I thought you loved me.'

'My aunt again? So I can add pity to your motivations now, as if I did not feel bad enough.' Clarissa looked up at Kit, her eyes full of unshed tears. It was so difficult not to run to him, not to soothe away his pain, no matter how temporarily, with avowals of her eternal devotion. 'What I feel is of no import, Kit. You don't really want to marry me. You are merely trying to do the right thing by me, and there is no need. You say you believe me now you realise that I tell the truth. Well, if that is the case, remember what I said in the letter I left you. You did not take what I was not happy to give. You have no need to feel guilt.'

'Clarrie darling, please. I know I hurt you, forced you, frightened you. And I'm sorry. I'll spend the rest of my life feeling sorry. But I can make amends. Please, just listen to me. You *must* listen.' Kit reached for her hand, but she wrenched free.

'No! No, I won't. I don't want your pity or your apologies, I won't listen any more, for you say nothing that I want to hear. Now please leave me alone, for I can't take any more. I will deal with my aunt, and your sister will no doubt forgive you in time. It was a lovely adventure, Kit, truly it was, and I enjoyed every minute of it. But it is over.'

'I see.' His voice was cool, his mouth a grim line of anger and hurt. Bewildered and confused as he was by her rejection, he could think of nothing else to say, nothing else to persuade her. Letitia must have misunderstood Lady Constance. He had been too quick to make assumptions himself. She didn't really love him. And it was no wonder, after the way he had treated her. He could not blame her. 'Very well, I will relieve you of my company. Please be assured, however, that you can count on me in the future if you ever need anything—anything at all.'

The touch of his lips on her hand was cool. He did not meet her eyes, but turned and left. It was almost too much to bear, knowing that she had caused such hurt. But it would be harder, so much harder, to see him repenting for his behaviour every day of their lives together, bound to her through obligation, tied to her side when all she wanted was for him to be free to be himself.

Clarissa swallowed the protest that rose to her lips as he closed the door, and tottered into a nearby chair, her legs unable to support her. This time it was final. There would be no more Kit. She should be pleased that she had not given in, pleased she had not humiliated herself with an admission of love.

Desperately reviewing his proposal, seeking some trace of emotion, some hint that he felt for her even a tiny part of the love that she felt for him, Clarissa had to admit defeat. He had asked her from a sense of duty, bullied into it by his family, no doubt relieved to have been refused. She could not build a future on such flimsy foundations. The thought was cold comfort. Distressed far beyond tears, Clarissa sat alone in the cold room, unable to move, lost in a world without Kit.

Chapter Thirteen

Robert, Marquis of Alchester, was also contemplating life without Kit Rasenby, but in his case it was a state of affairs much to be desired. In fact, he had been extremely busy making arrangements over the last twenty-four hours to bring about exactly that outcome. Envy of his childhood friend had turned over the years, like milk gone sour, into bitter hatred. Plotting Rasenby's downfall consumed almost every waking moment. Not everything that was afoot was absolutely clear, but Alchester was satisfied none the less that at last he had enough information to put his plan into action. His network of spies and outlay on bribes was finally starting to pay dividends.

The exact nature of Clarissa Warrington's place in Kit Rasenby's life still taxed him. The visits to his house in Grosvenor Square and the sojourn at Thornwood Manor, on each occasion without an escort, were not the actions of a respectable female. On the other hand, Rasenby was not in the way of asking his mistresses into his homes. There could be no doubt in Alchester's mind that the pair were lovers, but what intrigued him was Kit's intentions towards the wench. She was Constance Denby's niece, not one of his common flirts. Rasenby had called on her today, leaving those showy chestnuts of his to be walked in the cold for more than an hour. It was not like him to be so careless of his horses. Whatever Rasenby's ultimate intentions, Alchester had seen enough to know that Clarissa was important to him, and that would suffice. In Clarissa he now had a tool with which to extract his revenge.

Faith, it was satisfying, the thought that he'd finally be taking something away from his enemy. Something so obviously highly prized. Something whose loss would definitely pain him deeply. Someone whose disappearance would cause him to suffer agonies. Alchester almost rubbed his hands together with glee at the thought, his weak mouth set in a malicious grin. When Rasenby found the chit had been abducted and seduced it would pay in some part for all the humiliations Robert had suffered at his hands over the years. It was perfect. With profound satisfaction, Alchester set about making his final preparations.

Clarissa received his letter later that day. The Marquis of Alchester requested her presence at a meeting to discuss the settlement of her mother's debts. An office in the city was named, and the time of the appointment given for early the following morning. Exhausted and heavy hearted from her interview with Kit, Clarissa looked at the contents dully, convinced that it meant her mother was doomed to an early death in prison. This terrible thought failed to shock—Clarissa was numb—and she merely noted the address and time and thought no more of it. So clouded was her mind that it did not even occur to her to wonder why the letter was not addressed to Lady Maria direct.

* * *

She spent a listless day and could only toy with her dinner, scarcely aware of her sister's unusually animated prattling to Mama beside her. The meeting between Lady Constance and Edward had gone well, it seemed, and Lady Constance had intimated that she would not be averse to pulling the strings necessary for Edward's promotion. Amelia was transformed by happiness—although oblivious as ever to the cares of others.

'And I must have a decent trousseau, Mama, for I am like to mix with many of Edward's new clients, to say nothing of having to give my own parties as a married lady. Edward says that I must not expect too much, but with Aunt Constance behind him, I know it won't be long before we are rich. Oh, Mama, I am so happy. Edward says—'

'I am going to bed.' Clarissa rose abruptly from the table, scarcely glancing at the two faces staring at her in consternation.

'Yes, dear, but we were discussing Amelia's trousseau. We would welcome your views.'

'Your time would be better spent discussing how we are to pay the butcher's bill, Mama. And as to Amelia's trousseau—perhaps we should wait to see if Edward will actually propose before buying anything.'

'Clarrie dear, that is most cruel and very unlike you. Are you quite well, dear?'

'Oh, never mind her, Mama, she's just jealous because I have a beau who wants to marry me and hers doesn't. Even though she has tried quite *everything* to persuade him—is that not so, sister?'

As she watched Clarissa turn pale at the remark, even Amelia realised she'd gone too far. 'Clarrie, you mustn't worry, must she, Mama? We don't need Kit Rasenby or any of his sort now, do we? Perhaps once I'm married I'll be able to help find someone for you.'

'It doesn't matter. I don't care. I'm going to bed.' With a shrug, Clarissa left. Almost nothing touched her. She felt as if she was seeing the world through a thick wall of glass, which naught could penetrate. Nothing mattered, save that she would never see Kit again. Blinking away a single lonely tear, she took to her bed and fell into a deep, haunted sleep.

Awaking the next day, the future seemed bleaker than ever. Listlessly, she got ready for her trip to the city, barely glancing in the mirror as she thrust her hair into a simple knot and donned a cloak over her plain cambric gown, dressing rather for the weather than the vogue. Expecting to return before either Lady Maria or Amelia rose from their bedchambers, Clarissa decided against leaving any word of her whereabouts, for Mama would only get into a state. She left the house for her meeting with the Marquis of Alchester unnoticed even by the maid.

Twenty minutes later the hackney cab deposited her in the busy animated bustle of the streets of the Fleet in the heart of the City. Clarissa stood, bewildered by the multitude of cries from the streetmongers offering up pint pots of ink, bundles of faggots or pecks of oysters for sale. Directly above her she spotted the sign of Coutts Bank, and remembered her father had once mentioned doing business there. She wondered if they served Kit, and reminded herself that it was none of her business who he banked with. All these people going about their business, making money, drawing up contracts, with hardly a glance at her. To the world, it's as if I neither exist nor matter, she thought with unaccustomed bitterness. For one mad moment Clarissa felt an overwhelming urge to scream aloud, *Does no one know or care that my heart is torn asunder!* Repressing the thought, however, she instead stepped into the address she had been given, to be shown into a dingy office by a clerk.

As she sat opposite a desk, alone in the stuffy room, Clarissa grew ill at ease, realising for the first time that the requested interview was rather unorthodox. Why had the letter been addressed to herself and not Mama? Why was the Marquis of Alchester meeting her here, in this run-down office? And what could they have to discuss when the debt was not yet due? A slight tremor of fear ran through her. Something was amiss here. No one knew where she was. She should leave now and go home. But even as she rose to go the door opened and a man appeared, closing it firmly behind him as he entered.

He was slight of build, seeming neither young nor old. His face showed signs of dissipation, his eyes hooded, the lids pulled downwards by an intricate network of lines. His nose was long and thin and his gaze darted this way and that even though there was no one else in the room. His skin was pale, the colour of one who does not often see the sun. His movements were nervous and fidgety. The Marquis of Alchester reminded Clarissa of nothing so much as a small rodent.

But he was impeccably dressed and smiling, a tight smile, thinning his already narrow lips into a straight line. 'Miss Warrington? Robert, Marquis of Alchester, your servant, madam.'

The touch of his hand was cold as a corpse, his lips barely grazed her glove. Clarissa shivered, her fear taking shape as he bent over her. Whatever this man's intentions, they were not noble. She must escape.

'I am afraid there has been a mistake, my lord. I should not have come. Forgive me for wasting your time, but my mother is waiting for me outside. I came only to inform you to write to me with your terms that I may consider them on my mother's behalf. Now, I must bid you good day.' Clarissa gave a small bow and moved towards the door.

'I'm afraid I must ask you to stay for a moment, Miss Warrington. I'm sure your mama can spare you.'

'I'm afraid not, my lord. We have a morning call to make, we are expected, and I am late already.' Her voice trembled, but she stood her ground.

'Sit down, Clarissa. You are not going anywhere. You may spare me your pathetic attempts at lies. Your mama is not waiting for you outside. You are quite alone. You don't think your arrival went unnoticed, do you?'

His voice was cold, like a breath from a cadaver. Fear clutched her insides. She sat down, silent, unable to trust her voice, cursing her stupidity for not having informed anyone of her intentions.

'Your mama owes me quite a little sum, doesn't she? And I doubt she has the means to pay it, am I right?' Robert Alchester looked at the woman before him. She was terrified, he had no doubt about that, though determined not to show it. He liked a bit of spirit in a woman—that augured well for later. She was not beautiful in the common way, but there was something about her, a challenging look, a tilt to her face, and a curvaceous body despite her slenderness—yes, he could see why Kit Rasenby found her to his liking.

Clarissa cleared her throat to speak. Her voice was quiet, but resolute, despite the shaking that was threatening to prevent her from moving. 'The debt is not due for some time. There is nothing to discuss at present. I must leave now.'

'You are going nowhere, my dear. At least, not home in any event.'

'What do you mean?' Clarissa got quickly to her feet and tried to push past the Marquis, but he caught her arm in a firm grip, his bony fingers showing surprising strength. She stood without struggling, repulsed by his proximity, her breath coming in shallow, sharp gasps. 'Unhand me at once, sir!'

Robert Alchester merely laughed, a soft, low, vicious growl that made her skin prickle. 'Very good, but you will learn to be more—accommodating—unless you wish to be harmed. I have no wish to hurt you, Clarissa, but I will do so if I need to.'

His face was close to hers, those cold, icy eyes watching her like a hawk, his mouth a thin, sneering line. She had no difficulty in believing him. He looked like the type to inflict pain for pleasure, would no doubt enjoy seeing her suffer. The mixture of distaste and disgust showed clearly on her expressive face.

'Yes, I can see you believe me. Now sit down and I'll explain all.'

Clarissa thought it prudent to obey and sat back down without a word.

'Directly, we will leave this building. My carriage is waiting, you will accompany me into it without a struggle. If you do struggle, I have the means to overpower you—thus.' He held up a small brown vial. 'You will not like to be unconscious, will you? No, I thought not. We are going on a short journey to one of my estates—you will be familiar with the terrain, for you have already visited my neighbour, Lord Rasenby, at Thornwood Manor.'

'How do you know that?'

'There's little I don't know, Clarissa. I know you've been to France with him, and I know you are lovers.'

Her gasp of surprise and her blush confirmed this. 'This doesn't make sense. Wait a minute.' Suddenly she remembered. 'It was you, wasn't it? You who informed the customs men that night. But I still don't understand. What have my mother's debts to do with all this?'

'A lucky chance only, my dear. I took them in lieu of payment from a less fortunate opponent at hazard. I confess, at the time I would much rather have had the money. But when I realised what they were I decided that after all fate was smiling on me. For they brought you to me. And when Lord Rasenby knows I have you, I will have my satisfaction at last.'

'So, you have some sort of grudge against Kit—Lord Rasenby—is that it? But that still doesn't make sense. I am nothing to him, cannot influence him, you can achieve nothing by kidnapping me.'

'You underestimate your charms, Clarissa. I am sure that Kit Rasenby will be extremely upset to find you have decided to keep company with me, rather than him—for that is what I shall tell him, you know. It will give me immense satisfaction, knowing I have taken something he treasures. To say nothing of the pleasure that your company will afford me too, of course.'

The lascivious smile that accompanied this remark left Clarissa in no doubt about his ultimate intentions. She had to act quickly if she was to save herself—but how? Of a certain to be unconscious would be fatal, she could not risk it. Her best chance would be during the journey, for they must change horses at some point. He would not ravish her in a coach, surely? 'Very well, I'll come with you, my lord. But I warn you I am expected at home, and will be looked for soon, if I do not return.'

'Yes? Now, why do I not believe you? It is of no matter—we will be gone from here and no one knows our direction. If you are ready, madam, we will leave.'

Her knees were shaking so much she could barely stand, but Clarissa brushed Alchester's arm away angrily. 'I can walk, my lord, I have no need of your support.'

Slowly, unable to quite believe what was happening, Clarissa descended the steps from the building and climbed into the waiting coach. The Marquis of Alchester followed, close enough to ensure she could not make a run for safety, pausing only to hand a sealed note to the small boy waiting with the postillion. Once inside the coach however, he took the seat opposite, making no attempt to touch her. Deciding to feign sleep, Clarissa closed her eyes and focused all her thoughts and energy on escape.

Kit woke late. He had fallen asleep as dawn broke, having spent most of the night going over and over that final interview with Clarissa in his mind. It had all gone so horribly wrong, nothing he said had come out right. He could not believe she didn't care. Could not believe how miserable he felt at the thought of a future without her. Could not see the attraction of a world without Clarissa by his side. The image of her as he left her house yesterday haunted him—her beautiful little face set like stone, her eyes brimming with unshed tears, her luscious mouth held in a stern line, the words she was biting back lost to him for ever.

He had done this to her. The only person in the world whom he loved beyond words. He had been so overwrought yesterday he hadn't even told her so. But she knew, she must know, it had been implicit in all he said. Still, the actual words had not been spoken. He would go back today to try again, do it properly this time. And if she didn't listen today, then tomorrow. And the day after that. And every after that, if it took a lifetime to win her back. With this invigorating thought, Kit got out of bed.

He was breaking his fast when his butler came in, looking apologetic. 'Forgive the intrusion my lord, but there is a visitor demanding to see you urgently. A Lady Maria Warrington.'

Assuming that she had come to berate him again, Kit rose from the table wearily. 'Faith, Hodges, I am weary of these women and their early morning tirades. Can you not be more effective at keeping them at bay, man?'

Kit read the reproachful look on Hodges's face only too well. 'Oh, very well, I take your point. It would take a platoon of the dragoon guards to dissuade the unholy triumvirate of my sister, Miss Warrington or her mother from their stated course. You had better show her in, then.'

Lady Maria entered the room in a breathless state, her hat askew, her scarf, which had come loose, trailing on the floor, threatening to trip her over. 'Where is she, my lord? I demand to know, what have you done with my daughter.'

Firmly closing the door on his fascinated butler, Kit hastened over to Lady Maria. His experience of her was limited, but it was suffice to know that a fainting fit was imminent.

'Won't you sit down, madam, and take a moment to calm yourself.' A firm hand on her back guided her to a chair, into which she tottered gratefully.

Looking up at Kit, her mouth trembling, Lady Maria heaved a great sob and waved an accusing finger in his direction. 'Where is she? Where is my Clarissa? Oh, say you have not murdered her, you assassin! My poor dear, she does not deserve such a fate as this.'

Realising that there was actually something more drastically amiss with Lady Maria than a need to vent her spleen, Kit bit firmly down on his temper. 'Madam, I can see that you are distressed, but there is no need for histrionics. I haven't seen Clarissa since yesterday. Do you mean to tell me she has gone missing?'

'Missing! Likely dead of a broken heart and hidden in your attics, if nothing else. You blackguard! I know you have her here. Let me see her. Oh, was ever a poor widow more badly treated. First it is the butcher, demanding settlement before I have even had my chocolate. Then it is Amelia, demanding money for a trousseau when she has not yet received a proposal, although I am sure that Edward *will* propose, for he is not the type to be leading innocent girls astray—unlike *some* people, my Lord Rasenby.' A black look accompanied this remark. 'And now my darling, my sensible, my poor ruined Clarissa has disappeared, and you stand there denying responsibility when it is all your fault, and what am I to tell Lady Constance, when I promised I would look after her?' Breaking into sobs, Lady Maria leaned back into the chair and for some minutes cried heartily, oblivious of Kit's attempts to revive her.

'Madam, I need to understand your meaning fully. I beg of you, tell me what is wrong that I may help. Where is Clarissa?' Kit was becoming increasingly angry, concerned and frustrated in equal measures.

'You cannot fool me. I know she's here. I've come to fetch her. My poor lamb, strayed from the fold under such a vile influence as you. You monster!'

'For God's sake, will you be calm and tell me what is going on.' Looking up to see his butler had entered the room, Kit let go of Lady Maria's hands, which he had been chafing. 'Hodges, fetch some brandy. This lady is not well.'

'Yes, my lord. This note came for you just now, my lord. I thought it may be important.'

'Yes, thank you. Now go and get me some help before this—this lady becomes hysterical.' Abandoning Lady Maria to her tears, Kit snatched the note from the salver. He broke the seal and glanced at the contents, then sat down abruptly. Robert, Marquis of Alchester, sent his compliments. He felt it only fair that Kit should be informed, in the light of *his previous relationship*, that Clarissa Warrington had agreed to submit to Robert's *protection*. Miss Warrington wished Kit to understand that he should withdraw *forthwith* from any attempt at future contact with her *in the light of her new circumstances*. The Marquis and Miss Warrington were leaving town for a short period away from the distractions of society in order to *enjoy the fruits of their liaison*.

Kit looked at the note, completely dumbfounded. The words leapt out from the page, taunting him. His first coherent thought was that he had not known Clarissa and Robert Alchester to be acquainted. His next was closer to the truth, and he felt a cold fear clutch at him as he took in the import of what had been written. Alchester was using Clarissa in revenge against him. She would not have gone willingly. Kit's emotions were everything that the Marquis had hoped for when he had so gleefully penned the note a few hours previously.

Clarissa was in danger. And he didn't know where she was. And she was in danger only because of him. My God, could he do any more damage if he tried? He was finally paying for his years of raking, that was for sure—and paying a price beyond anything he had thought possible. Kit clutched at his hair and groaned, tempted for an instant to join with Lady Maria in hysterics.

The despair was short-lived. He would find his Clarissa, he would rescue her—he had to. The situation could not possibly be as hopeless as it appeared. He would not allow it to be.

A racking sob reminded Kit of Lady Maria's presence. Grabbing the tray of brandy that Hodges proffered and thrusting his butler from the room again, he decided that extreme measures were needed. Bracing himself, he administered a ringing slap to Lady Maria's face.

The effect was immediate. She stopped crying and gasped, staring up at him in astonishment. Forestalling any speech, he held a glass of brandy to her mouth and forced her to take two large gulps.

'Before you accuse me of either assault or making you drunk, madam, listen closely,' Kit said, as Lady Maria gasped, fish-like, in her chair. 'This letter is from the Marquis of Alchester. He has kidnapped Clarissa. Can you think of any reason why she would have gone to meet him, for I cannot understand it? Were they acquainted in any way?'

Subdued by the harsh treatment and stirred by the genuine concern in Kit's voice, Lady Maria sat up. 'Alchester, you say? Alchester? No, she has never mentioned that name before. Unless—no, it's not possible. But stay, let me think. Alchester? Yet the name is familiar. Why— oh, I have it. Oh my goodness. But surely... No, no, he would not. But then he might—and of course, Clarissa would—'

'For the love of God, madam,' Kit said through gritted teeth, 'speak slowly and clearly, I have no wish to strike you again. What is the connection between them?'

'Well, there is no need to be so harsh, my lord.'

'Madam, your daughter has been kidnapped. Do you not wish to find her?'

'Well, of course I do, my lord. I am just as keen to find her this time as I was the last time she was kidnapped. By yourself, in case you need reminding.'

'I can't waste time on discussion, madam, Clarrie is in danger. Alchester is not a man to be trifled with. I need to know why she was persuaded to meet him.'

'Oh dear, what have I done? If it is indeed the same Alchester, I owe him a terrible amount of money. I borrowed some money, and then the nice man I borrowed it from passed on the debt to another man at the hazard table. And he wanted to be paid much sooner. And I thought I should have to go to prison. Except Clarissa said not to worry because she would take care of it. And since she always *does* take care of things, I didn't worry. Except that Constance—Clarissa's aunt, you know— Constance told me only yesterday that the man who is dunning me is the Marquis of Alchester. So perhaps she also told Clarissa, and Clarissa has gone to meet him because of me. And, oh dear, it is all my fault—what am I to do?'

Kit struggled to make sense of Lady Maria's confession before dismissing it as irrelevant. 'You should go home, madam, and await word from me. I think I know where he might have taken her. Don't worry.'

'Don't worry? What do you intend to do?'

'I am going to fetch her back and I am going to marry her, madam. But I cannot stay to discuss this with you. Every moment is precious.' As he left the room, calling to Hodges to summon his groom, Kit heard Lady Maria give way again to tears. He made a mental note to inform

Clarissa that he very much regretted her mama could not form part of their future household. He would buy her a house of her own. In the country. As far away from him as possible.

Rapping out a stream of orders, Kit pulled on his hat and picked up his riding crop. He had no doubt as to Alchester's destination, his estate next to Thornwood Manor being the only one within a day's journey of London, but he had no idea how much of a head start they had. Knowing the state of Alchester's finances, it was unlikely that they would make the journey with more than two horses, however, so Kit reckoned he had a good chance of catching them if he went on horseback. And knowing his Clarissa, he had no doubt she would do everything in her power to delay the Marquis in the hope of rescue. He would not allow himself to consider the possibility that he might be too late.

Urging his horse into a gallop as soon as they were free from the traffic of the town, Kit reviewed Lady Maria's revelations. That she had been so foolish as to get into debt beyond her means did not surprise him, for Clarissa's mama was as stupid a woman as he had yet come across. She had uttered but one thing of interest, that she thought her daughter likely to die of a broken heart. Clarissa *did* love him. *Of course she loved him.*

How very foolishly he had behaved yesterday, Kit realised. He hadn't once said the only important thing—that he loved her. He had attempted explanations when he should have swept her into his arms and kissed her. He had assumed Clarissa knew how he felt, had been so devastated at her refusal as to leave without telling her. Promising himself he would tell her every day for the rest of their lives together if only he could reach her in time, Kit spurred his horse on, their fast pace eating up the miles from the town and south into the open countryside in record time.

Fortunately for him, Alchester was in no hurry. As Kit had correctly deduced, his coach was driven by a team of just two horses. Inside, Clarissa continued to pretend sleep as she racked her brains for a plan to escape. She had come up with no idea other than to make a break from her abductor at the first posting inn, and had been occupying her mind this past half-hour in wondering how long it would be before Mama would miss her, and what, if anything, she would do when she did. They had been on the road about two hours when the blast of horns warned her that they were pulling up for a change.

Clarissa yawned, as if just awakened. Alchester watched from the seat opposite, a lazy smile on his cold face.

'Where are we, my lord?'

'We are stopped for a change of horses. You may descend, madam, if you wish, and partake of some refreshment. But don't, I beg of you, try to escape. The landlord is known to me, and will ensure that we are private with no interference. Any noise or fuss will lead only to embarrassment.'

'I'll be discovered eventually, my lord. You had as well stop now, before it is too late. Let me return home and I will say no more of this outrage.'

His soft laugh made her shiver. 'You have a deal of courage my dear; it will be a positive pleasure to tame you. I pay you the compliment, even, that I would enjoy it without the spice of knowing I am taking Rasenby's property.'

They descended from the coach. Alchester urged

Clarissa towards the ramshackle inn and directly into a parlour at the back. The ostlers, busy with the change of horses, had their backs turned—deliberately, Clarissa could not but think—and there was no sign of anyone else. Coffee and brandy awaited them in the parlour.

Clarissa took her time, stripping off her gloves, sitting down, pouring herself some coffee with an almost-steady hand. 'I repeat my lord, you have mistaken your mark. I am nothing to Lord Rasenby, he cares naught for my fate. Whatever your plan is, to rouse him by kidnapping me is bound to fail.'

Alchester kissed the tips of his fingers and bowed. 'Bravo, my dear. Really, with every minute of your delightful company you make me happier to have found you. But I know you are lying, you see. You have set far too many precedents with Rasenby for me to believe you mean nothing to him. Any fool can see that. And I am not, I assure you, a fool.'

'What do you mean?'

'Dining alone with you in Grosvenor Square. Taking you to Thornwood Park. The trip on the *Sea Wolf*, of course. Your visit to him the other day. His visit to your home yesterday.'

Alchester smiled contentedly at Clarissa's shocked expression. 'Yes, you have been watched every step of the way. Maybe now you will take me seriously. You see now why I cannot believe, my dear Clarissa, that the gentleman could spend so much time with you and have no feelings. You make too little of yourself. But this discussion is become tedious. Let us turn our minds to more pleasant topics.'

'I have no wish for conversation, sir. You've kidnapped me, and my mother will be searching for me. Please, I beseech you, let me go. Let me go at once.'

She was frightened. This couldn't be happening. Forcing herself to calm down, thinking only to delay the moment when they had to go back into the coach, Clarissa tried a different tack. 'Why do you hate Kit—Lord Rasenby so, my lord? How can he have so wronged you so as to drive you to such desperate acts?'

Alchester's voice was bitter, the venom in his words clear. 'You wouldn't understand. I've known him all my life. All my life he's taken everything I've ever wanted, been everything I've ever wanted to be. He's bested me at everything, at every turn. But this time I'm victorious. This time I've won.'

'Not necessarily, Robert.' Kit stood in the doorway, mud splattered, his hair in disarray, his riding crop clutched in one hand and a grim look of controlled fury darkening his handsome countenance.

'Kit!'

'Rasenby!' Before she could move, Alchester had Clarissa in a firm grasp, one hand clasped around her waist, the other at her throat. 'She's mine, Rasenby. You are too late.'

'No, Kit, no. It's not true.'

But Clarissa's words fell on deaf ears. With a snarl of rage, Kit crossed the room. In one fluid movement he wrenched Alchester's hands from Clarissa, pushed her to the side, and landed a punch so hard on Alchester's jaw that he staggered back against the settle by the fire, knocking over a set of irons. It was a blow of which even the champion, Gentleman Jackson, would have been proud.

Recovering quickly, Alchester pushed himself upright, at the same time grabbing a poker with his left hand. As Kit moved in to land another blow, Alchester raised the poker. Clarissa screamed and ran at him, pushing with

all her might. Her attack deflected his aim. The poker
missed Kit's head, but hit him a glancing blow on the
shoulder, causing him to fall back, the punch he was
aiming finding only air.

The poker clattered to the floor. Alchester searched
for it with one hand, keeping an eye on his opponent. He
knew that he was no match for Kit without a weapon. As
his fingers felt the edge of the fire iron, Kit recovered his
balance and moved forward, kicking it out of Alchester's
reach. This time Kit's punch hit Alchester's nose, drawing a spurt of blood. Giving him no time to hit back, Kit
planted a second punch square on Alchester's jaw. He
went down heavily, almost without a sound, and lay on
the wooden floor with his eyes closed.

'Oh God, you've killed him.' Clarissa went to kneel
at Alchester's side, grasping his wrist to feel for a pulse.

'Don't be ridiculous, Clarrie, you can no more die of
a punch to the jaw than you can of a scratch on the arm,
more's the pity. Let him be and come here. Are you safe?'

She looked up, taken aback at the raw edge in his
voice, and saw the worry reflected in his strained face.
Kit's dark blue eyes searched her countenance anxiously, his mouth a grim line. He was concerned for her. A
flicker of hope sprang to life in the darkness of Clarrie's
heart. What if Alchester was right? What if she really
did mean more to Kit than she realised?

But she had been here too many times before. 'I'm
fine. I promise you I took no harm from him, save fright
and embarrassment at my own stupidity for falling into
such a simple trap. Give me a handkerchief, Kit, I must
staunch some of this blood.'

'He can look after himself. Come here, Clarrie.' Kit
leaned down to grasp her hand, and pulled her to her feet.
'I was worried. Really worried. You wouldn't believe just

how worried, you stupid girl. You really must break this habit you have of allowing yourself to be abducted.'

'Were you, Kit, really worried?' Clarissa smiled wanly, looking up into his eyes. She blinked at the blaze of emotion she saw in their dark depths. 'Kit?'

'Clarrie. Clarrie, I…'

Alchester groaned, startling them both, and tried to sit up. Reluctantly, Kit pulled back from Clarissa's gaze, turning to view his adversary. 'Get up,' he said grimly. 'Get to your feet and get out of my sight. You are lucky to escape so lightly. Take heed, Alchester, you get just this one chance. If I ever hear of anything, any rumours, any word at all, of your doings today, or if you breathe one word of scandal concerning Miss Warrington, I will ruin you, I swear. I have the means, I know you're in debt up to your scrawny neck. So get out, and crawl back into whatever hole you came from.'

Alchester stood, clutching Kit's bloodied handkerchief to his face, his eyes burning with hatred and impotent rage at his ignoble defeat. Reluctantly, he realised he had no choice but to obey. A brief bow to Clarissa and he left the room, cursing under his breath. Not only had his plan failed, he had been revealed in the cold light of day as Kit's enemy. He knew Rasenby too well to argue. He had no wish to be ruined or ostracised.

Kit shut the door firmly behind him. 'Now, Clarissa fair, we can be sure of no further interruptions.'

'Kit, take me home. Mama will be worried.'

A brief smile crossed his face at that. 'You have no idea how worried. She accused me first of murder, then of hiding your body in my attics.'

'Oh, please tell me she did not. I will die of embarrassment.'

'She called me a blackguard too.'

A small gurgle of laughter escaped from Clarissa. 'Oh, no, surely not.'

'I assure you. And that was on top of vile seducer from yesterday. Oh yes, and monster. I don't think I stand in very good stead with your mama, although even she could not find a way to blame me when she realised you must have been tricked into meeting Alchester in order to discuss her debts. What can you have been thinking of, you foolish child, it's not like you to be so easily taken in?'

'I know, I realised it was a trick, but it was too late. I don't suppose Alchester will be dunning Mama now, after today. It doesn't matter though, they are gaming debts and must be paid somehow.'

'As your husband, it will be my responsibility to sort that out.'

'Kit, don't let us go through all that again. You don't want to marry me. And I don't want you to hate me.'

'So that's it, my absurd, darling Clarrie. I wondered what prevented you from saying yes when I had been assured, first by your Aunt Constance and then by your dear mama, that you were dying of love for me.'

'Oh!' Clarissa flushed. 'I am *so sorry*. What you must think of us all. Please believe me, I told them again and again that it wasn't your fault, but they wouldn't listen.'

'I know you did. And I was so stupid I didn't listen to you either. But when I did finally come to my senses, I realised the truth. You would only have behaved the way you did, my darling love, for one reason. But it was the one thing that I didn't think possible. Forgive me.'

'No, there's *nothing* to forgive. We must go back. I must go home. And you must forget about me.'

'But don't you see, I can never forget about you. You silly girl, I'm not proposing to you because I feel guilty or because I'm worried what my sister might think. I don't even care much about what your precious Aunt Constance thinks. I'm proposing for very, very selfish reasons. I need you. There will never be a time when I wake up feeling anything other than glad that you're by my side. In my bed. In my head. And in my heart. Darling, dearest, Clarrie, how could I ever hate you when I'm so in love with you I can't imagine life without you. I got it all wrong yesterday, said all the wrong things, didn't say the most important thing. But I won't ever get it wrong again with you by my side to keep me right. I love you, Clarrie. Please, Clarissa, don't turn me down again.'

Giving her no time to respond at all with words, Kit pulled Clarrie towards him and kissed her ruthlessly, devouring her mouth like a man drowning, clinging to the rock of their love like a man saved. Crushing her to him, and pushing her bonnet back, he looked into her beloved green eyes, eyes so honest they could never lie, eyes that told him everything he needed to know. 'I love you. I love you. Clarrie, say yes. Say yes now, or I swear I'll wear you down with the asking.'

The tiny flame of hope in her heart ignited, but still her mind urged caution. She wanted to believe him. *She so wanted to believe him.* But how could she be certain?

It was as if he read her mind. 'You're wondering if this is just some sort of temporary infatuation, aren't you? You're thinking I'll grow bored with you, regret this one day, aren't you, Clarrie?'

She could manage only a nod.

Kit looked down at her pale face, the strain of the past few days showing in the dark lines under her beautiful green eyes, eyes that were looking at him with hope, with doubt, seeking reassurance. He wanted to kiss it all away, to hold her, make love to her.

But she deserved an answer. Their whole lives depended upon this moment. 'If I had a magic wand, I'd cast a spell and you'd never doubt again. But in truth, my own darling Clarissa, I don't know what it is that makes me so sure. I can't put into words, not properly, what it is that's so different about how I feel for you. I just know that it is. In the same way as I just know, with deep and unshakeable certainty, that I need you by my side to make me complete.'

Pulling her closer, Kit wound a finger round one of her curls, then tucked it behind her ear. Giving in to the temptation of those soft lips, that beloved face, he kissed her softly, tenderly, pouring all his love, channelling everything into the kiss, feeling her respond to him in the same way. Feeling not just passion, but love, true love, enveloping them in its warm cloak.

Slightly breathless, he pulled back. 'I can't explain it, but I can feel it, and I know you feel it too. I know I love you because I just do. I know I'll never leave you because I know I'll never want anyone else. You're the other part of me, what I've been looking for all my life, and you make me whole when I didn't even know I was missing something. But I've found you now, my darling, and I won't—I can't—let you go again.'

'Oh, Kit, I've never heard anything so lovely.' Once more, Clarissa dissolved into tears, but this time they were of joy, for she believed him. He was right, and she felt it herself after all, this illogical certainty, this completeness, this simple and overwhelming love. 'Kiss me, Kit, for I love you so much.' Without waiting, she reached up and pulled him to her. This time their passion held no restraint. On the hard floor in front of the fire in a remote inn, Kit and Clarrie consummated their love.

Later, dishevelled, tired and glowing, they righted their clothing. Looking in the mirror at her face, Clarrie laughed. 'I'm afraid you've left your mark all too clearly on me, Kit. The landlady will have no doubt what we've been up to.'

Looking at her heavy lids and flushed cheeks, Kit felt a familiar stirring. He smiled lazily, his own satisfaction reflected as clearly in his disordered hair, a necktie past recovery, the sated curl to his sculpted mouth. 'I'll gladly have you branded as my property, my beautiful Clarrie, for I can't resist you. With a ring, I think, and quickly. A special licence. Tomorrow, the next day at the latest. We can shop for your trousseau later—I don't intend for you to have much need of clothes for a while.'

'Just so that we're absolutely clear this time, Kit.' Clarissa was laughing up at him, unable to believe it. 'What *exactly* am I saying yes to?'

'Just so that we're absolutely clear…' the answering smile in his eyes took her breath away '…you're saying yes to a lifetime of me, me and no one else but me. You're saying yes to being loved more than anyone has been loved before. You're saying yes to me beside you always. I'll be the first thing you see every day, and the last thing you see every night. You're saying yes to a passion that will light up the sky. To sharing every part of my life. To being my better half. And on top of all that, you're saying yes to being my wife.'

'Yes. Oh, Kit, yes.' There was nothing more that needed to be said and nothing else that mattered. Their kiss said it all, a kiss that had a new tenderness, a breath-taking prelude to a lifetime of passion and fulfilment, a promise that would never be broken.

* * * * *

THE RAKE'S
REBELLIOUS LADY

ANNE HERRIES

Anne Herries, winner of the Romantic Novelists' Association romance prize 2004, lives in Cambridgeshire. She is fond of watching wildlife, and spoils the birds and squirrels that are frequent visitors to her garden. Anne loves to write about the beauty of nature, and sometimes puts a little into her books—although they are mostly about love and romance. She writes for her own enjoyment, and to give pleasure to her readers.

Chapter One

'My word, Freddie, that pair of yours are out-and-outers,' George Bellingham said, admiring the thoroughbred chestnuts that Sir Frederick Rathbone was driving in Hyde Park that May morning. 'You are an excellent judge of horseflesh. I shall come to you next time I decide to improve my stable.'

George was walking, Sir Frederick having pulled over to oblige him. He now offered the reins, inviting him to climb into the high-wheeled phaeton.

'Care to try them yourself?' he asked. 'They have as sweet mouths as any you'll find in London. I was lucky to get them. Came from Farringdon's stable. He sold them to me after a run of ill luck at the tables.'

'Had some of that myself recently,' Bellingham said, pulling a wry face. 'We can't all be as fortunate as you!' He looked thoughtful for a moment, then, 'It surprises me that Farringdon sold them; I thought they were his pride and joy.'

'Needs must when the devil drives, I dare say.' Freddie laughed, a gleam of mockery in his dark eyes. He was a handsome devil, arrogant, wilful and the bane of match-making society mamas, for at eight and twenty, he had managed to avoid all the traps set for him with consummate ease.

'Lucky at the tables, unlucky in love, is that not what they say?' Freddie's look challenged and provoked his friend. He did not add that the chestnut horses had been in settlement of an overdue gambling debt and that he had offered to take them at an inflated price well above their true worth.

'Not in your case!' Bellingham retorted. 'Your latest high-flyer is a beauty, Freddie. There isn't a fellow in London who doesn't envy you the magnificent Yolanda.'

'An expensive hobby,' Freddie remarked grimly; his mistress might be a spectacular beauty, but she had a decided partiality for expensive baubles. 'As greedy in bed as out. To be honest, I weary of her. She is too predictable.'

'Good grief, man! What do you expect? She is a courtesan of the first line. They say she has consorted with crowned heads in Europe—perhaps even Bonaparte himself!'

'You don't say?' Freddie said, pulling a face. He had heard the rumour and knew it to be untrue, but could not resist teasing his friend. 'Why did I not know this before? Boney, indeed! I do not know whether to be flattered or horrified.' He shook his head as he returned to the subject of his mistress. 'I dare say she is well enough in her way, George, but she is not… Perhaps I am too particular.'

'You would not want a simpering society miss? Perhaps the lovely Miss Avondale—if you are on the catch for a wife?'

'God forbid! That insipid fairness—and that lisp! I would be bored within days—hours!' Freddie laughed mockingly. 'No, I have no thought of marriage, George. Yet I sometimes yearn for a woman I can talk to as I do to you. A partner in more than a physical sense.'

'If such a woman exists, she's mine,' Bellingham said, taking up the challenge instantly. 'A woman like that *would* be something out of the ordinary. I might consider marrying her myself.'

'Come, come, old fellow,' Freddie chided, for his friend was four and thirty, and a confirmed bachelor in his own words. 'She would have to be special indeed to tempt you.'

George nodded, but looked thoughtful. 'As you say, though I have wondered of late…' He shook his head as the horses moved restlessly, impatient at being kept waiting. 'Since neither of us is likely to meet such a lady, it is mere speculation.' He gave the reins a little flick, allowing the high-spirited horses to move on at a trot. 'Do you attend Almack's this evening?'

'Good grief, no!' Freddie said, revolted at the idea of such a wasted evening. 'When you see me there you will know that I have discovered the paragon we spoke of.' He laughed softly deep in his throat. 'I believe that you may safely assume that hell will freeze over first.'

'Oh, you will fall in the end,' George murmured, more for the sake of provoking his companion than anything. He grinned at Freddie. 'You don't care to sell these beauties, I suppose?'

'No—but I will wager them against your greys.'

'On what?' George was surprised. His greys were very good horses, but not the equal of the chestnuts.

'That a woman who could tempt me to marriage does not exist.'

George grinned, for they were in the habit of making such bets, and often on a simple thing like the turn of a card,

Freddie the winner at least three out of four times. However, he bore his friend no ill will; he could afford to gamble, and, often, the stakes were trivial. 'I'll willingly put my greys up against your pair—but we must have a time limit.'

'Christmas,' Freddie said, a wicked glint in his eyes. He had made the bet for sheer devilment, as a cure for the slow, creeping boredom that had come over him of late.

'Done!' George cried instantly. 'But you must attend all the main affairs of the Season, no running off to hide in the country or disappearing to your club until you've met all the new hopefuls.'

'Fair enough,' Freddie agreed. 'But I draw the line at Almack's. When you see me there you will know that you have won your bet.'

'Indeed I shall,' Bellingham said for he knew his friend too well. 'I would not be attending myself, except that my sister is bringing her daughter to town and I have agreed that I will escort them. I assure you that Miss Julia Fairchild is not the lady you are seeking. She is seventeen and a shy child, so I must do my best for her—but we have the whole Season to look forward to, Freddie. Who knows what may happen?'

'Precious little, if past experience serves me true,' Freddie said and wondered why he had made such a bet, when it meant that he would have to attend many tiresome affairs that he usually avoided like the plague.

He yawned behind his hand, wondering what he could find to do with his evening. There was no denying that he was bored with Yolanda and a visit with her did not engender any feeling in him. It would be best to make an end. His tastes had altered of late, and he thought that it might be time to start making changes to his lifestyle.

He would buy the lovely Yolanda a handsome present, perhaps the diamond necklace she had been angling for these many weeks. Yes, he would give her the necklace and make an end to it.

'Mama, do we truly have to stay with Aunt Louisa?' Caroline Holbrook asked of her mother that morning. It was more than two years since Caroline's father, the Honourable Mr Anthony Holbrook, had passed away, and his grieving widow was only now coming to terms with her situation. 'Could we not take a house for ourselves for the Season?'

'You must know that that is impossible.' Marianne Holbrook sighed deeply. She was a thin, pale lady with a fragile air. Having given her husband two sons and a daughter, she had suffered a series of unfortunate miscarriages, which had left her a semi-invalid for some years. Her bereavement had taken its toll of her too and, never a strong-minded woman, she had fallen under her elder sister's influence. 'Your father died owing considerable amounts of money, and your brother has had difficulty in holding the estate together. I do not feel able to ask him for such a large amount of money.'

'Poor Tom probably hasn't any to spare,' Caroline said regretfully. She was fond of her eldest brother and had no wish to make life more difficult for him. She sighed because it seemed that there was no escape for her. Her aunt, Lady Taunton, had married to advantage and though she had been widowed a few years previously, she was in possession of a generous independence, which enabled her to live as she chose. It was kind of her aunt to offer to pay their expenses, but she had such an overpowering manner that Caroline was

dreading the experience. 'Couldn't we afford a short stay—
if I did not spend too much on my clothes?'

'Please do not be difficult, Caroline,' her mother requested.
'I have a headache coming on. You know my health is not
what it ought to be. I should not be able to escort you to all
the balls and affairs you would wish to attend.'

'Forgive me, Mama,' Caroline said, suddenly feeling
wretched for upsetting her mother. 'I suppose we must accept,
but I hope that Aunt Louisa will not try to dictate to me, especially on the subject of whom I should marry.'

'Of course, my dear, but you must choose someone
suitable—if you receive offers, of course.'

Marianne Holbrook gazed at her daughter doubtfully. She
was certainly very striking, though not in the particular
fashion of the day, which seemed to be for slight, fair girls
with gentle manners. Caroline was a flame-haired temptress
with a seductive mouth and challenging green eyes. She was
tall and filled with a restless energy that made her mother feel
distinctly weary around her. Sometimes, she wondered how
she had managed to give birth to such a spirited creature. She
must be a throwback to the old marquis, Caroline's grandfather, now a recluse, who had been a rake, a gambler and
highly disreputable from all accounts. Certainly she in no way
resembled any of Marianne's family.

'You married for love, did you not, Mama?'

'Yes, and have regretted it since,' Marianne said ruefully.
'Louisa married for position and wealth. I chose a younger
son with only a small estate and have suffered the consequences. I should not wish to see you in a similar situation.'

'Poor Mama,' Caroline said. 'But I think you were happy
enough while Papa lived, were you not?'

'Yes, perhaps…' Another sigh escaped her mother. 'Yet I do not care to see my son worn down by worry. And Nicolas has gone to be a soldier. I cannot sleep at night for thinking of him in danger.'

'The war with Bonaparte is surely over, Mama, for he has been confined on Elba,' Caroline said. 'Besides, Nicolas is not the kind of man who would be happy staying at home. You know that he was always into some adventure when a child.'

She and Nicolas had been born a matter of eleven months apart. Although not particularly alike in looks, for he favoured their mother, they had been kindred spirits. It was Nicolas who had taught his sister to climb trees, to swim in the river in her shift and to ride her horse astride. All of these unladylike pursuits had of course landed her in hot water first with her nurse, and later her governess. She had learned to be more sensible as she grew older, but secretly envied her brother his freedom.

'You always encouraged him in his wayward behaviour,' her mother said a little unfairly. 'But I suppose you are right. A mother may not keep her son in leading strings for ever. However, it is my duty to see you settled with a husband and a home of your own, and therefore we shall accept Louisa's invitation to stay with her in town. It is my intention to go up next week.'

Caroline gave up the attempt to dissuade her mother. It was not often that Mrs Holbrook set her mind to something, but on this occasion it seemed that she was determined. However, Caroline was equally determined that she would not allow her aunt to dictate to her in the matter of the gentleman she accepted as her husband—if anyone actually offered for her, of course.

* * *

'Very suitable,' Lady Taunton said, approving her niece's attire for that evening. 'Yes, I was right to insist on mainly white for your gowns, Caroline. The emerald you favoured would have been too bold with hair like yours. It is a pity that you are not more like your mama, but it cannot be helped.'

Caroline gritted her teeth, but kept her thoughts to herself. She had been in town for three days now and already she was finding her aunt's overbearing manner hard to accept, especially in matters of dress, which should surely have been her choice. She believed the white gown was less becoming than the emerald she had wanted, but her aunt was paying for most of her clothes and there was little she could do but accept her choices. Mrs Holbrook wanted only to keep the peace, and Caroline was forced to mind her tongue.

'Well, come along then, Caroline,' Lady Taunton said and swept ahead out to the waiting carriage, leaving her niece to follow in her wake. 'It is a pity your mother did not feel up to attending the ball this evening, but she will be better resting at home with her maid to cosset her.'

Caroline did not answer, for she knew it was not required. Her mother had accompanied them to a musical evening and two small dinners, and then declared herself exhausted. It was clear that she had abandoned the task of finding her daughter a husband to her sister, and that she would not bestir herself unless it was truly necessary.

During the carriage drive to the house of Lady Melbourne, who was holding one of the most prestigious balls of the season, Caroline was forced to endure another lecture from her aunt.

'I dare say I have no need to remind you not to be too free

in your manners, Caroline,' Louisa Taunton droned on. 'It was a fault I observed in you when you were younger, but I expect that you have learned how to behave since you left the schoolroom.'

Caroline made no reply; she felt that if she did she might say something rude, and therefore it was best to say nothing at all.

'Did you hear me, Caroline?'

'Yes, Aunt, of course.' Caroline folded her hands primly in her lap.

'Indeed,' Louisa Taunton said, eyes narrowing suspiciously. 'I do hope you are not sulking. I cannot abide gels that sulk.'

'No, Aunt, I am not sulking.' Caroline held on to her temper by a thread. If she was forced to endure much more of this, she would rather go home and never marry! She was fuming inside, and found it difficult to produce more than a polite smile when she was introduced to her hostess. However, as she followed her aunt's progress through the reception rooms, her mood began to lift.

Music was playing in the furthest room, which was the ballroom, and there was an atmosphere of excitement that communicated itself to Caroline. She looked about her, admiring the lovely gowns some of the ladies were wearing, and the flash of costly jewels. Overhead, a shower of sparkling light fell on the company from the massive chandeliers.

'Caroline, pay attention,' Lady Taunton said, recalling her thoughts sharply. 'This gentleman is Sir Henry Forsythe and he has just asked you for the honour of the next dance.'

'Oh…thank you,' Caroline said, relieved that the gentleman was in his middle years and quite attractive. She dropped a curtsy. 'How very kind of you.'

'No, indeed, Miss Holbrook,' Sir Henry said with a smile of approval. 'It is my pleasure and my privilege.'

Caroline gave him her hand, feeling a little spurt of excitement as he led her through to the ballroom. The black cloud that had hung over her dispersed as she was swept into the throng of dancers, and suddenly she was feeling wonderful.

The feeling continued after the dance ended, because she was besieged by gentlemen begging for the favour of a dance and her card was filled in no time at all. She laughed as she gazed up at her partners, for most of them were young and some were rather handsome.

The hours seemed to fly by with never a dull moment. She was the centre of a small group of ladies and gentlemen for the whole evening. It was not until the dance before supper that she was claimed by a gentleman she had rather liked when he asked for the privilege earlier.

'George Bellingham,' he told her, making his bow. 'You were kind enough to grant me the pleasure of this dance, I believe?'

'Yes, I remember,' Caroline said, giving him a dazzling smile. 'I have been looking forward to it, sir.'

'Have you?' Bellingham raised an eyebrow, a quizzing look in his eyes. 'But you have danced with all the young bucks, Miss Holbrook. I fear I cannot compete with the likes of Brackley or Asbury.'

'Indeed, I disagree, sir,' Caroline said at once, forgetting her aunt's strictures not to be too free in her speech. 'I do not think you need fear either of them—they are young rattleheads, are they not? Charming, of course, but interested only in horses and sport.'

'But one the heir to an earldom, the other to his uncle the

Marquis of Northbrooke.' Bellingham's mouth twitched, for she had described the pair of young bucks to perfection.

'Oh, that!' Caroline made a face at him. 'As if I cared for such things. I think a gentleman of your mode might possibly take an interest in poetry and reading, as well as sport, of course. Do not think I have anything against such pursuits, for my brother Nicolas is a rare goer at many things and I have enjoyed fishing for trout with him.' Her face sparkled up at him as she recalled her childhood adventures with pleasure.

'Have you indeed?' George was intrigued—she was not quite in the ordinary way. He recalled his wager with Freddie Rathbone and smiled inwardly. 'You must tell me more…' He was disappointed as the music ended. 'Oh…it has seemed but a minute…'

'Do you not think time always flies when one is enjoying oneself and drags when one is forced to do something utterly tedious?'

George disguised his laughter as a cough. It was on the tip of his tongue to ask her to have supper with him, but as soon as they left the floor, she was surrounded by four splendid young bucks dressed in the height of fashion, and all with the same question in mind.

'Miss Holbrook, may I take you in?'

'Ignore Brent, Miss Holbrook. I am sure you promised the privilege to me.'

'Oh, Asbury, she damned well said nothing of the kind—she is promised to me,' another gentleman claimed entirely falsely.

'No, no, gentlemen,' Caroline said and laughed, her eyes dancing with mischief. 'I have promised no one, but I shall yield to the gentleman who can quote Richard Lovelace to me—accurately, mind.' She looked at them expectantly.

There was stunned silence for a moment, their faces falling as they struggled to bring a word to mind; though most had subscribed to books of more modern authors, they were unable to remember the lines of the seventeenth-century poet.

'Stone walls do not a prison make,
Nor iron bars a cage;
Minds innocent and quiet take
That for an hermitage;
I'll have freedom in my love,
And so in my soul am free;
Angels alone, that soar above,
Enjoy such liberty.'

'Oh, well done, sir!' Caroline clapped and turned as the deep voice finished his quotation. 'That was excellent…' Finding herself having to look up at the newcomer, she discovered that he was the most devastatingly handsome man she had yet met. His hair was the colour of a raven's wing, almost blue-black where the light from the chandeliers touched it, his eyes very dark, just now mocking her, his mouth strangely enticing as it curved in a smile that made her heart jerk and then race on at frightening speed.

'Good evening, Miss Holbrook,' Freddie Rathbone said and offered her his arm, a glint in his eyes as a murmur of protest came from the other gentlemen when she took it. 'The honour is mine, I think. Better luck next time—George, gentlemen.' He inclined his head to them, his manner a nice blend of mockery and arrogance, as if he had claimed the prize by right.

Caroline laid her hand on his arm. She was laughing inside, though she did her best not to show it. 'I do not believe we have been introduced, sir?'

'Sir Frederick Rathbone at your service,' he said and smiled at her. 'I came late and was reliably informed that your card was full—young Asbury supplied the details. You must be aware that you have made a hit with that gentleman, and a few others, I dare say.'

'They have been amazingly kind,' Caroline said, a faint blush in her cheeks. She did not often blush, but there was something about this man's gaze that made her a little uncomfortable. He seemed to demand her thoughts, and she was not sure that she wished to share them with him. There was something about him that seemed to challenge her. To accept that challenge might prove dangerous.

'Come, now, no false modesty,' Freddie said, his eyes seeming to dare her to respond in a way that was not at all fitting. 'You must know that you are a sensation. I might almost say you are the belle of the evening, perhaps of the Season, though it is early days yet, I think.'

'This is my first ball,' Caroline said, her enthusiasm bubbling over. 'I have been lucky enough not to sit down for one dance as yet, but I do not think I am the only lady to have been popular this evening.'

'True enough, but people are talking about you. Everyone wishes to know where you came from—perhaps you were wafted here from some distant paradise? You are a siren come up from the depths of the sea to weave your spell over us poor mortals…'

'You mock me, sir,' Caroline reproved. She was a little uneasy—there was something about him, a glint in his eyes that told her he might be dangerous if she were to like him too much. And yet despite that she was drawn to him, much like a moth to an open flame. She tilted her head, deliberately challenging him. 'If we are to speak of looks, I dare say yours have won you more than your fair share of attention from the ladies? And if you should be wealthy, of which I have no idea, I am sure you are much sought after—unless you are already married, of course?'

'Oh, rich as Croesus,' Freddie said and grinned at her. Her bold manner was immediately attractive to a man of his humour, intriguing him. He wondered how she would respond to his teasing. 'And not married—a fact that some find irresponsible, for it must be the first object of a gentleman to marry, must it not?'

'Must it?' Caroline said, wrinkling her brow. He *was* clearly mocking her. She threw him a daring look, a flicker of defiance in her eyes. 'I do not see it. Much better to remain unwed unless it is for the further happiness of both partners—do you not think so? It would be tedious to marry just for the sake of it, I imagine.'

'Absolutely,' Freddie said, much amused. He had not met such frankness in a young lady of her class before and found it refreshing. 'Unfortunately, the match-making mamas of too many young ladies do not see it from your point of view. Now, what shall we have of this fine supper provided for us, Miss Holbrook? Please do not say you are not hungry. Surely you must fancy some of that delicious ham—or the chicken? Perhaps with a few green peas?'

'I would prefer one of those savoury pastries, and a syllabub,' Caroline said. 'But you must certainly have some of that beef, sir. It is rare and I know gentlemen like their beef that way—at least Nicolas does and so did my papa, although my other brother, Tom, likes the first slice from the cut.'

'Your father is dead, Miss Holbrook?'

'These two years past,' Caroline said and sighed. 'I miss him sorely, sir, but, truthfully, I miss my brother more. Tom has taken on the estate, of course, but Nicolas has gone to become a soldier. I just wish that I might have gone with him. I think it must be a fine thing to wear a handsome uniform and march to the sound of the drums.'

'Do you, indeed?' Freddie hid his smile at her naivety. 'I have had my share of it, Miss Holbrook. I can assure you that it is not all drums and flying colours.'

'Were you with Wellington when Napoleon was defeated?'

'No, I had resigned my commission, but I was with him at Salamanca.'

'Truly? Did you resign because you were wounded?'

'I was wounded several times, but I resigned because my father died and I had commitments at home.'

'Ah, yes, you are the elder son, I assume. I think poor Tom wishes that he were Nicolas at times. He has all the burden of the estate, while Nicolas may do much as he pleases.'

'Within reason, I dare say, but he will have to make his fortune—or marry into one. I dare say he has not much fortune of his own?'

'Oh, no,' Caroline said candidly, unaware that she was being quizzed for information. 'None of us has. Poor Papa was not a good manager, you see.'

'Ah…' Having gained all the information that Asbury had not been able to give him earlier, Freddie was satisfied. The girl clearly needed to marry well, which in her case should not be difficult, even without a fortune. She was undoubtedly beautiful and her easy manner had made her a favourite with the gentlemen. He found her amusing company himself, but could not help wondering if there were some artifice behind her easy manner. It would be interesting to discover more about her. 'Now, we must eat, Miss Holbrook. Please seat yourself, and I shall arrange for our supper.'

Caroline saw that a table by the window was still free, and she went to sit there. Before Sir Frederick could bring her her supper, Mr Bellingham came and sat down, supplying a third chair for himself.

'Freddie looking after you?' he asked. 'Decent chap, but rather stole my thunder. I was recalling what I know of Lovelace when he jumped in. I dare say he won't mind my joining you. We are close friends, you see.'

'I set the question, thinking that you might answer it,' Caroline said truthfully. 'I particularly like his letter to Lucasta—do you know it?'

'"Tell me not, Sweet, I am unkind…"' George quoted, raising an eyebrow. 'Is that the one?'

'Oh, yes, written to Lucasta when he was about to go to war. I find that period so romantic, do you not agree? I have a book at home, which tells the story of a lady defending her home in her husband's absence. It was a brave age, less polite than today, I imagine.'

'Yes, indeed,' George Bellingham agreed and smiled.

'George,' a voice said from behind him. 'What is this, my dear fellow—stealing a march on me?' Freddie waved the servant forwards who had brought various plates of the delicious food on offer. The servant deposited them and bowed, leaving the company to serve themselves. 'Please do join us…feel free to eat whatever you wish, but not the syllabub.'

'Very well, I shall,' George said, impervious to the sarcasm in his friend's voice. 'Miss Holbrook and I were discussing Lovelace—and the Civil War, a brave age.'

'Really?' Freddie said drily. 'With the whole country in arms and most of the aristocracy ruined for years?'

'Oh, you have no soul,' Caroline said, throwing him a challenging look. Her eyes were bright with mischief, making both men aware of her wayward spirit. 'The men were so gallant, and the ladies very different from the ladies of today, would you not say?'

'In what way?' Freddie asked, a gleam in his eye as he realised that his friend had been quoting her views, not his own. It seemed that this young lady was not afraid to voice her opinions.

'Oh, we are hedged about with convention,' Caroline said. 'I think it was easier to speak one's mind then than now.'

'Indeed?' Freddie was hard put to it not to answer in kind, for she was speaking quite freely. 'What would you like to say that you dare not, Miss Holbrook? Please do not hold back, for you are amongst friends. Neither George nor I will censure you.'

'Oh…' She looked into his eyes and saw the mockery. 'Have I been speaking too freely? My aunt forbade it, but I have been used to speaking as I find with my brothers. Forgive me.' A faint blush touched her cheeks.

'No, indeed, you have not. I find your frankness refreshing,' George assured her hastily. 'Do not let anyone tell you that you should be otherwise, Miss Holbrook.'

'Yes, well, perhaps I should not be quite so open,' she said, belatedly realising that her aunt might be right in some instances. 'Do you go to Almack's this week, sir? I believe I am to be given vouchers.'

'Then I shall certainly be there,' George said and shot a look of triumph at his friend. 'But I believe Freddie has other engagements?'

'Yes, I fear I have,' Freddie said and gave his friend a look that spoke volumes. The challenge was fairly joined and both men were enjoying themselves. 'But I shall be at Lady Broughton's rout—do you attend?'

'Yes, I believe so,' Caroline said. 'Indeed, we have so many cards that I am not sure how we shall manage to attend a half of the affairs we have been invited to.'

'You will no doubt simply make an appearance at some and then go on as many of us do,' Freddie said. 'But I shall engage to dance with you at least twice at the rout, Miss Holbrook. Please mark your card for me as you will.'

'Thank you, sir…' She looked at Mr Bellingham, for she sensed a friendly rivalry between the two and was amused by it. 'And for you, sir?'

'I believe two would be suitable,' he said, 'and I should like to take you driving in the park—perhaps tomorrow afternoon, if you have no prior engagements?'

'I know we are engaged for the evening, but I think there is nothing as yet for the afternoon. I shall be delighted to drive out with you, sir.'

'I shall look forward to it,' George assured her and glanced at Freddie. Their habitual rivalry was good-natured, but often quite fierce, and their friendship was all the stronger for the occasional clash of temperament.

Freddie was eating his supper. He made no comment, apparently leaving the field for the moment, though George did not doubt that he would re-enter when he chose.

Caroline looked up and saw her aunt bearing down on them. 'Gentlemen, I think my aunt may need me.'

The gentlemen got to their feet as Lady Taunton descended on them, but she smiled and indicated that they should sit. 'Please continue with your supper, gentlemen. I came only to see if my niece wanted to accompany me to the rest room?'

'Thank you, Aunt.' Caroline rose obediently, for she knew when she was being told to do something, however charmingly it was put. 'Excuse me, Mr Bellingham—Sir Frederick. I shall hope to see you at the rout we spoke of.'

She followed Lady Taunton from the room and up the stairs to the bedrooms that had been set aside for the comfort of the ladies, waiting for the tirade to begin. However, when they were alone, her aunt smiled at her.

'You have done well, Caroline. Mr Bellingham is a wealthy gentleman, though some think him a confirmed bachelor—but of course Sir Frederick is one of the catches of the Season. He has been for years, of course, but so far has shown no inclination for matrimony. If you were to receive an offer from either of those gentlemen it would be highly satisfactory, though Sir Frederick is the better catch of the two. He is his uncle's heir, you know—and will be the Marquis of Southmoor one day.'

'I am sure that they were just being gallant,' Caroline replied. 'They wanted to pass the time pleasantly.'

'I am not quite so certain,' her aunt replied, looking thoughtful. 'Rathbone's godmother is a friend of mine. I do not think you have met her—Lady Stroud?' Caroline shook her head. 'No, I thought not. She told me that he has been attending more of these affairs recently, something he hardly ever does. I imagine that must mean he has set his mind to taking a bride. You have clearly caught his eye. It might be to your advantage to make a push, Caroline.'

'We share an interest in certain poets,' Caroline told her,

'but I dare say that is all we have in common. Besides, there were many others who asked me to dance, and to take supper, Aunt.' Her aunt's untimely interference was irritating, for she had only just met the gentlemen in question.

'Yes, of course. You must not show neglect in your manner to any gentlemen who take an interest in you, my dear—but bear it in mind that Rathbone is a good catch.'

Caroline did not answer. Her aunt's words had the opposite effect of the one she had surely hoped for. If anything were calculated to set Caroline against someone, it was being pushed in his direction.

Freddie looked across the card table and sighed inwardly. He had been holding the winning hand for the past few minutes, but was reluctant to declare it. He would have preferred not to play Farringdon, but had been unable to refuse the challenge, having won from him only a few nights previously. He was aware that the fool was playing out of his depth, and could probably not afford to pay a half of the notes he had so carelessly thrown on the table. He toyed with the idea of throwing his hand, but that was against all the rules of play. Farringdon must learn not to gamble beyond his means.

He took a card from the pack; it was the one card that could improve his hand, which was now virtually unbeatable. He discarded and then laid his cards on the table. A groan broke from two of the other players; they complained of his incredible luck, but did so with a smile and a careless shrug, for both were well able to pay what was owed. Freddie looked at Farringdon's white face as he sat staring at the cards in disbelief.

The other gentlemen got up and left the table almost immediately, in search of wine or food, but Farringdon sat on, almost as though he were frozen to the spot.

'It will take me some time to raise the cash,' he said in a flat voice, the seriousness of his situation showing only by a slight nerve flicking at his right temple.

'Yes, of course,' Freddie said, gathering up the various gold coins and notes that had been tossed on to the table. 'Unless you would wish to toss for double or quits?'

'No, no, I think not,' Farringdon said with an attempt to seem casual. 'It is a temporary thing, Rathbone. I should be able to settle in a few weeks.'

'Yes, of course. There is no hurry, none whatsoever. You may take as much time as you please, sir. Will you drink a nightcap with me? It is my intention to walk home.'

'Thank you, no,' Farringdon said and got up. He left the table and walked from the gaming club without looking from left to right, his face set in a frozen expression that gave no indication of his state of mind.

'Have you won again?' George Bellingham wandered over to Freddie as he sat on for a moment in contemplation. 'Farringdon looked desperate. I heard a rumour that unless he finds some way to come about he may be forced to sell his estate.'

'The damned fool should have cut his losses earlier,' Freddie said with a frown of displeasure. 'I have no desire to ruin any man, George, and if he comes to me with the truth, I shall return his notes to him. However, he must retire from the tables. He should take a bolt to the country and stay there until he has the funds in his pocket. The rule is that if you can't pay do not play.'

'A gaming debt is a debt of honour,' George agreed immediately. 'Why do you not put the poor fellow out of his misery, Freddie? Send the notes back to him if you mean to do it.'

'He needs a lesson,' Freddie said. 'Had he lost to Markham or Lazenby, they would have demanded payment within the month. If I give him his notes, he may be tempted to play again with someone less lenient than I.'

'Well, yes, there is that to it,' George said. 'But he will hate you if you show him leniency—it will damage his pride.'

'Then he must hate me,' Freddie said. 'The man is not ruined yet—not while I do not press my claim. No, no, Farringdon must come to me, and then we may settle this thing like gentlemen.'

'Well, I dare say you are right, though you may make an enemy,' George said, and then grinned at his friend. 'Tell me, what did you think of *her*?'

'I am not certain what you mean?' Freddie said with a lift of his mobile brows, though he was perfectly aware of George's meaning. Caroline Holbrook had made her mark with him, even if he was not prepared to admit it. There was something very appealing about her, which had drawn him to her despite her youth.

'Miss Holbrook, of course,' George said. 'Do you not think she is everything we spoke of the other day, Freddie? She has beauty, a liveliness of spirit that one cannot but admire, and when she smiles the room seems to light up. Enchanting would not be too strong a word.'

'Ah, I see you have been smitten. When am I to wish you happy, my dear fellow?' Freddie raised his brows

'Oh, as to that…I am set in my ways, you know. I am not certain that I should be comfortable married to any lady…but I must admit that, if I were tempted to change my ways, I might ask Miss Holbrook if she would do me the honour. Not that I expect she would accept me. I am too old for her—and she may take her pick of a dozen or more gentlemen, I dare say.'

'All this on the strength of one ball?' Freddie looked incredulous. 'She is not quite in the usual style for one so young, I give you that, George—but you have met lively young ladies before.' He refused to allow that Miss Holbrook was anything out of the ordinary, even though she had unaccountably lingered in his thoughts these past few days. He had not yet decided if that ingenuous manner was genuine or whether it hid something rather less pleasant. The girl had been frank about her lack of fortune—but was she a fortune hunter herself? For the moment he was inclined to stand back and watch as others fluttered about the flame.

'Yes, of course,' George said. 'I am not sure what it is, Freddie—but does she not strike you as being remarkable?'

'She has an amusing turn of phrase,' Freddie conceded. 'But is that artlessness real or assumed? I am reserving judgement for the moment. You will not see me at Almack's just yet, George.'

'I shall certainly attend,' George said. 'Sally Jersey has been giving me hints for ages. She thinks I should bestir myself to find a wife before I sink into the murky waters of old age.'

'Good grief,' Freddie said, revolted. 'You are in your prime, George. But if you fancy the little Holbrook filly, I shall not stand in your way—though I warn you she has scant fortune.' Now why had he added that piece of information? It could make no difference to George, who had fortune enough not to need a rich wife.

'Where did you hear that?'

'She told me herself.'

'Well, you may be right, though…' George shook his head. 'It matters not a jot either way. I am not on the catch for a fortune. I may not have your luck at the tables, but I am not done up yet.'

'I never imagined you were, my dear fellow,' Freddie said, amused as much by his own feeling of pique as George's enthusiasm. 'Do you care to walk with me?'

'I have my carriage,' George said. 'Let me take you up, Freddie. It has started to rain.'

'Has it? I had not noticed,' Freddie said. 'Very well, then. I had thought to stretch my legs, blow the cobwebs away, but I do not care for a soaking.'

The two men smiled at each other, in perfect accord as always as they went out of the club and into the waiting carriage. Neither of them noticed the shadowy figure watching as they were driven away.

Chapter Two

'Damn it, Jenkins—' the Marquis of Bollingbrook glared at his valet '—I am not yet in my dotage. When I ask for brandy, I do not wish it to be mixed with water!'

His valet's face wore a martyred air, for, having served his master, man and boy, he was not like to resent his outbursts of temper. Especially since he, above anyone at Bollingbrook Place, understood the pain behind the anger.

'Begging your pardon, milord,' Jenkins said, 'but it was Dr Heron as told me your lordship ought not to drink so much.'

'Damn his impertinence and yours,' the Marquis said with a grunt of displeasure. 'Pour a smaller measure if you will, but do not ruin the damned stuff!'

'No, your lordship.' Jenkins retained his impassive stare. The Marquis was prone to severe bouts of painful gout, which another, more critical man might have considered a judgement for his sinful past—sins that had haunted the older man for too long. Jenkins, however, was devoted to his master, besides being privy to secrets that others did not share. 'It shall not happen again.'

'See that it doesn't.'

'I am sorry, milord.'

'No need to be sorry.' A weary smile settled over the old man's features. He knew that of late he had become almost impossible to live with. There had been a time when he was a very different man, but he had lived too long trapped in the pain of his memories. 'Damned if I know how you put up with me, Jenkins. It's a wonder you haven't walked out before this. I've driven my family away. None of them visit me these days.'

The Marquis had fathered three sons, all of them by different wives. He had been unfortunate in losing the last of them, a beautiful young lady many years his junior. She too had died shortly after childbirth from a putrid chill. The Marquis had not been the same since her death. However, the loss of his youngest son had almost finished him.

'Wouldn't know what to do with myself if I retired, sir,' Jenkins answered in the same flat tone as before. 'Can't blame your family for not visiting. You lost your temper and banned them from the estate the last time.'

'Do you think I don't know that?' Bollingbrook growled. His foot was causing him excruciating pain and there was nothing to be done about it. 'But I didn't mean her, damn it!' A look of regret came into his eyes. 'Caroline is the best of them all. She is very like *her*, do you not think?'

Jenkins understood perfectly. 'Yes, very like, my lord. You could write and invite her to stay…'

'Her mother and aunt have taken her to London,' the Marquis muttered. 'Had a letter from that wilting lily last week. Damned if I know what Holbrook ever saw in her. I blame her for his death, you know. Another woman might have steered him to a safer path instead of weeping buckets in her bedchamber! Still, water under the bridge now.' He glared at his valet. 'I won't have Caroline forced into a marriage she doesn't care for. I suppose her mother is feeling the pinch. That is my fault, of course. Should have done something for her. I ought to have done something for Tom before this.'

'Why not invite him here?' Jenkins suggested, braving his master's fierce stare. He knew him too well to quail in his boots, though others had been known to flee before such a look. 'If I may take the liberty, milord? Send him to town to look after his sister. He can keep you informed on her situation.'

'Excellent notion,' the Marquis agreed. 'He's not as weak as his mother, though I prefer Nicolas. Full of spunk, that lad! However, Tom is Holbrook's heir, so I must do something for him. Bring me pen and ink, if you will. I shall write the letter now.'

Jenkins obeyed, setting the well-used, mahogany writing slope on the Marquis' lap, as he sat in his high-backed chair before the fire.

'Is there anything else, milord?'

'Not for the moment. I shall ring for you later.'

Left to himself, Bollingbrook opened the secret drawer of his writing slope and took out the miniature of his third wife. Angelica was the only one he had loved, though there had been many women before her, some of them acknowledged beauties, but none at all had followed her. He had loved her dearly, and believed that she would survive him for she had been so much younger. She had been the delight of his life, and when he'd lost her he had wanted to die and to be buried in her grave with her. Only her dying wish had prevented him from taking his own life.

'Look after our son; look after Anthony,' she had whispered as she lay slowly wasting of the putrid fever. 'Love him for my sake, I beg you.'

He had loved Holbrook for her sake and his own—and he loved Caroline too because she was so like his lost wife; she had the same vitality, the same brave heart. For the rest of his family he had scarcely any affection. He disliked his eldest son, Sebastian. He thought it a damned silly name, and would have disinherited him if he could, but would find it difficult to break the entail. He liked Claude slightly better, but not enough to want him to visit.

The Bollingbrook estate must go to his eldest son by law, and Claude must have the London property. He had lived there for years and it would not do to put him out. Yet he had some money and property that had not come to him through the estate and was his to dispose of as he pleased. He would divide it equally between Caroline and her brothers. He should have done it before, but it was still not too late. Despite the constant pain, he was sound of mind and there were a few years left to him yet.

Caroline dressed in a green-striped carriage gown. At least she had been allowed to choose this for herself, she thought with some satisfaction. She knew the colour suited her and she was pleased with her appearance as she went downstairs.

Louisa Taunton was still in her room, but she knew of and approved Caroline's engagement to go driving with Mr Bellingham that morning. She had given her permission without hesitation.

'He will no doubt bring his groom with him. However, it is quite respectable to drive out unaccompanied with a gentleman of Mr Bellingham's reputation. I have known him for some years, and a more likeable gentleman could not be found, I am sure.'

'Yes, Aunt. I thought you could have no objection to the outing. He is a gentleman of good taste, would you not say?'

'Indeed,' her aunt replied and looked thoughtful. 'But he has no immediate prospects of a title. It is unlikely it will happen—there are several cousins before him—whereas Sir Frederick will undoubtedly inherit his uncle's title, as the present marquis has no living sons or grandchildren and he is not likely to marry again at his time of life.'

'I think I prefer Mr Bellingham,' Caroline replied, 'should he take an interest—but I do not think we should count on it just yet, do you?'

She spoke innocently, yet with a look in her eyes that her aunt suspected. Lady Taunton was no slowtop and she was well aware that her niece resented her interference.

'I am only reminding you of possible options,' Louisa said tartly. 'I believe that Sir Frederick might be on the catch for a wife, whereas Mr Bellingham is unlikely to marry. Everyone knows that he is too set in his ways.'

'Is that so?' Caroline asked sweetly. 'Well, I dare say there may be others, Aunt. We must be patient, must we not?'

'You are impertinent, miss,' Lady Taunton said with a sour twist of her mouth. She thought that if Caroline were her daughter, she would have beaten some of that sauciness out of her long ago. 'Do not ruin your chances to spite me, Caroline. You may get less than you imagine, despite your success so far.'

'Oh, I do not let such foolishness weigh with me,' Caroline replied. 'I dare say I shall be fortunate to receive any offers at all.'

'Well, you will make a push for Sir Frederick if you have any sense,' her aunt said and dismissed her with a wave of her hand.

Caroline was not sure why it should make her so out-of-reason cross that her aunt was trying to influence her decision. As yet, of course, there was no decision to be made, for she was barely acquainted with any of the gentlemen she had met. Perhaps it was her aunt's eagerness to rush her into marriage for the sake of a fortune that she found so distasteful. It had soured what might be simply a pleasant acquaintance. She shook her head, thrusting the irritating thoughts to the back of her mind as she heard someone arrive at the door.

The footman opened the door to admit Mr Bellingham into the elegant hallway. He was looking extremely fine in his blue coat and pale grey breeches, a beaver hat now removed from his fair curling locks. His face lit up as he saw her descending the stairs, clearly ready to accompany him.

'Good morning, Miss Holbrook. May I say how charming you look?'

'Thank you, sir. We have a beautiful day for our drive, do we not?'

'Very pleasant. There is a slight breeze but it is quite warm.'

They went outside to where his curricle stood waiting, his groom at the horses' heads. Drawn by a pair of fine greys, it was a smart affair with yellow-painted spokes to its wheels, and Caroline felt privileged to be taken up by him. He handed her up himself and then took the reins, the groom jumping up behind.

During the drive to Hyde Park, they made polite social conversation, but once they were within the park, they turned to poetry and books they had both read. From there it was an easy matter to progress to other pursuits they enjoyed.

'Do you ride much at home, Miss Holbrook?'

'As often as I can, before breakfast if the weather is good. My father put me up on my first pony almost as soon as I could walk—and of course I rode with Nicolas most days. I miss him greatly now that he has joined the army, but I know that it was what he wanted.'

'Nicolas is the younger of your brothers, I believe?'

'We are but eleven months apart in age. My elder brother Tom manages the estate, of course. I am fond of Tom, but it was Nicolas with whom I shared so much.' She laughed as she recalled some of the naughty escapades that had landed her in hot water when she was younger.

'Yes, I see,' George said. 'It is natural that you should feel closer to Nicolas with him being so near in age.'

'It is more than that.' A husky chuckle escaped her. 'Nicolas was sometimes a little high-spirited, and he encouraged me to do things of which my governess did not always approve. We escaped our tutors together, and he always shouldered the blame as much as he could, though I confess that the ideas for our adventures were not always of his making.'

George smiled inwardly. Her laughter was infectious and he thought her enchanting. She seemed to have no fear of speaking out, though some of her revelations might displease the old tabbies who considered themselves the arbiters of good taste and decorum.

'You were fortunate in having such a companion, Miss Holbrook. I, on the other hand, was an only—' He broke off as he saw who was approaching them on foot. 'There is Freddie. I think we must pull over for a moment…'

Caroline made no comment. She knew that he could not neglect to acknowledge his friend, but would have preferred to drive past with a polite nod. Something about Sir Frederick Rathbone unsettled her, whereas she was perfectly comfortable with Mr Bellingham.

'Good morning, George—Miss Holbrook.' Freddie's dark eyes dwelled on her face. With that flame of hair peeping from beneath her chip-straw bonnet, which was tied with green ribbons to match her gown, she was certainly a beauty. She would not lack for suitors, he thought, and wondered why the idea of her being pursued by all the young bucks should be slightly irritating. 'Are you enjoying yourself, Miss Holbrook?'

'Very much, sir, thank you. I have seldom seen a finer pair than Mr Bellingham's greys.'

'You haven't seen Freddie's fine chestnuts,' George said, generous to a fault. 'Miss Holbrook is a great rider, Freddie, and a judge of horseflesh. You must take her up in your phaeton one of these days. I am sure she would enjoy it.'

'Oh, yes, I should,' Caroline said without pausing for thought. 'Nicolas let me drive his phaeton sometimes, and we once raced a friend of his around the estate…though perhaps I ought not to have said so? I believe it might be frowned upon by some?'

'You have just damned yourself in the eyes of the old tabbies,' Freddie said, amused. Her way of confiding in one was attractive, for she did it with such innocence that one could not help being charmed. 'But fear not, Miss Holbrook. Neither George nor I shall betray you.'

'Thank you,' Caroline replied, a faint blush making her look touchingly vulnerable for a moment. That was the second time he had said something of the sort. Had he taken her in dislike? She lifted her head defiantly, meeting his gaze.

'I think my tongue will land me in trouble one of these days. I should learn to curb it, but it runs away with me.'

'No, no,' Bellingham assured her, but Sir Freddie remained silent. His silence made her feel that he disapproved of her and that made her want to challenge him. For why should he censure her? She had done nothing outrageous, and his manner had pricked her pride. 'Though you might offend the tabbies without meaning to.'

'Who are these tabbies?' Caroline asked innocently, though she was well aware of their meaning. Her eyes were bright with mischief, bringing a laugh from George and a thoughtful look from Freddie. 'Please do tell, for I am all at sea.'

'You are a minx,' Freddie told her and now there was a hint of amusement on his lips, which caused her heart to flutter oddly. 'I think you mean to tease us, Miss Holbrook. George, I shall not keep you. I am certain you are wishing me to the devil.'

'Not a bit of it.' George smiled. 'All is fair in love and war, they say. I shall see you later at White's…' The words died on his lips, for at that moment Caroline gave a little cry and jumped down from the carriage, lifting her skirts clear to avoid stumbling as she ran across the grass. 'What the devil is she doing?'

Sir Freddie did not answer—he had seen what had caused Caroline to risk life and limb and dash off so suddenly. A youth was tormenting a puppy, kicking at it cruelly, and the creature was yelping with pain. Without reference to George, he set off after her, arriving just as Caroline rounded on the youth in a fury.

'How dare you?' she cried as the animal cowered away from yet another blow. 'Stop that at once or I shall teach you better manners, sir!'

'What yer gonna do, then?' the youth asked, leering at her. He was a dirty, ragged boy and his face was smeared with dirt. 'Can't stop me. Master told me to get rid of it—and he'll kill me if I go back with the flea-ridden brute.'

'Then go back without it,' Caroline said. 'Touch it again and I shall have you beaten!'

'Yeah? How yer gonna do that, then?' the youth asked, squaring up to her. He lifted his fist as if he would strike her, only to have his arm caught in an iron grip. Looking up, his face turned white beneath the dirt and his eyes darted to Caroline in fear. 'Call him off, miss. I weren't gonna hurt yer.'

'No, you certainly were not,' Caroline said, head up, eyes glittering. 'For I should have hit you with my parasol. Let him go, sir.' She addressed Freddie in a tone of command. 'He may run back to his master and say what he will. This poor thing shall not be tortured again.' Turning her back on them as though neither were of the least importance, she did not notice Sir Freddie give the youth a sharp clip of the ear before sending him off. Caroline was on her knees beside the puppy, stroking its head softly as it whimpered and shrank away from her hand. 'Oh, you poor little thing. He has hurt you so, but he shan't do it again—no one shall, I promise you.'

'The creature may well have fleas as well as broken bones.'

Caroline turned to look up at Freddie. 'The fleas are a matter of indifference to me, and may soon be cured with a warm bath—the broken bones are a different thing. He must be looked at by someone who understands these things and then…' She faltered, for she had suddenly remembered that she was a guest in her aunt's house. Lady Taunton would not welcome a bedraggled puppy in her home. 'He is not the prettiest dog, perhaps, but he deserves to be cared for, do you not think so?'

Freddie bent down and picked the puppy up carefully. He ran gentle hands over its quivering body, but, though it whimpered at first, it seemed to quieten at his touch.

'I believe he likes you,' Caroline said. 'Do you think—?'

'Oh, no,' Freddie said instantly. 'I do not wish to be saddled with a mongrel—and he most certainly has fleas.'

'I was going to ask only if you could direct me to a place where I can arrange for him to be cared for until I can claim him. I can pay for his keep and when…when I go home he shall come with me.' Her eyes were bright and filled with unconscious appeal that placed him on his mettle. Freddie struggled and lost. She saw it in his eyes and gave him a dazzling smile. 'I promise I shall claim him as soon as I can.'

'Very well,' he said reluctantly. 'I shall take charge of the wretched thing—but only until you can find a home for it. I have several dogs at home and they would make mincemeat of the creature. It can go to my stables. The grooms will know what to do for it.'

'You are generous, sir. I am grateful.'

'The dog remains your responsibility,' Freddie said gruffly, for something in her look had touched him. 'You should be aware that your dress has become stained, Miss Holbrook—and I would advise you not to throw yourself down from a carriage so precipitously in future. George was about to move on and you might have been injured.'

'What can that signify?' Caroline asked with a toss of her head. She bent her head to kiss the puppy's neck. 'Please take care of him, won't you?'

'I have never neglected any animal,' Freddie said a trifle haughtily. 'I do not think you need fear for this one.'

'No, of course not. And thank you for your assistance, though there was no need. I should have hit him if he had tried to attack me.' Her eyes flashed defiantly.

'Next time I shall remember,' Freddie said, a flicker of amusement in his face. 'I think you should go now, Miss Holbrook. George's horses begin to fret.'

'Oh, yes, I had forgot,' Caroline said and flushed. 'I did not mean to sound ungracious—thank you.'

She ran towards the waiting curricle and was handed up by George while his groom held the now impatient horses.

'You know you owe your good fortune to her, don't you?' Freddie murmured, scratching the puppy behind its ear. It had now settled in his arms and he was inclined to optimism about its condition. Painfully thin, it had obviously been starved, but with some good food and care… 'Ridiculous!' he said aloud, causing a passing lady to stare at him. 'I do not know who is the greater fool.'

Freddie stood watching as his friend drove on by with a wave of his hand. The girl was an original, there was no doubt of it. She would either become the latest rage or fall foul of some sharp tongues. It would be interesting to watch her progress.

He was not likely to be caught in her toils though, he told himself. She was lovely, intelligent and lively, and it seemed that she was both brave and compassionate, but he was not in the market for a wife. Though Miss Holbrook had certainly enlivened what had looked like being a damned dull Season before her arrival. He tipped his hat to a passing acquaintance, deciding to visit the club of a certain pugilist he favoured after he had handed the puppy to his groom. He was feeling oddly restless and in need of some exercise before he kept his appointment with George later that afternoon.

Tom Holbrook frowned over the letter from his grandfather. He had not been expecting it, but he was not averse to visiting the old gentleman. He had never been afraid of Bollingbrook, as some of his cousins were, though he had thought it wise to hold his tongue. The Marquis had a volatile temper, and had never hidden his dislike of Tom's mother.

Left to his own pursuits with nothing but a pile of debts to keep him company, Tom had been thinking that he might take a trip to town and visit his mother and sister. It would not bother him to make a small detour to visit his grandfather. The Marquis had said there was a matter of business to discuss, which did not sound promising. It was quite likely he was to be taken to task for putting up a part of the Holbrook estate for sale, but there was little else he could do in the circumstances. Tom had been forced to sell or risk losing everything, for his father had made some foolish investments.

He instructed his valet to put up a travelling bag for him and send his trunk on, and then had his groom bring round his curricle.

Within three hours of receiving the letter from his grandfather he was walking into Bollingbrook Place. It was an old house, but both the building and grounds were immaculately kept, which Tom knew must be expensive. The estate was clearly flourishing. Tom had not given much consideration to it in the past, but now he wondered where his grandfather's money came from.

'Master Tom, it's good to see you, sir,' Jenkins said. He

had just come into the hall as the footman opened the door and smiled his approval at the young man. 'Milord wasn't sure you would answer his call, but I thought you might— and here you are.'

'Of course I came,' Tom said. 'He threw Mama out with instructions never to darken his door again, but I was pretty sure that he didn't mean it. How is he, Jenkins? The gout playing him up as usual?'

'His lordship is in some pain,' the valet told him, 'but not as bad this morning as it has been for the past few days. I try to keep him from his port, but you know how it is, sir.' Jenkins sighed heavily, his long face wearing an expression of extreme martyrdom.

'I do indeed,' Tom answered and grinned; he knew the man had much to bear, but he also knew that nothing would prise him from the Marquis' side. 'May I go up and see him, do you think? His letter sounded important.'

'I believe it would do him good to have company, sir. He dwells too much on the past when he is alone.'

'I'll go up, then,' Tom said and nodded to Jenkins as he ran up the stairs. Outside his grandfather's door, he paused and knocked, waiting until a gruff voice invited him in. 'Good morning, sir. How are you?'

'No better for your asking,' the Marquis grumbled, but then thought better of it. He had, after all, invited the young man to call. 'Not so bad, thank you, Tom. It was good of you to come to see me.'

'I had nothing better to do,' Tom said frankly. He saw shock and then amusement in his grandfather's face, for it was unlike him to answer so. 'I was considering taking a trip to London, thought I might escort Caroline to some of the affairs, save Mama the trouble—that's if she has troubled herself, which I dare say she may not very often.'

'I take leave to doubt she will do so at all,' Bollingbrook growled. 'Featherhead! Still, she produced the best of my grandchildren—the rest of them are a pack of ninnies! I won't have them here; they argue and whinge and I can't stand that at my time of life. However, I want to see that gel of mine— Caroline. It's an age since she was here. I know she's gadding about town at the moment, and I don't want to spoil her fun, but I should appreciate a visit when she can spare the time. I want you to tell her that, Tom.'

'Yes, sir, of course. I shall go up in a few days—that's if you will put up with me in the meantime?'

'I hope you won't run off too soon,' the Marquis said gruffly. 'I didn't get you here just to talk about Caroline. I have some things to discuss with you. It concerns the future— you, Nicolas and my gel. I have been remiss, but I intend to put things right. In fact, I have already had my lawyer here and the thing is done, a day or two back as it happens. It can't be explained all in a moment. Concerns secrets that most of 'em don't know—and are not to be told, do you hear me?'

'Yes, sir.' Tom was surprised and yet flattered that he was to be let into that part of his grandfather's life that was never spoken of, though he knew the old reprobate had been a high-flyer in his heyday. 'You may rely on me to do as you wish on the matter.'

'Good, thought I might,' the Marquis said. 'Do you see that chest in the corner? The one with the iron bands? It is locked and this is the key.' He took it from his waistcoat pocket and held it out to Tom. 'Open it and bring me the packet you see lying on top. You may study it at your leisure, and then we shall talk…'

* * *

Caroline saw that Sir Frederick had entered the ballroom, which was overflowing with people and far too hot. He had such presence and such an air that she could not help thinking him the most distinguished man of her acquaintance, and her heart suddenly beat a little faster.

His gaze seemed to travel round the room, and then settle for a moment on her. She dropped her own gaze immediately, for she would not like him to think she was staring, even though she had been. However, in another moment her next partner claimed her and she was whisked into the middle of the dancers. For the following few minutes, she forgot about Sir Frederick; when she was returned to her aunt's side, he had moved from the place he had been standing earlier. Perhaps he had preferred the card room, she thought, deciding to put him from her mind.

'I should like to tidy myself,' Caroline told her aunt. 'Would you tell Mr Asbury that I shall be only a few moments, please?'

'Yes, though you must be quick,' Lady Taunton said with a look of disapproval. 'It is rude to keep partners waiting.'

Caroline left the room immediately, going upstairs to the room that had been set aside for the ladies. She made herself comfortable as quickly as she could and left the room, beginning to descend the stairs once more, but as she reached the bottom she met Sir Frederick. He had been about to go up, but stood to one side to allow her to pass. Caroline did not know what prompted her, for she ought simply to have nodded and passed him by, but some little imp was on her shoulder.

'You do not dance this evening, sir?'

'I seldom dance unless I particularly wish to,' he replied. 'And George told me that I had no hope of securing a dance with you, since your card was full soon after you arrived.'

'I am afraid that is so,' she said, 'but there are others who may have a space left, sir.'

'Of little use when I came only for one purpose.'

Caroline caught her breath. Was he saying that he had come merely to dance with her? Surely not! She smiled at him and went to pass him, but now he would not permit it and caught her arm, his fingers seeming to close on her like bands of steel so that she could not move without pulling away from him. His touch seemed to burn her and she trembled inside, wondering why he should have such an effect on her senses.

'You wanted something, sir?' She looked back at him, eyes wide and clear, a hint of challenge in their depths. 'But perhaps you came to give me news of the puppy we rescued?'

'Well, it would seem my groom has taken rather a fancy to the creature, which fawns on him in a ridiculous manner, and would like to take it home for his children—if you have no objection?' Freddie raised his brows. 'I was not sure what you would wish—unless you expected me to care for it personally? I am assured it will be well treated.'

'That is excellent news.' Caroline smiled. 'How very kind of your groom to take the poor little scrap in. Tell him that I am grateful for his kindness.'

'So would you like to name the pup or shall we leave it to Jacob and his children?'

'I should think his name ought to be Lucky,' she said, 'for he undoubtedly is to find such a good home, but it must be for your groom to decide, sir. I am in your debt for relieving me of what might have proved a problem in my present circumstances.'

'Yes, indeed you are,' Freddie said, his expression seeming to mock her. 'But I fear that if I asked you to walk with me in the gardens for a few minutes you would refuse.'

'We hardly know each other well enough for that, sir.'

'We do not know each other at all, Miss Holbrook.' He let one finger trail down her arm, sending a *frisson* of sensation shooting through her. For a moment as she stared into his dark eyes, she felt as if she were drowning, being sucked down and down into a swirling pool and out of her depth. 'I am not sure that it would be to the benefit of either of us to be become more intimately acquainted…despite our mutual interest in a lucky dog.'

'Then please allow me to pass,' Caroline said and gave him a frosty stare. Until that moment she had been revising her opinion of him, and liking what she had discovered, but now she was once again aware of the danger of allowing herself to like such a man. If she were foolish enough to develop a *tendre* for him, he would be sure to break her heart. 'My partner is waiting and I am already late for our dance. As you said, all my dances are taken.'

'Just so,' Freddie said, releasing her. He felt the reserve in her and mentally drew back. If he were not careful he would find himself drawn into a situation that could lead to only one end. He liked her enough to enjoy a light flirtation—but marriage? No, he had no thought of it! He reverted to the mocking stance that was his habitual manner. 'You intrigue me, for I do not believe that you can be all that you seem, Miss Holbrook. You have made an impression. I dare say you could marry one of several gentlemen, all of them titled and wealthy.'

'Do you think so, sir?' Caroline lifted her head. 'Perhaps you imagine that I wish to marry for fortune and position? If that is so, I think you may regard yourself as safe. I believe a marquis is as high as you can aspire in the future? I have only to encourage it and I may become a duchess one day…' She walked off, her back straight, leaving Freddie to watch her in wry amusement.

The devil of it was that she was probably right! He was annoyed that she intrigued him, holding his thoughts more often than he liked. What was it about her that had caught his attention? She was a beauty, but there were other ladies as lovely who aroused no more than a flicker of interest in his mind. It seemed that the only way he might free himself was to develop the acquaintance, for he was sure to find her out in the end. She could surely not be as innocent and pure of mind as she seemed.

Caroline returned to the ballroom. Had she been a cat, her tail would have been twitching, for he had managed to get beneath her skin. Sir Frederick Rathbone was a sight too sure of himself for her liking. He had deserved a set down, and that was the only reason she had spoken in a way that might be seen as bragging. It was true that a young gentleman, who was the second in line for a dukedom, had paid her considerable attention, but she would not normally have dreamed of drawing anyone's notice to it—and she had no intention of encouraging Sir Frederick to make an offer. Indeed, she had done her best to discourage it.

She wished that she had thought of some other way to put Sir Frederick down, for she did not wish him or anyone else to suppose that she was hanging out for a title. It was the furthest thing from her mind. At the moment she did not precisely know what she wanted from a husband. He must be an educated gentleman, able to discuss poetry and literature and to appreciate music and art. She thought that he must also have a sense of humour, for she did not think she could bear to be married to someone who was serious all the time.

For a moment her thoughts turned to Sir Frederick. She smiled at the thought of him giving into the seduction of a helpless puppy, allowing it to inveigle its way in to his good graces. Perhaps he was not as reserved or haughty as he sometimes seemed…and perhaps she did quite like him after all. At the back of her mind the thought hovered that, perhaps if her aunt had not been so very keen to see her marry Sir Frederick, she might have liked him quite a lot…

The next morning, Caroline had almost forgotten the little incident of the previous evening. She had decided to go to the lending library to take out a book one of her new friends had told her about. She went early, escaping without her maid, though she knew that her aunt would not approve of such behaviour. However, since the library was only a few streets away, she thought that it was quite safe for she would be at home again before her aunt was aware that she had been out.

It was as she emerged from the library, her parcel of books held by the string the assistant had obligingly tied for her, that she almost bumped into the man she had been thinking about despite her struggle to put him from her mind. He lifted his hat to her, and she could not but admire the way he looked in his dark green riding coat and pale breeches. It would seem that he had been riding earlier, for he still carried his whip. It was impossible to avoid him, so she smiled and wished him good morning.

'You are about early, Miss Holbrook.' He glanced at her books, a flicker of amusement on his lips as he saw that she had chosen not only a book of poetry, but also a rather lurid gothic novel that was just then causing quite a stir amongst the younger ladies. 'Ah, I see you have fallen victim to a great piece of nonsense, mistakenly described as excellent stuff.'

'You do not like Ann Radcliffe's work, sir?'

'I do not find it particularly entertaining,' Freddie said, 'though I can see it might appeal to the female mind.'

Caroline's eyes glinted with anger. 'I think you are patronising, sir. The female mind is equally capable of understanding more worthy works of literature, but a novel of this kind is meant for entertainment.'

'Yes, I dare say,' Freddie said, amused by how easily she had risen to his bait. 'Personally, I prefer the Marquis de Sade—but that would not be fit reading for a young lady, of course. If you wish to read gothic novels, may I recommend Gregory Lewis's novel *The Monk* to you?'

'Had I not already read it, I would have been pleased for you to do so,' Caroline said, lifting her chin. She suspected that he was teasing her and it brought a hint of defiance to her lovely face. 'I thought it a little shocking, but it was very well written, did you not think so?'

'Indeed, yes,' Freddie said and laughed softly, for he had read the hint of challenge in her eyes. She looked just like an angry kitten! 'Have you not guessed yet that I am teasing you, Miss Holbrook? It is a fault in me. My godmother often takes me to task for levity. She says that, if I were ever to conquer the need for such foolishness, I might become a better man.'

'Yes, of course,' Caroline said, sheathing her claws. 'Then may I take it that you have read Mrs Radcliffe's book *The Mysteries of Udolpho*?'

'Indeed, I have, some years ago,' he agreed. 'I found it

the best of her work—though I dare say others are tolerably readable.'

'I have not yet found it on the shelves,' Caroline said. 'It seems to be popular still, even though it was published some years ago.'

'Ah, then perhaps I may be of service to you,' Freddie said. 'I believe I still own a copy. Allow me to lend it to you, Miss Holbrook…'

Freddie became aware that she was not attending. Her eyes seemed to be fixed on something behind him, and he turned, taking in the incident instantly, for he saw the young boy being attacked by a group of older boys. Seeing that Caroline was about to plunge recklessly into the path of an oncoming dray wagon, he took hold of her arm, restraining her so violently that she yelped with pain.

'Forgive me,' he said, 'but I beg you, leave this to me. Stay here!'

The instruction was given in such a severe tone that Caroline remained where she was while he crossed the road, dodging between the traffic. She watched as he spoke to the lads, sending them off about their business, and noted that he slipped a coin into the hand of the one that had been attacked.

'What happened?' she asked as he returned to her. 'Was he much hurt?'

'It was merely a spat amongst brothers,' Freddie told her. 'The boy had lost some money one of the others had given him to buy their supper—nothing for you to be distressed about, Miss Holbrook.'

'You gave him money,' she said. 'That was kind of you, sir.'

'It was an easy task.' He gave her a severe look. 'May I

recommend you to be less impulsive, Miss Holbrook. You could easily have been injured just now.'

'You are good to be concerned for me,' she replied with a toss of her head. 'I assure you that I was aware of the wagon and felt that I was quite able to avoid it. I am not one of those fragile young ladies who faint at the slightest thing, sir.'

'Indeed you are not, but your behaviour is sometimes reckless in the extreme,' he said severely. 'If I may say so, Miss Holbrook, you are far too pretty to end your life crushed beneath the wheels of a heavy-goods wagon. But before you grow cross with me again, I believe I had just asked if I might lend you a book you wished to read?'

Caroline hesitated, for he had seemed critical, but her desire to read the novel overcame her pique. 'Thank you, I should like to read it for it has been recommended to me by a friend.'

'I shall send it round to your aunt's house,' Freddie said. 'In the meantime, may I walk you home?'

'You are kind, sir,' Caroline replied, 'but I am but two streets from my home and I dare say you have other things to occupy you.'

'Then perhaps we shall meet again soon.'

Freddie tipped his hat to her and set off down the street.

Caroline successfully managed to slip back into the house without being discovered by her aunt, though Mrs Holbrook had been to her room to inquire for her and was a little upset that she had been out alone that morning, even though it was merely to the lending library.

'It will not do for you to visit these places alone in town, my dear,' she scolded her daughter, though without malice.

'I am not sure it is safe, for who can tell what might happen to you, dearest? You might be snatched from the street and then I should never see you again.'

'Oh, Mama!' Caroline laughed. 'I do assure you that I was quite safe, and the only person I met was Sir Frederick, who had been out riding.'

'Oh, well, I suppose it was perfectly respectable,' her mother said. 'But I know that your aunt would not approve, my dear.'

'Aunt Louisa does not approve of anything I do.'

'Caroline!' Marianne reproved her daughter with a shake of her head, and then sighed. 'But do you know, I do not believe Louisa approves of much I do either.'

'Oh, Mama!' Caroline said and went into a fit of giggles for she had never expected to hear her mother say such a thing. 'Do be careful or she will give us both the most frightful scold.'

'I dare say she may,' Marianne said. 'Do you know, I think I shall accompany you this afternoon. You are going to visit some friends, I believe?'

'Yes, Mama. Mr Bellingham has asked me to take tea with his sister, Mrs Fairchild, and her daughter, Julia, and I have agreed. If you come with me, Aunt Louisa need not, and I know she had another appointment for she spoke of my going with just my maid.'

'If I come with you, there will be no need for a maid to accompany us,' Marianne said. 'Now, my dearest. The reason I came to look for you was that I have received some silk I ordered from the merchant a few days ago, and the seamstress is coming later this morning to discuss styles and fashions. Do come and look at the fashion plates she left for me to peruse. I need your advice.'

Caroline followed her mother obediently to her bedchamber, where various bales of silk were spread out on the bed. She was delighted to find that her mother had purchased some colours as well as grey, and there was not even a black ribbon to be seen.

During the next hour before the seamstress arrived, they had a pleasurable time discussing the styles that would most suit Marianne, and the colours she ought to choose for each ensemble.

Caroline left her mother when the seamstress arrived, retiring to one of the small parlours overlooking the garden at the back of the house to read her book. She returned to her bedchamber before the bell sounded for nuncheon and she was joined by her aunt and her mother, to partake of a cold meal.

After they had eaten, Caroline went up to change into an afternoon gown of pale green. She put on a bonnet tied with matching ribbons and a pelisse of creamy white, adding a pair of white gloves and a green reticule. She had hardly reached the bottom of the stairs when Mrs Holbrook joined her and they went out to the carriage.

'Well, this is nice, my dear, just the two of us,' Marianne said. 'Perhaps we should do this more often.'

Caroline forbore to answer that they might do it as often as she chose. It was nice to see her mother looking better and to know that she seemed to have begun to throw off her grief at last.

Mrs Fairchild welcomed them to her At Home, and invited Mrs Holbrook to sit opposite her, while Caroline shared a small sofa with Julia. There were only three other guests: Mr Bellingham, Mr Milbank, a gentleman of mature years, and also a gentleman Caroline had not particularly noticed before this day. She was introduced to him as Mr Farringdon, a man of some thirty-odd years, attractive but not as gentlemanly in his manners as Mr Bellingham in Caroline's opinion. He seemed to her to be ill at ease, and she disliked the way he spoke to her, as though trying to claim an intimacy that did not exist.

When Julia got up to help her mother by serving tea and cakes, Mr Farringdon came to sit beside Caroline. He began by being very complimentary to her, remarking on her dress and asking if she was enjoying her stay in town. Caroline replied politely, but did not smile or allow her tongue to run away with her as she so often did. She was glad when Julia looked at him expectantly, and he was obliged to relinquish his place to her. He took his leave soon after, and Caroline was pleased that he had gone. The tea party now became more intimate, and she was entertained by Mr Bellingham, who was relating a saucy tale that was going the rounds of London's drawing rooms.

'Well, you can imagine what Prinny made of that,' George said. 'He asked the lady to remove herself if she could not control her excess wind and she went off with her cheeks the colour of puce.'

'Oh, how embarrassing for her,' Caroline said. 'We should not laugh, for it must have been awful for her.'

'Think of poor Prinny. He was seated next to her, you know. I think it must have been just a little unpleasant for him.'

'Oh, my dear,' Mrs Fairchild said. 'I am not sure you should repeat that tale in mixed company. You may have offended Mrs Holbrook.'

'Not offended,' Marianne said. 'Surprised might be a better word—for I had not thought the Regent would mind his words to that extent…'

Silence greeted her sally, and then they all laughed. It was unlike Marianne to make a jest, but she had certainly attempted it and was given generous approval for her efforts.

'There, you see, it was quite acceptable,' George said and turned his attention to his niece. 'I am glad that you did not encourage Farringdon, Julia. I have every reason to believe that he is hanging out for a rich wife. From what I hear, he is all but done up.'

'Oh, I need no warning against that gentleman,' Julia declared. 'He asked me if I would take the air with him at Mrs Peterson's musical evening, but naturally I refused.' She laughed, a look of unusual naughtiness in her eyes. 'In any case, I believe he has turned his attention to Caroline—so I shall not receive a proposal after all.'

'Oh, dear, I do hope not,' Caroline said and gurgled with laughter. 'If he has hopes of me, I fear he will be sadly disappointed on two counts. I do not care for his manner so very much—and I am not the heiress he needs.'

'Caroline, my love,' her mother reproved. 'You are from a good family, and you have a small trust fund from your father. And your grandfather may give you something when you marry.'

'He might if he chose,' Caroline said. 'But I do not expect it.'

'I dare say your face is your fortune,' Julia said and looked at her admiringly. 'I wish I were as beautiful as you, Caroline.'

'Oh, I am not beautiful,' Caroline said, 'and you are very pretty, Julia. You must know that you are?'

'Pretty is not beautiful—is it, Uncle George? Caroline is beautiful, do you not think so?'

'Oh, most certainly,' he replied obligingly. 'But Caroline is right, Julia. You are very pretty, and you have your share of beaux so you do not need to pull caps with each other.'

'Oh, we shan't do that,' Julia said. 'I like Caroline best of all my new friends, and I intend to see a lot of her while she is in town.'

'Do you intend to stay in London long, ma'am?' Mr Milbank asked of Marianne. 'I myself have come only for a short visit. I find Bath suits me better and I have only come up to visit my tailor—there is no one to rival a London tailor, you know.'

The conversation immediately turned to the merits of various tailors of note, and the time passed quickly. Indeed, they stayed for much longer than the polite twenty minutes, and Julia was reluctant to let Caroline leave.

'You are coming to my dance tomorrow evening, are you not?' she asked. 'Please, you must say yes, for if you do not I shall be so disappointed.'

'Yes, of course we are coming,' Marianne said before her daughter could answer. 'We are looking forward to it very much—but now we must go. Lady Taunton has arranged a dinner party this evening, and we must not be late.'

She stood up and Caroline followed her, Mr Bellingham coming out into the hall to say goodbye to them.

'It was a pleasure to have your company,' George told her. 'It is seldom that one gets the chance to talk as we have this afternoon. I do not dine with Lady Taunton this evening, but I shall look forward to seeing you tomorrow evening. May I beg that you will reserve two dances for me, Miss Holbrook?'

'Yes, of course,' she said. 'I shall be honoured, sir.'

She followed her mother into the carriage, accepting Mr Bellingham's hand as he came to assist her. She sat forwards and waved, and then relaxed against the squabs as they were driven away.

'Well, that was very pleasant, was it not?' Marianne said. 'I thought I should be quite tired, but do you know, I feel very well. I think the air in London must agree with me. It is not as damp as the air at home, I believe.'

Caroline thought that it was perhaps being out in company that had helped her mother recover her spirits, but she said nothing. It was too soon to be sure of anything, and she would not embarrass her mother for the world.

When they arrived home, Caroline found a package waiting for her on the hall table. She knew immediately that it was the book Sir Frederick had promised her, and picked it up with a pleased smile. He had brought it as promised, which was kind of him, and improved her opinion of his character even more.

She was a little sorry that she had not been at home to thank him personally, but decided that she would send a polite note of thanks to the address on his card, which was tucked inside the package. As she went upstairs to rest before changing for dinner, she wondered if she would see Sir Freddie at Julia's dance…

Lady Taunton was somewhat indisposed the following morning, and announced that she would not be able to attend the dance that evening.

'Something must have disagreed with me last night,' she said, rubbing at her chest. 'I am sorry to disappoint you, Caroline, but I believe you must prepare yourself for an evening at home.'

'I am very sorry that you are feeling uncomfortable, Aunt,' Caroline said. 'However, Mama is to accompany me. She had already decided on it, and I believe she is looking forward to wearing her new gown.'

'Very well,' her aunt said, looking sour. 'It is all this junketing about I have been doing on your behalf, miss. It does not suit me. Your mama may do her duty by you for once and we must hope that she is not prone upon her bed in the morning.'

'I do sincerely hope she will not be,' Caroline said. 'And I hope that a rest this evening will cure your indigestion, Aunt.'

'If it is merely indigestion,' Lady Taunton said, looking much as a martyr might being led to the stake. 'I think I shall send for my doctor just to be on the safe side.'

However, nothing untoward happened, and Caroline set out with her mother at the appointed time. It was just a small dance, not one of the important affairs of the Season. Julia was greeting her guests, looking delightful in a white dress with spangles embroidered over the skirt. She stood with her mother to welcome everyone, but once Caroline arrived she was released and soon after the dancing began.

Despite it being a small affair, there were several gentlemen present, most of whom Caroline was beginning to know quite well, for she had met them at most of the affairs she had attended. She was, however, a little surprised when she saw Mr Farringdon walk in a little later, and asked Julia about it.

'Mama invited him before George told us that he was in financial difficulty. I wish she had not, for I do not like him. I had hoped that he might not attend, but it seems that he does not know when he is not welcome. I just hope he does not try to get me to go outside with him.'

'If he does, you must simply refuse,' Caroline said. 'Is your card full yet?'

'Almost,' Julia said. 'Oh, look, here comes Sir Frederick. I shall ask him if he will dance with me twice. That will leave no space for Mr Farringdon.'

She smiled beguilingly as Sir Frederick came up to them and offered him her card, asking if he would write his name in the only two spaces available. He did so and returned it to her, turning to bow to Caroline as Julia's next partner came to claim her.

'May I hope that you have a space left for me, Miss Holbrook?'

'Yes, I do have two, as it happens,' Caroline said. She had left them deliberately, but she was not going to admit it. 'One is just about to begin—and the other is just before supper.'

'Then I shall claim them both,' Freddie said and held out his hand to her. 'I hope you found the book you took from the library as enthralling as you hoped?'

'I have managed to read only one chapter as yet,' Caroline said, 'but I am sure I shall enjoy it. Mama says that she wants to read it when I have finished—so you see, I am not the only empty-headed female to be seduced by the delights of Mrs Radcliffe's work.'

'I assure you that I have never thought you empty-headed, Miss Holbrook,' Freddie said, a gleam in his eyes; he knew that she was being deliberately provoking. 'A little reckless, perhaps? Or is that simply a disguise to fool us all?' His manner was decidedly provocative and received the answer it deserved.

'Oh, you are unkind, sir,' Caroline came back at him challengingly. 'What makes you think that I would pretend to be other than I am?'

'It was simply a thought that popped into my head,' he murmured, attempting innocence. 'I dare say I was wrong?' Caroline was silent and he raised his brows. 'Have I offended you, Miss Holbrook?'

'Oh, no, not at all,' she said and looked up at him. 'Please continue what you were saying.'

'I think I meant to ask if you will come driving with me one morning, Miss Holbrook,' Freddie said. 'I was hoping that you might say yes…if you are not otherwise engaged?'

'Oh…' Caroline was a little surprised, for she had not expected it. 'Yes, I do not see why not, sir. I have driven out with Mr Bellingham several times, but, yes, thank you. I should be happy to do so.'

'Perhaps the day after tomorrow?'

'Yes, I believe that will suit. My aunt never makes engagements for the mornings. She prefers to stay in her room until eleven or twelve, but I like to go out early.'

'So I have observed,' Freddie said. 'I shall call for you at ten, if that is not too early?'

'No, not at all,' she said. 'I shall look forward to it.'

Their dance was ending and Sir Frederick escorted her back to Julia, who was to be his next partner. Caroline was momentarily alone, and she saw that Mr Farringdon was making his way towards her. Fortunately, her next partner arrived before he could do so and she was swept back into the throng of dancers.

As the evening progressed, Mr Farringdon made two more attempts to reach her, but Caroline avoided him, and it was not until she stepped outside on the terrace to cool herself for a moment before the supper dance that he succeeded in speaking to her. She had not seen him standing in the shadows, and, as he moved towards her, turned away, intending to return to the ballroom.

'Miss Holbrook,' he said. 'I have been wishing to speak to you. I had hoped that I might be given the honour of a dance with you this evening?'

'Forgive me, but my card was filled almost at once. Excuse me. I must go, for my partner will be waiting.'

'Surely you can spare a moment?' He moved to block her way, sending a little shiver of alarm down her spine.

'No, I must go,' she said and tried to move past him, but he laid his hand on her bare arm, making her jerk away instinctively. His eyes glittered and she thought he was about to say something more, but then his face froze and he took his hand from her arm.

'Miss Holbrook—I believe this is our dance?'

Caroline had never been more relieved in her life as she saw Sir Frederick standing in the doorway. Her face lit up and she moved towards him eagerly, offering him her hand.

'I had not forgotten. I was about to return, sir.'

'Nothing has happened to disturb you?'

'Oh, no,' Caroline said, for she did not wish to make something out of nothing. 'Excuse me, sir.' Farringdon stood back, nodding to Sir Frederick, who was regarding him sternly.

'And that,' Freddie said in a low voice as they went inside, 'was extremely foolish of you, Miss Holbrook. There are some gentlemen you would be safe with on a desert island, but not that one. What made you go outside with him?'

Caroline glanced at him, a hint of temper in her eyes. 'If you imagine that I went to meet him, you are mistaken, sir. I do not like the gentleman and would not even grant him a dance!' The expression on her face hinted that at that moment she did not particularly like Freddie either.

A smile flickered in his eyes as he inclined his head to her. 'I stand corrected, Miss Holbrook, and I am happy to admit it. I jumped to conclusions, but I happen to know that Farringdon is not ideal as an admirer for a young lady like you. Neither is he possessed of a great fortune. I do not imagine your family would think him suitable, for I dare say they expect you to make a good match.'

'Do you, indeed?' Caroline tossed her head at him as he led her into the dance. 'I thank you for your advice, sir. In this instance I believe the advice was not needed, but please do feel free to give me the benefit of your superior knowledge on these matters whenever you wish. As you say, it is imperative that I marry well, and I dare say you may know to a penny what any particular gentleman is worth.' Since he clearly thought her a fortune hunter, she might as well encourage the thought!

Freddie's mouth twitched at the corners, but he made no further remarks on the subject as he led her into the dance. Caroline relaxed as she felt his hand at her waist, and for some reason her anger vanished instantly. She looked up at him a little uncertainly.

'I have distressed you. Forgive me, Miss Holbrook.'

'I think that perhaps I have been rude? I am the one to ask for understanding, Sir Frederick. I was upset and spoke too hastily. Indeed, I was glad to be rescued.'

'No forgiveness is needed,' he assured her. 'I would have you no other way, Miss Holbrook. I prefer that a young lady should speak her mind—and I find you most refreshing.'

Was that another way of saying that she was ill mannered,

but to be forgiven because of her youth? Caroline was not sure if he was mocking her or not, because she was sure that he was laughing inside. She decided that the best thing to do was to retain a dignified silence, which she did for the remainder of their dance, but when he asked if he might escort her into supper she was obliged to smile and thank him.

'And thus might Saint Joan have looked as she was taken to the stake,' he said in a low voice, and as she looked up she saw that his eyes were bright with laughter. 'Am I still to be permitted to take you driving, Miss Holbrook?'

'Do you still wish to?'

'Yes, certainly,' he said. 'I believe…'

What he had been about to say was missed, for they were joined by Julia and a party of young bucks, and after seeing that Caroline had all she needed, Sir Frederick soon left them to the enjoyment of their supper. When she looked for him later, she realised that he must have gone.

She could not help feeling piqued, because she did not know what she had done to give him such a poor opinion of her. It was true that if she married well she might be able to make Mama's life better, and she would like to do something for her brothers too—but she would not wish to marry exclusively for money. Indeed, she could not imagine herself married to most of the gentlemen she knew…

Chapter Three

Caroline was thoughtful as she went to bed that evening. She was aware that the evening had been very pleasant, and she was enjoying her stay in town—but for some reason the sparkle had gone out of things after Sir Frederick had left the ball. Now why should that be? She had continued to dance all evening and many of her partners were very personable young men—but somehow none of them made her feel quite as alive as Sir Frederick.

Why had he left early? She wondered if she had offended him by being a little sharp and was sorry that she had been hasty. He'd seemed to imagine that she was interested in making an advantageous marriage and that had made her angry. What had she done to give such an ill opinion of her? Caroline pondered the question, but could not think that she had done anything. It was hardly her fault if she had attracted the attention of several important and wealthy men. She ought not to have said anything about being a duchess, though; the memory made her feel ill at ease with herself.

Sir Frederick had said that he still wished to take her driving, but she was afraid that she might have given him a dislike for her company. She was at heart a very well-behaved young lady despite being sometimes reckless. She decided that the next time they met she would be more careful of her behaviour.

The following day was quite taken up by shopping and appointments with the seamstress, and in the evening they attended a musical event. There was no sign of either Sir Frederick or Mr Bellingham, and Caroline wore a rather fixed smile all evening, and was rebuked by her aunt for being above her company.

'You may be bored, Caroline, but if you show it so plainly you will soon find that you are no longer invited anywhere.'

'I am sorry, Aunt,' Caroline said. 'I did not mean to offend anyone, but I am feeling…' She sighed, because she did not know why her spirits were at a low ebb. She ought not to feel as if the evening were pointless just because her particular friends were not present. 'Perhaps I am a little tired.'

It was merely an excuse, she knew, but she was glad when it was time to leave and she could be alone in her own room. She was a little on edge, and she wondered whether or not Sir Frederick would keep his appointment to take her driving the next morning.

She need not have worried, for he arrived at the appointed time. He looked extremely handsome in his blue coat and pale breeches, his boots having the kind of shine that only a valet of the first order could bestow on them.

'Miss Holbrook,' he said as the footman announced him, showing him into the downstairs parlour where Caroline was pretending to read a news sheet that had just been delivered. 'You look charming this morning, if I may be allowed to say so?'

'Thank you, sir. You are very kind.'

'You are ready?'

'Yes, of course.' Caroline smiled, allowing none of her uncertainty to show as she picked up her gloves and went out into the hall. 'You will not want to keep your horses waiting.'

She was assisted with her pelisse, and, tying the ribbons of her bonnet, followed him outside. The young lad Freddie employed as his tiger was walking the horses and brought the phaeton back to them.

'Thank you, Jim. Up with you now, lad.' Freddie turned to Caroline as the lad obeyed. She had noticed that he was driving a pair of perfectly matched greys.

'Mr Bellingham told me that you had some fine chestnuts, sir. Have you changed your horses recently?'

'No, but I had a chance to purchase these and thought they would be a splendid addition to my stables. One can never have too many horses.'

'Oh, I agree. I should imagine anyone would be pleased to own these.'

'Not all young ladies take such an interest in horses. You are a rarity, Miss Holbrook.'

'Am I?' Caroline looked at him as he handed her up. 'I have loved horses since I was first able to walk down to the stables with my father…dogs, too. Proper dogs, I mean, not the fancy lapdogs that many ladies dote on. At home I like to walk with them, sometimes for hours at a time.' She laughed. 'Indeed, I think I prefer being out with my dogs to talking to some of the people I have met in town.' She drew a sharp breath as she realised what she had said. 'Oh, dear, that was not well said. Now you will think me a country bore and I shall be ruined.'

'Not at all,' Freddie said. 'You have too much intelligence and vivacity to be a bore.'

'I shall take that as a compliment.'

'Well, you may do so, for it was meant as one.'

'Thank you. Do you have a country estate, sir?'

'I have three at the moment,' Freddie said. 'A hunting lodge in Oxfordshire, my family seat in Derbyshire and a shooting box in Scotland, which I seldom use. It was set up by my maternal grandfather and came to me on his death, but I prefer to spend much of my time in London.'

'Oh…yes, I see,' Caroline said. 'I suppose the country does not appeal to everyone, though I believe I prefer it.'

'The countryside can be pleasant enough if one has the right companions. But I do not care to spend too much time alone there when my friends are in town.'

'Yes, of course. Do you have no family, sir?'

'I had an elder sister, but she died of a putrid fever when a child.' His eyes darkened as if the memory still held echoes of pain for him. 'My parents had both died some years earlier, so that meant I was left to the mercy of the servants—and occasional visits from my uncle and grandfather. Grandfather died when I fifteen, but my uncle still lives. As does my godmother, Lady Stroud.'

'I had no idea.' Caroline glanced at him, for she guessed that he must have felt lonely as a child, but his face was a mask that showed no sign of emotion.

'Why should you? It was a long time ago. However, you must not be sorry. If I have few relatives, I have some good friends and many pleasant acquaintances.'

'Oh, yes,' Caroline agreed. 'I believe you are very close with Mr Bellingham, are you not?'

'We have been friends for some time.'

They were entering the park gates now and Caroline saw several ladies and gentlemen she knew. Some were in carriages, but most were on foot.

'Would you count that gentleman as a friend?' Caroline asked after they had been driving for some minutes. She had noticed Mr Farringdon. He was on foot and seemed to be staring fixedly in their direction.

'An acquaintance. I believe his estate is not far distant from my hunting lodge, but I would not count him a friend. We meet at the card tables and at various functions.'

'Yes, I suppose you must play with so many gentlemen at the tables,' Caroline said, looking thoughtful. 'Papa was not lucky at cards. I think it is not always wise to gamble too much.'

'You are very right, though the golden rule is to play only if you can pay.'

'Ah, yes, very true—but I think that gaming has brought more than one gentleman to ruin.'

'I am sure that is so. The devil of it is that one can do nothing to prevent it. When someone has the need for self-destruction, no cautionary words will help.' Freddie was thoughtful for a moment and then he glanced at her. 'But tell me, do you go to Lady Rowe's affair tomorrow?'

'Yes, indeed we shall,' Caroline replied, allowing his wish to change the subject. 'Shall you be there, sir?'

'It was my intention, but I have business that takes me to Oxford, though I hope to return within a few days.'

'Oh…' Caroline knew a pang of disappointment. 'Well, I suppose you must settle your affairs.'

'I must speak to my agent urgently,' Freddie told her. 'There are certain things that must be seen to at my estate and…elsewhere.' He smiled at her. 'Do you intend to stay in town until the end of the Season?'

'I am not sure…' Caroline wrinkled her brow in thought. 'For some weeks yet, I believe, but it depends…on many things.'

'Just so,' Freddie agreed. 'Tell me, Miss Holbrook, have you progressed with your reading?'

They began to discuss the merits of Mrs Radcliffe's writing, passing on to the discussion of literature and poetry. The park was full of people that morning, and, as they made their rounds, they were hailed by Mr Bellingham, who was driving Julia that morning.

Caroline was sorry when they completed their turn of the park and returned to her aunt's house. She smiled and thanked Sir Frederick for his company, and went in feeling oddly out of sorts with herself. She had enjoyed driving with him, but was still uncertain whether, if asked, he would count her as a friend or merely an acquaintance.

Freddie left town that afternoon, his thoughts much exercised by his conversation with Miss Holbrook. She had begun to pop into his mind too often of late, but he had not yet come to a decision concerning his future plans. If he cared to marry, Miss Holbrook was exactly the kind of lively young woman he would wish to make his wife—though he would not wish his offer to be accepted simply for the sake of his wealth and rank. He supposed that in time he must marry, for it was his duty to produce an heir, as his uncle had no children to carry on the family name. However, he would not wish to marry for such a reason.

It would be unfair to the lady and to him. He firmly believed that there must be genuine respect and affection on both sides for a marriage to work—and therein lay the rub, for he could not suppose that he had found much favour in the lady's eyes even if she had caused him a restless night or two. He knew that her careless remark about becoming a duchess had been made out of pique, but it might not be far from the truth. He had noticed that one or two of her suitors were more than a little interested and some were his equal in birth, if not quite in wealth. Was it possible that Miss Holbrook—or her mama—was waiting for the highest bidder? Caroline might be feigning indifference so as to arouse his interest the more.

Freddie had been used to living much as he pleased, and was answerable to no one for his actions. If he were to marry, he would need to make changes to his lifestyle and his various houses. What would do for a bachelor would not do for a lady, particularly one with modern tastes and a lively mind.

Yes, he must consider carefully while he was away. In the meantime, however, he had other more pressing matters on his mind…

It was as well for Caroline that the next few days were too full to allow her time for reflection. It seemed that she went from one affair to the next, sometimes attending more than one event in the same evening. If it was not Almack's, it was a private dance or a card evening, and she met the same people with amazing regularity.

She had begun to realise that there were very few gentlemen she would be happy to see every day of her life. Most of them seemed good mannered and pleasant, but that spark was missing, the vital element that made her feel so much more alive. There were actually no more than two or three in whose company she felt truly able to be herself. Mr Bellingham was perhaps the kindest of her acquaintance and she was usually happiest when with him and Julia Fairchild, who had become a particular friend.

Nearly a week had passed before she saw Sir Frederick again. However, he was with Mr Bellingham and Julia as she entered Mrs Ashton's large drawing room that Saturday evening. Her breath caught in her throat, and all at once her heart began to beat very fast. It was so very pleasant to see him again. She fanned herself delicately, for she believed that her cheeks must be flushed.

Oh, no, this was foolish! She must control her feelings. It would not do for her to show any sign of partiality this early in their acquaintance. He would think she was setting her cap at him! Even though Julia was making signs to her, she would not go to join them just yet.

They had all been invited for the pleasure of having supper, listening to music or playing cards. Some of the gentlemen were already playing cards at tables set up at the far end of the room, but Sir Frederick, Mr Bellingham and Julia were standing near the French windows, which opened on to the terrace, possibly because the room was already warm. She smiled at Julia, and then turned to the elderly lady who had come to greet Lady Taunton, schooling herself to patience. In a little while she would excuse herself and join her own friends.

However, before she could do so, she was joined by three other friends: a young lady by the name of Helen Telford, her brother Henry and her cousin Stephen Rivers. Caroline joined in the animated conversation, for they had all attended a balloon ascension that morning, and there was much to say on the subject. It had truly been a marvellous sight, and Mr Rivers was telling them that he had spoken to one of the balloonists and hoped to take a trip in a balloon himself very soon.

'You will not do so, sir,' Helen said, and looked shocked.

'Oh, you lucky thing,' Caroline said at almost the same moment. 'I should love to go up in a balloon. It looked so exciting. Just think how wonderful it would be to float across the sky and look down on what is happening below.'

'Do you not think that you might fall over the edge?' a voice asked from behind her. She felt a tingle at the nape of her neck and turned to see the person she had somehow expected. 'Or are you so intrepid that you would dare anything, Miss Holbrook?'

Caroline looked into Sir Frederick's dark eyes and saw the mockery there. 'I believe I should like it of all things,' she replied, challenging him. She had a feeling that he was trying to provoke her deliberately and, as before, she was aware that to let herself like him too much might be foolish. 'I think it would be almost impossible to fall out unless one were very stupid, sir—unless it was to crash, of course, but I do not believe that happens so very often.'

'I am certain it would not dare with you on board,' Freddie said, much amused by her answer. He had been watching her from across the room, fascinated by the play of emotions on her expressive face, and he knew he was not the only one to think her exceptional. She was certainly a hit, for you could not go anywhere in society without hearing her name. If her artlessness were real, she was truly a pearl amongst women.

'Now, be truthful, Miss Holbrook,' he said and studied her face, trying to probe beneath the surface. She intrigued him. She must marry well, for she had no fortune, but her manner seemed to say that she would as lief take a nobody as a duke, which had added greatly to her popularity. Was that the real Caroline or just an act? 'Would you truly wish for a balloon flight? I believe I could arrange it if you dare?' His brows rose, answering her challenge with one of his own.

'Do you really mean it?' Caroline was ecstatic, her face alight with pleasure. 'Oh, if only I could. My aunt would not approve, naturally, but perhaps she need not know exactly what I have been doing. We could arrange to drive out to Richmond…Mr Bellingham, too, perhaps?'

'May I be one of this party?' Mr Rivers asked. 'If Helen and Henry came too, it would be quite respectable. A picnic in Richmond Park and a balloon ascension, too. I'm sure your aunt could not object—and she need not know the whole of it, of course.'

Freddie groaned inwardly. He had made the suggestion idly, believing that Caroline would withdraw at the last moment, but from the expression of delight on her face it was clear that she was all for the excursion.

'Oh, I should love that,' Caroline declared with enthusiasm, 'and if we are to go in a party, my aunt will not think it her duty to come with me. When shall you arrange it, sir?'

'For next week,' Freddie said, pulled in by some force stronger than his will. 'On Thursday if it is fine. I shall call for you myself at ten in the morning, Miss Holbrook.'

'Oh, thank you!' Her eyes were glowing. 'You are so kind, sir. I cannot thank you enough.'

'I believe you may change your mind when it comes to it,'

Freddie said. 'But for now, will you do me the honour of becoming my partner at a game of whist?'

'Yes, why not?' Caroline said. She laid her hand on his arm, giving him a brilliant smile. Freddie almost blinked— he had the impression that the sun had just come out and it sent him a little dizzy. She was truly an enchantress, whatever else she might be. 'Tell me, who are we to oppose?'

'George and Julia,' Freddie said. 'She is very modest about her skill, and tells me she plays whist with her grandmother for peppermints.'

'Oh, does she?' Caroline nodded happily. 'I used to play for humbugs with Nicolas. He usually won all the sweets from my jar—but I think he cheated. When I played with Tom I usually won.'

'Ah, yes, your brothers,' Freddie said. 'Do you think either of them will join you in town?'

'I do not think so,' Caroline said wistfully. 'Tom would if he could afford it, I think, but Nicolas is in France at the moment. He was sent as a liaison officer and I have not heard from him for almost a month now.'

'Well, perhaps he will surprise you on his return,' Freddie said. It would be interesting to observe her with her brothers, he imagined. 'Ah, George, you see I have captured Miss Holbrook. I told you I should persuade her to join us.'

'Oh, good,' Julia said and then blushed shyly. 'I should like that of all things, that is if Miss Holbrook chooses.'

'I believe we are to oppose each other, Julia, and I must wish you good fortune, though I dare say you will not need it with Mr Bellingham as your partner.'

'Julia is a demon card player,' George said and laughed.

'Do not be deceived by her modesty, Miss Holbrook. I warn you, at the card table she is ruthless.'

Caroline laughed. She felt fortunate to have been singled out as a fourth at their table, for some of the other company were not likely to be as much fun as her companions.

Someone had begun to play the pianoforte as they settled at their table. As the room was so large they were able to hear the music without losing concentration on their game, or disturbing those who wished to listen to the music. It was a very comfortable, pleasant arrangement.

'It is such a nice large room,' Caroline remarked. 'Of course, not all houses are built so obligingly.'

'Deuced difficult to heat in the winter, I imagine,' Freddie observed. 'I prefer separate rooms if the play is serious, but for an evening like this it could not be bettered.'

'Yes, though it is too warm for my liking. Not like your barn of a place, Freddie. That is cold even in summer,' George remarked.

'You are right, George,' Freddie replied. 'I am thinking of making some changes for the future.'

'You will need to when you marry.'

'If I marry…'

'My dear chap,' George said. 'Your uncle would be damned annoyed if you do not produce an heir, I should imagine. You owe it to the family, you know they are relying on you.' George coughed behind his hand. 'I beg your pardon, ladies, I forgot myself for a moment. Remiss of me. Mixed company, you know.'

'Oh, you need not fear,' Caroline said and dimpled at him. 'You must know that I have heard far worse from my grandfather. When his gout is playing him up the air is like to turn blue. Poor Mama almost fainted one day—the things he said to her!'

'Grandmother is a little like that, though she lowers her voice so that I shouldn't hear,' Julia said. 'But of course I do.'

'I do not believe I know your grandfather,' George said, wrinkling his brow. 'No one has mentioned him in my hearing.'

'Really, George,' Freddie drawled. 'Surely you've heard of the Marquis of Bollingbrook?'

'Good lord!' George looked astonished. 'Everyone knows—or has heard—of the Marquis, of course. I hadn't connected the two.'

'I believe Grandfather was a rake,' Caroline said. 'At least when he was much younger. I know there are some mysteries, secrets in his past, but of course he has never told me anything.'

'No?' Freddie raised his brows. 'You surprise me, Miss Holbrook. I would have imagined quite otherwise. However, perhaps I can unravel at least one of those mysteries for you. I know that your grandfather once took part in a bare-knuckle fight that lasted for twenty rounds. That is one of the few of his escapades that it is permissible to repeat in polite society.'

'How did you know that?' Caroline asked, her mouth quivering as she quizzed him with her eyes. 'Tell me, sir—did he win?'

'Yes, I believe he did.'

'Oh, well done, Grandfather!' Caroline said and calmly laid her trump card, taking the trick. 'I must ask him about it when I next see him…if I ever do.' She sighed.

'Well done,' Freddie said, as she collected her cards and laid a small club. 'A gentleman perhaps paying for his misdeeds. However, there were many other escapades that might not be so admirable as that fight, as I understand it.'

'You must tell us,' Caroline cried, taking the next hand with a nine of clubs. 'I have heard he was a gambler and…well, perhaps I should not say.' She glanced at Julia and then down at her cards.

'No, perhaps not,' Freddie said.

'I think we should change the subject, Freddie,' George observed with amusement. 'It is Julia's birthday dance this weekend. I trust you will be there, Miss Holbrook—and you, Freddie?'

The subject was successfully turned and they applied themselves to the cards. When everyone began to drift into the dining room, several other young people joined them at their table, and the conversation became very animated. Someone mentioned the balloon ascension and somehow the party grew to three carriages, to include Mr Bellingham and his niece Julia.

After supper, Caroline suggested to Julia that they should join forces against the gentlemen at cards, an idea that was taken up with pleasure. Luck must have been with them, for they won two games to one and enjoyed the feeling very much. Despite her shyness, Julia had true character, gathered no doubt from the long hours she had spent playing cards with her formidable grandmother, and she could be ruthless when it came to taking a trick.

Caroline asked Julia if she would care to go shopping with her the next morning. An arrangement was made to meet, and they parted on good terms.

Caroline was feeling very pleased with herself as she joined her mother, who had consented to accompany them that evening. However, her smile faded as Aunt Louisa came up to them, looking very satisfied with herself.

'I am pleased to see that you have taken my advice,' she said, her smug tone making Caroline itch to quarrel with her. 'I observed Sir Frederick's manner towards you this evening. I think he is taken with you. If you continue as you are, I am certain that he will come up to scratch before the Season is done.'

'I am not sure that you are right, Aunt,' Caroline said, containing her irritation with commendable control. Her aunt's comments made her uncomfortable, for she had certainly not set her cap at Sir Frederick. Indeed, until recently she had not been sure that she liked him. She had now revised her opinion and was secretly afraid that she was beginning to like him rather a lot, which only made her cross. She certainly would not wish him to think that she was angling for a proposal! 'We are becoming better acquainted, but there is nothing to show an attachment on either side.'

'You must listen to your aunt, Caroline,' Marianne Holbrook said nervously. She had sensed the friction between them and it made her uneasy, because she knew that her sister would lecture her on her daughter's faults when they were alone. Of course Caroline was a trifle headstrong and wilful, but she was also kind and thoughtful and her mother did not wish to be lectured on the subject. 'I am sure she knows best.'

'Yes, Mama, of course,' Caroline said, though her face was set like thunder. 'I dare say my aunt knows much more than I on a great number of things—but perhaps on this I may be allowed to judge for myself.'

'You are a stubborn, ungrateful girl,' her aunt said. 'Well, I shall not argue with you, Caroline, but you will see that I am right soon enough.'

Caroline's dreams were peaceful enough, though when she woke she did so with a start. She had been dreaming of a room filled with gentlemen playing cards, and a deadly game was taking place between two men, one of whom was Sir Frederick. The reason it had caused her to shiver upon waking was that she knew it was she for whom they were playing.

She laughed as she realised that the dream must have been because of the talk of her grandfather and his reputation last night. What a dreadful rake he must have been in his youth! And by the sound of things, it was not the worst of his escapades by half.

She had always been fond of the old reprobate, though as a child she had seen little of him. He had begun to take more interest in her as she grew up, and on her last visit she had spent some time with him in his library, looking at his books and pictures. However, he had lost patience with her mother and they had left under a cloud. Since then she had heard nothing from him.

She thought about it and then sat down at the writing desk in her bedchamber, deciding to write to him about her visit to London. If he did not wish to read her letter, he could throw it into the fire. However, she thought he must sometimes be lonely, for she knew that his family seldom visited him.

She smiled as she sanded and then sealed her letter with wax and a beautiful gold seal ring that her father had given her as a keepsake shortly before his death. Taking her letter downstairs to be left with the others for franking and posting, she then collected her pelisse and bonnet and, with her maid in attendance, set out for her appointment with Julia Fairchild.

They were to meet at a fashionable milliner's shop and from there would go on to a shop that sold delightful shawls and other pretty trifles. Julia had told her that she had seen a beaded purse that she particularly admired, and Caroline had been thinking of a rather attractive green bonnet she had seen when out with her aunt the previous week. She meant to purchase it if she could, though her aunt had thought it too dark for her.

When she arrived at the shop, she discovered that Mr Bellingham had accompanied his niece, and, as they went in to look at the delightful bonnets on offer, she saw Sir Frederick cross the road. He entered a few moments after them, she thought by prior arrangement with his friend, for Mr Bellingham was not at all surprised to see him.

Caroline was before the mirror, trying on the bonnet she had seen in the window, and Sir Frederick stood behind her, nodding his approval.

'You should wear more green,' he told her. 'I particularly like that on you, Miss Holbrook. You have the colouring for it.'

'You are very kind, sir,' she said and laid it down. 'But I am not sure that it is just what I want.' She wandered away, determined not to let him influence her. Was her aunt right? Was he paying her attention with the notion of asking her to marry him? Mr Bellingham had mentioned that he must marry to oblige his family the previous evening. Did she wish to be married simply for the getting of an heir? She was not sure how she felt about that and she would not allow herself to be rushed into a more intimate acquaintance. She picked up a deep blue velvet hat and perched it on the back of her head. It was becoming but slightly racy, more suited to an older lady, perhaps. She was about to put it down again when she saw Sir Frederick shake his head at her, registering disapproval, and on a spurt of independence, she held it out to the assistant. 'I shall take this if you please,' she said defiantly.

'Do you think you should?' Freddie said, hoping that his expression gave no hint of his satisfaction. She was ravishing in that hat, but he had learned his lesson earlier. 'I think Lady Taunton will not approve. Perhaps you would do better to think about it for a while?'

'I shall mostly certainly buy it,' Caroline said, a militant sparkle in her eye. 'I do not allow anyone to dictate to me if I can prevent it, sir.'

'Very sensible of you, Miss Holbrook,' he said innocently, but she detected a gleam of mockery in his dark eyes. 'But I will wager she forbids you to wear it.'

'What do you wager?' she demanded at once, her eyes bright with challenge.

Sir Freddie thought for an instant before answering. 'If you succeed in wearing it tomorrow when I call for you to go driving, I shall grant you one wish, Miss Holbrook—and if you are forbidden to leave the house with such a wicked thing on your head, you must grant me my wish.'

Caroline was a little taken aback, for she had imagined he would make a small wager of a guinea or some such thing. A wish might mean anything, but, since she had no intention of letting her aunt dictate to her in the matter, she had no hesitation in taking his wager. In her pleasure at thinking of what she would demand from him, she did not realise that she had agreed to drive out with him. It was not until much later that day that she began to wonder just what he had in mind should she lose the wager…

Chapter Four

Tom was thoughtful as he took leave of his grandfather and set out for London that morning. He had stayed for ten days, because the contents of the package given to him to examine had taken some serious thought on his behalf, and because he sensed his grandfather was feeling lonely. Lord Bollingbrook had put some propositions to him, which would mean a journey overseas if he accepted them. He had been given time to think them over, and to consider what they might mean to his life. Meanwhile, he was in possession of sufficient funds to pay the most pressing of his debts at home, and the news that both his brother and sister would shortly come into modest fortunes of their own.

Caroline was to have twenty thousand pounds on her wedding day, and she would also be given some rather valuable pieces of jewellery, which were not heirlooms, but had been bought for her grandmother at the time of her wedding. It meant that, far from being almost penniless, his sister was now a considerable heiress. However, Tom had been forbidden to inform her of her good fortune. His grandfather had made that plain as they sat together the previous evening.

'You are to say nothing to the gel or her mother—and certainly not to that aunt of hers, Tom. What you will tell your mother is that I shall not have my gel forced to a marriage she cannot like. I wish to be informed before anything is settled, do you hear me, boy?'

'Yes, sir, of course. May I tell Caroline that, sir?'

'You may tell her to come to me if she is in trouble,' the Marquis said. 'And make sure that her mother understands she must ask me before she gives permission for Caroline to marry. You are the head of your immediate family, Tom—but in this matter I stand on my rights as head of our family. You understand me?'

'Yes, sir, perfectly.' Tom gave him a smile of perfect good humour. 'I can assure you that I have no wish to see Caroline unhappy. Indeed, I should forbid Mama to bully her into something she disliked.'

The Marquis nodded approvingly. He had hopes of this grandson, for there was a wrong done many years ago, a wrong that needed to be put right, and it was too late for him to do it himself. 'And do not forget that I wish to see Caroline when she has the time.'

'No, sir, I shall not forget.'

Leaving the Marquis to the ministrations of his faithful valet, Tom went out to find his groom waiting for him. He took the reins himself, allowing the man to sit beside him as they drove through the estate at a spanking pace.

He had promised his grandfather that he would give him an answer in three weeks. In the meantime, he intended to enjoy himself in London.

'And what, miss, is that on your head?' Lady Taunton looked at her niece in outrage. 'I hope it is not your intention to leave this house wearing such a piece of nonsense? It is far too old for you and it makes you look fast.'

'Oh, no, Aunt, does it?' Caroline wore a face of innocence, her eyes as guileless as a babe's. 'And to think that Sir Frederick encouraged me to buy it—insisted that I wear it for him today. However, if you think I should not, I shall go up and take it off, though I believe he will be disappointed. You know, Aunt, I do not imagine that he would be interested in a milk-and-water miss—perhaps I should be a little bold if I am to capture his interest? But pray tell me if you disagree, ma'am?'

'I imagine you think yourself clever,' her aunt said and scowled at her. 'Very well, my girl, make a show of yourself if you choose. If you get a reputation for being fast, you will ruin yourself, and then no one will offer for you.'

'Oh, Aunt, if only I could believe you,' Caroline said to herself and went quickly down the stairs as she heard the doorknocker.

Her aunt stood at the head of the stairs, watching as Sir Frederick entered and swept off his hat to her niece. He glanced up at her as she stood at the head of the stairs, a flicker of amusement in his eyes, for her annoyed expression told much. He bowed his head to her and then turned to look at Caroline.

'You look beautiful, Miss Holbrook,' Freddie said in a voice that carried to Lady Taunton, who snorted her disgust and walked away as Caroline laid her hand on his arm. 'That hat becomes you well—and I believe I have lost our wager…' He lowered his voice as they went out to the waiting carriage. 'What would you have of me?'

'May I have a little time to think?' Caroline asked, her head to one side. Her eyes were filled with wickedness, making him laugh softly, for he sensed her mood of defiance. She really was enchanting, a girl of spirit! But could he be certain that she liked him for himself—if she liked him at all, that was? 'What would you have demanded of me had I lost?'

'I had thought of something entirely suitable,' Freddie said, 'but I take leave to keep my secret for the moment. I think you have the gambling spirit of your grandfather, Miss Holbrook, and I may win next time.'

Caroline tipped her head to one side, for she saw the mockery in his eyes. 'Perhaps you have already won, sir,' she suggested. 'For you wished me to buy this hat all the time, did you not?'

'I have observed that deep colours become you,' he said. 'I dare say that you are under the influence of others, but I should like to advise you on matters of dress, Miss Holbrook. Be bold in your choice, for it suits you. Do you know that you are considered an original? At this moment you may say and do almost as you wish, for you are the darling of society.'

'No, am I?' Caroline was astonished. She looked at him hard to see if he was quizzing her. 'Are you funning, sir? I know that people have been amazingly kind, but I had not thought to cause a sensation. After all, I have very little fortune.'

'Which matters not a jot in your case,' Freddie said, enjoying himself immensely. He was beginning to accept that she meant what she said, and that artless as her manner was, it was genuine, not assumed. 'I have it on the best authority that there are ten wagers on the books at White's concerning you, Miss Holbrook.'

'No? How terribly shocking,' she said and gave a gurgle of delight. 'Pray do tell me what they are for.'

'No, no,' he said. 'For then you would make up your mind before you were asked and that would prejudice the wager.'

'Oh, that would be even more shocking,' she said, her eyes dancing with merriment as he handed her into her carriage.

'Yes, indeed,' he replied with a straight face. 'Gambling is a serious business, Miss Holbrook. Fortunes have changed hands for a foolish wager when gentlemen have been imbibing recklessly. One gentleman placed a bet that he could shoot the king of spades in the eye when drunk one evening, I recall. He was an excellent shot when sober, but just a trifle off when in his cups. He lost a small estate in Kent that night.'

'How awful,' she said. 'I do not think I should care to gamble so much on such a business.'

'Come, come, Miss Holbrook,' he said. 'Where is your fighting spirit now?'

'Perhaps if I were wealthy,' she said, 'but I should not be able to honour such a bet, for I have no property.' She looked up at him. 'Tell me, have you ever made such a reckless wager?'

'I just told you of it,' Freddie said and laughed. 'But that was when I was much younger and more inclined to wildness. However, I did not much care for the place and I later won something I liked better.'

'Are you usually fortunate at the tables?'

'Oh, yes,' he said carelessly as he drove them through the busy streets. 'Observe that gentleman in the rather odd purple coat there to your left—but do not let him see that you are staring. I won ten thousand guineas from him the other evening. I offered to throw the dice for double or quits, but he would not take it.'

'I dare say he could not afford it, sir.'

'Oh, yes,' Freddie said. 'The fellow has more blunt than he knows what to do with. His uncle recently left him a huge estate—half a million, they say—though he will probably run through it before he has done.'

'Then he is very foolish. I think that gambling for high stakes may be the cause of much suffering amongst the families of those who are addicted, but also unlucky.'

'You are perfectly right, Miss Holbrook,' Freddie said and looked serious for a moment. 'A great friend of mine was ruined that way, and there was nothing I could do about it. Had he gambled only with me, I might have saved him, but he went to low dives where the stakes are sometimes too high. Only the most reckless would play in places like that, I think.'

'You do not?'

'No, no, I am a mild gambler, Miss Holbrook. I usually prefer wagers that are not always for money.'

'Then my forfeit was not to have been monetary?'

'No, indeed.' He arched his brows at her. 'But you will not coax it from me, Miss Holbrook. I am determined that I shall win next time. Have you made up your mind what you would have of me?'

'I think…' Caroline was about to say that she wanted nothing when they were accosted by one of the young bucks walking in the park. He came up to them, sweeping his hat off and smiling at her.

'You look particularly lovely today, Miss Holbrook,' he said. 'But it was Sir Frederick I particularly wanted to address. Have you heard about the mill, sir? It is to take place on the Heath next Tuesday and they say that Gentleman George will win this time. Are you to attend?'

'I imagine I may,' Freddie said and frowned at him. 'However, this is a matter for discussion at another time, Blakeny.'

The younger man looked at him and then flushed. 'Oh, I

see what you mean, Rathbone. But I'm sure Miss Holbrook isn't offended over a small thing like that.'

'No, indeed,' Caroline said, but Freddie merely frowned and flicked the reins, moving on. 'I truly did not mind, sir.' She glanced at him sideways and saw that he was frowning. 'Why are you annoyed?'

'It was not the subject for a young lady's ears. That young idiot should have known better than to speak of it in your presence.'

'Oh, pooh,' Caroline said, and on impulse, 'I should like to see a fight—will you take me to watch it, please?'

'No, indeed I shall not,' Freddie said. 'The scene of a bare-knuckle fight is not the place for a young girl. It is out of the question.'

'But you must,' Caroline said because she was piqued by his attitude. Why did gentlemen always think a lady was too delicate for such things? She had seen her brothers scrap when they were young and had been none the worse for her experience. 'You promised me a forfeit and that is what I want…to come with you to watch the fight.'

Freddie turned his head to look at her in disbelief. Did she know what she was asking? 'You cannot mean it, Miss Holbrook? It would be most improper and your aunt would have a fit if she heard of it.'

'Well, she need not,' Caroline said. 'I shall not tell her, and neither will you—so how will she know?'

'Because everyone would talk of it,' he replied and shook his head at her. 'There would be a terrible scandal and you would be ruined. No, I shall not do such a thing. I do not think you have considered the consequences.' He gave her a severe look. 'This is foolish in the extreme.'

'But you know that paying a gambling debt is a matter of honour,' Caroline said, tipping her head to one side. Her eyes were bright with devilment; though in her heart she did not particularly wish to see the fight, she was determined to get her own way. He could not wriggle out of it, because his sense of fair play would not allow it. 'And there is a solution…if I came dressed in a youth's clothes and hid my hair, everyone would think I was your groom.'

'I do not believe that you dare,' Freddie said, but there was a sudden gleam in his eyes. The plan could just work. Her boldness amused him, and he found the idea appealed to him, against his better nature. Indeed, the idea was so intriguing that he decided to see if she would actually dare to carry it out. 'How would you slip away—and where would you get the clothes?'

'I imagine the fight is to be held early in the morning? I could slip out and perhaps return before my aunt had risen.'

'Yes, I dare say…' Freddie was caught—this was beyond anything he had expected from her and he was tempted to see just how far she would go. 'Of course, I could give a parcel of clothes to your maid, if you truly wish to go through with this—but think carefully. Supposing you were discovered?' He raised his brows at her.

'Both Mama and my aunt scarcely ever rise much before noon. I dare say we might be back home before then.'

Freddie gazed at her doubtfully. It was madness and he knew that he should refuse, but he had always paid his gambling debts… No, no, that was merely an excuse. He could not wrap this in clean linen. In truth he was tempted by the prospect of discovering whether she was really as bold as she claimed.

'If you gave your maid some of your own clothes for me, it might work,' he said. 'You may change back into them after we have left the fight, and then go home as if we have merely been for a drive together…if you truly wish to take the risk?' His eyes were intent on her face.

Caroline was on fire for the idea had appealed to her. It would be an adventure and she had been feeling restricted by her aunt's constant grumbling, the need to behave circumspectly at all times. 'If the clothes are suitable for a groom and I dirty my face, no one will even notice me.'

'How will you slip out of the house?'

'Oh, I shall manage it,' Caroline said. 'I have done it before…at home in the country. It may not be quite as easy in town, but I dare say I can manage it.'

'Very well,' Freddie said. 'We shall make another wager, Miss Holbrook. If you play your part I shall take you to the fight, but if you change your mind you will owe me a forfeit.'

'I think you will owe me yet another forfeit,' Caroline said, her eyes sparkling with mischief. Her head was up, her face alight as she challenged him. He thought her more lovely than he had yet seen her. 'I shall be there—and you must be on time, sir. I do not wish to miss anything.'

Freddie laughed, for she was undoubtedly a temptress. Would it be possible to take her to such an event and return her to her home with no one the wiser? That, of course, was his responsibility and he would certainly find it a challenge.

'I dare say you attend the ball on Monday evening?' She nodded. 'You may oversleep and forget the fight if you wish. I should not blame you.'

'You will not win your forfeit so easily,' she said, her face alight with excitement. 'We shall talk about this again, sir—but now you must pull over, for I see some friends and we must not ignore them.'

Caroline said goodbye to Sir Frederick at the door of her aunt's house. She asked him if he would care to come in for some refreshment, but he refused, saying that he had another appointment. She smiled at him, giving him her hand, which he kissed gallantly before returning to his curricle.

Caroline went into the house. She was still feeling pleased with herself for she had made him give her her own way, and, though she knew the escapade might cause her problems, she was excited at the idea. It was a long time since she had done anything so rebellious and at times had been feeling rather constricted at having to behave in the ladylike manner that was expected of her. Why did ladies always have to be so particular in their behaviour when gentlemen could do much as they pleased? There was so much she would have liked to do that was forbidden her. It was not fair and she was tired of being scolded by her aunt for things that were completely trivial.

'Caroline,' her mother's voice called to her as she walked up the stairs. 'Come here, my love. We have a visitor.'

Mrs Holbrook was standing in the doorway of the parlour she used most while a guest in her sister's house. It suited her because it was small and prettily furnished, and so seldom used for entertaining by her sister that she might think it her own. She looked very pleased with herself, almost excited about something.

'What is it, Mama?' Caroline's heart skipped a beat. 'Is it Nicolas?'

'No, it is your brother Tom,' Mrs Holbrook said, seizing her daughter by the hands and drawing her into the room. 'He is in his chamber changing, for he has just this minute arrived—and with good news. Bollingbrook has settled the most pressing of his debts. There—what do you think of that?'

'I think it wonderful news,' Caroline said, surprised and pleased. 'I am so glad for him, Mama. Do you know why Grandfather decided to do something for him?'

'I have no idea,' Marianne said with a frown. 'After the last time we visited him I thought he would not wish to see any of us again—but Tom says that he has asked particularly for you, Caroline. It would be wonderful if he were to do something for both you and Nicolas.'

'Oh, Mama, why should he?' Caroline said. 'It is quite enough that he has helped Tom to recover from his debts. Besides, Nicolas has found a life for himself and we are well enough as we are, are we not?'

'If your grandfather means to do something, you should visit him,' her mother said, hardly listening to her daughter's disclaimer. 'I know you are engaged for the next three weeks or so, but after that you might go down for a few days. I would stay here, of course, and you could always return. Your brother intends to visit Bollingbrook again in three weeks. He could take you down, and perhaps your grandfather would send you back in his own carriage. Yes, that would be quite acceptable, Caroline.'

'I have no objection to visiting Grandfather,' Caroline said. It would be pleasant to spend a few days with the Marquis. 'But you must not expect anything more, Mama. I dare say Grandfather thought it his duty to help Tom, but I do not need anything. I am quite content as I am.'

'Do not be so foolish,' Mrs Holbrook said and frowned at her. 'Louisa tells me that there are prospects of a marriage between you and a certain gentleman—but nothing is sure, Caroline. I dare say you would receive many more offers if you had a decent dowry.'

'From fortune hunters?' Caroline raised her eyebrows. 'Surely I may find someone who truly cares for me, Mama— and if I should not, it is hardly the end of the world. I may stay at home and be a help to you.'

'Do not be ridiculous,' her mother said and looked cross. 'It is as Louisa told me. You are too stubborn for your own good, my girl. I cannot afford to keep you in a home of my own, and your brother will not want us once he decides to marry. Louisa has offered me a home with her once you are settled; though I am not sure that would serve. However, you must marry, Caroline. Besides, every woman wants a home, husband and children.'

'Do they? Is there truly no other life for a woman, Mama? I have sometimes thought it unfair that we are not allowed to live as men do…' She saw her mother's shocked expression. 'Well, not quite in the way some gentlemen do—but at liberty to please ourselves. Why can we not be lawyers or doctors or some such thing? Why must we limit our expectations to being wives and mothers?'

'Caroline, you are ridiculous,' her mother cried, looking distressed. 'No wonder your aunt complains of you. She says that you might have been engaged by now had you made a push.'

'Mama, it is barely three weeks since we came up,' Caroline said. 'Surely you would not wish me to rush into some misalliance without consideration?'

'No, of course not,' Mrs Holbrook said. 'I did tell Louisa

that I thought it too soon, but she says you will ruin your chances by being too proud—and by speaking too freely. I hope your aunt has no real cause for her fears, Caroline? You have been much indulged at home, but you must understand that you should be careful what you say in society, my dear.'

Caroline felt a pang of remorse as she saw her mother's anxious face. What would her aunt—or her mother—think if they knew of the arrangement she had made with Sir Frederick? She knew that what she had agreed to was very shocking, but she had been driven by a wildness that now seemed very ill advised.

Perhaps it might be better if she allowed Sir Frederick to win his wager—and yet she would dislike having to do so, for she could imagine the mockery in his eyes if she did not go through with the dare.

'Of course, Mama,' she said. 'And now if you will excuse me, I should like to change before nuncheon.'

'Caroline,' Tom accosted his sister as she came downstairs later that day. He looked her over, noting the town bronze she had acquired with approval. She had grown up quickly, and he liked what he saw. 'You look well. Are you enjoying yourself more than you thought?'

'Yes, it has been pleasant,' Caroline told him truthfully. 'I have made so many friends, Tom, and it would be altogether wonderful if…well, you know my aunt. I know I should not complain, for if it were not for her generosity I should not have had a Season at all.'

'Well, I am not so certain of that, and I do know my aunt well enough,' he said and smiled ruefully—he had already fallen foul of Lady Taunton's tongue. 'But the good news is that Grandfather says you are not to be forced into a marriage you cannot like. He will not have it, and he has charged me to make sure that it does not happen, which I should have done anyway. But now we have his blessing. And that means that you cannot be bullied into an alliance just because Aunt Louisa wishes it.'

'That is exceedingly good of him,' Caroline said. 'I would not have thought he would wish to be bothered with such trivial matters.'

'Truth is, we don't know him as we ought,' Tom said and frowned. 'Mama sets his back up, because he thinks her too timid. I believe he blames her for Papa getting into debt the way he did. It is completely unfair, of course, but she irritates him and you know his temper. He has kept himself to himself for too long and now regrets it. If you knew him better, Caroline, I think you would like him.'

'Oh, but I do like him,' she said, surprising him. 'He has always been perfectly pleasant to me—I think it is just Mama he does not care for, which is unkind in him. However, she is a little milk-mannered sometimes and that is what sets him by the teeth, you know. He likes it when you stand up to him, give him back a little of his own mustard.'

'Yes, I see you do know him better than I thought,' Tom said. 'He has been a bit of a dark horse, though…secrets I had never guessed. Nor would have had he not told me himself.'

'Do tell?' Caroline begged, but her brother shook his head. 'Oh, that is not fair. Why am I not to know—because I am a mere female, I suppose?'

'No, certainly that is not the reason. I was told in confidence,' Tom said, 'and I may not break my word, Caroline. You would not expect me to?'

'No, not if it was in confidence,' she admitted with a sigh. 'Are they very dreadful, Tom? Grandfather's dark secrets?'

'Some of them are surprising—but one is rather dreadful,' her brother said. 'At least, some people would find it shocking, though I thought…' He shook his head. 'No, I must not say, forgive me. I ought not to have mentioned it at all, but Grandfather has asked me to do something for him, and if I agree it means that I must go abroad for a while.'

'Go abroad?' Caroline was startled. 'But whatever can you mean?'

'It is just something our grandfather wishes to put right… an old wrong, as he called it.' He laughed and shook his head. 'No, I have told you enough and I shall say no more, tease how you choose. Tell me, where do you go this evening, and shall I be welcome, do you think?'

The conversation was successfully turned, though Caroline's curiosity was merely deflected for a moment. She sensed that there was something very much on her brother's mind, and she had no doubt that she would eventually prise it out of him.

Over the next few days Caroline attended several functions with her aunt and sometimes her brother, at which Sir Frederick was for some reason present. Her determination to accompany him to the prize fight had wavered on several occasions. However, each time she saw him, he asked her if she had changed her mind with a look in his eyes that immediately renewed her courage. She knew that he was expecting her to default and that was the very thing needed to be certain that she did not draw back.

* * *

On the Monday morning, her maid, Mary, brought a bundle to her room, which had been handed to her by Sir Frederick's groom. Caroline had been obliged to take the girl into her confidence, and to give her a handsome shawl, which she had known Mary coveted. It was not the first time she had taken one of the servants into her confidence, and she had no reason to think that Mary would betray her. She had arranged that the girl would open a door at the back of the house and then lock it again, so that Caroline could escape through the mews, to where Sir Frederick would be waiting.

The ball that evening was a serious crush. Caroline was much in demand, dancing twice with Sir Freddie, and twice with Mr Bellingham, also once with her brother as well as many others. However, she took care to keep several of the dances after supper free, and complained frequently to her aunt of the heat, telling her when the clock struck eleven that she had the most dreadful headache and asking if her aunt would mind their leaving early.

'You do look a bit flushed,' Lady Taunton observed. 'You have been racketing around town these past few days. It may be best if you have a lie in tomorrow, Caroline. We do not want you taking sickly.'

'No, Aunt, I am sure I shall not—but I may sleep in if you think it sensible.'

Lady Taunton looked at her suspiciously, for it was not often that Caroline answered her so meekly. However, she put it down to her niece feeling unwell, and, having sent for the carriage, escorted her home an hour sooner than they would normally have left.

'Do you wish for a tisane to help you sleep?' she asked as they parted at the top of the stairs. 'We do not want you taking sickly—that would blight your chances of making a good match.'

'Thank you, but I am sure I shall sleep once I can put my head down.'

Caroline's heart was racing wildly as she went up to her room. Her maid had hidden the youth's clothing in a trunk, but Caroline took it out after locking her door, and tried it on. It fitted her remarkably well. She looked at herself in the mirror, twisting her hair up into a flat pleat that would not be seen beneath the cap, and pulling it tight over her head. She pinned it securely, for she did not want it to come down and betray her. Looking at herself in the mirror, she decided that she made an excellent youth. Anyone looking at her closely might think her features a little fine for a boy, but most people hardly glanced at a groom, and she thought she might get away with it, providing she did not speak.

She decided to keep the clothes on, pulling a light cover over her as she lay down. She was afraid of sleeping late, though Mary had promised to wake her if she did.

In the eventuality, however, she was awake and ready when her maid came to her room with a tray bearing a pastry and a glass of milk.

'I thought you might wish to eat something before you went, miss,' she said. 'If something is bothering you, a full stomach is better than an empty one.'

'Thank you,' Caroline said and took a bite of the pastry and two swallows of milk. 'If anyone should inquire for me, I am sleeping in this morning.'

'Yes, miss,' Mary said, looking at her doubtfully. 'Until

later, when you've gone out driving with Sir Frederick—is that it?'

'Yes, thank you.' Caroline saw the concern in the girl's eyes and pulled a wry face. 'There is not the least need to look like that, Mary. It is just a lark—the same kind of thing as I used to get up to with my brother Nicolas.'

'Begging your pardon, miss, but it ain't the same.'

'No, well, perhaps not,' Caroline agreed. Her stomach was tying itself in knots and she had no idea why she had thought it such a capital notion in the first place. Had it not been for the challenge in Sir Frederick's eyes each time she saw him, she would probably have withdrawn long before this. However, her pride had kept her courage high and even though she was feeling scared at this moment, she was determined to go through with it. After all, she reasoned uneasily, there was nothing so very terrible about going to a prize fight with a gentleman she knew well, was there?

She lifted her head and went out of the room, her maid hurrying after her. Mary unlocked the door for her and then Caroline reminded her to lock it again so that no one would guess that anyone had gone out early. Mary gave her an odd look as she slipped out, and it crossed her mind that the girl might be thinking she was going to meet a lover—which was so foolish it did not bear thinking of! As if she would do such a thing!

Once outside in the cool air of early morning, she hurried through the small garden, out of the gate and into the mews where the horses and carriages were kept. She saw immediately the curricle drawn up just outside the arch, and walked quickly towards it.

'Mornin', milord,' she said in her best mimicry of a stable

lad, which was amusing but would fool no one. 'Was your lordship looking for assistance?'

Freddie looked at her, a gleam of appreciation in his eyes. She made a pretty youth, and he realised that if his friends saw her up beside him they would begin to wonder what he was up to, and his reputation might suffer a blow.

'Good morning, imp,' he said a trifle ruefully. 'Take some dirt from the ground and smear your face a little. You look too clean and sweet for a stable lad.'

'Oh, yes, I forgot,' Caroline said and bent down to scoop up a little mud, smearing her face and neck, also her hands. 'Is that better?'

'A little,' he agreed. 'If we meet any of our acquaintances, keep your head down and do not speak, unless forced.'

'No, milord,' Caroline said.

'Are you ready?' Freddie said. She gave a slight nod of her head. 'You are certain you wish to continue?'

'Yes, quite certain.' Caroline tossed her head, her eyes clear and bright as she gazed up at him. 'I do not know why you are so concerned, sir. It is merely a lark, after all.'

Freddie frowned, for he suspected bravado. Indeed, until this moment he had thought that she would not show, and he was a little taken aback that she seemed so careless of her good name. Surely she must understand what the tabbies would make of it if it ever came out? But of course it was up to him to make sure that it did not!

'Climb in, then,' he said, making no attempt to help her. Unless she could manage it herself they were stumped. He saw that she made nothing of it, seeming as if she obeyed such orders every day of her life. 'Well, then, we shall go—but if you find the sight of blood sickening you must tell me and we shall leave.'

'Blood…' Caroline had hardly thought about the fight until this moment. For her it had all been about adventure, the excitement of doing something she knew was forbidden. 'Yes, well, I suppose there will be some.'

'You may depend upon it,' Freddie said and shot a glance at her. His expression was severe. Caroline, aware that he was expecting her to show some emotion, schooled her features to show none, lifting her chin. 'But we need not stay long if you do not wish it.'

Caroline made no answer. In fact, neither she nor Freddie spoke much for the next hour or so as they made their way to the scene of the fight, which was on Hounslow Heath. It had been scarcely light when they set out, but by the time they had reached their destination the sun had begun to fight its way through the clouds.

Some forty-odd carriages had drawn up at convenient intervals about the spot where the fight would be held. Bare-knuckle fighting wasn't exactly illegal, but it was frowned upon by many and usually took place in secluded locations at an hour when there was least likely to be any interference.

Looking about her, Caroline saw that the carriages belonged mostly to young men, though there were one or two older gentlemen of the sporting persuasion. There were, of course, no ladies of quality present, though she saw a couple of females who could in no way be called ladies. They were dressed in gaudy, revealing gowns and looked as if they might have been out all night, their cheeks painted with rouge. They were laughing loudly with the gentlemen who had brought them, and from their manner looked as if they might be intoxicated.

Caroline had not known what to expect, and she was a little shocked by such free manners, and by some of the language the gentlemen were using. It was the language of the stables, and though she had heard such cant before, somehow she was not prepared for it.

Besides the gentlemen's carriages, there were wagons and men dressed in shabby clothes walking about, at their heels a pack of dogs, some of them hounds and lurchers, also a bull terrier or two with ferocious-looking mouths. The atmosphere was one of excitement and anticipation, and as her eyes travelled round the arena, she saw that men were placing bets and also buying tankards of ale from a stall that had set up some distance away from where they were stationed.

Freddie looked at her speculatively. 'Well, lad, what do you think of it?'

'It is strange,' Caroline said. 'Different…exciting, I think.'

'Exciting?' His smile mocked her. 'A rough place for a lad like you. But it was what you wanted, though we can leave if you wish?'

It was on the tip of Caroline's tongue to tell him that she had seen enough when a voice hailed him, and two gentlemen came over to speak to him. She was thankful that they seemed to have been drinking, and did not glance her way as they talked about the merits of the fight they had come to watch.

The two gentlemen, both of whom were known to Caroline, though only by sight and not by acquaintance, seemed in no hurry to move on. They were making wagers with each other, and drew Sir Frederick into it, asking him his opinion of the outcome.

'I would lay my blunt on Mason,' Freddie told them. 'But I have not seen Gentleman George fight, so I may be mistaken.'

'What will you wager on it?' one of the gentlemen asked.

'Oh, fifty guineas,' Freddie said. 'You may come to me at my club if you should win.'

'Naturally,' the gentleman replied, glancing briefly at Caroline. 'What does the lad say? Who will win, lad?'

'His name is…Sam,' Freddie said, 'and he has no opinion on the matter—do you, Sam?'

'Come, come, let the lad speak for himself, Rathbone. Tell me, lad, what is your opinion?'

Caroline shook her head, keeping her eyes down, aware that she was being studied rather too intently. She averted her gaze. A short distance away she saw that two dogs were squaring up to each other, and in another moment they were at each other's throats, growling fiercely, their fangs bared as they entered a bloody conflict.

It was a horrid sight, and one that Caroline disliked very much, but it diverted attention from her, for instead of trying to separate them, their owners urged them to it and started to make bets on the outcome. The two gentlemen who had come up to Freddie walked off to watch and hazard their blunt in the betting. Freddie glanced at her, raising his brows.

'Do you wish to leave?'

'No, certainly not,' Caroline said, though she had found the dogfight unpleasant, but it was over now and the pugilists were being announced to the crowd. 'I am not so easily distressed, though I do not like to see dogs hurt.'

'Nor I,' Freddie agreed. 'Men have a choice whether to fight or not. Animals are not so fortunate. Personally, I abhor such sports. Well, I dare say we may as well watch the fight since we are here.' Caroline watched as the two men began to square up to each other, thinking that both looked very strong and well matched in size and weight. They began by circling each other, making occasional jabs at each other and ducking. Around them loud voices were raised, urging the men to close with each other and eventually the blows began to land with regularity.

At first Caroline was struck by the excitement and the science of the way men ducked and weaved, and the skill it took to land a punch on their opponent. However, after some rounds, when they were both reeling from the effect of so many blows, she began to hope that it would soon be over. However, she said nothing, for she was not prepared to let Freddie think her a weakling after all. It was towards the end of the thirteenth round that he turned to look at her.

'I believe I have seen enough. Mason will undoubtedly wear his opponent down,' Freddie said. He began to back his horses and in a few moments they were leaving the Heath. He glanced at Caroline again, noticing her thoughtful expression. 'You did not wish to stay for the end, did you?' he asked after they had driven for a few minutes on the road.

'No,' she admitted, meeting his gaze then, a little flush in her cheeks. 'At the start it was rather fine—two men of equal skill matched in a display of pugilism—but I must admit that it became a little too bloody towards the end—foolish of me to be so squeamish, I know. I am glad to have had the experience, but I do not think I should wish to attend another fist fight.'

'I never expected you to come,' Freddie said. He was unsmiling and Caroline thought that he disapproved of her behaviour. 'You have more pluck than most, Miss Holbrook. I admire you for it, but I should never have allowed you to go through with this mad escapade. Now we must think how to get you home with no one the wiser.'

'I shall have to find somewhere to change my clothes.'

'And wash that dirt off your face,' Freddie said. 'But there is a quiet inn I know of where we may take breakfast in a private parlour and you may retire to the landlord's best chamber to make yourself tidy.'

'You are very thoughtful for my sake,' Caroline told him, a faint flush in her cheeks. 'I have been a little reckless, have I not?'

'My fault, I think,' Freddie told her. 'I should not have provoked you into it.' He raised one eyebrow. 'What of the balloon ascension—shall we call off your part in that?'

'Oh, no, indeed not,' Caroline said instantly. 'I am not so pudding-hearted! You must not think it.'

'I assure you that I do not,' Freddie confided with a smile that lifted her spirits. His smile had set her heart racing rather fast and she knew in that instant that she liked him very much. 'To be honest, I am not particularly enamoured of bare-knuckle fighting. Boxing in a ring with gloves is quite another thing. I doubt very much that I should have bothered to attend this morning if we had not made our little wager. I see no sport in two men hitting each other until one or both can no longer stand up. The sport must have rules and be conducted in a gentlemanly fashion if it is to be watched with any pleasure.'

Caroline made no answer, but she thought a great deal. His behaviour that day had been so considerate, so generous and kind, that she could not help liking him much more than she had thought possible. He seemed to think just as he ought on so many matters that she was inclined to believe him a very sensible and charming man. His mocking air and habit of seeming never to take anything seriously was possibly a mask to hide his true nature, which was perhaps more sensitive than others might realise. However, she naturally kept her thoughts to herself, and, since he seemed to be thoughtful too, they continued in silence until they came to the inn he had spoken of.

He ordered breakfast for them both in the private parlour, and Caroline discovered that she was hungry, eating some cold ham followed by bread and honey, which she washed down with a mug of watered cider. After they had eaten, Caroline took the bundle of clothes Freddie had had from her maid and went up to the bedchamber he had mentioned. She washed her face, tidied her hair and dressed in a green carriage gown and a straw bonnet.

She glanced at herself in a rather grey-looking mirror on the wall, and then went downstairs to the hall, where she saw that Freddie was in conversation with the landlord. He shot a startled glance at her, but then smiled as Freddie pressed some gold coins into his hand.

'I believe he thinks we are eloping,' Caroline said as they went outside. This time Freddie handed her into his curricle, taking care to stop her gown from snagging on the wheel.

'I dare say he may, but we do not need to care for his opinion,' Freddie said as he flicked his reins to give the order to his horses to walk on. 'It seems that we may have brushed through this without much trouble, Miss Holbrook.'

'Oh, do call me Caroline,' she said, as she threw him a speaking glance. 'I do not think we can stand on ceremony now—do you?'

'Perhaps not,' Freddie said. 'Very well, Caroline it shall be, at least when we are alone. And now I shall get you home before your family begin to wonder where you have been.'

Neither of them were aware of a curricle that had just that moment pulled up at the far end of the inn yard. The two young gentlemen, who had come in search of the prize fight, but decided that they would stop for breakfast, glanced at each other in surprise.

'Was that Miss Holbrook with Freddie Rathbone?' Asbury asked of his companion. 'They are somewhat out of the way, are they not?'

'It is a trifle unusual,' Mr Bellows agreed. 'You do not suppose that they have been to…no, no, of course not.'

'To the mill?' Asbury asked and shook his head. 'No, I cannot think it. Not but what she is game enough—but Rathbone has more sense than to take a delicate lady there. Or has he?'

'He has always been a trifle unsteady,' Bellows said. 'At least…he has done some reckless tricks in the past, so I've heard. But surely even he wouldn't do such a thing? Take a lady to a prize fight? No!' He looked shocked, disbelieving, as well he might, for it was unheard of.

'No, I can't think it,' Asbury said. 'But what in the world were they doing here—at an inn like this? I mean, a drive in the park is one thing, but…you don't suppose that…?'

'An assignation?' Bellows said. 'You're off the mark there, Asbury, old fellow. I know she is free in her talk, but she ain't fast. I admire her. I won't believe there was anything havey-cavey about it.'

'I am sure you are right,' Asbury said, but frowned. He wouldn't care to think anything unkind of Miss Holbrook, for he liked the spirited beauty very well, but it had put some doubt in his mind concerning her character. He had wondered if he should make her an offer, but now he thought that perhaps he would not. A gentle, biddable girl might be more suitable as the mother of his children. 'There must be some perfectly reasonable explanation for them having just come from that inn…though I am damned if I know what it might be.'

Chapter Five

It was not to be hoped that she would escape her aunt's eagle eye when she returned to the house—it was past noon and Lady Taunton had already been to her niece's room to ask how she was feeling that morning. Having been met by a maid who stumbled over her words of explanation and looked guilty, her suspicions had been aroused, though Caroline's appearance was just as it ought to be and, when questioned, she answered innocently enough.

'Oh, I had quite forgot an appointment to go driving with Sir Frederick when I said that I might rest,' Caroline said, feeling guilty as she lied. She knew herself to be in the wrong, for she had indeed been foolish. 'Besides, my headache had completely gone this morning, Aunt.'

Louisa Taunton looked at her with dislike. 'I think you enjoy flouting me, Caroline,' she said, her mouth twisting. 'I do not know what mischief you have been up to, but I should warn you that it will come to my ears eventually, miss. You can do nothing in society that remains a secret for long, and if you have acted unwisely it will rebound on you. I have told you often enough that you are too free in your manners. You believe that you may do as you like, but go too far and you will discover that I was right.'

'I must be such a trial to you, Aunt,' Caroline said. 'Why did you agree to bring me out this Season if you so heartily disapprove of me?'

'For your mother's sake. She has no more idea of control than a nodcock, and less sense than a peagoose. You have been much indulged as a child, Caroline. Had you been my daughter, I should have taken a cane to you long ago.'

'Perhaps it was as well for me that you are not my mother,' Caroline replied. She lifted her head, meeting her aunt's angry gaze. 'If you will excuse me, I shall go up and change my gown. Mama wishes to attend an exhibition of art this afternoon and I have promised to accompany her.'

Lady Taunton snorted her disgust and turned away as Caroline walked up the stairs. The stubborn girl would go her own way, it seemed. She was heading for a fall, but there was no telling her, and her aunt sustained some satisfaction in thinking of how much she would enjoy dealing with Caroline's eventual disgrace.

Caroline entered her room, shutting the door and locking it behind her. She put her hands to her heated cheeks, for her aunt's criticism had struck home more deeply than usual. She was aware that she had behaved badly that morning, though she seemed to have brushed through it with little more than a scolding. Her spirit was not crushed, nor her determination to take part in the balloon flight on that Thursday, but she admitted now that there were some things she ought not to dare, and she told herself that she would be more sensible in future. She did not care what her aunt thought of her, but she would not like to bring shame and distress to her mother. And she could not help wondering if perhaps her reckless behaviour had lowered her in Sir Freddie's estimation. That would indeed be a heavy price to pay.

She washed her face in cold water, and then changed into a pretty walking gown of patterned green muslin before going downstairs to partake of a simple nuncheon that had been prepared for them in the dining room. Her mother and aunt were already seated, Marianne looking up with a smile as she entered.

'You are better this morning, my dear,' she said. 'I do hope you will not be like me, Caroline. I suffer with dreadful heads from time to time.'

'Oh, I think it was just the heat last night,' Caroline replied and dropped a kiss on top of her neatly dressed head. Her mother was wearing a fetching cap of Brussels lace and in truth looked much younger than her years. 'I am perfectly well, dearest Mama—and looking forward to attending the gallery with you this afternoon.'

'Yes, I am looking forward to it, too,' her mother said, giving her a look of affection. 'I was speaking to Mr Herbert Milbank about it last week. He told me that there were some fine watercolours to be seen, as well as oils, and you know that I paint a little, dearest—though of course nothing I produce could ever be thought good enough to be shown.'

'But of course they are,' Caroline told her. 'It is just that you are too shy to allow it. I think you have a good eye for landscapes and some of the portraits you have done are so like the subject it is unreal.'

'You flatter me, dearest,' her mother said, but looked pleased. 'Sit down and have something to eat, my love. This ham is very good and I think you missed your breakfast, did you not?'

'Oh, Mary brought me a pastry,' Caroline said with a little flush. She had eaten heartily at the inn with Sir Frederick, for the cold air had given her an appetite. 'I am not very hungry just now.'

'Eat something to please me,' her mother urged. 'This cold chicken is very good.'

Caroline helped herself to a small piece of the meat and some green peas, but pushed them around her plate, feeling unable to swallow even this small morsel. However, she drank a cup of tea, and then went upstairs to put on her pelisse and bonnet.

'Is everything all right, miss?' Mary asked as she helped her to find the gloves she needed to complete her ensemble. 'Lady Taunton was that suspicious earlier, I was sure she guessed something was wrong.'

'She knows nothing,' Caroline said. 'It is mere speculation.'

'No, miss, but if it were to happen again…'

'Do not worry, Mary, it shall not.' She smiled at the girl, picked up her reticule and went along the hall to her mother's bedchamber.

Mrs Holbrook was looking doubtfully at herself in the mirror. She had put on a green velvet bonnet trimmed with black ribbons and turned to her daughter as she entered. 'Do you think this is wrong for me, dearest? Ought I to stick to black entirely?'

'No, indeed, Mama, you should not,' Caroline said at once. 'You look very nice, very respectable—and it is two years since we lost Papa.'

'Your poor father,' Marianne said and sighed. She blinked hard and then turned back to the mirror. 'Well, I think it is quite suitable, and Papa would not have wanted me to mourn for ever. Besides, he could not expect it in the circumstances.'

Caroline wondered what her mother meant, but forbore to ask. She felt a little tingle at the nape of her neck. It was unusual for her mother to say anything of the kind, and the green bonnet was new—something that made her wonder.

The carriage was waiting for them when they went downstairs. Jeremy the coachman helped first Mrs Holbrook and then her daughter inside. Caroline glanced sideways at her mother's face—she had sensed that she was oddly nervous and wondered why that should be.

The art gallery was not overcrowded, though several ladies and gentlemen were walking about the large room, looking at the pictures, most of which were reasonably priced works of art. The artist was a newcomer to the scene, and giving his first show, but already his work had aroused considerable interest and Caroline had noticed that several of the pictures had been marked as being sold.

'This is rather nice, isn't it, Mama?' Caroline stopped in front of a portrait in oils of a young girl playing with a hoop. 'Isn't she pretty?'

Her mother did not reply immediately, and, glancing at her, Caroline saw that her cheeks were quite pink. And then she saw that a gentleman was staring at them. She recognised him at once, though she had not spoken to him for some weeks.

In his middle years and of medium height, he was still an impressive man. He came towards them, raising his beaver hat to reveal a head of thick dark hair. He was stoutish though not fat, his impressive moustache flourishing under a patrician nose, his eyes grey and just now smiling at…her mother.

'Ah, Mrs Holbrook,' he said. 'How very pleasant to see you

here. I had hoped that you might attend today.' He inclined his head politely towards Caroline, but it was obvious that her mother was the object of his interest.

'Mr Milbank. I remembered it most particularly,' Marianne told him, blushing like a young girl. 'For you told me you were the young man's patron, did you not?'

'Yes, indeed. I saw some of his work when I visited Lancashire a few months back. Not in an exhibition, you know, but hanging on the wall of a modest home. I've had the devil of a time persuading him to show his work, but I managed it at the last, and it seems to be a success. It was that portrait of a young girl that took my eye, you see—she is older now, for I met her, but just as beautiful, I assure you.'

'The picture has no price tag,' Mrs Holbrook remarked.

'No, for he does not wish to sell it,' he told her. 'But there are many pretty pictures that are for sale—if you care to see them?'

Mrs Holbrook said that she did, taking his arm. Caroline remained looking at the picture for a while—there was something in the girl's smile that intrigued her. She did not notice the gentleman approach until he spoke to her.

'Charming,' Freddie said, 'and a little like you in some ways, Miss Holbrook.'

'Oh…' Caroline was startled, a blush coming to her cheeks as she glanced at him. 'Do you think so? I was not expecting to see you here this afternoon, sir.'

'Were you not?' His eyes quizzed her. 'Did you imagine that I had no interest in such things?'

'Oh…well, I would not have expected you to attend the show of an unknown artist, though I am sure you have many valuable works of art.'

'Perhaps…' Freddie smiled oddly. 'But it is amazing what one finds at these affairs. I think I shall buy this picture.'

'Mr Milbank says that the artist does not wish to sell.'

'Does he not?' Freddie smiled. 'Well, then, I may have to persuade him, for I am determined to have it.'

'And do you always get your own way?' Caroline met his gaze boldly, a hint of challenge in her eyes.

'Usually,' he said. 'When I truly want something I am not often denied. Ah, here are George and Julia—shall we join them, for it was to meet them that I came this afternoon?'

Caroline suddenly felt a little disheartened at the thought that Sir Frederick had not come to the gallery with the sole intention of seeing her, but brushed the feeling aside. 'Yes, I knew they might come,' Caroline said, 'but you must excuse me, sir. I believe my mother needs me…'

'Then I shall not keep you, but do not forget that we are engaged to each other on Thursday, Miss Holbrook. I am looking forward to our excursion very much.' Caroline met his challenging look, her cheeks a little warm, for she knew that she was being mocked.

'As I am, sir,' she said. 'Please excuse me for the moment.'

She walked away, conscious that his eyes were on her, wondering why her heart was beating so very fast. Was she imagining it, or had his manner become just that little bit more reserved towards her?

Caroline looked at her mother with approval that evening. Marianne was dressed in a simple grey gown, but had a spangled shawl draped over her arms, and was wearing the pearls she had been given as a wedding present when she had married Mr Holbrook. Her hair had been dressed in a new, becoming style that was swept softly off her face and finished in an attractive coronet on her head, which had been dressed with a scrap of exquisite lace.

'Mama, you do look lovely,' Caroline said. 'I can see that I shall have a rival this evening.'

'Do not talk such nonsense,' Marianne said. 'I thought that perhaps it was time I began to wear something other than black.'

'More than time,' her daughter agreed, but when they went downstairs together, Lady Taunton's expression was one of disapproval. She gave her sister a speaking glance, but said nothing as she led the way out to the carriage. Her silence spoke more than words could have done, and mother and daughter were aware of her displeasure.

It was clear from her manner that she did not approve of her sister's new touch, but Caroline thought that her mother looked happy for the first time in an age. However, once they were at the dance, her usual court soon surrounded her and it was a while before she noticed that her mother was talking animatedly to Mr Milbank. She smiled inwardly, believing that she understood the change in her mother's manner of late, and feeling pleased by it. If her mother were to find happiness with that gentleman, she would be delighted.

It was not until quite late in the evening that Caroline realised Mr Asbury was present. He had not asked her to dance, which was unusual, and she noticed that he was paying a great deal of attention to Julia, who was looking very pretty in her pale pink gown. Caroline wondered whether she might have done something to offend him. However, when Julia brought him over to join her and Mr Bellingham just before supper, he seemed as polite as ever—but he still did not ask her to dance.

Caroline was not concerned enough to be troubled by his neglect for she already had more than her share of partners. However, she wondered why Sir Frederick was not in attendance, for he had said that he would see her later that evening.

'Oh, Freddie was called suddenly to his uncle,' George said when she asked. 'However, he says that he shall return tomorrow evening so you need not worry over the excursion on Thursday.'

'What excursion is that?' Caroline turned in surprise as she heard her brother's voice. 'Where are you off to?'

'Sir Frederick has arranged for us to watch a balloon ascension on Thursday,' Julia said. 'There is a party of us going, Mr Holbrook, and we shall have our nuncheon in the park at Richmond if the weather is fine.' She smiled at him shyly. 'Why do you not accompany us, sir? I am sure there is room for one more.'

'Yes, I should think I might,' he said, looking pleased to have been invited. 'I was going to take a look in at Manton's, you know; had an appointment to discuss what might suit me, but I can do that another day. It was just a little matter of purchasing a pair of pistols and there is not the least hurry.'

'Are you sure you wish to come?' Caroline asked her brother with a little frown. 'Will you not find it rather tedious? I imagined you were busy with your friends.'

Since his arrival, some gentlemen who were generally considered to be rakish young bucks had taken Tom into their circle.

'Oh, lord, no,' Tom said with an ingenuity that immediately endeared him to every one but his sister. 'I can visit my clubs any day, but a balloon flight sounds the greatest fun—and I shall be with you and Miss Fairchild, and that will be exceedingly pleasant.' He bestowed an admiring glance on Julia, which made her blush with pleasure.

Caroline knew that she could do no more to dissuade him without appearing churlish. It was an unfortunate occurrence—he would be sure to frown on the idea of her going up in the balloon, more from a point of safety than anything else. She smiled and said that she was glad he had nothing better to do, smothering a sigh. She still meant to take her chance in the balloon, but it would probably earn her a scolding.

She danced with her brother next, for he had asked her to reserve a space for him, and tried not to feel disappointed that Sir Frederick had had to leave town so suddenly. However, if his uncle had sent for him, it was probably important and she must not mind that he had not found a way of letting her know. Still, she could not help wondering if her fast behaviour had earned his disapproval. If he had been thinking her a suitable wife, he had quite possibly changed his mind.

Later that night, as she sat brushing her hair before she went to bed, she was thoughtful. Sir Frederick's absence had brought one fact home to her—without him her evening had seemed less enjoyable. Was it only that he had not been there, she wondered, or was she beginning to tire of attending so many society affairs?

She wondered why Mr Asbury had been a little reserved with her too. She had seen him looking at her oddly once or twice, but could not imagine what she had done to offend him. He had been one of the acquaintances she liked best apart from Mr Bellingham and Sir Frederick—and his desertion was perhaps a little hurtful. However, the rest of her court was as attentive as ever, and she had received two proposals that evening. One from a young gentleman she thought far too intoxicated to know what he was doing, and another from a gentleman she completely disliked.

She had been relieved to escape from both of them, and wished fervently that she had not granted them even one dance each—which she might not have done had Freddie been there. There was only one more day before she saw him again, but it seemed an age away. She knew that he had been attentive to her, but they struck sparks from each other more often than not, and, unlike her aunt, she did not believe that he was looking to take a wife just yet. At least if he were, he had given her no indication that she might be his chosen bride.

Still holding her pretty silver-backed hairbrush, Caroline gazed at her reflection. When she had first arrived in London she had believed that she preferred Mr Bellingham and had almost made up her mind to it that she would accept him if he offered for her. But now she seemed to have crossed some sort of line and felt much closer in spirit to Sir Freddie than she had... Yes, Sir Freddie was the way in which she thought of him now, she realised, a smile on her lips. He was no longer merely an acquaintance, but a close friend. She liked it that he had not mocked her for her foolish insistence on being taken to the fight, confiding in her that he did not much care for bare-knuckle fighting himself. It might have been said simply to please her, but he had made her feel better and she was grateful to him. And yet after that he had seemed to become more distant and Caroline struggled to understand why.

She was not sure exactly what her feelings were towards him at this minute, but she knew that the evening had seemed flat without him. She was sighing as she put down her hairbrush and went to bed. What was so important that it had taken Sir Freddie from town at such short notice?

* * *

'What was it that made you send for me so urgently?' Freddie asked of his uncle that evening after they had dined. 'I half-expected to see you taken ill and I was very relieved to find you as hale as ever, sir.'

'I'm not about to give up the ghost just yet, my boy,' his uncle told him with a wry grimace. 'I know you ain't exactly short of the readies, so I've no hold over you, and no doubt you would resent any suggestion from me about your marriage.'

'It depends what kind of a suggestion you meant to make,' Freddie said, looking at him guardedly. He was his uncle's heir only because the Marquis had lost two sons to a hereditary weakness that had come to them through their mother's family. As for fortune, he had sufficient of his own and was not hanging on for his uncle to shuffle off this mortal coil. However, he was too much his own man not to feel his hackles rise as he saw the expression in his uncle's eyes. 'I am aware that as your heir I owe you a duty, sir. My mother was fond of you, and you may have considered that she married beneath her. However…'

'Selina married on the rebound,' the Marquis said and frowned again. 'She was in love with someone I did not approve of and I told her that she would be letting the family down if she married him. He was on the catch for his second wife and I believe she turned him down after I gave her my opinion. I never knew all of it, but she was very distressed for some months—and then she married your father.'

'I knew there was someone else,' Freddie said, looking thoughtful. 'She told me once that she had loved someone, but was unable to marry him. She came to love my father in time, but not in the way she had loved her first choice.'

'I may have been wrong to interfere, but she was my sister,' Southmoor said and grunted. 'I realised later that I might have wronged her. It made us enemies, which was a shame, for I always liked him, even though I thought him unsuitable for your mother. However, he had three wives and managed to kill 'em all off…though I think he cared for his last. She was a gel of spirit. Almost half his age she was when he married her, but they were happy until she died. I think her death almost killed him…'

'Forgive me, sir, but I do not quite follow you. Of whom are we speaking—and what has it to do with my marriage?'

'Bollingbrook, of course. You've been squiring his grand-daughter about town, so I've been told. I wanted to know what your intentions were towards her.'

'Indeed?' Freddie's tone became reserved, slightly chilling. His eyes narrowed menacingly, for he did not allow anyone to question him on matters of a private nature. 'And where did you obtain this information, sir?'

'It hardly matters who told me,' his uncle said. 'Don't give me that top-lofty stare, Freddie, for it won't wash. I'm merely asking whether or not you intend to make Bolling-brook's girl an offer?'

'And what if I do so intend?' Freddie asked, a glint in his eye that would have made anyone else shudder and retreat.

'Bollingbrook was once a friend of mine,' Southmoor said. 'I dare say he was a bit of a loose screw at times, but we were close at one period. I warned your mother against marrying him because I thought he would make her unhappy. I thought you should be aware that he is unlikely to welcome an offer from you. I am happy enough for you to marry the gel if she's the one you want, but you may get short shrift from Bollingbrook.'

'I see—then perhaps I should thank you for the warning,' Freddie said, a glint in his eyes. 'I do not say that I should wish to marry her, but if I did I should not care too much for Bollingbrook's objections—or yours, sir.'

Southmoor stared at him for a moment and then laughed. 'No, sir, I do not suppose that you would. But if you are determined on her, then there is something else I think you should know…'

'Very well, I shall listen if it is important,' Freddie said. 'Though I doubt it will weigh much in the scale of things.'

Caroline woke to the excitement of knowing that she would see Sir Freddie later that morning. She ran to the window to look out, feeling relieved when she saw that the sky was a clear blue and it promised to be a beautiful day— just right for the balloon ascension. She decided to dress at once and was already struggling into her gown when Mary came in with her tray.

'Miss Caroline, what are you about?' the girl asked. 'You'll never fasten them hooks like that, miss. Stand still and let me do them for you.'

'Oh, Mary, I am so excited,' Caroline said, her eyes bright. She turned her back so that the maid could fasten the row of hooks at the nape of her tailored gown, which had a slender skirt and small puffed sleeves and would be ideal for climbing in and out of the basket of a balloon. 'It is such a lovely day, isn't it?'

'And what mischief are you about today then, miss?' Mary looked at her doubtfully, for she had seen her mistress like this before. 'You ain't excited for nothing and that's a fact.'

'I am going to a balloon ascension,' Caroline said. 'It will be so thrilling…' She laughed in delight. 'You will never guess…but I am going to go up in one if everything turns out as it should.'

'You never will, miss!' Mary was shocked. Her mistress was too reckless in her opinion and would, she felt sure, land in trouble one of these days. 'Them things is mighty dangerous. You might fall out and break your head.'

Caroline's laughter pealed out. 'Oh, Mary, of course I shan't fall out—but you won't mention this to anyone?'

'You know I wouldn't, miss. I shan't betray you, though they might put me to the rack and torture me with hot irons.'

Caroline was too well bred to laugh at the girl's solemn avowal, though she was very much pleased by Mary's show of loyalty.

She was downstairs waiting by the time the knocker was raised and the footman admitted Sir Frederick. Her brother Tom had arranged to drive to the meeting in his own carriage, though she knew he was hoping that he might have a passenger on the return—and it was not his sister. She had seen a certain look in his eye as he addressed Julia, and she rather thought her friend preferred him to many of her suitors.

'Miss Holbrook,' Freddie said, his eyes going over her appreciatively as he saw the stylish gown she was wearing. It was fashioned of a pale grey, soft material and she was wearing the infamous blue hat on her head. She was quite magnificent, a vivacious woman and very much in her own style, he acknowledged and noted the bright sparkle in her eye. 'I see that you are ready and waiting.'

'Yes, sir. I was up early, for I am eager not to miss a moment of the treat you have promised us.'

'You are still of the same mind, then?' His eyes seemed to challenge her and she raised her head defiantly.

'Yes, sir. Did you imagine that I would change my mind?' She tipped her head on one side.

'No…' Freddie looked at her thoughtfully. 'I believe you to be as brave as you are beautiful, Caroline. Shall we go?'

'Yes, please.'

Caroline happily accepted his hand as he helped her into the seat of his new phaeton. It was extremely racy with high wheels and painted in yellow and black. The pair of horses drawing it were coal black and, if anything, more spirited than his greys; they were, he confided, a new acquisition.

'I think I may have to part with my chestnuts soon,' he told her. 'Having heard of these, I decided to buy them…just in case.'

'They are adorable,' Caroline said. 'Somewhat of a task to handle, I dare say, though you make nothing of it, sir. I have noticed before that you have exceptional hands. I thought no one could rival Nicolas, but I believe you would be a match for him.' She shot a mischievous glance at him. 'My brother allows me to drive his phaeton occasionally, did you know that?'

'Oh, no, miss!' Freddie said swiftly. 'You won't wheedle round me with that one, so don't think it. These brutes are too strong for you. It takes me all my time to handle them.'

'Which you do beautifully,' she said and laughed as she saw the expression in his eyes. She was feeling on top of the world— she had discovered that it was very amusing to tease him as he teased her. 'We shall just have to have another wager, sir.'

'None that concerns these horses,' he replied, a flicker of amusement in his eyes. 'However, should we discover a wager that pleased us both, I would not be averse to letting you drive me—though I think with the greys, not these devils.'

'That would indeed be a good beginning,' she murmured, a husky gurgle in her throat as she saw the little nerve flick at his temple. 'But first things first, sir. Today will provide quite enough excitement—and you know, next time we wager, you may very well win.'

'I am not sure that I should ever best you, minx,' he said with a mock scowl. 'However, it may be amusing to try.'

'Just so, sir.' Caroline's air of innocence was patently false, bringing a little snort from the gentleman beside her.

'At least you might call me something other than sir,' he said in assumed outrage. 'You said that we were friends—or do you wish me to return to calling you Miss Holbrook?'

'Only when my aunt or one of the old tabbies is by,' Caroline said. 'To be honest, I think of you as Sir Freddie— if you would not mind me using your name in that way?'

'As you wish,' he said, a gleam in his eyes. 'What happened when you returned home the other morning? Did you escape detection?'

'My aunt was as cross as crabs,' Caroline said. 'She suspected something, for she had questioned my maid—who assures me that hot irons would not make her betray me! However, there is nothing Aunt Louisa can do, for she has no idea of what happened.'

Freddie looked thoughtful and said, 'I dare say we got away with that little escapade—but you know that it will be different today, do you not? Your friends will see you enter the basket and it will not long remain a secret.'

'Oh, but there is nothing so very shocking in it,' Caroline said. 'Mama might be anxious if she knew that I intended it, for she is of a nervous disposition, you know—but I dare say I shall not be the first lady to go up in a balloon.'

'No, there have been others, but the flights took place at private estates. I think your aunt may censure you, Caroline.'

'I do not mind that so very much,' she said and looked at him, her expression serious now. 'But I should not like to incur your ill opinion, sir. Do you think it very fast of me?'

'Good lord, no,' Freddie said. 'A little reckless, perhaps— but I do not censure you. What made you think I might?'

'Oh, I do not know…' She considered telling him that Mr Asbury had seemingly turned against her, but decided that she would keep it to herself. It was her problem, not his, and she might find that she was mistaken another day.

'Well, you may forget any such foolish notions,' he said and smiled at her in a way that made her heart jerk. 'I do not think that anything could make me think ill of you, Caroline.'

'Oh…' She blushed slightly and looked down at her gloves, which were a fine York tan leather, smoothing at the fingers for a moment. 'I trust you found your uncle well, Sir Freddie? Mr Bellingham told me you were called away unexpectedly.'

'Yes, I broke my word to you, did I not?' Freddie said and frowned. 'I thought he might be unwell, but it was just a small matter of business—nothing important at all.'

'Oh, I am pleased to hear that,' she said. 'I was a little anxious for your sake. It is awful to lose someone of whom you are fond.'

'I suppose I am fond of the old reprobate in a way,' Freddie said. 'I must admit that we sometimes have words, but it usually blows over. Neither of us is one to hold a grudge.'

'Oh…' She looked at him inquiringly, but no further information was forthcoming. 'My grandfather wishes me to visit him soon. I think my brother intends to go down at the end of next week. Mama thinks that I should go with him, and return after a few days. She says she shall make my excuses to everyone.'

'She does not go with you?'

'Grandfather does not care for her. They fell out some years ago. She is terrified of him and I think that annoys him somewhat—and he suffers greatly from gout, which does not sweeten his temper.'

'Ah, yes, the curse of many a rake at the end of his days, I think,' Freddie said. 'I dare say he likes his port too well.'

'I am sure he does,' Caroline said. 'No, Mama does not go with me—though I think she may have other reasons for remaining in town.' She smiled as he arched his brows at her. 'I believe she has a beau…'

'Indeed, that must be a happy turn out for her,' Freddie said.

'Yes…if I am not mistaken, which I think I am not.' Caroline began to recount the story of her first meeting with her mother's admirer, her conversation lively and entertaining. In this way their journey was accomplished and they were soon meeting up with their friends as arranged.

Freddie steadied his horses as they approached the park and smiled at her. 'Do you know, I think we are almost there.'

Chapter Six

Caroline was a little shocked to see how large the company had grown by the time they arrived. It had been meant to be a private affair, but somehow the secret had got out and at least thirty of their acquaintance had turned up in their carriages to watch. Not only were so many of their friends there, a small crowd of interested onlookers had arrived to watch as the balloon was being made airworthy by the appliance of hot air into the great canopy. Indeed, so many people were crowded around it that it was difficult to actually see it when they first arrived.

'Oh, there is quite a crowd,' Caroline said as Freddie drew his phaeton to a standstill, and assisted her down. 'It is very exciting, isn't it?'

'Yes, very,' he said, amused by the bright look in her face. He wondered when she would realise that it was impossible to go through with her avowed intention, but said nothing to discourage her. He had no doubt that she would dare to do it, for he thought that she was afraid of nothing, but she must see that it would come to her aunt's ears in no time at all. 'Ah, here is your brother.'

Caroline looked at Tom as he came up to them. He looked excited and she suspected what he was about to say before he spoke.

'I am told you mean to go up, Caroline—and there is one more place available in the basket. I should very much like to go with you. It would look much more the thing if I accompanied you.' He glanced at Sir Freddie a trifle uncertainly. 'I think perhaps you may have wished to take that place, sir—but it would wash better if it were me, do you not agree?'

'Yes, I do, as it happens,' Freddie said. He saw by Caroline's expression that she was disappointed, but believed that if anything could get her through this without too much censure, it would be her brother's presence in the basket. 'You are very welcome to take my place, for I have been up before—several times, as it happens.'

'Oh, you did not tell me,' Caroline said, gazing at him in surprise. 'But I suppose that is why you were able to arrange this…' She saw something in his eyes. 'Why, it is your balloon, is that not so?'

'I must confess that you have found me out,' Freddie said, amused. 'I am fascinated by the idea of flight, Miss Holbrook. I believe that this is just the forerunner and that one day we shall have a much more controllable method of flying.'

'No, do you, sir?' Tom looked at him with unconcealed enthusiasm. 'I have heard talk of it, but I thought it was all a hum. We must discuss this another day, when you have time, of course. I am very interested in anything scientific.'

'You must dine with me at my club one day,' Freddie said and frowned. In taking an interest in Miss Holbrook, he seemed to have landed himself with very much more than he had intended. 'We shall arrange it. And now I think the balloon is almost ready. You should make your way through the crush if you do not wish to keep the balloon master waiting.' He looked at Caroline, eyebrows raised, but did not ask again if she were sure. Now that her brother had agreed to accompany her, it should cause no more than a few raised eyebrows from all but the high sticklers. She might find herself less popular in some drawing rooms than before, but that might be repaired.

'Oh, yes, Tom, do let's go,' Caroline said and started off a little ahead of him. She knew that word of her adventure would reach her aunt swiftly, but she was determined to go through with it. Even her brother's presence would not make it all right in her aunt's opinion, though she thought that her mother might accept it as just another of her naughty tricks.

Caroline was helped into the basket by her brother. She had a feeling of tremendous excitement as she looked at the man who was preparing to take them up. He introduced himself as Mr Jackson, smiling at her as he began to explain the principles of hot-air ballooning, which she listened to with interest.

'Oh, this is so exciting,' she cried as there was a roaring sound above her head and the balloon began to lift off from the ground. For the moment they were still attached to the anchor ropes, because they were not quite ready to cast off. 'How high shall we go, sir?'

'It depends on the currents of air,' Mr Jackson was explaining to her when all of a sudden there was the sound of something snapping and one of the ropes gave way. Because they still had another rope tethering them to the ground it made the balloon shudder and tip to one side, and then go crashing downwards.

Caroline screamed as she felt herself falling. The shock of a hard landing sent the basket lurching over to one side and she stumbled, but recovered her balance quickly. She realised immediately that there could be a danger of fire and scrambled quickly over the sides of the basket. She saw Mr Jackson do the same and called to him. All around them there was noise and confusion, and it was only when Caroline felt strong hands pulling her clear of the ropes and debris that had fallen on top of them that she realised she wasn't badly hurt. Shaken and bruised, she looked into the face of the man who had pulled her clear.

'Caroline!' Freddie cried. 'My God! You could have been killed! Are you in pain? Where does it hurt?'

'I'm all right,' Caroline said, shrugging off the shock as if it were nothing. 'Just a little bruised I think…but where is Tom?' She looked around for her brother and saw that he was lying on the ground a short distance away. It looked as if he had been thrown clear before they crashed, and he was lying very still. 'Tom! Is he dead?' she cried and now there was fear in her eyes as she ran to him. 'Tom…' She fell to her knees beside him on the ground, looking at him anxiously. 'Tom! Tom, my dearest…' she cried, horrified by the turn of events that had ruined their happy day. 'Oh, Tom, speak to me…'

'Let me have him.' Freddie was by her side almost at once, laying her brother down carefully and making an examination of him. 'He is still breathing,' he said after a moment. 'I think he may have broken his arm, and he must have hit his head, for he is unconscious.' Caroline had remained on her knees, watching him handle her brother with an expertise that spoke of his having done such a thing before. How sure and gentle he was, so reassuring in a crisis. Now his eyes met hers as Tom gave a moan of pain. 'It is as I thought, but I believe it might have been much worse. I think we may safely move him to somewhere more comfortable.'

'He will do better in my curricle than your phaeton.' George Bellingham had come up to them unobserved. 'Let us get him into it. I will engage to take him home and you must come after in your own rig.'

Behind them, shouting warned of fire and Caroline glanced back to see that the canopy was blazing. Mr Jackson was leading the efforts to put out the flames before they got out of hand, but it was certain that the balloon was ruined.

'Oh, Freddie, your balloon…' Caroline cried.

'It is of no consequence. I am grateful that none of you was hurt more. As for Tom, I think we should get him to an inn,' Freddie said, frowning. 'The sooner a doctor sees to him the better.' He glanced at George.

'As you say. I know of a small discreet place near by. The Henderson Arms. You may follow me if you wish.' He glanced at Caroline. 'I dare say you would wish to accompany your brother?'

'Yes, please.' She glanced at Freddie. 'You will forgive me? I must go with Tom.'

'Of course.'

Freddie bent over the half-unconscious Tom, lifting him in his arms and carrying him, with some slight assistance from George. Tom moaned and seemed to come to himself for a moment, his features registering extreme pain as they moved him. They laid him down in the curricle, Julia having vacated it for the greater ease of his comfort. She was white with distress, tears hovering on her thick lashes.

'It is too awful,' she said to Caroline. 'I know you wish to go with him, but I shall follow with Sir Frederick, if I may?'

'Yes, of course,' Caroline said. 'Oh, poor Tom. He was so looking forward to this trip—and to many other things, I imagine. This will quite ruin his visit.'

She climbed into the curricle, taking her brother's head upon her lap, and soothing his head with her fingers. She glanced round to see what Freddie was doing, but he seemed to be making arrangements with his tiger. He looked round just as the curricle began to move off, catching sight of her pale face, though by then she had turned her attention to her brother and was whispering words of encouragement. She was not sure that Tom knew she was there, for he seemed to have fainted again, but she continued to stroke his head and talk to him, believing that Freddie knew what he was saying when he said that it might have been much worse.

It seemed an age until they reached the hotel, though it was in truth only a short distance from where they had gathered in the park. George Bellingham jumped down, giving his reins to a groom who came running.

'Stay with Tom, Miss Holbrook,' he told her. 'I shall arrange for a room and a doctor, and then return. We shall have him carried to a chamber and then his hurts can be tended.'

'You are so kind,' Caroline said, her face pale and anxious. 'If anything happens to Tom, I shall never forgive myself. He only went up in the basket because he thought it would protect my reputation.'

'You must not blame yourself,' George said. ' No one could have known that a rope would give way like that…it was most odd.' He shook his head. 'Excuse me, I must waste no time in arranging all.'

Caroline watched as he strode towards the inn and disappeared inside. She continued to stroke her brother's head and counted the seconds until her friend returned. It seemed an age, but he brought several men with him, and, within moments, Tom was being carried inside the inn and up the stairs to a room where he was carefully deposited on clean sheets. Caroline hovered nearby, wondering what she might do for the best, but she had hardly had time to think of taking off his boots before she heard voices behind her and turned to see Freddie and another gentleman, who she realised was a doctor.

'We were lucky enough to find a doctor at the site of the ascension,' Freddie told her with a grim nod. 'We shall need to cut his coat off, Caroline—and Julia is waiting downstairs alone in the parlour. I think you should keep her company— it will not do either her or your reputation the slightest good to be seen in an inn parlour alone. You may be able to stand it, but she ought not to be exposed to undeserved censure.'

'Yes, of course,' Caroline said in a small voice. His tone had been harsh. He was clearly very angry and she felt that he was blaming her for her part in this affair. Indeed, it was all her fault and he was right to censure her! 'I shall do as you say, sir.'

He did not seem to have heard her, for he paid her no attention as he went to the bed and, with the assistance of the physician, began to cut away Tom's tightly fitting coat. Caroline threw an unhappy glance at the bed where her brother was just beginning to moan once more, clearly roused from his stupor by the pain their ministrations had caused him.

'Bear up, old chap,' Freddie said encouragingly. 'You will

be right and tight in a while. Doctor Fortescue has had practice enough at binding the wounds of soldiers. He will make short work of this.'

Caroline went down to the parlour. Sir Freddie's tone to her brother had been kind, which told her that he was angry at her alone. Her spirits had fallen to nothing, for she had taken the blame of Tom's injury upon herself and was distressed by his pain. There was no denying that he would not have been there had she not teased Sir Freddie into arranging the whole thing. It was no wonder Sir Freddie had lost his good opinion of her! She had behaved shamelessly in demanding to be taken to the mill and insisting on being taken up in a balloon.

Julia was the picture of dejection when Caroline entered the private parlour that their host had provided, but she was not alone, for George was with her. She jumped to her feet as soon as she saw Caroline, running towards her, her face wet with tears.

'How is he?' she asked. 'Please tell me that he is not dead—I do not think I could bear it.'

'Julia, do not be foolish, my dear,' George expostulated with a gentle smile for her. 'I do assure you that Freddie knows about these things. Tom may feel groggy for a few days, but I dare say he will come about and be none the worse for it.'

'The doctor is with him now,' Caroline said, taking Julia's hands and holding them tightly. She lifted her head, summoning her courage. 'I dare say he will soon have him patched up.'

'Do you think so?' Julia blushed for she realised that she must have betrayed herself. 'I was so distressed...it was a dreadful thing to happen. Sir Frederick says that Mr Jackson has examined the rope and it had been tampered with, but I am not sure what he meant…'

'Tampered with? In what way?' Caroline was bewildered.

'I thought it odd that it should just snap like that,' George said, nodding to himself. 'Freddie is always meticulous about things like that, as is Jackson. The rope had been frayed by a knife or some such thing.'

'Then it was deliberate…not an accident?'

Julia gave a cry of distress. 'Who would do such a wicked thing?'

'I do not know,' Caroline said, putting an arm about the girl and drawing her to a wooden settle to sit down. She could feel Julia trembling and sensed that the girl had been much affected by the accident, perhaps the more so because it was Tom. 'I did not truly see what happened, because it was all so fast. There was no time to think about anything.'

'It was quite deliberate.' George looked at her above the head of his niece, who was hanging her head and on the verge of more tears. 'Whoever the rogue was, he meant to cause a dreadful accident, though why I cannot say.'

'Why should anyone wish to harm poor Tom?' Caroline said, and turned as she heard an indrawn breath behind her. 'You startled me, Sir Freddie. Please do not tell me that it is bad news about Tom?'

'Nothing of the sort,' he said. 'It is as I thought. He has a broken bone in his arm, but the injury is not life threatening. We can only be grateful that no one else was badly hurt. It does not bear thinking of. You could all have been killed.'

'But who could have done such a terrible thing?' Caroline asked.

'Jackson did not see it happen, but there were so many people crowding about the canopy that it is not surprising. It is unlikely that we shall be able to trace the culprit, though I shall see what can be done.'

'You are sure that it could not simply have been an accident?' Caroline asked.

'Quite certain. It was the first thing that Jackson checked. He is meticulous in all his preparations—and the more so because he knew that you were to go up in the basket. I particularly stressed that all care must be taken.' His look was so severe that Caroline felt sick—he was clearly very angry.

'Oh, dear…' Julia swooned. George was just in time to catch her as she fell forwards and lowered her to the settle with gentle care. 'I am so sorry…' she whispered as her eyelids fluttered open. 'What a silly goose I am.'

'This has all been too much for you,' George said. 'I must get you home, for you are not well, Julia.'

She made a faint protest, looking apologetically at Caroline. 'I ought to stay with you,' she said, 'but in truth I do not feel well.'

'You must go home,' Caroline said. 'I shall stay with my brother for the time being.' She looked at Sir Freddie. 'Would you mind fetching my mother? I think she would want to be here and I cannot leave him.'

Freddie hesitated, giving her a hard stare. She was wondering if he meant to refuse her, when someone came into the parlour.

'The young gentleman is conscious now,' the physician announced. 'He is in some pain and will need nursing of the kind that I do not think may be procured here, for such injuries can sometimes turn infectious. Perhaps some arrangement could be made to convey him to his home?'

'Yes, I shall fetch his mother and a suitable vehicle,' Freddie said. 'You get Julia off, George. We don't want her fainting again…' His gaze turned to Caroline, seeming to her to become colder. 'Go upstairs to your brother and stay there until I bring Mrs Holbrook. It would only start a deal of point-less gossip if someone were to see you here. I shall be no longer than need be and until then you must stay with Tom. Do you hear me, Caroline? You are not to leave the bedchamber for anything!'

'Yes, yes, of course.' She left the room immediately, feeling chastened. It was obvious that Sir Freddie thought that the blame for this débâcle lay squarely in her court. But did he really need to be so harsh to her? She felt tears prick her eyes, but blinked them away.

She knocked softly at the door and then entered her brother's bedchamber. He was lying propped up against a pile of pillows, but opened his eyes and looked at her as she approached, attempting a weak smile.

'I'm sorry, Caroline,' he apologised in a faint voice. 'Seems I made a mess of the whole thing, ruined your day.'

'How could you think that? Besides, it was hardly your fault!' Caroline's throat was tight with emotion, for it was like him to think of her. 'I am merely distressed for your sake, dearest.'

'What happened?' Tom looked puzzled. 'There was an odd sound and then we just fell like a stone.'

'One of the ropes gave way. Sir Freddie says the rope had been tampered with deliberately.'

'Good grief! What fool would do a thing like that?'

Caroline agreed, giving a little shudder as she realised how close they had all been to a terrible death. 'Why should anyone want to harm you, Tom, or me? I do not understand…' A soft moan broke from him and she hastened to his side. 'Is the pain very bad?'

'I should like a drink of water, if you wouldn't mind,' Tom said. 'I think there may be some in that jug over there, on the washstand.'

Caroline went to investigate, but it was empty. She picked it up and turned to look at him. 'I am afraid there is none left, Tom. The doctor must have used it to wash his hands. I shall go and fetch some more.'

Tom seemed not to have heard her. He was lying with his eyes closed, clearly in some pain. She went softly from the room and down the stairs, wondering how best to discover her host, but as she hesitated at the bottom of the stairs he came out of a door to her left and saw her hovering uncertainly.

'Ah, there you are, miss,' he said. 'I was about to send the chambermaid up with a jug of fresh water. Is there anything else you would like for the poor gentleman?'

'Yes, please,' Caroline replied. 'I think a little brandy might not come amiss, sir, if you please.'

'Right you are, miss. You go up to him and I shall send it immediately.'

Caroline turned and ran up the stairs. As she did so, she heard a burst of laughter and some gentlemen came out into the hall behind her. She paused on the landing at the top of the stairs to glance back for a moment and then hurried down the hall to her brother's room, unaware that she had been recognised by one of the party.

Tom was looking for her as she came in, and she explained that the landlord was sending up water and brandy.

'It might help with the pain if it is very bad,' she told him.

'Yes, it might,' he agreed with a grimace. 'But you ought

to have rung for the maid, Caroline. It won't do for you to be seen here alone, love. You know what Aunt Louisa is like and the rest of the tabbies with her—they will put two and two together and make six.'

'I was only a moment,' Caroline said. 'Besides, you are my brother. Only a mean spirit could find fault with my being here with you, I believe?'

'Yes, well, most people would understand once they knew,' Tom said. 'But whispers can do a lot of harm, and people always think that there must be some truth in these rumours.'

'No smoke without fire?' Caroline said and smiled at him. 'I dare say you are right, but I shall not let it weigh too heavily, for truth to tell I do not care if some think ill of me.' Though in her heart she knew that she cared very much for the opinion of one person in particular.

Caroline sat with her brother for two hours before she heard voices at the door and then her mother came in, looking upset and anxious. Marianne had clearly shed a few tears on the way here and Caroline got up to go to her and embrace her as soon as she entered.

'It is all right, Mama,' she said. 'Tom is just sleeping. He was in some pain, but after he drank a little brandy he fell asleep and seems to be resting easily.'

'Is there any fever?' his anxious mother asked, and laid a gentle hand on his brow. A look of relief came over her face as she realised that he was resting quite peacefully. 'Thank God! We owe his safety to Sir Frederick, I am sure.'

'I believe it is merely a slight break,' Caroline reassured her. 'However, he will be better at home. Have you brought our own coach?'

'Yes, I have,' Mrs Holbrook said. 'I was out when Sir Frederick first came for me, but he found me on my way home from the lending library. I hope you appreciate how much he has done for us today, Caroline?'

'Yes, of course, Mama,' Caroline said, her manner a little reserved—she could not help thinking of Freddie's coldness to her earlier. 'It was very kind of him to help us as he did. Did he return with you?'

'No. He asked if he should, but I refused—I am sure he had something on his mind, though he would undoubtedly have come had I needed him. However, I have my coachman and two grooms, and I am sure we can manage well enough without him.'

A slight moan from the patient brought her head round to him at once, and for the next few minutes all her attention was for her son. She fussed over him, but, receiving a request not to do so, laughed in relief. Clearly Tom was feeling much better and when asked if he felt up to making the journey home was quick to say that he would do so if she could arrange for him to be helped down the stairs.

Mrs Holbrook rang for the maid and gave instructions. A chair was duly produced and Tom helped into it. Two strong men then carried him from the room and down the stairs. Caroline went ahead to alert the coachman, and her mother followed, urging the men to be careful and not to drop their precious burden. Her fretting possibly made their task that much harder, but it was accomplished without too much pain for the invalid, and within some ten minutes or so Tom was settled in his mother's carriage as comfortably as could be arranged.

Mrs Holbrook, inquiring what she owed for the care of her

son, was told that Sir Frederick had already paid for everything, including the doctor's fee, and she was overcome with gratitude, which she continued to pour into her daughter's ear all the way home.

'He is the perfect gentleman,' she told Caroline twenty times. 'Everything that is kind I am sure. He will make some fortunate lady a very satisfactory husband.'

Although she stopped short of saying that Caroline should make a push to gain his affections, as her aunt had many times, it was clear to her daughter that she thought it a perfect match. Caroline did not protest as she would have to her aunt's bullying, for there was little that she could say. It was perfectly true that Sir Frederick had done all that could have been asked of him, but his generosity was not a reason for marriage. Caroline liked him very well, had counted him one of her best friends. Indeed, she had wondered if she might like to be married to him, but she was not sure after that morning if he liked her as well as she had thought.

She was subdued on their return to the house, and followed the servants who carried her brother up to his own room. His arm had begun to hurt again, and Mrs Holbrook shooed her from his room, while retaining the services of the butler to help her settle her son as comfortably as possible. She then went down to the stillroom and made up a tisane to her own prescription, which she allowed Caroline to take up for him.

'It will help him to sleep,' she said to Caroline. 'I shall not go out this evening, for I could not bear to leave him in this condition, but you must go with your aunt to the soirée as arranged, dearest.'

'Do you think I could cry off for once?' Caroline asked. 'I would much rather not go this evening, for although I was not harmed I was a little shaken by the accident—and I could help you to sit with Tom.'

'Very well, my love,' Marianne said and looked at her with approval. 'Yes, it must have been a shock for you when the balloon fell, and I dare say it will not matter in the least if you miss one evening's pleasure. And it would be a help to me to have you here—just in case he should take a turn for the worse.'

Caroline did not believe that anything of the kind would happen, but she was pleased that she did not need to go to the musical evening with her aunt. Lady Taunton had not been pleased when they returned to the house, and Caroline could only think that she had done something to annoy her.

The next morning Aunt Louisa was still in a foul mood and her annoyance with both Caroline and her sister was not alleviated when she informed them that she had learned that rumours had begun to circulate concerning her niece.

'But you know the truth of it, Aunt,' Caroline said when she was subsequently questioned by the older woman. 'Tom was hurt in the accident, and that was the reason I was at the inn. It is unfortunate that someone saw me there, but you may easily scotch such tales by telling the truth.'

'Which I did, as you would expect,' Lady Taunton said with a scathing glance. 'I dare say we shall brush through this easily enough, but had you been a little more circumspect in your behaviour, miss, it might never have been thought possible in the first place. I have warned you. If you gain a reputation for being fast, you will lose more than you bargain for!'

'I do not think I have done anything particularly wicked,' Caroline said, crossing her fingers behind her back. Had anyone seen her dressed as a youth, she might have been in serious trouble. 'When our friends hear the tale and put their side of the story about, people will soon forget this nonsense.'

'Well, it is to be hoped so,' her aunt said. 'But once this kind of thing happens, the tales often linger. You must be particularly careful in future that you do nothing that could cause further gossip.'

They were in the small back parlour, to which her aunt had summoned her, and neither of them heard the knocker, so it was with some surprise when a visitor was announced. Caroline turned to look at the young man standing in the doorway and ran to him with a cry of delight. 'Nicolas dearest! It is so good to see you. I had hoped you might get leave while we were here, but I thought it unlikely.'

'Well, here I am, puss,' Nicolas said and embraced her in a bear hug. Looking up at him, she thought that he had grown since she had seen him, and he looked wonderful in his scarlet uniform. 'Now tell me, what is this I hear about Tom?'

'Oh, do come up and see him,' Caroline said, linking her arm through his. 'It will cheer him up immensely to talk to you. He is very annoyed that Mama has forbidden him to get up again for at least two days.'

Nicolas inclined his head to his aunt. 'I hope you are well, ma'am? I shall greet you properly later, but I am eager to see my brother—if you will excuse us?'

Caroline drew him from the room, hugging his arm. 'You arrived in the nick of time,' she confided. 'Aunt Louisa was giving me a fearful scold! I know it was my fault that Tom was hurt, for he wouldn't have been in the basket if it hadn't been for me, but I couldn't be blamed for being in that inn.'

'I suggest that you start at the beginning, puss,' Nicolas said, grinning at her. 'Then I might have a hope of understanding.'

'Oh, you!' Caroline said, but obliged him with the full story, which took them up to the landing where Tom's bedchamber was situated. 'So you see, she was quite unfair!'

'Yes, she was, but you should learn to dissemble, puss. You are defiant and it puts her in the right of it. Bite your tongue and think before you answer. There is no point in antagonising her. After all, she did stump up the blunt for this trip.'

'Yes, I know, and I am behaving very ungratefully,' Caroline said, feeling a little ashamed. 'I shouldn't wrangle with her, for no doubt she means well—but I cannot like her.'

'As to that, she is not my favourite person by any means.' He grinned at her. 'But let us see what Tom has to say, shall we?'

Caroline nodded, following her brother into Tom's bedchamber. He had been sitting up and reading a book, but he threw it down with a joyful cry as he saw Nicolas.

'Thank goodness you are here,' he said. 'Perhaps you can convince Mama that I am not on my deathbed, Nicolas. It is true that I have a little pain still, and my arm feels awkward in this splint, but I shall expire of boredom if I am forced to stay here for two days. I am promised to Bollingbrook next weekend and that only gives me a few days to enjoy myself.'

'Indulge her for one day,' Nicolas advised. 'By what I hear, you were lucky to escape so easily and will need to rest for a while, otherwise you may find yourself fainting. And that, dear brother, would cause our much-loved mama to go into a decline herself.'

'No, I do not think so,' Caroline said, eyes sparkling. Her mood of despondence had been lifted by Nicolas's arrival.

'She has seemed much better of late, brighter in herself and happier. I think she has a secret admirer…'

'Mama—an admirer?' the brothers exclaimed in unison. 'You are roasting us, Caroline!'

'No, indeed I am not,' she said. 'Please say nothing to her yet, for she has not told me anything, but I have met him once or twice now…and she likes him. I think he likes her very much, but I do not know how far they have progressed.'

'I thought it was you who came here to catch a husband,' Nicolas said and laughed in delight. 'Well, if I ever heard such a blessed thing! I should be much pleased if she were to take him. I think she and Papa went on tolerably well, but it wasn't all April and May with them, and she has been down in the dumps since he died. Yes, it would be a good thing for her.'

'That is how I feel,' Caroline said, 'but I am not sure there is anything to celebrate yet. It may all fall through.'

'Good for her,' Tom said. 'You may not know this, either of you—but Aunt Louisa has been bullying her into making a home with her when I marry or before that if she can persuade her to it.'

'Good grief,' Nicolas said and looked revolted. 'Poor Mama would be truly under the cat's paw. We must save her from that at all costs.'

'I think she would not like it at all,' Caroline said. 'She spoke wistfully of living in a cottage so that she might live as she pleased, but I think Mr Milbank is wealthy enough to provide her with a decent home of her own.'

'I can see you have been busy, little puss,' Nicolas said. 'Now tell me, how did you come to be in town, Tom—and why do you have to visit Grandfather next weekend?'

'Grandfather stumped up the readies to settle most of my

debts and allow me a short visit to town,' Tom said. 'He has asked me to do something for him in return, and I think I shall, though it means I shall have to go abroad for a while.'

'Shall you like that?' Caroline asked, recalling how upset Julia had been when he was hurt. 'Would it not affect plans for—?' She broke off because she had no idea whether or not her brother returned Miss Fairchild's affections.

'I have no immediate plans for the future, except to put the estate into good heart,' Tom said with a slight frown. 'I could not think of marriage until I could support a wife, if that is what you were wondering, Caroline. Mama has no need to rush into anything, though I would be happy to see her settled if she wished it—but I am not on the catch for a rich wife, or a wife at all for the moment.'

'Oh, I see,' Caroline said and felt sorry for her friend, because it was obvious that her brother was too proud to ask Julia to be his wife, at least until he had something more than a rundown estate to offer her. 'Well, you must do as you please, of course.'

As she finished speaking, their mother came into the room. She was delighted to see all her family together, and immediately charged Nicolas with taking his sister to the ball that evening.

'Tom was to have come with us, you see,' she said, 'but I am sure Lady Jersey will be only too happy to accept you in his place. I shall stay here, of course, in case my son needs me, but Louisa will go.'

'Why do you not let me stay with you, Mama?' Caroline asked. 'I am sure Nicolas may find his own amusement for one night.'

'No, dearest,' her mother said. 'It is a matter of choice, and I shall not be entirely alone. A friend has promised to call, just for a few minutes. We shall have a quiet supper together, and talk…'

'Mama, do tell,' Caroline said, mischief in her eyes. 'Is it Mr Milbank?'

Marianne flushed and then smiled. 'I can see you have guessed it, Caroline, and since we are all together, I must confess that Herbert has asked me if I will consent to be his wife. I have asked him here this evening to give him his answer—and now, perhaps you will all have your say?'

'You should marry him, Mama,' Caroline said. 'He seems a pleasant gentleman and likes you very well.'

'Take the fellow,' Nicolas said and grinned wickedly. 'You are too young to wear the weeds for ever, Ma.'

'Marry him if you wish,' Tom said, 'but there will always be a home for you with me, Mama, whatever happens.'

'Bless you, dearest,' Marianne said, looking at Tom. 'But I must tell you that I feel happier now than I have for a long time. Papa and I did well enough together, and I was fond of him until he died—I would not want any of you to think that I had entirely forgot your father.'

'We should not have thought anything of the sort,' Caroline said. 'I hope you will take Mr Milbank, Mama.'

'Well, it is you it will affect most,' Marianne told her daughter. 'If you do not form an attachment this time, you will be obliged to live under his roof, which he is very happy for you to do—so you must not think you are forced to accept an offer you cannot like. I think you would be well suited with a certain gentleman if he should offer, but there is no saying he will.'

'What is this?' Nicolas asked, mischief in his eyes. 'You did not tell me this, Caroline!'

'Well, there was too much else to say,' she replied. 'But if you would like to take me driving this afternoon, I shall tell you all there is to know.'

Chapter Seven

'George, a moment if you please!' Freddie hailed his friend as he saw him leaving the premises of a gentleman's hat shop in Brook Street. He ran across the road, dodging between the traffic to catch him. 'How is Julia today? I trust she took no harm yesterday?'

'No, no, I do not think it,' George said with a little frown. 'She was merely distressed. It was a shocking thing to happen. You do not know any more concerning the incident, I suppose?'

'I have made further inquiries and it is quite certain that the rope had been tampered with, as we suspected. It must have happened under our noses, for Jackson swears that it was sound when he began to set up the balloon and I trust him completely. However, with so many people milling around before the flight, it might have been anyone. I do not imagine we shall discover the culprit, for we have nothing to go on. It was fortunate that things were no worse. Despite her denials, I am sure that Caroline was much shaken, and bruised, and Tom must think himself lucky he is no worse.'

'Miss Holbrook was very brave and acted with calm good sense. But why should anyone want to hurt her—or her brother, for that matter?' George looked puzzled.

'I have no idea,' Freddie said with a frown. 'However, I intend to make inquiries into this affair. It will not stop here.'

'No, it cannot,' George agreed. 'I don't suppose it was aimed at someone else…?' He lifted his brows.

'Exactly,' Freddie said. 'I was meant to be in that balloon with Miss Holbrook.'

'Then you think it may have been aimed at you?' George was shocked and stared at him incredulously. 'Although she could easily have been killed—both of you might have died, to say nothing of Jackson. If that is the case, you have a dangerous enemy, Freddie. He is ruthless and cares not who he harms.'

'Yes, unless it was merely a malicious act from a mindless idiot who did not understand what he did.'

'You think it might be simply that?' George raised his brows. 'But why would anyone do such a thing?'

'At this moment I have no idea, but I intend to discover the truth. We want no more *accidents*, George. I shall set an agent to work to discover what he may and I think I may take a trip out of town myself.'

'Were you thinking of going immediately?'

'Why do you ask?' Freddie saw something in his friend's eyes. 'Spit it out, man. It clearly bothers you.'

'There are some spiteful rumours circulating, Freddie— about Miss Holbrook…'

'You mean because of that business with the balloon, I suppose? I know it was a little bold of her, but surely nothing that could cause her to be censured?'

'That and other things…' George frowned. 'Apparently,

she was seen alone at the inn, coming from the bedchamber. Obviously, she had been with her brother, so that may be set to rights easily enough, but it seems that she was also seen leaving an inn early one morning quite recently…with you.'

'Damn!' Freddie glared at him so fiercely that George was taken aback.

'Didn't mean to offend you, old fellow. Dare say it is all lies?'

'That is the devil of it,' Freddie said. 'I did take her to an inn—and that's not the worst of it, George. I took her to a mill and she was dressed as a youth.'

'That was somewhat reckless of you, Freddie.'

'I know it,' he said with a rueful smile. 'She demanded it of me in settlement of a wager, George—but that is no excuse. I admit that I was at fault. I wanted to see if she would dare and she did! Sneaked out in borrowed clothes, as game as anything. We left before the fight finished, as it happens— but she would have seen it out if I'd let her.'

'She is very spirited,' George said, 'but quite innocent, you know. It would be a sad thing if she were to lose her reputation for a lark, Freddie.'

'Yes, you are right, of course,' Freddie replied. 'This other business must wait for the moment. There is something I must do first…'

'That was no accident,' Nicolas said and frowned as he looked at his brother when they were alone. 'Caro told me the rope had been deliberately frayed. It must have been done in the hope of causing harm—either to you or Caroline.'

'But it was a last-minute decision,' Tom said, wrinkling his brow. 'That I should go up with her, I mean. It was to have been Sir Frederick.'

'Damn it!' Nicolas was concerned, angry. 'She might have been killed! I cannot think that Caroline has an enemy...but it might have been intended for Rathbone. Besides, he is to blame for risking her safety in that ridiculous thing!'

'No, no,' Tom said. 'I do not think you can blame him for this, Nicolas. Caroline teased him into letting her go up and he would have been with her had I not intervened.'

'Then the intended victim must have been Sir Frederick...' Nicolas frowned. 'Though I cannot think why anyone might want to harm our sister in the process.'

'It might have something to do with the money...' Tom mused thoughtfully. 'Grandfather has decided to leave a large chunk of his fortune to us—not the entail, of course, but it is a sizeable amount as I understand it.'

'You mean to suspect our uncles—cousins?' Nicolas looked dubious. 'I know they are not exactly fond—but murder?'

'No, of course not. Uncle Sebastian will get what is his, naturally. The entail cannot be broken, nor should it. Uncle Claude will also get something—the London house and a small estate in Cornwall, which came to Bollingbrook through his second wife, I believe. However, there is someone else who might stand to gain if we were not around when Grandfather dies.'

'I don't understand you,' Nicolas said. 'Who could possibly benefit?'

'I dare say Grandfather won't mind me telling you this much in the circumstances,' Tom said. 'There is a fellow in Jamaica who might benefit if the named heirs were dead. I suppose he *is* an uncle of sorts, though illegitimate. Grandfather wants me to sell the plantation out there and I'm to do something for this uncle fellow.'

'You mean the old gentleman had another son in Jamaica?' Nicolas was fascinated, his eyes bright with amusement. 'He hasn't been out to the plantation since before he married our grandmother. I understood he had left the management of his property there to his overseer…'

'It is a wonder that there is anything left to sell, for it has been shamefully neglected,' Tom observed. 'But it seems that the man was entirely trustworthy. Now he has died and Grandfather says it is time to sell. Whatever I get for it will come to me, and that may be very little. Apparently Grandfather had property elsewhere, which did not come to him through the estate. It was sold some years ago and the money invested safely. Caroline is to have something and you, I imagine—but there should be a couple of hundred thousand pounds, and Grandfather is determined that his elder sons shall not touch a penny of it. I think he intends to divide it between us and the fellow in Jamaica.'

'Good grief!' Nicolas ejaculated, feeling astonished at the size of the bequest. 'Now that alters things somewhat. As lazy as he undoubtedly is, even Uncle Sebastian might consider stirring himself for that kind of money.'

'No, you cannot think it? His wife was an heiress and both daughters married well. Come to think of it, Uncle Claude married to advantage and he has but one daughter. Grandfather gave her ten thousand when she married.' Tom frowned. 'I cannot say with any certainty that it was truly an attempt on Caroline's life or mine. Besides, Uncle Sebastian has no sons at present and the Bollingbrook estate may well come to me in the end—or you, if I die.'

'But if it were the bastard…surely he is in Jamaica? And surely you would be his intended victim, not Caroline!'

'He may not be in Jamaica. Apparently, he wrote to Grandfather a while back and told him that he intended to visit England and that he would call on him.'

'Do you think his letter was intended as a threat of some kind? I dare say he might think himself ill used if nothing has been done for him.'

'Yes, that was in my mind,' Tom said.

Nicolas frowned. 'Shall you risk going out to Jamaica?'

'I think I must. The overseer's daughter is to marry, and she wants to know if her future husband may purchase the estate. An offer has been made, but it is paltry. I must see what can be done elsewhere.'

'You will need someone to watch your back.'

'Any ideas?'

'I might have. I shall ask around and see if I can find a suitable man for you. You need an old soldier, Tom. A man you can trust in a fight.' Nicolas was thoughtful. 'Meanwhile, you must take more care—you and Caroline.'

'I trust I may rely on you to behave yourself this evening?' Lady Taunton looked at Caroline with something not far from dislike. 'We can only hope that the rumours circulating town have not become so strong that we shall be asked to leave. The patronesses of Almack's are extremely strict, as you very well know, and if you are treated with some coolness you have only yourself to blame. The very idea of going up in a balloon! It is not the behaviour expected of a respectable young lady, I can tell you. And as for being seen coming from the bedchamber of an inn alone…' She clicked her tongue in disgust. 'It is no wonder if people are talking.'

'I promise you that I shall be circumspect this evening,' Caroline replied, feeling unusually chastened.

'We must hope that that is an end to it,' Lady Taunton replied with a sour look. 'All I ask is that you do not disgrace me, Caroline.'

It was not to be expected that Caroline went with a light heart to the assembly that evening. Her mother had declined to accompany them, because she was worried about Tom, who seemed a little less well that day, but she would not hear of Caroline staying at home.

'You must go, my dear,' she insisted. 'Especially if there are silly rumours circulating. To stay at home might cause people to think they were true.'

Caroline knew that her mother was right. To stay away when she had been given vouchers would look as if she had something to hide. It was usually a very insipid evening, for she knew that Sir Frederick would not be there. Mr Bellingham had told her that Sir Frederick had never attended these gatherings, had not done so since he was first on the town. The most that she could hope for was to dance twice with Mr Bellingham and perhaps stand up for a waltz or two with others of her friends, for there was often more ladies than gentlemen present.

She wished that she might have seen Sir Frederick—she was afraid that he was still angry with her and that had left her feeling rather low. Since the incident at the balloon ascension, he had seemed to change towards her—what could have happened? And why did she mind so much?

Caroline was aware of something different as she went into the ballroom with her aunt. People turned their heads to look at her and she heard a little buzz of noise, as if they were whispering. For a minute or two she and her aunt stood alone, and then Mr Bellingham brought Julia across to speak to them.

Caroline's cheeks were a little warm, for her friends usually surrounded her as soon as she entered a room; she felt wretched, for clearly her aunt had been right. After a moment, one or two others drifted over to join them and she began to feel better. However, she was aware of an odd atmosphere, and even when Sally Jersey came over to speak to her, she felt that there was something a little chilly in that lady's manner.

Caroline lifted her head and danced with George, determined to brave the evening out whatever happened. He, of course, was just as usual, making her laugh and complimenting her on her gown so that she began to relax a little and wonder if she had imagined that she was being given the cold shoulder by some of the older ladies. It was just as their dance was drawing to a close that she heard a little gasp of surprise that seemed to echo from the assembled company as one. And then, turning her head towards the door, she saw that a gentleman had entered, accompanied by an elderly lady.

'Good grief!' Bellingham said, clearly startled. 'I never thought I would see the day. Freddie here and his godmother too! He intends business…'

'What do you mean?' Caroline asked, looking at him.

'Lady Stroud hardly ever attends this sort of affair these days,' George said. 'She was one of the leading hostesses of her day, of course—a stickler in all matters of propriety. Clever devil!' A look of appreciation had entered his eyes.

'I do not understand…' Caroline said, her voice fading as he nodded at her encouragingly, a flicker of amusement in his eyes. She began to see what he was getting at. 'Oh…'

'Trust Freddie to see you right, m'dear,' George said and smiled at her. 'Knows he got you into it, up to him to see you safe.'

'No, please…' Caroline said, her cheeks becoming hot. This was dreadful! George was suggesting that it was up to Freddie to make her an offer because he had compromised her, and that wasn't right at all. 'It was all my fault. He mustn't—'

'Freddie might be a bit reckless, careless, even, at times,' George said, still smiling rather oddly at her. 'But he knows what is expected of a gentleman—and he is fond of you, m'dear. He'll see you right and tight.'

Caroline knew that he was leading her towards Sir Frederick and Lady Stroud. She wanted to break away from him and seek a place to hide, but his hold on her arm was quite firm and it was clear that there was no escape for her.

'Lady Stroud,' George said. 'May I say that I am delighted to see you here this evening, ma'am. It is too seldom that we see you in company these days.' He looked at Caroline. 'May I present you to a young lady I admire, ma'am? This is Miss Caroline Holbrook.'

'I am aware of the gel's name,' Lady Stroud said a little testily, her steely gaze fixed on Caroline's face as she addressed her godson. 'Pretty enough, I'll grant you that, Freddie. I dare say you'll know how to steady her.' She fixed Caroline with a bayonet look. 'A spirited gel, so my godson says. He often talks a great deal of nonsense, but in this instance I have been prepared to listen to him. Miss Holbrook, I believe they are about to play a waltz. I give you permission to dance with Rathbone. Off you go, now, and try to look as if it pleases you.'

'Thank you, ma'am.' For once in her life Caroline did as

she was bid without demur. 'Sir, you are very kind.' She lifted her head, meeting his eyes without flinching.

'Caroline, my privilege,' Freddie said, taking her by the hand and leading her towards the floor. 'Do not look so scared. I promise you that her bark is much worse than her bite. She is actually on your side, though you may not think it.'

'Lady Stroud is very good,' Caroline said, a trifle pale though her head was up, her smile in place. 'But it was not necessary to ride to my rescue like a white knight, sir. I am quite able to manage for myself.'

'Caroline, do you not know what people are whispering—what they are thinking? You were seen leaving the inn with me on the morning of the fight.'

'Oh…' Caroline glanced up at him, her eyes wide. 'I thought it was just that I was alone at the inn when Tom was hurt.'

'No,' Freddie said. 'You might have ridden that out, but this is more serious—and it is my fault. Therefore I must do my best to see you clear of it. Lady Stroud still has significant influence in society and if she is seen to approve of you…'

'Yes, I see,' Caroline said and swallowed hard. 'I thought…Mr Bellingham said…thank you for thinking of it, sir. I know this is all my own fault, though I do not see that I have committed a terrible crime.' Her eyes were suddenly filled with defiance as her pride took over and she threw off her subdued mood. 'You did not seduce me, sir, and are therefore blameless.'

'No, not blameless,' he said honestly. His expression was serious, a little harsh. 'I have a way of teasing, Caroline—a provoking manner that sometimes leads others to recklessness that they would not otherwise think of, and I believe this is what happened in your case. Therefore, I must do what I can to—'

'No!' Caroline said quickly. 'I am not sure what you mean to say, sir, but I must tell you that I shall soon be leaving London on a visit to my grandfather. I think that it would be better if you waited until I return…if you have anything you wish to say to me.' Her cheeks were flushed and she concentrated very hard on the second button of his pristine shirt.

'Very well, if that is your wish,' he said. 'My own feeling is that Lady Stroud may do all that is necessary. I do have something to say to you, Caroline, but it may easily wait for a few weeks.'

'Thank you,' she said and smiled up at him. Her smile at that moment was so brave and so beautiful that Freddie was momentarily dazzled. 'You are very kind, sir, and I am glad that you are not cross with me.'

'Have I done something to make you think that I might be?' He raised his brows at her.

She took a deep breath. 'You seemed angry after Tom was hurt…at the inn.'

'I was angry at what had happened,' he said. 'You made light of the accident, Caroline, but you could have been badly hurt. And it is for this reason that I must leave town for a few days. If someone is trying to harm one of us, I think it needs investigating.'

'You are very kind to take an interest.'

'Anything that concerns you, concerns me, Caroline. Besides, whoever tampered with that rope may have had another victim in mind altogether.'

'Do you have an enemy, sir?'

'I dare say I have more than one,' Freddie said, looking

grim. 'He may do his damnedest as far as I am concerned, but when the safety of others—your safety, Caroline—is concerned, that is another matter.'

There was such sincerity, such anger in his eyes that her heart caught. She knew in that moment that there was a special feeling between them, but the dance was ending and she was unable to say more as Sally Jersey came up to them at that moment. She gave Freddie a look of pure mischief.

'Sir Frederick, this is indeed an honour. I had long given up hope of seeing you here, my friend.'

'As well you might,' he said. 'It took a great deal to bring me here, Sally—but I imagine I have no need to elaborate? I believe that my godmother will do all that is necessary.'

'Of course,' the lady replied and threw Caroline a speaking look. 'You are a fortunate young lady, Miss Holbrook. I believe I may not say more for the time being, but now that I understand you were visiting Lady Stroud that morning, there cannot be the least need for censure. It seemed a little odd that you should be seen leaving an inn with Sir Frederick at such an hour, but I understand that he was forced to stop because his horses had some trouble with their harness. It is all explained and shall be forgotten. Come along, Caroline. I want you to take pity on a young gentleman who is newly come to town. He is very shy and may tread on your toes, but I know that you will be kind to him.'

Freddie watched as Lady Jersey bore Caroline off with her. He smiled a little as George came up to him.

'The chestnuts are yours, my dear friend. I believe that was our bet—that when you saw me here I should have met my match?'

'You had no choice but to come in the circumstances,'

George said. 'The bet was a matter of marriage. You have until Christmas, Freddie…'

'Very well,' Freddie replied, frowning slightly. He gave his friend a quizzical look. 'You know, I am not sure that a few months will be long enough. I'm damned if I know if she will have me.'

Caroline sat staring out of her bedroom window. It was a wet day and the streets of London were unappealing. Her thoughts were running in a direction she did not like. She was almost certain that Sir Frederick meant to make her an offer of marriage. An offer he felt obliged to make because of the scandalous gossip that had been circulating about her.

He had left Almack's soon after his dance with her, though Lady Stroud had stayed on for two hours, keeping Caroline by her side most of the time and introducing her to everyone who came near as her new friend.

'My godson brought her to visit me early one morning recently,' Lady Stroud lied stoutly, 'and we took to each other like ducks to water. She's a gel after me own heart. I like a gel with spirit. Can't stand these milk-and-water manners today!'

Her sally had attracted polite laughter, which meant an end to the threat of scandal. Caroline had watched and listened, for it was soon clear to her that Lady Stroud was a martinet in the matter of proper manners and much respected. When she took her leave, she instructed Caroline to visit her soon, and told her that she expected them to become good friends in the future.

Caroline had thanked her for coming to her rescue and received a stern look in return. 'I don't make a habit of lying, young lady. Make sure that you give me no cause to regret this evening. I happen to be very fond of Freddie. He owes a duty to his family. He will be expected to provide the family with an heir soon, and his wife must be above reproach.'

Caroline had mumbled something appropriate. She was very grateful to the elderly lady for helping her, and even though she was forced to endure another lecture from her aunt on the way home, she knew that Lady Taunton was impressed.

'Of course you know what this means,' she told Caroline before they parted. 'I shall say no more—but I was right all the time.'

Caroline had not answered her, because she was very much afraid that Sir Freddie did intend to make her an offer. Not because he loved her, but because he thought it was the proper thing to do—and people would expect it after what had happened at Almack's. His coming there just to dance with her—when he had never done so before—was sure to be taken as a sign that he meant to marry her. She knew from Lady Stroud that he was looking to settle and she had been warned that his wife must be beyond reproach. Surely he could not truly wish to marry Caroline! Her reckless behaviour had aroused gossip, and she had nothing to offer him. It could only be a misplaced sense of honour that had prompted him to think of it.

She had prevented him from speaking that night, and perhaps once the gossip had died down he would reconsider. After all, it was not truly necessary—and she did not want to be married for the sake of her reputation.

She would miss seeing him over the course of the next few days, and she thought that she might not be in London when he returned. She was to visit her grandfather at the end of the next week, and Mrs Holbrook was talking of leaving London soon. She had spoken to Caroline of it the day after Mr Milbank came to supper.

'It may not be necessary for you to come back to town after your visit to Bollingbrook,' she had told her daughter. 'I am thinking of going down to Bath. Mr Milbank believes it would suit me better than racketing around London, and I think he may be right. I should naturally wish you to join me there. I am sure that you will make new acquaintances in Bath, Caroline, and anyone who wishes to see you will take the trouble of travelling there, I am certain.'

'Will Aunt Louisa accompany you to Bath, Mama?'

'No, I do not think so,' Marianne said. 'I have a little money of my own, Caroline. I have been reserving it for the future, but I think I shall not need it now. I have decided to accept Mr Milbank's offer. It is so that we may see each other comfortably, and make what arrangements we wish, that I have decided to go down to Bath. I am afraid that your aunt is not pleased by my decision.'

'But you will not let her displeasure change your mind, Mama?' Caroline looked at her anxiously, for in the past months her mother had been much influenced by Lady Taunton.

'No, I shall not,' Marianne said with more determination than her daughter had seen from her. 'I shall tell you now, Caroline. My first marriage was not all that it might have been—but I think that this time I am truly loved. I should be foolish to turn down this chance of happiness.'

'I am sorry that you were not happy with Papa.'

'It was only after my illness,' her mother said. 'Until then I think he cared for me as much as most men care for their wives. But I was ill and things were not right between us. He formed another attachment—a relationship that lasted until his death.' She lifted her head proudly. 'I did not know it, though I suspected it—and then, after his death, I received a very unkind letter. I showed it to Bollingbrook, but he told me not to make a fuss about it, and that was one of the reasons we disagreed. He was inclined to think me foolish. However, I did not think that an affair of long standing was something I could simply forget as if it had never happened.' She shook her head. 'It does not serve to dwell on these things. I shall forget it now, because it no longer matters.'

'I am sorry you were hurt,' Caroline said, understanding now why her mother had seemed to fade away after her father's death. It was not just a matter of grief, but also of hurt and disappointment. 'But I think you will be happy with Mr Milbank.'

'Yes, I am perfectly sure of it,' Marianne said. 'I did not think that I could ever feel anything for anyone again, other than my children—but it has happened and I feel young once more.'

'You look young,' Caroline assured her mother and hugged her. 'Yes, let us go down to Bath, dearest Mama. I believe it will suit both of us much better than London.'

'Yes, my dear, we shall do so. We must attend the masked ball at Lady Mannering's house, but after that we shall go.'

The ball had begun with Caroline being surrounded by eager partners as always, for it seemed that society had decided to think the best of her and her popularity was restored. Mr Bellingham had written his name in three spaces, her brother Nicolas in another two. Although everyone wore masks, it was easy enough to guess who most of the guests were, though one or two eluded Caroline.

The room became very warm as the evening wore on and the French windows were opened on to the garden to allow some air to circulate. Caroline felt the heat a little before supper and decided to slip outside to the garden rather than go into the dining parlour. She was not in the least hungry and she did feel very sticky, for it was an airless night.

It was not so much better on the terrace, but at least the air was fresh out here, and the gardens looked enticing in the moonlight. She thought that she could smell some kind of night-blooming flower and was about to go in search of it when someone came out onto the terrace.

'Ah, I thought I saw you come out,' George said. He removed his mask and Caroline did likewise, for she thought it was in part due to the silken mask that she felt uncomfortable. 'Were you thinking of taking a stroll in the grounds?'

'Yes,' Caroline said, welcoming him with a smile 'I was not in the least hungry and thought it would be pleasant out here.'

'The air has been heavy all day,' George said and offered her his arm. 'May I walk with you, Miss Holbrook?'

'Yes, that would be nice,' Caroline replied with a smile. 'Have you heard from Sir Freddie? Do you know when he will be returning?'

'I fear not. Has he said nothing to you?'

'He had some business out of town, I believe, but I do not know when he may return.' She was torn between wanting to see him again and dreading it—she was afraid that his sense of honour would make him offer for her even if he did not truly wish her to be his wife.

They had strolled some distance from the lights of the ballroom. George was struck by the look on her face, for he sensed that she was deeply troubled. Could it be that she did not wish to marry Freddie? He hesitated for a moment, then, 'If there is anything I can do for you, Miss Holbrook, you have only to ask. You must know that I…have a great admiration for you.' Caroline's head came up and he smiled oddly. 'I do not think that it can be a surprise to you.'

'Oh, Mr Bellingham,' Caroline said, her breath catching in her throat. 'I have appreciated our friendship greatly but…'

'You care for someone else?' he asked gently. 'You may speak plainly. I shall not be offended, my dear, for I have suspected it, but I know that you are leaving town for a while and that nothing is settled. Indeed, you seem a little unhappy—and I wished to speak. I have never thought of marriage. I am set in my ways, and I had thought that Julia would be my heir, for I have no title to consider. However, if you need me, I am at your service.'

'How kind you are, sir, but you must not concern yourself for me.' Caroline reached out to touch his hand. He had not quite proposed to her, but she knew that he might have done if she had given him encouragement.

'I think so well of you, sir. And I like you more than any other gentleman of my acquaintance except—' She stopped and blushed. 'I am not perfectly sure…'

'I understand perfectly, more than you imagine, I dare say,' he said. 'I should be happy if our friendship were to continue, my dear.'

'What a generous man you are,' Caroline said. 'I think myself very fortunate to have such a friend.'

'Thank you. I am glad to have your good opinion, Miss Holbrook.' George smiled at her. 'I think perhaps we ought to go in for your aunt will be looking for you.' Hardly had he finished speaking when they saw her brother Nicolas walking towards them across the smooth lawns.

'It was our dance, Caroline. Ah, I see you are with Mr Bellingham,' he said. 'Then all is well. I merely came to see if you had wandered out here alone, puss.' He grinned at her and nodded to George. 'Warm this evening, isn't it?'

'Yes. We came out to take some air, but we are about to return to the ballroom. I believe you are to go out of town in a few days?'

'Yes, that is perfectly right. My brother has to visit Bollingbrook and Caroline is to go with him. Tom isn't fit to drive yet, of course, though he is much recovered in himself, so I shall take them down.'

'I am thinking of travelling to Bath this coming weekend,' George told him. 'The road follows the same direction you must take for a while, I dare say. We may see each other on the way.'

'Indeed we may,' Nicolas said. 'My mother goes to Bath in a few days I believe. You will surely see her there, and us too after our visit to Bollingbrook. I have agreed to drive Caroline there before I return to my regiment.'

'Yes, I had heard of Mrs Holbrook's intention,' George said with a smile. 'My estate is on the way, not too distant from your grandfather's. I shall stay there for a few nights on my journey, I believe. I have a little business to attend to before I go on.'

'Then you must visit us at Bollingbrook,' Nicolas said. 'I dare say the old gentleman may like to give a dinner for his neighbours while we are there.'

'Perhaps. We shall see,' replied George, who knew Bollingbrook's reputation as a recluse these past years. 'And now I must bid you both good evening as I am engaged for the next dance…'

He went on ahead of them, leaving the brother and sister together in the garden. Nicolas looked at his sister thoughtfully.

'Bellingham is a decent chap,' he said. 'You might think yourself fortunate if he asked for you, puss.'

'He is very kind,' Caroline told him a trifle wistfully. 'And I do like him, but I am not sure who I wish to marry just yet.'

'It's this other fellow you've got your mind set on,' Nicolas said and frowned, for he had heard some gossip. 'I don't say as there's anything wrong with that, Caroline—but if he ain't come up to scratch yet, he may not.'

'I know,' Caroline said. 'I am not sure I wish to marry him if he does, Nicolas. Sometimes I have thought…and yet I do not know. This marrying business is more difficult than I had imagined. I had always believed Mama happy with Papa, but it seems that it was not so…and that upsets me a little.' It had made her wonder if there was such a thing as true love, and she was not certain that she could trust her own feelings. Was the most she could sensibly hope for a marriage of convenience with someone she liked?

'Well, I dare say there is time enough for you to find someone you can like.' Nicolas glanced over his shoulder as he heard a rustling noise behind him. He was not carrying his pistol, though it was in the pocket of his topcoat. 'I believe we should go in, puss—and I should tell you that I think it would not be sensible of you to venture out alone while you are in town.'

'Are you thinking of what happened the other morning?' Caroline saw the concern in his face. 'I know Sir Frederick thinks someone deliberately caused that accident to the balloon, though I cannot imagine why anyone would want to do such a thing.'

'It is difficult to know the reasoning behind it,' Nicolas agreed. 'But Tom and I think that you should take care, Caroline—just in case you were the intended victim.'

'I know that I might have been killed, but why should someone want me dead? As far as I know I have no enemies and my dowry is virtually nothing.'

'It may not be as insignificant as you think,' Nicolas told her. 'Grandfather may do something for all of us if he chooses.'

'Grandfather has a lot of secrets, doesn't he?' Caroline said. 'He hinted as much to me once, but when I asked him what he meant he became cross and told me to run away to my mother.'

'He certainly does—more than we could ever know!' Nicolas said and laughed. 'Well, puss, I think we have probably lost our dance, for here comes your next partner, if I do not mistake his look. I shall leave you now—I have an appointment elsewhere, but do not forget what I told you…the garden is out of bounds for you without someone to protect you.'

'Then I shall not venture out even if it is hot,' Caroline said. She glanced over her shoulder, for she had felt for the past few minutes that she was being watched…

'I shall miss you when you leave London,' Julia said, looking a little wistful. 'I am happier with you than any of my other friends, Caroline. I do hope we shall not lose touch?'

'Oh, no, I am sure we shall not,' Caroline said. 'I shall write to you and tell you all what is happening. Have I told you that Tom has to go abroad for a while?'

'Go abroad?' Julia looked surprised and then upset. 'Oh, I did not know. Will he be gone long, do you think?'

'I would not think it,' Caroline answered, for she could see that Julia had been greatly affected by the news.

'Mr Asbury has made me an offer of marriage,' Julia said. 'Please, do not mention it to anyone, for I have asked him for a little time. I am not sure, you see. I like him very well, and he is the only gentleman to have offered for me—other than Mr Farringdon.'

'Oh, yes,' Caroline agreed. 'You would not wish to marry Mr Farringdon…' She frowned as she realised something. 'He has not been in town for a week or more now, I think. At least I have not seen him.'

'George said he has been obliged to leave town in a hurry. His tailor had heard rumours of him being near to ruin and he was pressing for settlement.'

'Oh, that is unfortunate for him,' Caroline said, for even though she did not like the gentleman, she would not wish such a fate on anyone. 'However, I must admit that he had a way of looking at one that was most uncomfortable.'

'Oh, yes,' Julia said. 'It is strange how some gentlemen make one feel happy in their company—and others do not.'

'Yes, isn't it?' Caroline agreed. 'It is not easy to know one's own heart sometimes, is it?'

'I know my own heart,' Julia replied with a frown. 'But Mama wishes me to marry quite soon and she likes Mr Asbury…'

Caroline looked at her, feeling sorry because she knew that it was useless for her friend to have hopes of Tom. However much he might be attracted to Julia, he would not offer for her until he could afford to support her. She wished that she might say something to ease Julia's uncertainty, but she could not, for Tom had said nothing of his intentions to her and it would be wrong to arouse false hopes.

'Well, perhaps things will turn out as they ought,' she said and smiled at Julia. 'Oh, dear, sometimes I think it would have been very much easier to have been born a man, don't you?'

'Oh, yes,' Julia agreed. 'At least one could have asked the person one liked instead of having to wait to be asked.'

'Yes, that is unfair,' Caroline said, 'though I think that if I truly wanted to marry a gentleman who did not speak, I might just give him a hint.'

Julia looked at her and sighed. 'You are so much braver than I,' she said. 'All I can do is smile and hope…'

'Will you allow me to drive for a while?' Caroline asked her brother. They had been driving for some distance and the busy streets of London were left far behind them now. 'It is ages since you taught me to drive, Nicolas, and I have had no opportunity since you left to join the army, and I should be glad of some practice.'

'Very well,' Nicolas said and handed the reins to her. 'The road is quiet enough. Do you see that phaeton up ahead of us, puss? Let us try to overtake him before we come to the cross-roads. Do not be anxious—I am here to take over if you cannot manage it.'

'Oh, yes,' Caroline said, much amused. She was sitting up beside him, but she glanced over her shoulder at Tom, who was resting with his head back, his eyes closed. 'Wake up, Tom!' she cried. 'We're going to race that phaeton ahead of us.'

'God save us!' Tom said wryly. 'You were supposed to be saving me from more injury, brother—not exposing me to certain death.'

'Never fear, Tom,' he said with a grin. 'I am here and I shall take the reins if Caroline cannot manage it.'

Caroline's face was vivid with excitement. She could feel the wind in her hair as her bonnet blew off, hanging by its ribbons, and she cried out to her brother as they caught up with the vehicle in front of them.

'Go on, Caroline,' Nicolas urged. 'Pull out and pass him now. It is easy enough for we are at the crossroads and you have plenty of room.'

'Do you think I ought?' Caroline asked, knowing a moment of doubt. It had been fun catching the phaeton ahead of them, but she had recognised it and would have slowed up had Nicolas allowed it.

Seeing her hesitation, Nicholas snatched the reins back from her and flicked his whip over the horses' heads so that they sprang forward. The other carriage had increased its own speed and for a moment they were wheel to wheel. It was only when Nicolas saw the farm wagon coming from the right of the crossroads that he became aware of danger. It would have been wiser to drop back and let the phaeton have right of way but instead, he shot through and cut across to the left, causing the driver of the phaeton to curse and rein his horses in sharply.

Nicolas squeezed ahead, though it was only the skill of the other driver that saved them from an accident. Nicolas looked back with glee as he saw that they had left the phaeton far behind.

'It was a pity it was over so quickly,' he said regretfully. 'I should have liked to race him for longer. He is no mean whip, Caroline.' Realising that she was silent, he turned his head to look at her. 'Did I scare you, puss?'

'No, I was not frightened,' she said. 'But…that was Sir Freddie. I wasn't sure until we caught up with him, for there are other phaetons painted in those colours, but those were his horses and I caught a glimpse of his face as we shot past. He was very angry, Nicolas.'

'He came off all right,' Nicolas said, slightly shocked to discover who he had almost overset.

'By his judgement, not yours,' Tom said from behind them. 'You are completely mad, Nicolas. You should not have encouraged Caroline to drive like that on the open road. And you were reckless to pass him that way. I do not think I should want to be in your shoes when Sir Frederick catches up to us.'

'Well, I dare say he will not, unless I wish him too,' Nicolas said. 'I shall let them have their head for a while yet.'

'You will have to rest them eventually or change them,' Tom said and sat back, closing his eyes again. 'Besides, it is almost time we stopped for nuncheon. There is an inn no more than five miles ahead of us. I stopped there on my way up and it serves tolerable food.'

Nicolas glanced back over his shoulder. 'There is no sign of him. I dare say we shall reach the inn and eat our nuncheon before he catches up to us.'

Caroline was silent. She did not think that Sir Freddie would allow the incident to go without rebuke, and she was not at all surprised when a few moments later Tom called out that the phaeton was behind them. The driver caught up to them easily, keeping pace whatever Nicolas did in an effort to lose him, but did not attempt to pass. Though there were places that would have allowed it easily had Sir Frederick wished it, for even Nicolas was aware that Sir Freddie's blacks had the beating of him if their master chose.

When he turned into the inn yard at Tom's insistence, the phaeton followed. Nicolas jumped down, assisting his sister and then his brother, who was still not as nimble as usual. Sir Freddie was attending to his horses, speaking to the ostler who had come running. One of the grooms had attended to Nicolas's curricle, but it was clear that the preferred attention was being given to Sir Freddie.

'You go ahead,' Nicolas told Caroline and Tom. 'I had best have a word first. It will not do to come to blows in the inn itself. If we are to quarrel, it may be done out here.'

'But it was my fault in part…' Caroline began, only to find herself being firmly propelled towards the inn.

'Leave him to it,' Tom said, a firm hand at her elbow. 'Nicolas can handle himself, and it is his own fault if Sir Frederick gives him a set down.'

'Oh, but…' Caroline glanced back unhappily as she saw that the two men were closing on each other purposefully. 'I do hope they won't fight, Tom.'

'Well, I know who will feel sorry for himself if they do,' Tom said. 'Sir Frederick trains at Cribbs's Parlour. Nicolas is all pluck, but I think Rathbone is heavier, and has more science, I dare say. He is sure to give Nicolas a bloody nose if it comes to a mill.'

As they entered the inn, their host greeted them by beaming and welcoming them to his establishment. Tom asked for the private parlour, saying that there would be three of them for nuncheon. However, they had not been seated long before they heard voices and then the parlour door was flung open and Nicolas came in, followed by Sir Freddie. Caroline threw a scared glance at her brother, but was relieved to see that he did not have a bloody nose. He was slightly chastened, but did not seem resentful as he told them that he had invited Freddie to join them.

'I have apologised for stealing the road,' Nicolas said and grinned, a little shamefaced. 'But Sir Frederick has been dashed obliging about it.'

'No harm was done, though that was more luck than judgement,' Sir Freddie said and his eyes glinted as he looked at Caroline. 'However, it was not a fair race, for I had no idea of what you meant to do. Had I been aware that you meant to overtake me if you could, I should not have allowed you close enough and it would not have happened.'

'Oh, come on,' Nicolas exclaimed. 'That is doing it a dashed sight too brown. I shall not believe that you were not aware of me coming up behind you.'

'I did not think that you would be fool enough to try to pass at the crossroads,' Freddie said with a lift of his brow. 'If I were to meet you on the road another time, I should be more prepared.'

'Let us make a race of it,' Nicolas said. 'We are on our way to Bollingbrook—do you go that way?'

'Yes, as a matter of fact, that is exactly my intention. I have something I wish to discuss with Bollingbrook. I shall be staying at an inn nearby and will call on your grandfather in a day or so. If you are serious about this race, Nicolas, we shall come to terms. Besides, it will be best to rest the horses. I dare say yours are almost blown after the way you pushed them.'

'You are the most complete hand,' Nicolas said, for he had taken to Sir Freddie at once, despite being given a tongue-lashing in the yard for having risked the health of his sister and brother. He had loyally refrained from telling Sir Frederick that Caroline had been driving until the overtaking manoeuvre, perhaps because he sensed that it would have brought a further tongue-lashing. 'Yes, I agree. We shall make a wager when you come to Bollingbrook. Here's my hand on it.'

He offered his hand, which Sir Freddie took with a wry twist of his lips. He then sat down on the settle next to Caroline and looked at her, his brows lifted.

'Nicolas informs me that you were not in the least scared?'

'No, not of the race,' she said, 'but I thought you would be angry because of the way he cut you up at the crossroads.' She looked at him uncertainly.

'Had he been anyone else, I might have wrung his neck,' Freddie said lightly, though with a look that seemed to say he meant it. 'However, I shall hold my hand this time. I suppose that you will want to be a part of this race?'

'Yes, please,' Caroline said instantly. She was surprised, for she had thought he would forbid it. 'Indeed, I should!'

'Then we shall have the same wager as before?'

'Yes!' Her eyes sparkled—she suddenly felt much better than she had since the morning of the balloon ascension.

'Very well, Miss Holbrook,' Freddie said, a gleam in his eye. 'If I win, I gain my wish, and, if Nicolas wins, you shall have what you desire of me—but there is one condition to this race.'

'And what is that, sir?'

'You will be my passenger and not your brother's. At least then I shall be certain of you ending in one piece. And you will not be allowed to drive!' He fixed her with a piercing stare, which told her that he was not ignorant of the truth concerning her behaviour earlier that morning.

'Dash it all, sir!' Nicolas exclaimed. 'That's a deal too much! Caroline is my sister, after all, and I would never do anything to harm her.'

'Sir Freddie is in the right of it,' Tom agreed. 'You are both too headstrong by half! And I'll wager fifty guineas he beats you, Nicolas.'

'Fine brother you are,' Nicolas said with a wrathful eye. 'I'll take your fifty guineas, Tom! But as for whose passenger she shall be—that must be Caroline's choice.'

'Oh, I shall go with Sir Freddie,' Caroline said happily. 'For if I win my wager, he must teach me to drive his blacks—'

'The greys,' Freddie said, 'and it's a deal.'

Chapter Eight

Freddie had refused to accompany Caroline and her brothers, promising to meet with them again within a day or so. He had no intention of encouraging Nicolas to race him again while Caroline was his passenger. Instead, he put his feet up and thought about the girl he had made up his mind to marry.

He had been slow to come to his decision, but his mind was set now. She had seemed natural enough and pleased to see him—once she realised he was not going to quarrel with her brother—but he sensed it would not be easy to gain her consent to the marriage. Because of all the gossip in town she had taken it into her head that he meant to make her an offer as a matter of honour, whereas nothing could be further from the truth.

He would have to think of a way to persuade her… Thinking about the various methods of persuasion that he might use brought a smile to his lips. Some of them would, he was sure, prove extremely pleasurable.

'Well, girl, let me look at you,' Bollingbrook said as Caroline ran to kiss his cheek. His eyes dwelled intently on her face for a moment. 'You have become an elegant lady, Caroline. I think you must have all the young bucks by the ears.'

'Oh, Grandfather!' Caroline cried, her eyes bright with laughter. 'Of course I have not.'

'She has, sir,' Nicolas said. 'They were falling over themselves to dance with her when I accompanied her to a ball. I had to fight my way through the crowd to ask her for a dance.'

'That isn't true—tell him it isn't so, Tom.'

'Well, it ain't far from the truth from what I saw,' Tom said, smiling at his sister affectionately. He looked at his grandfather. 'And how are you, sir? Feeling a little better, I hope?'

'As a matter of fact, I am,' the Marquis said. 'Got myself a new quack. Heard of him by chance and sent for him to call. He prescribed a new mixture, which seems to have helped for the time being at least. But we shan't talk of me. I've had my day. I want to know what you young people have been up to. Caroline, come and sit by me and tell me if you have settled on a beau yet.'

Caroline moved one of the pretty gilt chairs nearer to his large wing chair and sat down. She proceeded to chatter about what she had been doing in town, which made her grandfather laugh. Seeing that he was in a good humour, Nicolas joined in, telling him about army life, and Tom watched in his own quiet way, letting them have their sway until his grandfather looked at him.

'What of you, sir?' The Marquis' eyes narrowed. 'You don't look as hale as you did when you were here last. Been overdoing it, have you? What's the matter with your arm?'

'Tom was hurt,' Caroline said defensively, for she would not have her brother criticised unfairly. 'There was an accident with a balloon and Tom's arm was broken.' She did not mention her part in the affair, for she thought it best that he should not be told it all. Fortunately, it did not occur to him that she might also have been involved.

'Lucky to be alive, are you?' Bollingbrook beetled his brows. 'Damn stupid thing to do. Any fool knows those contraptions aren't safe. Well, we shall talk later, Tom. Go and rest for a while before dinner. The journey must have done you up.'

'Yes, I think it has to a certain extent,' Tom agreed and got to his feet. 'If you will excuse me.'

'Humph,' the Marquis said as he went out. 'I didn't know he had the gumption. Why anyone would want to fly I can't imagine. Don't know what the world is coming to!'

Bollingbrook sighed before looking at Nicolas. 'Nicolas, get off and find something to do before dinner. I want a few minutes alone with my girl.'

'Yes, sir, as you wish,' Nicolas said and grinned at his sister. 'I shall see you later, puss.' He winked at her as he went out.

'Impudent pup,' the Marquis grumbled, but in a mild manner that told Caroline he wasn't truly annoyed. 'Now then, girl, tell me the truth—have you seen someone that you fancy? If you have, I shall want to look him over. I want to make sure he is good enough for you.'

'I think there may be someone, Grandfather,' she said, 'but he hasn't spoken yet and I am not certain that he will.'

'What's the matter with the fellow? Ain't he got eyes?'

'Oh, yes,' Caroline said and laughed. 'He is very handsome and a little arrogant at times, I think—but he is also kind and funny and…' Her words tailed off. 'I think I may be in love with him, but I don't want to be if he doesn't love me.'

'Can't dictate something like that,' her grandfather told her. 'Either you are or you ain't. I only ever loved one woman, and that was your grandmother. The moment I set eyes on her I knew I had to have her. There was opposition to our marriage from her family, but I wasn't going to be beaten. I couldn't have cared less what anyone said or did, she was mine from the moment I saw her.'

'She was very beautiful,' Caroline said, thinking of Angelica Bollingbrook's portrait. 'I wish I had known her, Grandfather.'

'I wish you had too. You are very like her—and you would have loved each other.' He sighed deeply. 'Yes, I have wished that she could have known you, all of you.'

'I wish that she might,' Caroline said.

'Well, well, it can't be helped,' the Marquis said. 'I've shut myself off from the world too long, but there's time enough to repair things. You and your brothers shall not be forgotten, miss, and there's my promise to you. Run along, now. I shall see you later.'

Caroline was glad that she had come down to visit her grandfather. It was good to be in the country again, and though she had enjoyed the whirl of social activities in London, she thought that perhaps she preferred a quieter life.

The weather had settled into warm, balmy days and she spent much of her time either walking or riding with her brothers. She had persuaded Nicolas to take her driving in the park and they had enjoyed themselves letting the spirited horses have their head. It was on the morning of the second day after their arrival at Bollingbrook Place that she pulled Nicolas's phaeton to a standstill in front of the house just as a visitor arrived. She knew at once that it was Sir Freddie, and that he had seen her.

'Well done,' he said as he handed his reins to his tiger and came to help her down. 'I see that you have been practising, and perhaps we shall make a whip of you yet.'

His words of praise brought a flush to Caroline's cheeks and she gave him a shy smile, looking away quickly as his eyes seemed to penetrate her thoughts. She must not let him see that she was head over heels in love with him!

'Do not encourage her, sir,' Nicolas begged, grinning broadly. 'Given the opportunity, I think she would set up her own rig and then we should none of us know what she was up to!'

'Well, I dare say a suitable vehicle would not be so very dangerous,' Freddie said. 'Miss Holbrook would not be the only female whip; there are one or two notables, such as Lady Cheshire and Selma Hamilton.'

'Now you've done it,' Nicolas said with a look of mock despair. 'We shall have no peace now until she has set up her own curricle.'

'Oh, I want a phaeton,' Caroline said, giving her brother a challenging look. 'Something a little racy with a high-stepping pair to give me a certain touch.' She peeped under her lashes at Sir Freddie, but he had not risen to the challenge.

'What did I tell you?' Nicolas shook his head. 'There will be no dealing with her now!'

Freddie laughed, but made no further comment as he accompanied the pair into the house. Tom had been reading in the front parlour, but, having seen them through the window, came out to greet Sir Freddie and invite him to nuncheon.

'That is very kind of you,' Freddie said. 'But perhaps I ought to speak with your grandfather first?'

'I should leave it until later if I were you,' Tom advised with a wry grimace. 'He has his quack with him now and I think there is a little matter of a new dressing. In an hour or two he will no doubt be restored and feeling rather better.'

'Very well, I shall take your advice,' Freddie said, and glanced at Caroline. 'When do you intend to go down to Bath?'

'The day after tomorrow,' Caroline told him. 'Grandfather wants me to stay longer with him next time, but my mother will be expecting me—and, as she may be planning her wedding, I do not wish to keep her waiting.'

'Shall we arrange our race for then, Nicolas?' Freddie turned to him with a lift of his brows. 'We may meet at the Waverly Arms, which is just five miles from Bath, and race to the Abbey. After Caroline has transferred to my phaeton, of course.'

'Yes, a capital notion,' Nicolas said and grinned at him. 'But we have not decided a wager, though you have one with Caroline.'

'The race is enough in itself,' Freddie said, 'but if you wish for a wager—shall we say twenty guineas to the winner?'

Nicolas agreed. 'Twenty guineas it is!'

The details settled, they repaired to the dining room.

They spent the next hour or so very pleasantly eating and drinking. The conversation veered from prize fighting to horse racing and the likelihood of Bonaparte staying put on Elba for long, and then back to town gossip. The time passed so pleasantly that it was almost three in the afternoon before they rose from the table.

'Will you walk with me for a while?' Freddie asked

Caroline as they went out into the hall. 'I am sure your brothers have other things to do…'

'I can take a hint,' Nicolas said and grinned at his brother. 'Come along, Tom. I dare say we know when we are not wanted. I'll give you a game of billiards if you're up to it.'

'What do you mean if I'm up to it?' his brother demanded. 'Tell you what, we'll settle on the best of three…'

'How are you feeling now?' Freddie asked as they left the house and began to stroll across the lawns towards the rose arbour. His eyes moved over her with some concern. 'I know the accident was an unpleasant shock for you the other day, though you claimed you were not hurt—and of course you were denied your trip in that balloon.' He said nothing of the affair at Almack's, for he knew she would shy away from it like a young filly being put to its first fence.

'As if I cared for that,' Caroline said. 'I should still like to go up one day, but my only concern was for Tom. I think we were lucky that more serious harm did not result from such an accident.' She stopped walking for a moment to look at him. 'For myself, I cannot understand why anyone would do such a thing as to tamper with that rope. Why should anyone wish to harm Tom or me? Or you, sir, for that matter?'

'Indeed, it was more likely so, for the change was made only at the last moment, and I think the damage must have been done earlier that morning.'

'Yes, perhaps,' she said, looking at him doubtfully. 'Have you any idea who it might have been, sir?'

'None at all,' Freddie said. 'But I have not been idle, Caroline. I shall discover the truth in the end, I promise you.'

Caroline nodded. 'I think that you would always do what you set out to do, sir.' She blushed and dropped her gaze as she saw the expression in his eyes.

'Miss Holbrook…Caroline,' he said and looked down at her face. 'You do not have to answer me now unless you wish, but I—'

He was interrupted by a shout from the house and then Nicolas came sprinting across the lawns towards them.

'I am sorry to interrupt you,' he said, 'but Caroline must come at once. Grandfather has had some kind of a seizure and he is asking for her.'

'Oh, no,' Caroline said and looked at Freddie anxiously. 'You must forgive me, sir. May we speak again another time?'

'Yes, of course,' he said. 'Go to your grandfather, Caroline. I shall come tomorrow to inquire how he is—perhaps we may speak then?'

'Yes, thank you,' she said. 'Please excuse me…'

She fled across the lawn towards the house, her heart racing. These past couple of days her grandfather had shown his true affection for her, and she had felt happy that at last she was getting to know him. It would be a sad thing if he were to die just as they were truly becoming acquainted.

'Forgive me for disturbing you,' Nicolas said to Sir Freddie after his sister had left them. 'But I had no choice.'

'Obviously my meeting with Lord Bollingbrook must wait for another time,' Freddie said. 'It is unfortunate, for there were one or two matters I wished to discuss with him. I shall return tomorrow and in the meantime I hope that your grandfather is not seriously stricken.'

'He is as tough as old boots,' Nicolas said with a grimace that hid his affection. 'At least he has been, apart from the gout—but of course there is always a first time. But please do feel free to call whenever you wish.'

'Thank you. I shall,' Freddie said and nodded. 'I trust we shall not have to postpone our race. Good day to you now, Nicolas.' He tipped his hat and set out for the stables to have his phaeton made ready.

Nicolas turned and walked back to the house. He was almost certain that Sir Frederick had been about to make Caroline an offer, and he wished it might have happened before he had interrupted them. It would have secured his sister's future.

Tom was talking about making arrangements for his journey to Jamaica and Nicolas would need to return to his regiment in just over a week's time—which meant that Caroline would have no one to look out for her. If Tom was right and the attempts on his life were down to money, she might also be in some danger.

The doctor was still with Bollingbrook when Caroline arrived. He turned his head as she entered, smiling and beckoning her closer, though he had a finger to his lips, warning her to speak softly.

'The Marquis is resting, Miss Holbrook. I have given him something that will help him to sleep for a while.'

'Will he be all right?' Caroline looked at him anxiously. 'He isn't going to die—is he?'

'It was fortunate that I was here,' Dr Harris told her with a frown. 'I believe that it was merely a slight seizure and he should be well enough in a few days. However, the next few hours are all important. He must rest—and he should not be upset in any way. However, you must be aware that it could happen again, and if it does…'

'Yes, I see,' Caroline said and looked at her grandfather, who was now sleeping soundly. 'It is odd, but I have never considered him old. He is always so full of pepper that we take him for granted.'

Doctor Harris looked at her kindly. 'Do not despair, Miss Holbrook. He may yet be spared to you for some years to come.' He took his large silver watch from the pocket of his waistcoat and glanced at it. 'I have another call to make—but if you should need me at any time, please do not hesitate to send for me.'

'Thank you, sir. You are very kind.'

Caroline brought a chair to the side of her grandfather's bed and sat down beside him. His right hand was lying on the cover and she reached out to touch it with her own, wondering what he had wanted to say to her so urgently. The doctor's medication had obviously worked before he could communicate with her, and so she would sit quietly with him until he woke from his sleep.

She let her thoughts return to the few minutes she had spent alone with Sir Freddie. She had sensed that he was about to ask her to marry him—but did he truly care for her or was he merely offering out of a feeling of responsibility?

She had tried to deny her feelings for Sir Freddie, but, as her grandfather had said, you either loved or you did not; if she admitted what was in her heart, she had loved Freddie from the very beginning. There was something about him that had drawn her to him as a moth to the flame, a certain look, his smile and the way his ready wit matched hers. Whenever he was with her she felt alive and happy. She had not wanted to admit it, but now she could no longer pretend to herself that she was not head over heels in love with him.

But she must not reflect on her own feelings now. She glanced towards the bed as her grandfather stirred restlessly in his sleep, and she thought she heard him murmur a name.

'Angelica…' The words were slurred, indistinct, but had a desperate ring to them. 'My beloved…do not leave me…'

He was calling for the young wife he had loved and lost, Caroline thought. None of them had truly understood his grief, she realised now, or the loneliness he had imposed on himself after Angelica's death. Why had he done that? Was it grief or for some other reason that he had punished himself? Feeling her heart twist with pity, she stood up and bent over him, kissing the papery softness of his cheek.

'I am here, dearest,' she said. 'Rest now. There is nothing to fret for. I am here…'

He murmured something, but the frown faded from his forehead and he seemed to rest easier. Caroline stroked his brow for a moment and then resumed her seat until he seemed to settle. She sat with him, watching as he slept peacefully until Jenkins came to tell her that her brothers wished her to go downstairs and eat dinner with them.

'I shall watch over him, miss,' the valet said, nodding at her encouragingly. 'He speaks of you often to me, Miss Holbrook. If there is any change, I shall send one of the maids to fetch you at once.'

'Yes, perhaps…' Caroline got to her feet. She bent to kiss her grandfather's cheek once more. 'I know he is safe in your hands, Mr Jenkins. I shall come again for an hour or so later this evening.'

She went down to the dining parlour, answering her brothers' anxious inquiries as they sat down to dine together. As children, they had found the Marquis daunting, a figure of awe, but of late they had begun to know him and a shadow of anxiety hung over them all. He had been a dominating figure in their lives, and it would seem odd if he were no longer there.

It was just as Caroline and her brothers were about to rise from a rather sombre meal that one of the maids came to tell her that her grandfather was awake and asking to see her.

'Oh, thank goodness!' she cried, feeling the relief sweep over her. 'I shall come at once.'

She went quickly up the stairs and hurried to her grandfather's bedchamber. She tapped the door and went in as she was bid, halting as she looked towards the bed, hardly knowing what she would find. However, the Marquis was sitting up against a pile of pillows, taking a little refreshment from a cup that his valet held for him. He waved Jenkins away as he saw her.

'Enough for now, thank you.' Lifting his hand, he motioned to Caroline to come forward. She did so, thinking that he looked a little weary, but seemed to be otherwise much himself. As far as she could see he had not been paralysed and it appeared that his doctor had been right in saying that the seizure had been slight. 'Well, there you are, Caroline. Jenkins told me you were anxious, so I thought it best to have you up to see for yourself that I am as right as ninepence. It was just a little unpleasantness, nothing to worry about at all.'

'I am glad to see you recovered, Grandfather,' Caroline said with a smile. He was clearly not as well as he claimed, but he was not at death's door, for which she was heartily grateful. 'We have all been a little anxious, you know.'

'Humph,' the Marquis grunted. 'I hope you had the sense not to send for the rest of the family?'

'We thought it best to wait, sir.'

'Good. I don't want Sebastian or Claude troubling themselves to come all the way down here. I've nothing to say to either of 'em!'

'Grandfather! You should not say such things.'

'No, you shall not pull caps with me, Caroline. I don't mince my words. Never have done and it's too late to begin now. There's no wrapping it up in clean linen. I don't give a fig for either of 'em and they care less for me. I ain't saying it ain't my fault, but that's the way of it.'

'I am sorry for it, sir.'

'Well, I ain't and we'll say no more of it. You and your brothers are here and that's enough.' He sighed and closed his eyes for a moment, but opened them again as she moved away from the bed. 'No, don't go yet, girl. I have something to tell you. It concerns you more than your brothers.'

She saw that his hand was trembling and she reached for it, holding it gently in her own. 'You should not distress yourself, Grandfather. Surely it may wait until you are feeling better?'

'I've been lucky this time,' the Marquis told her and grimaced, rubbing at his chest as if he felt some discomfort. 'It would be easy to put off what must be done, but if I do you may have grief of it one day.'

'I do not understand,' Caroline said and held his hand a little tighter as she felt him quiver. 'How does your secret concern me?'

'It is time that you knew the whole story. It may shock you, but I would not have you live in ignorance of the truth. You see, it concerns my Angelica. You will have heard stories of her, I dare say?'

'I know that you loved her very much, sir.'

'She was my whole world,' the Marquis said, his voice ragged with remembered grief. 'I loved her more than my life. Her happiness was my only concern and I would have done anything to please her—though I know that what I did was wrong. I make no bones about it. Guilt for my sin has haunted me through the years, but I did it because I loved her and I could not bear to deny her anything.'

Caroline sat on the edge of the bed, looking at him in pity as she saw his anguish. 'You do not have to tell me this now, sir. I see that it affects you deeply. Whatever it is, it may wait.'

'No, child, let me speak,' her grandfather said. ' I have told you that Angelica's family did not wish her to marry me?' Caroline nodded, wondering what was troubling him so much. 'She defied them and ran away with me because she loved me. She was brave, if reckless…'

'She loved you as you loved her, Grandfather.'

'It was her dearest wish to have a child,' the Marquis said. 'But I was older and I ought to have been wiser for her sake…it was my fault that she died.'

'What do you mean? I do not understand you, sir. I thought Grandmother died of a fever?'

'It is a long story and began the first time I saw her. My Angelica. She was so beautiful that I could not resist her. Even when her brother told me…' His voice faded to a harsh whisper and he closed his eyes as if it were almost too much for him.

'Tell me, sir. It may ease your pain.'

'I knew that she was delicate,' the Marquis said. 'Her brother did not wish her to marry at all. He warned me that she must never have a child…that the strain of it would be too much for her heart.'

'How could he know that for certain?'

'He claimed it was a hereditary weakness. I did not care for such things. I only knew that I wanted her…loved her. I had my heirs. I did not need or want more children, but Angelica did. I tried to avoid giving her a child, but she guessed what I did and she begged me to give her a baby. I gave in to her pleas and by doing so I killed her. I adored her and I killed her. She was not strong enough, you see, and caught a chill that finished her off. Before she died she begged me to love our son and I did love him more than any other. When he married your mama, I thought that he could have married better. I have not been fair to your mama—or to you and your brothers, Caroline. Now I would make recompense. I cannot make up for what I did to Angelica, but I shall do what I can for her grandchildren.'

Caroline was silent for some minutes after he had done. 'But you were not to blame for her death,' she said at last. 'Angelica wanted a child and you gave in to her pleas…that does not make you a murderer.'

'Her brother called me that and he was right,' the Marquis said. 'I was warned that she was not strong enough, but I stole her from her family. I married her and I gave her a child…a child that ultimately killed her. Her brother hated me for it, and I have hated myself…'

'I am sorry that you have suffered so much, Grandfather,' Caroline told him. 'But why do you feel that this concerns me?'

'Angelica's weakness was hereditary, Caroline. They told me that it does not pass to the male line, but only to the female…' His eyes were sad as they rested on her face. 'You are so very like her that I fear for you.'

'You think that I might carry Angelica's weakness?' Caroline glanced up at him, her eyes wide with shock. 'But that is foolish, Grandfather. I am as healthy as can be. You need not concern yourself on my account.'

'It did not show in Angelica until she caught a fever after giving birth…it might not come out in you until later.'

'It will not affect me,' Caroline said quickly. 'I know that it has worried you for my sake, sir—but I am quite well.'

'I do not say that you should never marry, child,' the Marquis said. 'But you must be aware that you might never be able to give your husband a child.'

'You cannot know that,' Caroline cried. The idea suddenly distressed her more than it should. She had been told by more than one person that it was imperative that Sir Freddie's wife gave him an heir for the sake of the family name. Now Caroline was confronted with the thought that she might not be able to marry the man she loved. 'No one can know such a thing. I am perfectly well.' Her voice rose as she tried to deny what he was telling her. It could not be true! It must not…

'Do not be angry with me, Caroline,' the Marquis begged. 'Angelica's death has weighed on me all these years and of late I have begun to fear for you.'

'I am not angry,' Caroline told him, but her thoughts were whirling in confusion. 'You must rest now, sir. You have told me what you think I should know, and I am grateful—but there is no need for you to worry for my sake.'

Caroline's heart was heavy as she left her grandfather and went to her room. If she did carry this mysterious illness in her blood, she could not in all honesty marry Freddie. He needed an heir and she might simply be too delicate to give him one.

Chapter Nine

After spending a restless night, during which she slept little, Caroline visited her grandfather's room to see how he was. Jenkins was with him, and she could see that it was not a good time to call, but at least she was able to reassure herself that he had taken no further harm.

She went downstairs, but did not join her brothers in the breakfast parlour. Instead, she walked down to the stables and asked the groom to saddle a suitable horse for her. He asked if he should accompany her, but she shook her head, allowing him to help her mount, and setting out at a good canter, which soon developed into a headlong gallop.

The wind in her hair and the exhilaration of riding helped to blow away the confusion of her thoughts. She covered much of the estate, passing two tenanted farms and a lake, and returning at a slower pace an hour or so later. It was as she was passing the Home Woods that something caught her eye, and instinct made her duck her head over her horse's neck. Her instinctive reaction may have saved her, for she heard the shot whistle harmlessly by as she raced on, her heart hammering wildly in her breast.

Arriving back at the stables at a fierce canter, she flung herself down and left the horse standing for the groom, while she ran up to the house. Her brother Nicolas was coming from the front door and he frowned as he saw her.

'Why didn't you ask me to accompany you if you meant to ride?' he asked, and then, seeing her white face, 'What happened, Caroline?'

'Someone took a shot at me as I passed the Home Woods. I caught a glimpse of him in the trees and ducked forwards over my horse.'

'Go into the house and stay there!' Nicolas commanded, his face like thunder. 'This thing wants sorting once and for all.'

Caroline did not stay to argue. She found Tom in the back parlour he favoured. He was reading a news sheet delivered from the Receiving Office with some letters. She related her story to him breathlessly. Tom shot up from his chair immediately, his expression a mirror image of his brother's.

'Where are you going?' she asked. 'You are still recovering from that damage to your arm, Tom.'

'I can walk and I can shoot if need be. I am going to help Nicolas look for this rogue,' her brother said. 'We'll take some of the men with us. It is time this fellow was stopped or we shall none of us be safe.'

'Oh, Tom…' she said but there was nothing she could do to stop him for he was clearly determined.

After he had gone, she tried to find something to occupy herself, but ended by pacing up and down in an agitated manner, until one of the maids came in to announce a visitor.

'Sir Frederick Rathbone to see you, Miss Holbrook.'

'Sir Freddie!' Caroline ran to him, her hands outstretched. She was so relieved to see him and it showed in her expressive face. He took her hands, his strong fingers closing round hers in a way that instantly calmed her. 'I am so glad you have come! My brothers have gone to look for a rogue who fired on me as I rode past the Home Woods, and I am afraid that something will happen to them.'

'Someone fired at you?' Freddie's expression darkened, becoming one of outrage.

'Yes, when I was out riding this morning.'

'You were alone?' Freddie swore beneath his breath. He had thought her brothers had more sense than to allow it, and yet he knew her well enough to be sure that if she wished to ride alone nothing would stop her. 'This becomes serious, Caroline. I think I shall go in search of your brothers and see if they have had any luck in finding this rogue.'

'Oh, please take care,' she said. 'Must you go? I dare say it was merely a poacher misfiring.'

'If we discover that it was so, I shall be relieved. I think there must be a more sinister reason behind these attempts and I must ask you to remain in the house for the moment. Please excuse me, Caroline. I came here for another purpose entirely, but that must wait for the moment. I shall return with your brothers…' He gave her a rueful smile and left.

Caroline stared after him as he walked from the room. It was almost more than she could bear to be cooped up in the house when everyone else was out searching for the rogue who had fired at her, but she knew that she must obey her brothers and Sir Freddie. They were risking their lives for her sake and she could not make things more difficult for them by flouting their wishes.

After a while, a maid came to ask if she would step up to visit her grandfather for a few minutes. She did so, finding him looking much refreshed after his valet had finished ministering to him.

'What is this I hear, miss?' he asked, frowning. 'Jenkins has it that someone fired at you from the Home Woods—is that true?'

'Yes, sir, though I wish he had not told you. The doctor said that you were not to be upset.'

'I should be more upset if I were not told something like that,' Bollingbrook said. 'I trust you were not hurt, girl?'

'Only frightened for a moment,' Caroline said. 'But it is odd that this has started happening now, is it not? It seems that someone wishes me ill, though I do not know why.'

'I dare say it is a matter of money,' her grandfather told her, looking angry. 'I have recently changed my will. You and your brothers will benefit substantially when I die, Caroline—and you are to have something when you marry.'

'But surely…' She looked thoughtful. 'Who would know that you had changed your will, sir?'

'No one ought to know anything,' he growled, 'and I shall have something to say to my lawyer if it turns out that this is at the bottom of it. Someone in his office must have spoken of it—and I shall want to know to whom he betrayed what should have remained secret!'

'But who would want us dead? Not my uncles or cousins?'

'I do not think it for the estate is entailed and they must have expected I might leave you something from my private fortune—but I have not always lived as I ought, Caroline. There is another: a child I fathered on a trip to Jamaica before I met my Angelica. I went there to see the property left me by my second wife, and had what most would call a shameful affair. Later, when I returned home, I learned there was a child, a son—but I was married to Angelica by then and I told my overseer to take care of it. I believe a good family adopted the child, and I know little more.'

'I see…' Caroline bit her lip. She had always known there were secrets in her grandfather's past, though she was shocked at this revelation. 'It is unpleasant, sir. To think that someone wishes to kill us for the sake of money—but, of course, we cannot be sure of anything.'

The Marquis looked thoughtful. 'A man makes mistakes in his life and there may be others with a grudge against me. Well, we must just hope that the rogue is found, whoever it is, and an end made to this affair.'

'Yes, Grandfather.' Caroline sighed. 'I must own I do not find it comfortable to be the target of someone's malice.'

The Marquis gave a shout of harsh laughter. 'I dare say you do not, girl. If I were younger I should be out there looking for the rogue now, but I imagine I may leave it to your brothers.'

'And Sir Freddie,' Caroline said. 'He has gone to help them.'

'Who the devil is he?'

'Someone I like very well, sir.'

'Ah, the wind is in that quarter, is it? Send him up to see me when he returns to the house.' The Marquis frowned. 'Do not forget what I told you, Caroline. He will have to be a certain kind of man to accept that you should not have a child.'

'You do not know that for sure, sir.' Caroline wrinkled her brow in thought. 'He wished to speak to you yesterday, sir— but was prevented by your discomposure.'

'Well, I am much recovered now, girl. I shall see him at his convenience. Give him my compliments and ask him to step up and see me if he will when he returns.'

'Yes, Grandfather, I shall do so—though I am not sure when that will be.'

His eyes narrowed as he looked at her. 'Caroline, Caroline,

you are so like your grandmother. You have her reckless spirit, her certainty…' His eyes shadowed with doubt.

'I am glad to be like my grandmother in so many ways,' Caroline told him. 'But please do not worry for my sake, sir.' She smiled at him as she prepared to take her leave. 'Is there anything I may do for you?'

'No, I am well cared for. Jenkins is a good man and I rely on him completely—but you will come and see me again before you leave?'

'Yes, of course.' She hesitated, and then, 'I had thought perhaps you might wish me to stay until you are on your feet again?'

'No, though I thank you for the kind thought. You must go to your mother, Caroline. I shall speak to Tom about this incident. I think he should put off his visit to Jamaica until this business is settled.'

'You must do as you think best, sir.'

'Yes, yes, I think I shall rest now. You may leave me, for I am sure you have plenty to do.'

Caroline left her grandfather to go downstairs again, and it was not long before she heard voices in the hall and then her brothers and Sir Freddie came into the parlour where she was sitting. She got to her feet, looking at their faces, sensing that they were pleased about something.

'Did you catch him?'

'Not quite,' Nicolas said, 'but Sir Freddie winged him as he went by on his horse. One of the grooms had spotted him in the woods and we went after him. We thought we had him cornered, but he got away after firing a shot in our direction— though I think he will not be bothering any of us for a while.'

'I merely clipped him in the arm,' Freddie said. 'But it may be enough to quieten him for a while—and in the meantime we must take what precautions we can to prevent something like this happening again.'

'But how can you do that?' Caroline asked.

'In London, I had you followed for the last few days you were there. I had made no similar arrangements for your grandfather's estate, but with his permission I shall do so—and in Bath something similar will be put in place.'

'You had me watched in London?' Caroline stared at him for a moment, and then laughed. 'Yes, I see…I thought that someone was watching me that night in the gardens. Do you remember, Nicolas? When I was speaking to George Bellingham and you came out to look for me? I thought then that someone was there, spying on us.'

Nicolas nodded. 'I went to search for her, because Tom and I had decided that she might be in some danger if she wandered off alone, but she was safe enough with George Bellingham. We thought all this bother might be down to the business in Jamaica…for the inheritance, you know.'

'You mean the son Grandfather had whilst in Jamaica,' Caroline said. 'He told me that you knew about that, Tom. I dare say it might cause a scandal if it came out—but that is nothing compared to what is happening now. If this person is trying to kill me…you and Nicolas may not be safe from his spite.'

'Good grief,' Nicolas said. 'Heaven knows what more scandals the old man has up his sleeve.'

Freddie smiled, lifting his brows. 'I dare say there are skeletons in the closets of a good many families, some of the very highest distinction. However, I agree that we must see that this remains a family secret.'

'A family…ah, I see,' Nicolas said and grinned. 'I think I

will go up and have a word with Grandfather before supper. The old reprobate has plenty to answer for, though I shall not make a fuss for he is not up to it. Tom, will you come with me? I have something particular to say to you.'

'Oh, very well,' Tom said. 'I shall speak to you later, sir. You will stay to dine with us, I hope?'

'Certainly, I should be very happy to do so.'

Freddie smiled and inclined his head as Nicolas steered his brother from the room. It was obvious that the younger brother had realised what was going on and would no doubt explain to Tom as they went upstairs.

Caroline had taken a seat by the window. She sat resolutely looking out into the garden, her cheeks a little pink, her hands clasped in her lap until she sensed that Freddie was beside her. As she turned her head to look at him, he went down on one knee.

'Oh, no, you must not,' she said, a little flustered. 'At least, there is no need… I am sure that the last thing you truly wish is to make me an offer, sir. Only think of the scandal it might bring to your family if this Jamaican connection were to come out.'

Freddie rose and fetched a chair so that he might sit next to her. He reached out and took her hand, looking into her eyes as she gazed at him, clearly anxious. 'What is this foolishness, Caroline? You must know that I care for you—that it has been my intention to ask you to marry me for a little while now?'

'I have thought perhaps…' She stopped and blushed. 'I had hoped you might…but this must alter things. I feel that you have been caught up in something that is not of your making, sir. If you felt obliged to make me an offer, this must set you free.'

'If I wished to be free.'

'Do you not?' she asked, looking at him uncertainly. 'Only think of the scandal, sir.'

'Was it so wicked, Caroline?' He raised his brows. 'Your grandfather is not the first gentleman to get himself a bastard son.'

'There is more…' Caroline hung her head. 'Grandfather told me last night.'

'Another skeleton in his closet?' Freddie smiled oddly.

'This one concerned his third wife—my grandmother…' Caroline hesitated, suddenly knowing that she could not bear to tell him and see the light fade from his eyes. 'It is something that I believe you should hear from him. I do not regard it myself, but it must be for you to make up your own mind.'

'Is it so very terrible?'

'No, perhaps not—but only consider, I have been reckless.' Caroline hung her head. 'I teased you into taking me to that prize fight and I would have gone up in the balloon if the rope had not snapped. And I fully intend to be with you when you race Nicolas tomorrow…' Her eyes were dark with emotion. 'Do you think that—considering what you now know of my family—I should make the right kind of wife for you, sir? What would your uncle say?'

'If I told him, he would probably say that it was a deuced coil but all for the best, Caroline. He told me that he and your grandfather had quarrelled years ago, but that he was prepared to make it up if Bollingbrook would agree.'

'Was that why you hesitated to speak?' Caroline asked, her eyes intent on his face.

'No, it was not. If I seemed reserved with you at any time, it was because I was not perfectly sure I wished to marry. I

had become accustomed to living in my own way and knew
that if I married I must make changes.'

'And are you sure that you wish to marry now? You must
not think yourself obliged in any way, sir. I know why you
came to Almack's that evening, but it cannot signify. I need
never go back to London unless I wish, and in the country no
one will bother about what I did there.'

He smiled at her. 'Believe me, I should not allow the
gossips to drive me into making an offer I did not choose to
make, Caroline. I do truly wish to marry you.'

Caroline felt a weight lift from her shoulders, but persisted. 'You must speak to Grandfather, listen to what he has
to tell you about my grandmother and then ask me again if
you still wish it.'

'Nothing he or anyone else could say would change my
mind.'

'But—'

Before she could finish, she felt Freddie's hands on her
shoulders. He turned her round to face him, and she trembled
as she saw the look in his eyes. The next moment, he bent his
head, taking her lips with a kiss that was soft and gentle at
the start, but became more intense, hungry, as he felt her
response. Swept away on a tide of feeling she had never experienced before, Caroline melted into his body, wanting this
wonderful feeling to go on and on. It seemed to her that the
kiss was endless, but when at last he withdrew, she felt herself
sway and might have fallen had he not held her.

'Oh…' she said in a bewildered tone. 'I did not expect to
feel like that…'

'No?' Freddie laughed huskily. 'You are a sweet innocent,
my dear one, and I adore you for it—but I must admit I have

not felt quite this way before.' His eyes quizzed her. 'So what are we to do, Caroline, my love? You are reluctant to marry me because your family may become the centre of a scandal—and yet we clearly have an uncontrollable passion for one another. Will it suit you better to become my mistress?'

'Sir! You are outrageous,' she said, stung by the suggestion. As she saw the laughter in his eyes, she realised that he had merely been teasing her. 'Oh, Freddie, I do love you. I think I should die if anything came between us…but is it really fair to you?'

'What is this foolishness, my love?' He questioned with his eyes.

'You must speak to Grandfather. I am not sure it would be right if I accepted your very generous offer. I wish you to think very carefully about what he has to say to you—and then ask me again.'

'This is very mysterious. Do you think I care for a little scandal? I have not been exactly without blame in my life, Caroline. Some would think that you were the one who had cause for complaint, not I.'

'It is not just the Jamaican business…though there is that, too.'

'Surely it cannot be so very terrible?'

'Oh, Freddie, it might be worse than you imagine,' she said, her mouth soft with love. She longed to accept his offer, but her sense of fairness held her back.

He took her hand, caressing the palm with his finger. The stroking movement was delicate but it brought her close to swooning with what she knew must be desire. She melted against him as he put his arms about her, gazing up at him longingly. 'I feel so strange and not at all as I ought. I think if you do not marry me, I might end by taking up your very disobliging offer to become your mistress…'

'Well, it must be one or the other,' he told her as he stroked her cheek with the tips of his fingers, making her shiver with excitement. 'I confess that I cannot live without you, my darling. If you refuse me, I may very well—'

They were interrupted by a knock at the door, which opened as they moved apart, to allow Jenkins to enter. 'Excuse me, Miss Holbrook—Sir Frederick. My master requests that you visit him for a moment or two before dinner, sir.'

'Very well, I shall come in one moment,' Freddie said, and as the door closed behind him, 'You know that I adore you, Caroline. What is your answer, before I speak to Lord Bollingbrook?'

'You know that it must be yes—if you feel the same,' she said, swept away on a tide of recklessness. 'I would marry you even if I had to elope with you, Freddie. My hesitation was for your sake, not mine—I shall be happy to be your wife.'

'Very well, that is settled,' Freddie said and there was laughter in his eyes as he looked down at her. 'We shall marry against all opposition and be damned to the tabbies!'

'Oh, Freddie!' Caroline cried, laughing as he dropped a light kiss on her forehead. 'I am so glad that we met.'

Freddie kissed his fingers to her as he left the room. Jenkins was waiting for him at the top of the main staircase and he was conducted along the passage to the Marquis' suite of rooms.

'Please go in, sir,' Jenkins said. 'His lordship is waiting for you.'

'Thank you,' Freddie said. 'Is his lordship well?'

'Yes, sir, better than might have been expected. The doctor said that he was not to be upset, but I have no fear that you will come to blows.'

Freddie smiled and nodded, going into the room that was indicated. He discovered that Lord Bollingbrook was sitting in a wing chair next to the fireplace, where a small blaze cheered the room. He was a man of some seventy years, his hair silvery white, as were his brows, but there was strength in his features, and he was clearly in possession of his wits, for his eyes blazed with a fierce vitality.

'Good evening, sir,' Freddie said. 'I am Sir Frederick Rathbone. I believe you asked to see me?'

The Marquis looked at him through narrowed eyes. 'Humph,' he said in a tone that boded very little good will. 'So you're the one, are you? What have you to say to me?'

'I hope you are feeling better, sir,' Freddie said. 'There is much I would wish to say to you at another time, but this may not be the right occasion.'

'Don't pass me off with that flummery,' Bollingbrook muttered sourly. 'What are your intentions towards my girl?'

'Ah…' Freddie nodded pleasantly. 'It is my intention to make Caroline my wife quite soon.'

'Not without my permission you won't,' Bollingbrook said and glared at him. 'I shall want to know a lot more about you before I give it. Who are you and what are your prospects?'

'My fortune is adequate, I believe—and in the fullness of time I shall inherit my uncle's title and at least as much of the estate as is entailed. For although we have our disagreements, he cannot avoid it.'

'Damned entails!' Bollingbrook growled. 'I'm in the same

boat meself—bound to leave this place to me eldest son, but he won't get a penny more, I can tell you. I'll leave most of the money where I please.'

'That is your prerogative, sir.'

'Well, go on then, sir—who is this uncle you mentioned?'

'The Marquis of Southmoor. He knows you very well, I believe?'

'Southmoor? I thought the fellow was dead—as he ought to be by rights! We fell out years ago over your mother. Selina would have married me had he not forbidden her. He had no right to do it, for I cared for her and should have treated her well. I married badly that time—and that was his fault.' Bollingbrook glared at Freddie. 'I demanded satisfaction when Selina turned me down, and we fought a duel. Not that it gave me much satisfaction.' He looked at Freddie, his expression harsh with dislike. 'Well, that's it then, sir. You can take yourself off and never darken my door again. I shan't give you my girl—not if you went down on your knees and begged for it. I won't have Southmoor's breed in my family! You can forget Caroline.'

'That I shall not do for you or any man,' Freddie said. 'Pray tell me why a quarrel between you and my uncle should prevent my marriage to Caroline? Surely it happened too long ago to matter now?'

'Insolent pup,' Bollingbrook snapped. 'This conversation is at an end. Please have the goodness to leave.'

'Certainly, sir. This is your house and I shall not enter it again without an invitation, but my intention remains the same. You are the head of the family, but not Caroline's guardian. There are others I might apply to for permission, and you may be sure that I shall do so.'

'I am the head of this family…'

'As you say,' Freddie said, a glint of steel in his eyes. 'I shall not say more at this time, but Caroline has a mother and brother who may think differently.' Bowing his head, he turned and walked to the door.

'Damn you, sir! What do you mean by that?'

Freddie glanced back at him, a slight smile on his lips. 'If you should reconsider, please feel free to let me know that you would like me to visit you again.'

'Never! Damn you!'

Freddie looked grim as the curse was flung after him. He walked along the hall and down the main staircase. At the bottom Nicolas was standing speaking to one of the footmen. He turned as Freddie came up to him, extending his hand.

'I believe I am to wish you happy?'

'You may do so, for I intend to be,' Freddie said and took his hand in a firm grip. 'However, you should know that Lord Bollingbrook has forbidden me to marry Caroline.'

'Why in God's name should he do that?'

'He once wished to marry my mother, but my uncle forbade it and they fought a duel over it,' Freddie said, his tone dangerous. 'I believe there is no love lost on either side, for my uncle tried to dissuade me from making Caroline an offer—but I have and Bollingbrook shall not stop me. I think I have your blessing and Tom's—and I shall apply to Mrs Holbrook.'

'Tom would not deny you, though he has recently had reason to be grateful to Bollingbrook.'

'Whether I have Tom's blessing or not, I intend to marry her.'

'Good for you!' Nicolas said. 'You may count on me, and as for the rest…I leave the details to you.' Nicolas frowned as Freddie picked up his hat, gloves and driving whip from the hallstand. 'You are leaving?'

'Your grandfather threw me out, figuratively speaking.'

'But what shall I say to Caroline?'

'Say that I was called away, but shall see her tomorrow.'

'Nothing else?'

'Only if the subject is causing her distress. If Lord Bolling-brook should upset her—then you may tell her that nothing is changed between us.'

'Oh…' Nicolas grinned. 'Like that is it? He will kick up a fine dust, I dare say. He's had his own way for years. It may do him good to discover that at last he has met his match.'

'He would already have discovered it had he not been so recently ill,' Freddie replied grimly. 'But one thing you may be certain of, Nicolas—I do not intend to give her up.'

Nicolas inclined his head. Had he been wearing a hat, he would have taken it off to the man he was beginning to like very much. Freddie nodded in return and then went out, leaving Nicolas to stare thoughtfully after him.

'But why did he leave?' Caroline asked. 'It seems strange that Freddie should go without a word to me.' Her eyes narrowed as she looked at her brother. 'You're hiding something from me, aren't you? It is something to do with Grand-father, isn't it?' Had he decided that it would not suit him to marry her knowing that she might not be able to give him an heir? For a moment her heart contracted with pain and she thought that she would not be able to bear it if he withdrew. Yet she must do so. Indeed, she ought to have expected it in the circumstances.

'Sir Freddie told me to tell you that he would explain tomorrow, Caroline.'

'Explain what? Has Grandfather made him angry?'

'He wasn't angry, merely determined. Oh, if you must have it—Grandfather refused permission, but Sir Freddie says that nothing is changed. He intends to apply to Mama, and of course both Tom and I like him.'

'But Grandfather is the head of the family…' Caroline was confused, upset by the news that the Marquis had refused his permission. She had expected something quite different. 'Why did he say we might not marry, Nicolas?' Caroline was very pale, for she suspected her grandfather's true reasons, whatever excuse he might have made to Freddie.

'Some tale of a quarrel between Rathbone's uncle and Grandfather,' Nicolas said. 'But you should not let it weigh with you, Caroline. He does not have the power to prevent you, though it would have been better to have his permission. I think he had promised that he would give you a substantial dowry.' Caroline made an impatient movement of her head. 'Well, I dare say it doesn't matter. Sir Freddie isn't short of the readies.'

'I do not care for the money,' Caroline said, 'but I feel hurt that Grandfather should wish to deny me this happiness.' Her eyes were stinging with unshed tears, but she lifted her head proudly, refusing to let anyone see how distressed she felt. Perhaps her grandfather had done the right thing. Oh, she did not know what she ought to do!

'Do not let it upset you,' Nicolas said, guessing at how she felt. 'Tom and I will support you and I dare say Mama will be glad if you are happy.'

Caroline heard a little cough behind her and turned to see

her grandfather's valet. 'If you would care to step up to his lordship's rooms, miss?'

'Miss Holbrook is about to dine, Jenkins. Say that she will come up later.'

'No, Nicolas, I shall go,' Caroline said. 'You and Tom must not wait. I shall come later, but I am not hungry.'

Nicolas cursed as he watched her run up the stairs. He had always liked his grandfather despite his testy ways and his faults, but he was damned if he would let the old devil ruin Caroline's life!

Caroline knocked at the door and went in, finding her grandfather sitting in his favourite chair. She was pleased to see that he was feeling well enough to leave his bed, but her heart was heavy as she saw his forbidding expression.

'I dare say you have heard the news?'

'Yes, sir. I do not understand why you have done this to me. It made me happy when Sir Freddie asked me to marry him—why could you not just accept that he was my choice?' She looked at him, feeling close to tears.

Bollingbrook did his best to ignore the signs of distress. 'There are plenty more fish in the sea, girl. He isn't good enough for you. Besides, he needs an heir and I told you that you might not be able to have a child.'

'You do not know that for sure, sir. Besides, it should be for me to decide whether or not I wish to be his wife. Did you tell him about the hereditary illness?'

'There was no point. He isn't the man for you. I shan't have it, Caroline, and there's an end to it.'

Caroline raised her head. Tears glittered in her eyes. 'I should never wish to hurt you, sir, but I do not think it is proper for you to decide. I believe my mama and Tom…' She quailed as she saw the anger in his face. 'I do not mean to be rude or disobedient, sir—nor to blame you for what happened so many years ago. But I cannot obey you in this. I love him…'

'Stuff and nonsense. You don't know what love is. Besides, in law I am your grandfather and the head of the family. You will obey me.'

'You told me yourself that love cannot be denied,' Caroline reminded him. 'You married Angelica despite everything. Why should you deny us the happiness you found with her? I would be willing to take the risks she did to give my husband his heir. Forgive me, but I cannot obey you. I do not wish to disoblige you, Grandfather, but it would break my heart.'

He gave her a stern look. 'If you disobey me, you will not get a penny from me, either when you marry or when I die.'

'I have never expected anything other than the small portion my father left in trust for me,' Caroline told him. 'If you think that I care for such things, you do not know me, sir.'

'Care for your brothers, don't you?' Bollingbrook growled. 'Well, if you go against me in this, they won't get a penny either!'

'But that is unfair,' Caroline gasped. 'How could you hold such a wicked thing over my head?'

'Didn't you tell me there were others who asked for you?' He glared at her. 'Take one of them and I'll keep my word to Tom—defy me and there's an end to his hopes.'

'You are very cruel, sir,' Caroline said, stifling a sob. 'I shall never forgive you…' She turned and ran from the room before the tears could fall.

Chapter Ten

Caroline had been lying on her bed, but sat up as her brother tapped at her door. Her tears had dried, but she knew that she must look dreadful and she asked Tom to wait. Leaving the bed, she went over to the washstand and bathed her face with cool water, then called out that he might enter.

'Nicolas told me what happened,' he said as he came in. 'When you didn't come down after dinner, I knew that I would find you crying. You must not upset yourself, Caroline. Grandfather has no real power to forbid you. I am the head of our family—the Holbrook family. I do not like to disoblige him, but in this I must think of your future. Besides, after the way he has behaved, I think he has no moral right to demand anything of us. He may decide to cut you out of his will—but you will be no worse off than before.'

'I know that,' Caroline said. 'As for myself, I do not give a fig for his money, though I would have preferred his blessing. I have always cared for him—but I cannot…' She shook her head, her voice catching. It was impossible to tell Tom what their grandfather had threatened.

'Well, I think you must make up your own mind,' Tom said. 'If you love Sir Frederick and wish to marry him then you must. Do not allow anything Grandfather said to influence you.'

'I must think about it,' Caroline said and forced a smile. She was torn in two. If she chose to follow her heart, she might destroy Tom's hopes of a future. She suspected that he liked Julia more than he let anyone see, but until his fortunes were settled he could not ask her to marry him. And there was the question of Freddie's heir. She must tell him that it was possible she could never give him a son. 'When are you going out to Jamaica, Tom?'

'Next week. I have discussed it with Nicolas and we decided that it would be best for me to go soon. As for this other business, Nicolas will shortly be back with his unit and does not fear that anything untoward will happen to him. If you were married, the threat to your safety would be at an end…one way or the other.'

'Yes, I see.' Caroline felt a surge of indignation. 'It would have been better if Grandfather had never changed his will in our favour, then we should not have this shadow hanging over us.'

'I must admit that I am grateful to him for settling the most pressing of my debts. Father had made a mess of things, Caroline. I imagine he spent much of his money on his mistresses and gambling. Not that I care for that so much. I am capable of earning my own living, I dare say. If this business goes well in Jamaica, I might even stay there for a while, see if I can make my fortune out there. Nicolas may take care of things here.'

'I do not precisely understand what it is you have to do in Jamaica, Tom?'

'Grandfather says that the estate must be sold, and that I am to have what it yields.'

'Oh…' Caroline wondered what would happen if she defied her grandfather. 'Supposing Grandfather changed his mind, Tom? Would you still wish to go?'

'I have the deed for the property and his authority to sell it,' Tom said. 'What makes you think he might change his mind?'

'Oh, no reason. I suppose he will not.'

'It is but a small part of what he intends to leave us,' Tom said as he saw her worried expression. 'Just what did he say to you this evening?'

'It does not matter,' Caroline replied and shook her head.

'You should have some supper,' her brother said and looked at her anxiously. 'Will you allow me to have something sent up for you?'

'No, please do not. I shall ask my maid for a glass of hot milk. I really need nothing more.'

'Very well,' Tom acquiesced and gave her a look of encouragement. 'I shall leave you now, but remember that Nicolas and I are on your side, Caroline. Do not let Grandfather make you unhappy.'

'No, I shan't,' she said and raised her head proudly as he went out.

After he had gone, she sat down at her dressing table and picked up a hairbrush, beginning to smooth it over her long bright hair, which hung about her shoulders in a cloud of red-gold waves. The action soothed some of her distress, but it could not prevent her mind from going round and round in circles. What was she to do? If she defied her grandfather, he had the power to deny her brothers the money that might have given them better lives. Yet how could she let him destroy her happiness? Would Sir Freddie even wish to marry her once he knew that she might carry a hereditary illness? If she had daughters, she might pass the curse on to them. It was a heavy burden her grandfather had laid on her shoulders.

At the very least, she must talk to Freddie and hear what he had to say on the matter. Even if he said it was not important, it would still not solve the problem of her brothers' inheritance. She could do nothing for the moment. She needed to talk to the one person she felt able to confide in. Having made up her mind on that point, she went to bed, and, after some initial tossing and turning, fell into a deep sleep.

Caroline did not take leave of her grandfather the next morning. When she inquired after him, Jenkins told her that he was out of sorts and did not wish to see anyone.

'You will please give him my good wishes for his health,' she said, her face pale and distressed.

'Yes, miss,' the valet said, looking at her sorrowfully. He was well aware of the dreadful ultimatum his master had delivered the previous evening, and had already tried to take the Marquis to task over it, for which he had had his head snapped off. 'He will come about, miss. Never you fear.'

'Yes, perhaps,' Caroline agreed, though she had no hope of it. 'I must not keep the horses waiting. Forgive me.'

'Keep your chin up, miss,' Jenkins said with the familiarity of a long-serving retainer. 'I shall do my best for you.'

Caroline smiled, but made no reply. She went down the stairs, taking a warm farewell of Tom, who was not accompanying them to Bath.

'If I do not see you before I leave, remember that you have my blessing, Caroline,' he told her. 'Grandfather will regret his unkindness. I think he will come to see that he has been unfair to you.'

'Thank you, dearest Tom,' she said and kissed his cheek. 'I love you. Take good care on your journey. You will write to us when you can?'

'Yes, of course. Tell Sir Frederick to take care in this mad race of yours, but no doubt he will. I have more faith in his driving than Nicolas's.'

Caroline smiled. The thought of the race lifted her spirits, for she liked nothing better than to be behind a bang-up pair of thoroughbreds, and Freddie's blacks were some of the finest she had ever seen.

She went out to join her brother in the curricle, for he had sent his phaeton on ahead with his favourite horses, and they were to drive the best part of the way in Tom's rig. A groom would stay with it when they left the Waverly Inn, and return it to the Bollingbrook estate the next day when the horses were rested.

Despite the shortcomings of his brother's pair, of which Nicolas complained bitterly at the start, they made good time and arrived at the Waverly Inn just in time for nuncheon, which had been their intention. Sir Freddie had arrived earlier, and he came out to greet them, having already secured the use of the landlord's private parlour.

He helped Caroline down, searching her strained face with a grim look of his own. 'I see that you know what took place last evening, my love. We shall discuss it at another time, if you please. It would be foolish to let such a thing spoil our pleasure in the day, would it not?'

'Yes, certainly,' Caroline replied, all heart. She gave him a sparkling smile, for her spirits had lifted at the sight of him.

'And I do not intend to do so. Tell me, Freddie—shall we put my brother to the blush?'

'Would you wish to do so—if it were possible?' he asked, a flicker of amusement in his dark eyes.

'I have always wished to beat my brother at some sport,' Caroline said, her face alight with mischief. 'I dare say it would do him no harm to lose for once. He was always faster and better at everything than Tom.'

Freddie laughed softly in his throat. 'Then we must see what we can do, must we not?'

The three of them had a pleasant lunch together. Caroline was amused to see that Nicolas drank only water, which was a sign of his respect for Freddie's driving skills. He knew that he needed all his wits about him to stand a chance of beating him. Freddie had one glass of wine, which he merely tasted as a toast to her and the future. Neither of the gentlemen ate a great deal, though they laughed and talked as if it were merely a normal day and nothing at stake.

'When are we going to start?' Caroline asked because it seemed that she was the only one impatient to be on their way.

'Patience, my love,' Freddie said, a flicker of amusement on his lips. He raised his brows at Nicolas. 'Well, shall we see what our grooms have been up to, Nicolas? It appears that at least one of us is in a hurry to be off.'

Leaving the inn parlour together, they saw that their grooms had been busy while they were dining, and had both phaetons ready to leave. Caroline looked at Freddie's blacks, which looked in the peak of condition. Her brother's greys were pawing the ground, seemingly anxious to be off, and she noticed that they were sweating slightly. Having driven with him behind them on several occasions, she knew them to be spirited creatures and she thought that the teams were well matched. It would be a close-run thing and possibly down to the skill of the drivers.

Freddie smiled at her as he handed her up. 'Are you ready, Caroline?'

'Oh, yes,' she said, her eyes bright. She had put all her problems to one side for the moment. 'I think it will be the greatest of good fun.'

Seated on the driving box beside Freddie, she glanced across at her brother. She could see that he was on his mettle, anxious to be off, and she waved to him, blowing a kiss with her fingertips.

'Good luck, Nicolas.'

He grinned at her and saluted as the grooms stood away from the horses' heads and then they were off. Caroline saw that her brother set off in a hurry, flicking his long driving whip at his horses, clearly intending to reach the turning that led to Bath in the lead.

Freddie, on the other hand, allowed his horses to begin at their own pace, holding the reins lightly, his whip propped up in the box at his side, apparently unconcerned that Nicolas had taken an early lead.

Had she been driving, she knew that she would have been pushing her horses hard to catch up, but Freddie kept his hand lightly on the reins. She frowned a little, for she thought that Nicolas would get too far ahead of them, but then she sensed that the blacks were gathering speed little by little. Freddie had done nothing that she could see, and as yet he had not touched his whip. She looked at the horses, the rippling strength of their muscles, the shine of their glossy coats, and knew that so far they were only cruising.

Freddie had not asked anything of them, but they were moving with such ease and grace that their pace was increasing effortlessly. The road ahead was quite narrow for a stretch of more than a mile or so, hardly wide enough to allow for one vehicle to pass another. And, with some sharp bends hiding any oncoming traffic, it would have been impossible to pass Nicolas even if they had caught up with him.

After they had been driving for some minutes without seeing more than a glimpse of her brother, the road ahead of them began to widen slightly. Freddie took his whip and cracked it over the heads of his team and all at once she felt the surge of speed. She glanced at him, for he seemed so calm, so certain, and it made her wonder at his patience. However, after a few minutes she saw that they were only a short distance behind her brother. Because of the difficult road, he had been unable to put enough distance between them, and now Freddie had him in his sights.

'You knew, didn't you?' she said. 'You knew that there was nothing to be gained by setting out at a cracking pace.'

'Nicolas will have found his horses hard to control on that stretch of the road at such a pace,' Freddie said, and glanced at her. 'He may have taken too much out of them at an early stage. We have some way to go yet, Caroline.'

Nicolas had clearly realised that they were behind. He was urging his horses on faster, and for the next twenty minutes or so he managed to increase his lead, the distance between them lengthening again. Freddie let him go, but then, after some fifteen minutes or so, he gave a little flick of his whip and the blacks responded gallantly. Caroline looked eagerly for some sign of her brother's vehicle, and then, just as they were approaching a crossroads, she saw it ahead of them.

'Oh, there he is,' she cried. 'We shall catch him again in a moment.'

Freddie smiled as he heard the excitement in her voice. He kept his horses steady as they approached the crossroads, which were clear on both sides, allowing both Nicolas and Freddie to maintain their speed. Ahead of them was a stretch of good clear road, with grassland to either side. Caroline felt the surge of speed as Freddie let his horses have their head, and she sensed that this was what he had been waiting for. Here at last was the space for the phaetons to race to their full potential.

She was on the edge of her seat with excitement as Freddie's blacks ate up the distance between the two phaetons; gradually, inexorably, Nicolas was being hauled back. She could see that he was using his whip frequently now, trying to urge that extra bit of speed from his horses, but he had driven them hard for the past four miles and now they had no more to give. The blacks were fresher, having been spared for the better part of the way, and now Freddie cracked his whip over their heads and they responded willingly.

Caroline hung on tightly as the phaeton seemed to almost bound forwards, holding on to her bonnet with one hand and to the carriage rail with the other. They had caught Nicolas now, and then, with a slight flick of his wrist, Freddie edged his phaeton out slightly to perform one of the neatest overtaking manoeuvres that she had ever witnessed. She held her breath as for a moment the wheels of both vehicles were side by side. A false move now and they could all be overset, but Freddie judged it to a nicety and in another moment they were past. Freddie kept up his speed for long enough to gain the lead into the next stretch of road, which was too narrow to allow for Nicolas to pass them.

Caroline looked back at her brother. For a few minutes he continued to urge his horses on, but then he seemed to realise that the race was over, for he let his pace slow and dropped behind. They were entering the outskirts of the fashionable spa town now, and the press of traffic would have made it impossible for the race to continue. As they passed the Abbey church, Caroline looked back and her brother saluted her.

She laughed and turned to Freddie. 'Nicolas has just saluted you, Freddie. He acknowledges that yours were the better horses.'

'I doubt there was much between them,' Freddie said. 'I knew the road well, perhaps better than your brother.'

'Oh, no, I do not think it was only that,' she said. 'You have the best hands I have ever seen, Freddie. It was your driving that made the difference.'

'I would not advise you to say as much to your brother,' Freddie said and grinned at her. 'I trust you are pleased, Caroline—though I noticed that you wished Nicolas luck, but did not do the same for me.'

'You did not need luck,' she said and her eyes were mischievous. 'I had every confidence in your driving, sir.'

'Thank you. I shall take that as a compliment,' he said. 'I believe I shall have to take your driving in hand before I allow you to handle my greys.'

'I love to drive,' Caroline said. 'I only wish I were able to practise more.'

'We may soon put things right when we are married,' Freddie said. 'You shall have your own rig, Caroline. Something suitable for a lady, and then you may drive yourself when you wish.'

'I wish that I might,' Caroline said, suddenly rather sad. 'I know that I said I would marry you, Freddie, and you mustn't think that I don't want to. I do love you with all my heart— only I am not sure I can marry you in the circumstances.'

Freddie glanced at her. 'You mean because of what your grandfather said, I suppose. You know that we do not need his permission? Your brothers have already signified their approval, and I dare say Mrs Holbrook will look favourably on my suit.'

'Yes, I am sure Mama will say yes,' Caroline said, but hesitated. 'But…Grandfather threatened to change his will again if I disobeyed him. For myself I care nothing for it, but Tom has had such a difficult time since my father died. And then there's Nicolas. He has only a small trust fund from his maternal grandfather, and must support himself.'

'Bollingbrook threatened to disinherit them if you married me?'

'Yes,' Caroline said, pleased that he had grasped the situation at once. 'It kept me awake all night, for I could see no way out of the predicament. I dare say you will not mind if I have no dowry, but how can I deprive my brothers of their fortunes?'

'Do you know the size of this inheritance?' Freddie had slowed his horse to a walk now. He raised his hat to an acquaintance passing in a similar vehicle.

'I believe Tom said it may be in the region of two hundred thousand pounds—divided between us and the son in Jamaica.'

Freddie whistled softly. 'That is indeed a considerable sum of money. I had not realised Bollingbrook was in possession of such a fortune—and that, I imagine, does not include the entail?'

'Oh, no, that is entirely different, and not worth the half of it, I dare say,' Caroline said. 'Nicolas wondered if my uncles might have got wind of the change to his will, and if they could possibly have commissioned the attempts to kill Tom—and me.'

'What happens to the money if you or your brothers should die before your grandfather?'

'I believe the money would go to the fourth beneficiary.'

'The Jamaican?' Freddie nodded thoughtfully. 'I think that there may be something in it after all. Two hundred thousand pounds is a great deal of money.'

'Yes, that is what Tom has always said,' Caroline told him, frowning. 'It might have been better had Grandfather never altered his will.'

'Yes, perhaps,' Freddie agreed, 'but we must not jump to conclusions too soon, Caroline.' He was drawing to a halt in front of one of the fashionable houses in the Royal Crescent. 'As for this other business—does your grandfather's blessing mean a great deal to you?'

'I would have been pleased to have it if he had given it freely,' Caroline admitted. 'I have always been fond of him—but it is Tom and Nicolas that matter most.'

'Yes, I see,' Freddie said and smiled as he handed her down. His groom, who had gone on ahead of him with the baggage coach, was waiting for them, and came to take the reins from him. Freddie knocked at the front door and stood with Caroline on the pavement as they waited for an answer. 'Do not worry too much about this for the moment, Caroline. Bollingbrook may have been bluffing—and when he thinks about it, he may wish to reconsider. I shall call another day to speak with Mrs Holbrook—but for now I shall leave you. There are some matters of business I must attend to.' As the door was opened by a maid wearing a neat black gown and white apron, he nodded to Caroline and, lifting her hand to his lips, dropped a kiss within the palm. That and the smile which accompanied it sent a little shiver of pleasure down her spine.

'Thank you for the pleasure of your company, Caroline. It was most enjoyable.'

Caroline felt a thrill of delight. She could only agree with him, returning his smile before entering the house. Her mother came into the hall as she did so, running towards her with outstretched arms.

'Caroline, my love. It is so good to see you! I had your letter about your grandfather and I wondered if you would feel that you must stay with him for a little longer?'

'He would not have it so,' Caroline said and embraced her. 'Besides, I fear that he is not pleased with me at the moment. I have a great deal to tell you, Mama.'

'Well, put off your bonnet and then come into the parlour,' Mrs Holbrook said. 'I am alone at the moment, though Mr Milbank dines with us this evening. I did not wish to go out on your first evening in Bath—but where is your brother?'

'He will be here shortly,' Caroline said. 'I came with Sir Frederick and Nicolas…followed us.'

'Sir Frederick brought you?' Mrs Holbrook was somewhat surprised. 'There was no mention of that when your baggage arrived earlier.'

'No, Mama. But I wanted to tell you…' She followed her mother into the small parlour, but just as Mrs Holbrook had finished telling the maid that she was to serve them tea and buttered muffins in twenty minutes, there was a commotion in the hall and Nicolas came striding in.

'Ah, there you are, puss,' Nicolas hailed her in high good humour. 'Sir Freddie is not here, I gather? I must seek him out to pay him the twenty guineas I owe him. That was a capital race and the way he passed me was a masterpiece. I declare he is a fine whip, one of the best I've met.'

'What is that?' Mrs Holbrook looked from her son to her daughter. 'Please tell me that you do not mean… Caroline! You did not take part in a curricle race?'

'Well, Sir Freddie was driving a phaeton, but, yes, I did, Mama.'

'You were with Sir Frederick on the high road—racing your brother?' Mrs Holbrook made a moaning sound and put a hand to her face. 'You might have been killed…both of you. Not to mention the scandal…'

'But no one knows,' Caroline said, her cheeks warm. 'And we are perfectly safe, Mama. Sir Freddie took no risks, I promise you. He has the best hands of any whip I've seen and he has promised to teach me to drive so that—' She was silenced as she saw her mother's expression. 'Honestly, Mama, no one will know that we raced.'

'Depend upon it, someone saw you,' her mother said and looked at her accusingly. 'You must know that you were the subject of some gossip in town, Caroline. We brushed through that right and tight thanks to Lady Stroud—but it is enough that you drove here with Sir Frederick alone, for I dare say you did not have a maid or a groom?' Caroline's guilty look was enough to confirm her fears. 'That on its own would cause talk—but if anyone should learn that you actually raced…' She sank down into one of the comfortable chairs with an air of despair. 'I think you have ruined yourself.'

'No such thing, Mama,' Nicolas said, guiltily aware that in his excitement he had given his sister away. 'I dare say Caroline may drive with her fiancé, may she not?'

'Her fiancé?' Mrs Holbrook stared at her, anxiety and hope warring in her breast. 'Do you tell me you are engaged to him?'

'Yes,' said Nicolas.

'Well, perhaps…' said Caroline.

'Which is it?' Mrs Holbrook asked and fanned her cheeks with the ladies' magazine she had been reading before her children arrived. 'You have quite overset me, Caroline. I am not at all sure that I should wish you to marry him. It seems to me that he is hardly a suitable husband for a young lady— where is his notion of propriety?!'

'I wanted to be part of it, Mama,' Caroline said. 'I was not frightened and it is not fair that I should be excluded from all the fun just because I am a girl.'

'I am glad that you did not say lady,' her mother said, 'for your behaviour has been anything but ladylike. I would send you to your room to reflect on your waywardness—but please explain, are you or are you not engaged to be married?'

'Freddie has asked me and I have said yes,' Caroline said, 'but Grandfather has forbidden it. He says he shall not give me a dowry if I disobey him. And…' she glanced at Nicolas '…he says he shall change his will again. You and Tom will get nothing if I marry against his wishes.'

'A fig for that!' Nicolas said and snapped his fingers. 'I ain't saying that it wouldn't be a fine thing to inherit some money—but I ain't prepared to be the cause of your unhappiness, puss. Tom would say the same.'

'I am not sure that he would,' Caroline said. 'He has had so much trouble to pull the estate together and he would have been the main benefactor, I think.'

'Well, there's no telling that the old gentleman wouldn't

pull caps with him over something else,' Nicolas said. 'We all know what Bollingbrook's temper is. He may change his will fifty times before he's done for. Besides, I should not let it worry you, puss. He will regret his harshness to you when he has thought it over. And then he will send to make things up to you, I imagine.'

'Freddie said as much,' Caroline said. 'He does not care for my dowry, no more do I—but I do care for you and Tom, Nicolas.'

'I wish that one of you would consider my feelings in all this,' Mrs Holbrook said in a faint voice. 'I declare that I have a headache coming on. You really are the most troublesome of children. I shall go up to my room and lie down.'

'Sorry, puss,' Nicolas said as the door closed behind their mother. 'I never thought she would cut up rough like that over it.'

'It does not matter,' Caroline said. 'Poor Mama. We must be such a trial to her. You will not tell her about the Jamaican business? I fear that she would be distressed by it.'

'Lord, no!' Nicolas ejaculated. 'Sir Freddie said that it was not so very terrible, but it would cause rather more scandal than the fact that you took part in a race.'

'Yes, I think it would. What Grandfather did was perhaps not so very bad, but it is best if Mama does not hear of it.'

'She shall not from any of us.'

'Do you think this other thing…the attempts on my life…? If indeed it was truly an attempt to kill me. It might simply have been a poacher misfiring, you know.' Caroline sighed. 'I do not think we should tell Mama that someone tried to kill me, Nicolas. It would upset her.'

'We did consider that it might have been a poacher, but Sir Freddie was of the opinion that it was unlikely. As for telling Mama, I would not dream of it. I dare say she would make a run for home and keep you under lock and key. Though for myself, I think you may be safe enough for a while,' Nicolas said. 'Sir Freddie winged the fellow who shot at you. We cannot know if it was merely a hired assassin or the originator of these crimes himself, but it must give whoever it is pause for thought either way.'

'Well, I shall certainly be careful not to go far alone,' Caroline said. 'Sir Freddie is coming to see Mama in a few days. If she gives her permission…'

'You must consent to an engagement,' Nicolas said. 'You cannot give up your chance of happiness for a whim of the old gentleman. He has no right to demand it of you—and to hold such a threat over your head is wicked. I think I shall tell him he may keep his money, for the promise of it has brought nothing but trouble.'

'Oh, Nicolas…' She looked at him unhappily. 'Do not burn your boats for my sake.' He must not throw his chances away, especially as it was not yet certain that Freddie would wish to marry her once he knew she might have some dreadful hereditary illness.

'I dare say I shall get along without it,' he said and grinned at her. 'I shall have to hang out for an heiress, puss.'

'Oh, dearest,' she said and laughed. 'When do you return to your regiment?'

'I shall stay with you for two days, and then I must leave,' he told her. 'I'll see if I can bring Mama round this evening. I dare say she will have forgiven us by the time she has dressed for dinner.'

* * *

Caroline watched her brother leave. She sat down and waited until the maid brought the tea tray, asking her if she would carry something up to Mrs Holbrook's room.

After the maid had gone she bit into a delicious fruity muffin, the butter dripping on to her chin as she stared at nothing in particular. What ought she to do for the best? Nicolas had been so supportive over her predicament, but she knew that her grandfather's money would go a long way to helping both of her brothers. Could she really deprive them of their inheritance? And there was the matter of her grandmother's weak heart. She did not think that she could bear to live without Freddie for the rest of her life. Even the thought of it brought tears to her eyes.

'Damn you!' the Marquis growled as Jenkins brought him a small measure of brandy. 'What is that supposed to be?'

'With your lordship in a state of choleric, brandy is the worst thing you can have,' Jenkins said imperturbably. 'And it ain't a bit of good glaring at me that way, sir. It ain't going to change a thing.'

'Do you think I don't know that?'

'Well, you ain't been thinking much of late, sir.'

'Impudent rogue! I should dismiss you instantly, do you know that?'

'That's as may be, sir,' Jenkins said without turning a hair. 'And I ain't saying as I wouldn't mind retiring to a little cottage I've had my eye on for a while. My sister is a widow and has been for this year past. I dare say she would be glad to keep house for me for what years remain to us—but it don't alter your case, sir. You've driven your sons away, and now you've seen off Miss Caroline, and I think you are going to regret that for a long time. Especially if you cut the young gentlemen out as well, sir.'

'Know everything, do you?' the Marquis said and muttered furiously to himself. 'Well, I ain't such a fool as you think. I know that girl. She won't see her brothers disinherited. She'll come back and say she's sorry.'

'Give you pleasure, will it, sir—to see her wretched? She loves the man. Stands to reason. 'Sides, I saw her woebegone face, poor little lass.'

'How dare you speak of my granddaughter so familiarly?'

'Well, seeing as you're about to set me off, it don't make much difference, does it, sir? I might as well say my piece while I'm at it. You ain't been exactly an angel, sir.'

'Are you threatening me?'

'I wouldn't dare, sir,' Jenkins said with an air of inno-cence. 'It strikes me that you ought to do something about all this trouble. You wouldn't want Miss Caroline's death laid at your door?'

'And what do you mean by that?' The Marquis started up out of his chair.

'Stands to reason, sir. Someone knows you changed your will and, whoever that may be, he doesn't much like it.'

'Claude or Sebastian?' the Marquis demanded.

'I should doubt it, sir. Mr Sebastian wouldn't stir himself, and Mr Claude would think it beneath his touch. It may be that Jamaican business…'

'Yes, I dare say you are right. I shall have to think about this carefully.' Bollingbrook held out his glass. 'Now fill that up and have done lecturing me, man. I'll not have harm come to Caroline, but she must come to me and apologise before I change my mind about that damned fellow!'

'Hell will freeze over first,' Jenkins said, ignoring his master's scowl as he took the glass and filled it with a more generous measure. 'Not that it makes much difference what you do. I dare say you'll finish yourself off before you have time to change anything.'

He walked to the door, leaving Bollingbrook to scowl into the glass before setting it to one side. The man was an impudent rascal, but the devil of it was he was right…

Chapter Eleven

Caroline accompanied her mother to the Pump Room the following morning. She was feeling easier in her mind, because Marianne had mellowed towards her children. She had been suffering a little irritation of the nerves lest they should not approve of Mr Milbank on closer acquaintance with him. However, Nicolas had charmed all her fears away, and she was now happily describing her plans for her wedding, which was to take place the following week. For, as she had told her children, there was no point in delaying it at her time of life.

'Mr Milbank is to take me on honeymoon to Italy,' she had told her daughter before they retired to bed the previous evening. 'You have a choice, Caroline my love. You may come with us or…I had thought you might stay with your grandfather, but you might prefer to return to your aunt?'

'Perhaps I could simply go home, Mama? I should be quite happy there by myself.'

'I am not sure that that would serve,' Marianne said. 'However, we might find another alternative. I could write to my cousin and ask her if you may visit with her for a few weeks. We do not intend to stay longer than six weeks or so abroad. Mr Milbank is having some work done at his country house, and of course you will join us there as soon as we are in residence.'

'Unless I were to marry, Mama.'

'Well, yes, I suppose.' Her mother sighed. 'If you do wish to marry Sir Frederick, it might be arranged before I leave. But you were quite against it at one time, Caroline. And I am not at all sure that he is the right husband for you.'

'I know he is the one,' Caroline said. 'I love him, Mama, but as I told you yesterday, Grandfather is against it.'

'Bollingbrook may be the head of the family,' Marianne said, her feathers ruffling indignantly, 'but I am your mother, Caroline. I think I may be trusted to decide your future. Besides, Nicolas told me that Tom has given you his blessing. Bollingbrook cannot lawfully forbid the marriage.'

'I know that, Mama,' Caroline agreed. 'But would it be fair of me to take my happiness at the expense of my brothers?'

'As to that…' Marianne smiled her satisfaction. She had been at the mercy of her father-in-law for too long, and he had done little for her. Now at last she was about to become truly independent of him. 'Mr Milbank is possessed of an adequate fortune. He has already offered to set some of it aside for your brothers—and to give you five thousand pounds when you marry.'

'Mama!' Caroline was astonished. 'That is too generous. I cannot accept so much. It is kind, but—'

'Nonsense, my dear.' Marianne looked extremely pleased with herself. 'Mr Milbank suggested it without a hint from me. As I told you, he has no family of his own, and he is delighted with mine. I am sure we shall all go on very well together.'

Caroline kissed her cheek. 'Thank you, Mama. You have relieved my mind, for I do not need to feel so very guilty if I disobey Grandfather's wishes.'

'You have yet to gain my permission, Caroline. Sir Frederick may call upon me when he chooses. If I am satisfied that he can be trusted to take proper care of you, I may allow it—or perhaps an engagement. Yes, that would be much better. The wedding may wait upon my return.'

Caroline kept her thoughts on the matter to herself. Lord Bollingbrook was fond of calling his son's wife a peagoose, but Marianne could be stubborn when she chose. If she decided that Caroline must be content with an engagement until her return from Italy, there would be no changing her.

If she had known that her decision might place Caroline in danger, Marianne would have been horrified. However, her children had agreed to keep her in ignorance of the truth, and she was quite justified in thinking that if her daughter waited for a while it could do no harm. Given time to think, Bollingbrook might come to his senses and seek reconciliation.

'Yes, I think that will do very well,' Marianne said, believing that she had settled things nicely. 'If you do not wish to accompany us, you may stay with your Aunt Louisa or Cousin Amelia. And perhaps you may marry at Christmas.'

Caroline had thought about her mother's decision for much of the night, but she could see no way of changing things. With the wedding so close, something must be arranged for her, and she thought, of the two alternatives open to her, she would prefer to stay with Cousin Amelia.

Amelia Postlewaithe was the unmarried daughter of a bishop and lived with her companion and servants in an old and crumbling country house, together with her cats, dogs and a rather rude parrot that someone had taught to swear. Caroline suspected that that someone was her brother Nicolas, and the parrot had been a source of much amusement when they visited—though not shared by Cousin Amelia.

Although life would undoubtedly be rather dull with her mother's cousin, who seldom entertained, Caroline thought that she would prefer it to another stay in London with her aunt. She had no interest in continuing her Season, and wished that she might look forward to a settled future with Freddie. However, her mother's wedding must take precedence and therefore she would just have to wait.

Venturing to the Pump Room with her mother the next morning, Caroline looked around her with interest, for it was her first visit. Several ladies and gentlemen were drinking from small cups of the spa water, which was said to be beneficial for health. When Caroline took a sip, she pulled a wry face, for it did not taste as pleasant as it might.

Marianne Holbrook did not venture as far as the baths themselves. She was not in need of their healing properties and would have thought it most improper to bathe in mixed company. She knew that ladies of unimpeachable reputation did so, but she had already made it clear to Caroline that neither of them would bathe.

'For you know the water makes one's bathing dress cling to the form and is shockingly revealing,' she had confided to her daughter in the carriage earlier. 'No, Caroline. Mr Milbank does not approve and nor do I.'

Caroline was fast discovering that her mother's conversation was liberally punctuated by references to Mr Milbank. His likes and dislikes, his manners and goodwill, were all dwelled upon and examined with too much regularity for Caroline's taste. She was grateful to him for delivering her mother from the sad decline into which she had fallen, but thought that she would not care to accompany them on their honeymoon trip.

They saw nothing of Freddie at the Pump Room and Caroline was feeling low in spirits when they returned home. They were to dine with some of her mother's friends that evening, and the only entertainment offered would probably be a hand of whist.

The evening was worse than Caroline could have imagined, for it seemed that one of the ladies had heard something she thought a little odd concerning her. As yet there was no talk of the race, but Caroline had been observed arriving in Bath with Sir Frederick.

'I was told that she was with a gentleman and that they had neither a maid nor a groom with them,' Mrs Selwyn said to Marianne. 'I was sure that that could not be the case, for I know Caroline to be a properly behaved young lady. To arrive looking a little windblown and in a phaeton…I thought that some mistake must have been made?'

'Oh, she was with Sir Frederick Rathbone,' Mrs Holbrook said airily as if it were no great matter. 'You must know that he is a great friend and…' She looked coy. 'Well, I must not say more at the moment, but I assure you that it was quite proper for her to be with him. Besides, her brother was not far behind her. They met on the way to Bath, and Sir Frederick took Caroline up with him for a short distance.'

'Ah, I thought there must be some explanation,' Mrs Selwyn said, nodding at Caroline in a satisfied way. 'You are to be congratulated, Miss Holbrook. I believe Rathbone is quite a catch.'

'Well, as to that…' Marianne put a finger to her lips. 'We must wait and see, must we not? I am sure I can rely on your discretion, Susan.'

'Yes, of course. Absolutely!'

'And that means she will tell everyone that I am to marry Freddie,' Caroline said as they were driven home later. 'How could you do it, Mama? When Freddie has not even spoken to you.'

'I was left with little choice,' Marianne said. 'You will have no reputation left if the gossips hear of that infamous race, Caroline.'

Caroline crossed her fingers. She placed no reliance on her brother's keeping mum concerning the race, and it could not be long before it was noted that she had been with Freddie when he drove into Bath, her brother following shortly behind. The gossips would put two and two together, and she would be labelled as being shockingly fast, if nothing worse.

She spent another uncomfortable night, dwelling on her thoughts.

In the morning, just before they were about to set out for the Pump Room once more, the knocker sounded and Sir Frederick Rathbone was announced. He was shown into the small parlour where Caroline sat with her mother. Her heart leaped as she saw him, looking particularly handsome in his blue coat and cream pantaloons. His cravat had been tied in what was called the Waterfall style, and he looked very much the gentleman of fashion.

'I am glad to have found you at home, Mrs Holbrook,' he said and smiled at her. 'I was afraid you might have gone out.'

'We were to leave in a few minutes,' Marianne said, 'but no matter. I have no pressing appointments and we are pleased to see you, sir.'

She indicated a chair, but Freddie preferred to stand. He glanced at Caroline. 'I trust you are well? Would you wish to remain—or return in a few minutes? You know the reason for my call, I believe?'

'I shall stay, if you do not mind,' Caroline said. 'I have told Mama of the situation with Grandfather.'

Freddie inclined his head, turning to her mother. 'Then you know my purpose, Mrs Holbrook. I applied to Bollingbrook as the head of the family, but was refused on grounds which I do not think valid. Tom was good enough to say that I had his blessing, but I think Caroline will wish to have yours, ma'am.'

'I dare say,' Marianne said, but did not smile. 'However, I must pull caps with you, sir. I cannot approve of Caroline's being with you during the race you and my reckless son took part in. Not only is it shocking, and may well harm Caroline's reputation, but it could have been dangerous.'

'I assure you that at no time was Caroline's life or wellbeing in danger,' Freddie said. 'Forgive me if it distresses you, but I took care to do nothing that would risk her. She is far too precious to me.'

'Yes, well, that may be the case,' Marianne said. 'But it makes me a little uneasy. Can I trust you to take care of her? You may love her—and I believe that she loves you—but love is a fleeting thing. I believed myself loved when I married Mr Holbrook and was sadly disappointed in later life. I do not wish my daughter to suffer as I did. Her husband must be a man of character and responsibility, sir.'

'Oh, Mama, there was never any danger,' Caroline said. 'And it was I who teased Freddie into letting me be a part of the race.'

'Caroline dearest, do not,' Freddie told her gently. 'Your mama is perfectly right to make these inquiries. I understand that she may feel a little uneasy, but you know, ma'am...a young lady of Caroline's nature may fall into more trouble if her spirits are denied. Had I not taken her up with me, I dare say her brother might have been persuaded.'

'Oh, you do not need to tell me that she is reckless,' Marianne said. 'It has always been the same with that pair—and Caroline as naughty as her brother.' She looked at the gentleman standing before her, seeing the mischief in his eyes. 'And I dare say that you are another such one, sir. You will not bamboozle me! I believe that I must not deny you, for my daughter might very well do something outrageous if I tried—but you must prove yourselves to me. There is already some scandal concerning the pair of you, and an engagement would be just the thing to nip that in the bud before it goes too far—but you must be prepared to wait until my return from Italy for the wedding.'

'Thank you, ma'am, you are very generous,' Freddie said and leaned forwards to take her hand, raising it briefly to his lips. 'Do I have your permission to take Caroline driving now? When she returns I hope she will be wearing my ring. Do you go to the Assembly this evening?'

'Yes, that was my intention.'

'Then we may let it be known there, ma'am. It should help to steal the gossips' thunder, and I shall know how to deal with anyone who dares to speak ill of my intended wife.'

'Yes, that will do very well,' Marianne said and relented as she saw the pleasure leap in his eyes. 'Go along the pair of you!'

'Thank you, dearest Mama,' Caroline cried and flew to embrace her. 'I knew that you could not refuse us.'

'Well, I have always liked him,' Marianne said. 'And if he cannot control you, then I dare say no one will. But the wedding must wait—is that clearly understood?'

'Yes, Mama,' Caroline said and looked at Freddie. 'It will take me one minute to put on my bonnet and pelisse…'

As she hurried away to get ready, Freddie looked at his future mother-in-law. 'You need not fear for her future, ma'am. It has taken me a long time to find a lady that I wished to make my wife. I may not have been as circumspect in the past as I might have—but all that is at an end. Caroline's happiness will be my first concern, and I shall do everything that I deem necessary to protect her.'

'Then you have my blessing, sir.'

'I have received a letter informing me that Lady Stroud arrives in Bath tomorrow, ma'am,' Freddie said. 'She will be delighted to learn that you have consented to our engagement for I know that she liked Caroline very well.'

'I shall be delighted to renew our acquaintance,' Mrs Holbrook said. 'And I shall call as soon as she is in residence.'

'I know that Lady Stroud will be pleased to see you, ma'am.'

On that note they parted, Freddie going into the hall as Caroline came flying down the stairs to meet him.

Freddie had driven out to a local beauty spot. He stopped his phaeton and told his tiger to watch the horses while they got down to walk for a few minutes.

'So, my love,' he said when they had wandered a sufficient distance from the lad's curious gaze. 'Are you happy?' Caroline smiled up at him. Her heart was beating very fast and she was excited by his nearness.

However, there was one thing she had to do before she could accept her happiness. 'Yes, Freddie, I am happy—but there is something I must tell you. I thought Grandfather would tell you, but he did not…'

'You mean the quarrel with my uncle?'

'No, something more unfortunate…' Caroline hesitated, then, 'You may have heard of Grandfather's third wife. He loved her very much and she was my grandmother.'

'Yes, I had heard that he was very fond of her.'

'Did you know that her family refused permission for the marriage and so she ran away with him?'

'Yes. Someone told me recently.'

'Grandmother's brother told Grandfather that she was too delicate to have a child…he warned that she might die in the attempt.'

'As she did, unfortunately,' Freddie said. His eyes narrowed. 'It happens sometimes and is always tragic. Are you thinking that you might have inherited her weakness?'

'Grandfather fears it. I was afraid if you knew that I might not…be able to give you an heir…'

'If I thought it for one moment, I should be careful not to give you a child. I must tell you at once, Caroline—you are more important to me than any child could possibly be. If we were fortunate enough to have a son, I should naturally be delighted, but if I lost you…it does not bear thinking of, my dearest.'

'But surely it is important for you to have an heir—for the sake of your family?'

'It would please my family,' Freddie told her. 'But you may put such fears from your mind, Caroline. In the first place I am fairly certain that your grandmother's illness was due to a fever she caught in childhood that weakened her heart, and, secondly, I am marrying you because you are the only woman I have ever wished to marry.'

'So you would still choose me even if I could not bear a child?'

'Yes, of course. I know this must play on your mind, Caroline. Bollingbrook should never have told you the story. However, we shall arrange for you to visit an excellent doctor I know once we are married. I am certain that he will put your mind at rest. If he should confirm your fears, I shall make certain that we never have a child.'

'And you truly would not mind that?'

'I should mind it more for your sake than my own, since I believe you might be unhappy if you could not have children—but I should try to make you happy despite it. We might in those circumstances even adopt a poor child who needs a home and family.'

'Freddie…' Caroline's throat caught with emotion. 'You are so good…'

'I am selfish,' he told her and took her hand. 'I want you, Caroline, and I would move heaven and earth to get what I want.' He raised her hand to his lips, dropping a kiss in her palm. 'Are you content now, dearest?'

'Yes, Freddie. How could I not be after what you have just said to me? I must be the most fortunate of women!'

'I believe I am the fortunate one, my love. I cannot wait for the day when I can claim you for myself.'

'I hope Mama may be persuaded to allow us to marry

as soon as she returns from Italy, but Christmas is not so very far away.'

'Shall you stay with your aunt while Mrs Holbrook is away?'

'Mama says she will write to her cousin, Amelia. She is a little deaf and does not entertain much, but I think I would prefer to stay with her. She lives in Yorkshire, so it may mean that we shall not often see each other.'

'I have an idea that might suit us better—if it appealed to you, dearest?'

'Please tell me,' Caroline said, smiling up at him as he reached out to touch her cheek. The look in his eyes made her sigh, for she wished that they might be married almost immediately. Her heart was racing wildly, her lips anticipating his kiss. She felt that she could swoon with the delightful sensations he was arousing in her. 'I hope it means that we do not need to be separated?'

'If you would consent to be Lady Stroud's guest at her country house, which is not much more than twenty miles from Bath, I might also visit her—and then, you know, we should be in each other's company as often as we pleased.'

'Oh, I think that is a very good suggestion. Do you think that Mama will agree?'

'I think that she might listen to my godmother, don't you?'

'Oh, yes.' Caroline laughed as she saw the mischief in his eyes. 'You wicked thing, Freddie! You always make me laugh—and to think that I did not particularly like you when we first met. I thought you arrogant and too sure of yourself— but I like you very well now…despite your faults.' Her eyes sparkled with mischief as she waited for him to take up the challenge, but he replied in a more serious vein.

'I knew that I found you very attractive at the start,' Freddie told her. 'But I was determined to hold back. I was not sure that I was ready to marry anyone, but then I realised that nothing else would do.'

'When did you know that you truly loved me?'

'I believe it was after the balloon accident. I realised that it could so easily have been you that was injured or killed—and it terrified me.'

Caroline blushed. 'I thought you were angry with me…that you had formed a disgust for my reckless behaviour, which was the cause of the trouble. For it was surely my fault that Tom was injured.'

'That is ridiculous,' Freddie said, a grim line to his mouth. 'How could you have been to blame? I was angry that it had happened and anxious, for I did not understand why.'

'It is very difficult to understand,' Caroline said. 'Tom and Nicolas seem to have settled on Grandfather's illegitimate child in Jamaica, but I cannot see why it should suddenly happen now. I know that Grandfather changed his will in our favour, but surely that cannot be the cause of these attempts on our lives? How would that person be so quickly aware of the changes?'

'Do you have any other ideas?' Freddie asked. Having turned the various theories over in his mind, he had as yet been able to come to no real conclusion. Had the attacks been made on him he might have understood their cause—but why Caroline? 'My one concern in waiting for our wedding is that this unknown assassin might try to kill you again.' He frowned as she shook her head. 'I know that you do not wish your mama to be upset over this business, but if you were my wife I could make certain that you were safe.'

'I promise you that I shall be careful,' Caroline said. 'I

think I must be quite safe staying with Lady Stroud in the country.'

'Yes, perhaps. I own I think you will be safer there than in London.' He reached out, drawing her into his arms and bending his head to kiss her. His mouth took possession of hers in a hungry yet tender kiss that made her weak with longing. 'I confess that I shall find the next few weeks very trying, my love.' He smiled at her, tracing the line of her cheek and laying his finger for one moment at the pulse spot at the base of her throat. 'I have never wanted anyone this much, Caroline. I do not know how you managed it, little minx, but you have wound yourself about my heart and it beats only for you.'

'Oh, Freddie,' Caroline said, feeling that she wanted to melt into him, to become a part of him. 'I do so wish that Mama would consent to a wedding before she leaves, but I know that she will not.'

'Then I must be content to wait,' Freddie said, 'which means that we should go now, for I am tempted to sweep you up in my carriage and run away with you to Gretna Green.'

Caroline laughed, her eyes bright with mischief. 'Oh, yes, Freddie! I should love that of all things. What an adventure that would be—to be married over the anvil and be together always.'

'I dare say you would regret it afterwards and long for all the trimmings of a big wedding?'

'No, I do not think so,' Caroline said. 'We should be able to give a dance and dinners for our friends whenever we felt like it—and, in truth, I do not care so very much for the constant round of society. It is well enough to invite one's true friends, but I was happy enough to go down to Grandfather's estate.'

'But you would not truly wish to elope?'

'Yes, I should like to…but it would hurt Mama, and we have promised that we shall wait,' Caroline said. 'So I suppose that we must.'

'Yes, I suppose we must,' Freddie said and laughed. 'Besides, I wish to let the world see how much I love and honour my bride, so we shall restrain our impatience. Hold out your left hand, my love.'

Caroline did as she was bid and he took a small pouch from his coat pocket, extracting a beautiful square emerald surrounded by diamonds and set on a gold band, which he slipped on to her third finger.

'Oh, Freddie,' she said. 'It is so beautiful. Thank you very much.'

'I am glad that you like it,' he said. 'There are many items of family jewellery residing in the bank, which I shall give you when we are married—but this ring has never belonged to anyone else. I commissioned it for you before I left London.'

Caroline tipped her head to one side, challenging him. 'Were you so certain that I would say yes?'

'I hoped that you would,' he said. 'But had you refused, I should not have given up, Caroline. When I want something, I am not to be denied—and I want you for my wife.'

Caroline lifted her face for his kiss, melting into his arms once more, feeling the wave of desire she was beginning to expect whenever he touched her. She let her hands move up the back of his neck, spreading out into his hair and holding his head as he would have moved away. Her body was demanding so much more, and she felt bereft when Freddie broke free, holding her from him.

'If we continue like this, I shall not be able to keep my

word to Mrs Holbrook,' he said. 'Come, Caroline, we must return to the carriage. Your mother will be anxious if we are gone too long.'

Caroline knew that the news of her engagement had gone round the ballroom like wildfire. She suspected that it had already been talked of, and, as soon as she walked into the room with her mother and Sir Freddie, it had been noted that she was wearing a ring on her left hand.

She had imagined that she would not know anyone, but soon discovered that several of her acquaintances had come down to Bath. The Season in London had passed its height, and some of the older ladies had decided to visit the spa for their health after so much junketing around in London.

Lady Stroud was evidently delighted. She nodded with approval as Freddie brought his fiancée to her. 'Kiss me, my dear,' she said, offering her cheek. 'Yes, it will do very well, Freddie. I am pleased that you have at last decided to oblige your family. I shall enjoy having you both to stay with me for a few weeks before the wedding.'

Caroline was congratulated on her engagement by almost everyone she met, though one or two of the ladies looked at her askance. Nicolas told her that rumours of the race were circulating, but the news of her engagement had overtaken it, and most of the younger set found it a huge jest and were applauding her courage. It would, of course, have been very different had she not become engaged to Freddie, and Caroline was a little chastened as she realised that she might have been in serious trouble.

However, no one actually cut her, and she enjoyed the evening more than any similar affair that had preceded it, for she was able to dance with Freddie as often as she liked. She did dance with one or two other gentlemen out of politeness, but her true happiness came from being with Freddie.

George Bellingham came to them as soon as he arrived, congratulating Freddie and wishing Caroline happy. He had taken a house in Bath for a few weeks, and Julia and her mother had come down to stay with him.

'It is a great pleasure to me to see you settled, Freddie,' he said. 'And I am happy that you have a good man to care for you, Miss Holbrook. Freddie is the best of good fellows and we shall all get on famously.'

'Thank you so much, sir,' Caroline said. 'You are very kind.'

George looked at his friend. 'There was something I wished to discuss with you, Freddie. It will do tomorrow, if you will call at my lodgings?'

'A little matter of business?' Freddie said, amused. 'I assure you I fully intend to settle my debt, George.'

'Oh, you mean the chestnuts?' George said and frowned. 'No, this is rather more urgent, Freddie—but it will keep for tomorrow.'

Freddie nodded, sensing that George had something of importance to impart—something that he did not wish Caroline to hear.

'Yes, of course. At about ten?'

'Excellent,' George said. 'Caroline, you will give me the pleasure of this dance, I hope?'

'Yes, of course,' she said and gave him her hand. She looked up at him as he led her into the dance. 'You and Freddie are very good friends, are you not?'

'The best,' he agreed. 'I have long wished to see him happy, Caroline—and I believe he is at last.'

Caroline enjoyed her dance with him, and when he returned her to Freddie, they talked for a while before he left. She looked at Freddie curiously when they were alone.

'What do you suppose is so important?'

'I have no idea,' Freddie said. 'Do not tease yourself over it, my love. I dare say George wants my advice on some horses that he wishes to purchase.'

Caroline thought that he was being a little uncommunicative, but was too happy to press for more information. If it was a matter of business, it was unlikely to concern her.

'What I have to say concerns Farringdon,' George said when they met the next morning at his lodgings. 'I happened to dine at the same inn as him on the way down here. He was looking most odd—not at all his usual self. And that evening he became quite drunk and abusive. He said some rather unpleasant things concerning you, Freddie.'

'Such as?' Freddie raised his brows.

'He practically accused you of cheating him out of his fortune.'

'Rubbish! No one would believe him. He is a careless gambler, reckless—and I have always been meticulous in matters of play.'

'You are perfectly right, Freddie, that was not what worried me. He seemed to be so bitter, to hate you so much. He was muttering in his cups, threatening you. Of course it was all nonsense, but I felt that you should be aware.'

'Thank you, George. What was the nature of his threats?'

'He said something like…*he will discover what it feels like to lose everything he cares for.* Clearly he was drunk, but I did not care to hear him speak so bitterly of you. I believe he means you some harm, my friend. Can it be merely a matter of his gambling debts—or have you done something more to make him hate you?'

'Nothing I can think of…' Freddie frowned.

'It may be the loss of his horses,' George said thoughtfully. 'He was very proud of both his chestnuts and the greys. He cannot enjoy seeing you driving them.'

'I do not fear Farringdon. He is a fool and might have cut his losses had he been honest. I told you that I was prepared to forgive the debt if he was straight with me, but he lied— told me that he had no debts on his estate and that he would pay in full. I had my agent investigate and he discovered that hardly anything was left. Farringdon knew that when he sat down to play. He knew that his notes were worthless. I did not wish to be lumbered with a failing estate and would gladly have returned it had there been anything to return. As it was, I took his greys in settlement of the debt and as far as I am concerned that was an end to it.'

'And he may think himself fortunate, for if you had chosen you might have had him arrested for debt or fraud, whichever you preferred—but instead of being grateful, he has dwelled on his misfortunes and now blames you for all his ills.'

'Well, he may think as he pleases,' Freddie said. 'He was already set on the path to ruin before I won a guinea from him.' He smiled wryly. 'I must settle my debt to you, George.'

'There is no hurry,' George said. 'I am happy to see you so well suited, my friend. I think she is just the woman for you.'

'How could it be otherwise?' Freddie said and offered his hand. 'The chestnuts are yours and I wish you joy of them.'

'I think I shall give them back to you as a wedding present,'

George said, shaking his hand. 'I would not wish to win such a wager, for it was taken lightly. Yes, you shall keep them, and in return you will ask me to be godfather to your first child.'

'Yes, of course. Thank you, George. I am glad to know what is in Farringdon's mind, though I set little store by it. The man is a loser by nature and I shall not let his bitterness disturb my peace of mind.'

'Well, I dare say it was merely a drunkard's loose talk,' George said and smiled. 'Tell me, when are you to be married?'

'As soon as Mrs Holbrook allows,' Freddie said. 'I am on my way to the Pump Room now, for she takes the waters most days. Perhaps you would like to accompany me?'

Caroline saw the two gentlemen come in together, and, leaving her mother to talk to companions of her own generation, she went to join them, her face alight with mischief.

'Have you come to take the waters, Freddie?' she asked innocently. 'I believe they are beneficial for all manner of ailments. Especially the rheumatics, they say…'

'Minx!' he said, giving her look of mock outrage. 'You deserve a spanking, miss, and the time is coming when you may get all that you deserve.'

Caroline went into a peal of delighted laughter. 'Have you come to take me driving? I was about to go to the lending library, for Mama has asked me to return a book for her. If you accompany me, we may go driving afterwards—should you wish for it?'

'As it happens, George and I are both on foot this morning,' Freddie said. 'But we should both be delighted to accompany you, Caroline. Afterwards we may stroll for a while and perhaps gaze in the shop windows or take a cup of chocolate and some of those delicious cakes they sell at a little shop nearby—if that would please you?'

'Oh, yes, that sounds delightful,' Caroline agreed. 'I must just tell Mama what we plan, and then we may leave. I confess I find the prospect of chocolate more appealing than a cup of this water.'

Freddie and George exchanged a few words with Mrs Holbrook and then the three set out together. Caroline found the two gentlemen good company, for they teased each other unmercifully, and made wagers on the silliest things, but only for amusement's sake.

'Shall you attend the theatre while you are here, Miss Holbrook?' George asked her. 'I believe there is a very good play on this coming week. Does Mrs Holbrook approve of the dramatic art?'

'Oh, yes, I think so,' Caroline replied, a naughty twinkle in her eye. 'You see, Mr Milbank particularly likes to visit the theatre, especially for something of a light-hearted nature— and Mama approves of most things that Mr Milbank likes.'

'Perfectly proper,' Freddie told her with mock severity. 'I hope you are taking a lesson from your mama, Caroline? I shall expect you to agree with everything I say when we are married.'

'Shall you truly?' Caroline said, tipping her head to one side. 'Oh dear, I fear you shall be sadly disappointed, sir.' She laughed softly, her eyes bright with mischief. 'Oh, do look,' she said. 'I believe that is Julia over there with her mama. I must speak to them...'

She let go of Freddie's arm, and went to step out into the road, but, remembering that he had once scolded her for being impulsive, hesitated as she saw a heavy wagon rumbling quite fast towards them. Then, as she hovered at the kerb, she suddenly felt something knock into her and she gave a little cry, almost falling from the pavement into the path of the oncoming vehicle. She was within a hair's breadth of being crushed under its wheels, for her ankle had twisted and she could not keep her balance. Fortunately, Freddie was standing close to her and he grabbed her pelisse, pulling her back out of harm's way and into his arms as the wagon thundered past over the cobbles.

'Oh,' she said as he held her. She was trembling, for the accident had shocked her. 'What happened? What is George doing?' she asked as she saw that their companion had taken off after someone who was clearly running away. 'I think… did someone push me?'

'Yes, Caroline,' Freddie said, looking grim. 'I did not notice him, for I was concerned that you meant to dash across in front of that wagon. I was watching you and only saw the rogue as he pushed you, but I think George realised what was going on, for he was after the man like a shot.'

'Oh, how horrid,' Caroline said, feeling shocked and a little sick. 'Do you think…I mean, did he actually mean to push me or was it an accident?'

'I cannot be sure,' Freddie said, though he did not believe it could have been an accident. 'Miss Fairchild has seen you, Caroline. She means to come to us. It may be best if we say nothing to anyone just yet. Invite your friend to take chocolate with us, and then we shall see what George has to say when he returns. I hope he may catch the fellow, but I make no reliance on it.'

'Caroline!' Julia said as she came across the road to them. 'What happened—did that fellow push you? I thought you were going to be hurt!'

'Oh, no, I believe it was a mere accident,' Caroline said. 'We are going to have some chocolate and cakes, Julia—do say you will come?'

'Yes, of course. I should love to,' Julia said. 'I have been to the lending library, but the book I wanted was out.' She looked at Freddie. 'I hear you are to be congratulated, sir— and you, Caroline. I wanted to tell you how very pleased I am for you both. Of course I expected it—we all did.'

'Thank you,' Caroline said and blushed as she glanced at Freddie. 'I was not aware that anyone knew until recently.'

'It was commonly talked of in London,' Julia told her and smiled a little coyly. 'I know for a fact that some of our friends had a wager that you would be married before Christmas. Everyone remarked on it, because Sir Frederick had never been known to take so much interest in a young lady before. Besides, it was obvious that he was in love with you.'

'Oh, no…' Caroline glanced at Freddie, and saw that he was looking thoughtful. 'Was it so easy to see? I confess that I did not know it myself for some time.'

'Oh, here comes my uncle,' Julia said, her attention turned. 'Did you catch that wicked fellow, sir?'

'I fear not,' George said, a trifle out of breath. 'He went into an inn and escaped out the back somehow. I'm sorry, Freddie. I should know the fellow again if I saw him, but that isn't of much use to you.'

'You did your best, George,' Freddie said. 'As it happens, Caroline was not hurt. I dare say he must have been after your purse, Caroline. It is over now—shall we all have our chocolate and cakes?'

George offered Julia his arm and the four of them went into the chocolate shop together. Caroline glanced at Freddie, for she sensed that he was playing the incident down to try to avoid gossip, which would have been bound to reach her mother's ears sooner or later.

'What are you thinking?' she asked in a low voice.

'That I must do something about this business, Caroline. That is the third time you have been attacked and it really cannot go on.'

'But what can you do?'

'Trust me, my dearest,' he said and smiled at her. 'When does Nicolas return to his regiment?'

'In the morning, I believe.'

'I must speak to him before he leaves,' Freddie said. 'But Julia is looking at us. We must behave as if nothing has happened.'

Caroline went to join her friend by the counter where delicious-looking cakes had been set out on various plates and stands. Freddie certainly had something on his mind, but there was no use in asking. He would tell her when he was ready for her to know.

When she glanced over her shoulder, she saw that Freddie was talking earnestly with George about something, and the two of them looked serious. However, when the ladies walked to join them at the table, having made a selection of cakes that they would all enjoy, they were laughing over some jest and she thought that perhaps she had imagined it.

After enjoying their chocolate, they parted company, George having agreed to escort Julia to join her mother, who had gone on to the Pump Room, and Freddie to deliver Caroline to her lodgings.

'I shall see you this evening, my love,' he told her, kissing her hand. 'Please take care of yourself until then.'

'You are very worried about what happened this morning, are you not?'

'You could have been killed or at least badly injured,' Freddie said. 'The time has come when I must do something, Caroline—but do not worry your head over it, my love. I am taking certain steps to make sure it will not happen again.'

Caroline stared after him, wondering what he meant to do. She sighed as she went indoors. It was most unpleasant that these things should be happening, and she could not help wishing that her grandfather had never thought of changing his will.

'I believe it must be for the best,' Nicolas agreed when, a little later that day, Freddie finished telling him what he planned. 'The sooner she is removed from harm's way the better, in my opinion. She should be safe enough at Lady Stroud's house, particularly if you have employed certain measures to protect her.'

'I shall be with her,' Freddie said. 'I have been giving the matter a great deal of thought recently, Nicolas. Something George told me earlier today has made me wonder if we were wrong to consider the Jamaican connection. I think that business may have rather more to do with me than your grandfather's will.'

'Yes, it had crossed my mind,' Nicolas agreed. 'But why is Caroline his target?'

'I imagine at the start it was meant to be me, for I was due to fly in that balloon, not Tom. He may have had no idea that Caroline was to be involved—but when he realised that I was planning to marry her, he turned his hand against her, thinking to cause me more grief.' Freddie looked grim. 'It is fiendishly clever, Nicolas, for I would rather die than have harm come to her.'

'Yes, I understand you,' Nicolas said grimly. 'I am very fond of Caroline and I think I might kill this rogue if I got my hands on him—whoever he may be.'

'You may stand in line,' Freddie said, a glitter of anger in his eyes. 'I have agents working on this affair, Nicolas. Do not imagine that I have been idle. They will discover who is behind all this bother and the culprit will be punished. Until then, Caroline must be protected. You must return to your regiment tomorrow and that means I must be the one to see that she is watched constantly. I shall do that best if I have her near me at all times—and there is only one way to be sure of it.'

'Yes, that is very true. Your plan is the best that can be achieved, sir. I understand what you mean to do—and I pray that all will go well.'

'If Caroline is safe, I care little for anything else,' Freddie said, and on that note of agreement they parted, Freddie to complete his plans for that evening, and Nicolas to prepare for his part in the plot.

Mr Milbank had given a small party for a select number of friends that evening. It was Nicolas's last evening with them in Bath, and was to be a celebration, for he would not get leave to attend his mother's wedding. Tom had driven over from Bollingbrook to join them, for he was about to set out on his journey to Jamaica and had been invited to the party. Naturally, Freddie was invited as Caroline's fiancé. Amongst others, Mr Bellingham, Julia and her mother made up the company that sat down to a very good dinner.

The conversation flowed easily, helped by the fine wines

and delicious food served at table. It was quite late in the evening when the party finally began to break up. Nicolas took his mother aside, asking if he might escort her home in his curricle, for there was something he wished to say to her.

'Yes, of course, dearest,' Marianne said, smiling at her son, who was her favourite, though she had always tried to love her children equally. 'Caroline may come with Tom if she pleases. Or perhaps Sir Frederick will bring her…'

'Yes, of course I shall take Caroline,' Sir Frederick said and smiled at her. He turned to Tom and shook hands with him. 'I am glad to see you again. You are looking much better. I trust nothing more has happened to disturb you?'

'No, I am sure thanks to you,' Tom said. 'I have noticed a few extra rather brawny men about the place recently. Grandfather knows and said to tell you he appreciated your interest in the business. He hasn't quite got round to sending you his apologies, but I think he may do so before long.'

'Well, I am not perfectly certain of that,' Freddie said, a flicker of a smile in his eyes. 'I may be in his bad books again soon, and in your mama's—but Nicolas will fill you in, I am sure.'

He turned to Caroline, seeing that she had her velvet evening cape about her shoulders, smiling at her as she came up to them. 'Ah, there you are, my love. Are you ready to leave?'

'Yes, thank you,' she said, and took a step forwards, standing on her toes to kiss Tom's cheek. 'I shall not see you for some weeks, perhaps months, dearest. You will promise me to take care of yourself while you are away?'

'Yes, as best I can,' Tom told her and gave her a one-armed hug, his other arm still in a sling, but no longer painful.

'Freddie sent me someone I might trust—an old soldier. He swears worse than Cousin Amelia's parrot, but I shall walk safer with him at my back.' He nodded to her. 'Go with Freddie now, Caroline. You will be married when I next see you, and I shall leave a gift for you with Mama.'

'Thank you,' Caroline said, 'but my best gift will be to see you safely home again, Tom.'

She became aware of Freddie waiting for her, and went to him, tucking her arm through his and looking up at him. 'I am quite ready now.'

'Then we must be off,' Freddie said. 'My curricle is waiting, I believe.'

'Your curricle?' Caroline asked curiously, for she knew that he more usually drove his phaeton in town. 'I thought you walked here this evening?'

'Yes, that is true, but my groom has his instructions.' Freddie offered her his arm. 'Are you tired at all, my love?'

'No, not at all,' she said. 'It was a very pleasant evening, but I do not feel like going to bed.'

'What would you like to do?' Freddie asked with a flicker of a smile.

'Oh…walk with you under the stars perhaps,' Caroline said and laughed. 'Yes, I know I am being foolish. It is just that…it becomes harder and harder to part every night.'

'Does it, Caroline?' Freddie took her hand, helping her into his curricle. His groom was driving that evening and he climbed in after her, sitting next to her and taking her hand in his. 'Why do we not take the long way home?'

'Oh, may we?' Caroline was pleased, for though she had enjoyed her evening, she did not wish to say goodnight to him yet. 'That would be lovely, Freddie.'

He kept her hand in his, stroking it idly with his thumb so that she felt her blood rush wildly through her veins and turned to him as he drew her towards him, his lips brushing hers in the softest of kisses.

'You do know that I love you and that I would never do anything to harm you?'

'Yes, of course,' she said and gazed up into his eyes. 'I love you, too, Freddie.'

He touched her cheek, his fingers shaping the contours of her face and then going behind her head as he pulled her to him for a kiss that was deeper and more hungry than any she had yet had from him. Caroline melted into him, her body aching for the release of something she hardly understood, but knew would come from being one with him.

'Oh, Freddie…' she whispered. 'When you kiss me like that, Christmas seems a very long way away.'

'Yes, it does,' he agreed. 'But we are leaving for my god-mother's home this evening, and that means we shall be together constantly until we are married.'

'What do you mean?' Caroline looked at him. She was suddenly aware that they were leaving Bath. 'Freddie, this isn't the way home. What are you doing?'

'We are leaving Bath, my love,' he said and gave her a wicked smile. 'My godmother travelled home this morning and will be waiting for us.'

'No, Freddie, we must not,' Caroline said, startled and anxious. 'Mama will be so worried—and there is her wedding… No, we must not do this.'

'She will know of my intentions by now,' Freddie reassured her. 'Do not distress yourself on Mrs Holbrook's account, Caroline. Nicolas has promised to talk to her and explain why I have taken this desperate step. It is to protect you, my dearest one. I told you that I could not allow the situation to continue any longer. You were not safe in Bath, but you will be safe with me at my godmother's, I promise you. In the meanwhile I shall try to mend fences with your mama—and possibly your grandfather, if he will see us.'

'Oh…but Mama will be so upset,' Caroline said. 'Poor Mama…you really should not have done this, Freddie.'

'I am sorry if it distresses you, Caroline—and I would not have done it had I not believed it was the only way. I took precautions to protect you at Bollingbrook Place, but even though I was with you in Bath you were still attacked. I shall feel safer in the country for your sake—just until this thing is settled.'

'Yes, I see,' Caroline said. She was silent for a few moments, absorbing what he had told her, and then, 'Do you not think Mama might have agreed to our marriage sooner had you told her the truth?'

'She might,' Freddie said. 'She knew that you were to stay with Lady Stroud, though she did not know that I intended to leave Bath this evening. I did so for reasons of secrecy, of course.'

'You took a great deal on yourself,' Caroline said, for she was too disturbed to give in immediately. 'I am a little cross with you for not telling me what you planned.' She looked at him anxiously. 'Of course I do not mind—as long as Mama is not worrying about me.'

'I believe Nicolas may bring her about,' Freddie said and smiled at her. 'It will not be so very bad, my love. Your mama may tell everyone you have gone to visit friends. And then we shall invite them all to our wedding when your mama returns from her honeymoon trip.' He touched her hand briefly. 'Have I your forgiveness, my love? You do know that I have done this for your sake?'

'Yes, I know,' Caroline said and turned to face him. She leaned forward to kiss him softly on the lips. 'I still wish that we might be married sooner…'

'You are a temptress, my love,' Freddie said ruefully and eased her away from him. 'I may have spirited you away, my dearest, but I am not going to seduce you. We shall wait until my wedding ring is on your finger.'

'Shall we really, Freddie?' Caroline said and reached up to touch his face. She traced the line of his mouth with her forefinger, bringing a groan from him. 'I do not truly see why we should. We are so soon to be married…'

'And then I shall put you across my knee and give you the spanking that your mother obviously did not,' Freddie growled. 'I have no intention of giving in to you, minx, no matter how you try to tempt me.'

'Oh, dear,' Caroline said and gurgled delightfully. 'What a sad disappointment you are, Freddie dearest. I had not thought you were such a flat…'

'A flat?' Freddie looked at her incredulously. 'No, no, Caroline, I shall not have that.'

'Well, a slow-coach then,' Caroline said and pouted at him. 'I am not perfectly sure what the right word may be, but—' She gasped as he pulled her into his arms, kissing her so ruthlessly and with such determination that she could do nothing but melt into his arms. 'Oh, Freddie…' she breathed, well pleased with the result her teasing had brought. 'I do love you.'

'And I love you, my darling,' he said, grinning at her. 'I am not sure that I shall ever say no to you again, but this time I am determined on it.'

'Oh…' Caroline smiled and leaned her head against his shoulder. 'In that case, I think I may as well go to sleep for a while.'

Freddie smiled as she lay against him. He slid his arm about her, holding her more comfortably as the curricle drove on through the night. She did not fool him for one moment, and he was very much aware of an uncomfortable tightness in his breeches. It was exquisite torture to have her near like this, to know that she was ready to surrender her sweetness to him, and yet refrain from taking all that he so desperately wanted of her.

And yet he was determined that he would wait for their wedding night. Caroline was such a lovely innocent, and he would not give the gossips more fodder than he needed. Though if Mrs Holbrook played her part, there was no need for anyone to know where Caroline had gone…

Chapter Twelve

'Nicolas!' Mrs Holbrook stared at her son in shock and horror. 'Do not tell me that you were a party to this terrible deceit? I cannot believe that you would treat me so hardly…' She held a scrap of lace kerchief to her eyes. 'It is quite, quite shocking that Caroline should run off with him at the dead of night…'

'It was not Caroline's fault,' Nicolas said loyally. 'Sir Freddie and I planned it together. It was the only way to keep her safe, Mama. Caroline has been attacked three times. There was the balloon accident and then she was shot at when riding at Grandfather's estate—and this latest incident. Freddie said that he must remove her from danger and the best way to do that was to leave Bath at once and secretly.'

'Why didn't any of you tell me?' Mrs Holbrook demanded. 'If I had known…' She smothered a sob. 'I think it is most unkind of you all to keep this from me.'

'We didn't want to upset you,' Tom said, coming into the parlour at that moment. 'Stop crying, Mama. Caroline will be all right with Sir Frederick.'

'This means I must cancel my wedding,' Mrs Holbrook said dramatically. 'It cannot go on as planned…'

'That is nonsense, Mama,' Tom said. 'You will be married at the appointed time. Nicolas must return to his regiment, of course, but I shall put off my journey for a few days to see you wed.'

'Oh, Tom dearest…' Mrs Holbrook threw herself on his shoulder, weeping into his coat. 'You alone of my children even attempt to consider my feelings.'

Tom patted her shoulder, nodding at his brother over her head. 'You had best get to bed, Nicolas. You have to leave early in the morning. Leave Mama to me.' He smiled at his mother, putting her from him. 'Tell me, Mama—would you have Caroline safe at Lady Stroud's home or fatally harmed?'

Marianne gave a little shriek, her face turning pale. 'Was it truly the only way to keep her safe, Tom? Not just one of her mad pranks?'

'I am convinced that Caroline did not even know of it,' Tom said. 'Indeed, I think only Nicolas and Freddie knew what was happening. I am perfectly sure that George Bellingham did not, for he caught up with me when I was walking home. Apparently, he had just received some information that he thought Freddie should know.'

'Oh, dear,' Marianne said, looking at her son. 'Do you think it is more bad news?'

'I have no idea, but I intend to speak to Bellingham as soon as possible myself. He will be wondering what has happened, and if this concerns Caroline in any way, then I want to know about it.'

'This is all Bollingbrook's fault,' Mrs Holbrook declared,

a wrathful look in her eye. 'And the next time I see him I shall certainly tell him so!'

On that note she departed to her bedchamber, leaving the brothers together. Nicolas looked thoughtful, because he sensed that Tom was anxious about something.

'I wish I could help you out, Tom—but if I am not back on time I shall be declared absent without leave, and that will not do.'

'No, no, you must get off right and tight. My journey may wait a few days. I must keep my promise to Mama, and, if Caroline is in some fresh danger, then I must warn Freddie of it.'

'Yes, of course,' Nicolas said, frowning. 'Has it occurred to you that this business may be nothing to do with Grandfather's will?'

'Well, I have wondered lately,' Tom said and looked thoughtful. 'It may be that Sir Frederick has an enemy himself. I am damned if I can puzzle it out.'

'Sir Freddie has some idea, I believe,' Nicolas said thoughtfully. 'However, when you speak to Bellingham in the morning, you may learn something new. You will write and let me know what comes out of all this, Tom?'

'Yes, of course,' his brother assured him. 'Try not to worry about it, Nicolas. There is nothing you can do—and you may be certain that Sir Frederick knows what he is about. I dare say there is nothing for either of us to worry about at all.'

'Thank you for coming,' George said the next day when Tom called on him. 'I was worried when I found that Freddie was not at his lodgings last night. However, now I understand—and you may be sure that I shall not say a word to anyone.'

'Thank you. You may imagine that Mrs Holbrook is very distressed about all this, but she has accepted it because she believes, as my brother and Sir Frederick do, that it was the only way to keep Caroline safe.'

'That was undoubtedly his reason for carrying your sister off in such a high-handed way,' George said and looked anxious. 'The devil of it is that I think it is exactly what he ought not to have done.'

Tom felt a coldness at the nape of his neck. 'What do you mean, sir? Surely she will be safe enough at Lady Stroud's home?'

'Perhaps,' George said. 'Sir Frederick has an enemy—a man who is determined to bring him to his knees if he can. And, though I believe it would please him to see Freddie dead, I think he wants to punish him first.'

'By taking away the person who is most precious to him?' Tom nodded. 'Yes, that makes sense to me. All the attacks have been on Caroline of late. Indeed, since I took Sir Frederick's place at the balloon ascension at the last minute, he may have been the intended victim. A hired assassin would not know of a last-minute change of plans...'

'Yes, quite possibly. We have all been chasing our tails, thinking that you and Nicolas were targets as well as Caroline, but I am fairly certain that we were wrong. As I left Milbank's party last evening I met a man who had been working for Freddie. He had important information, which I persuaded him to give to me...and it transpires that I was right after all. I mentioned my fears to Freddie a day or so ago, but he shrugged it off as unimportant.'

'You know who has been threatening Caroline?' Tom asked.

'Yes, I believe so,' George said. 'It was a matter of money, but not of Bollingbrook's will. Freddie won a considerable sum from someone a short time ago. He thought he had settled the affair, for he took far less than was owed, merely warning the gentleman concerned that if he saw him gambling again he would make public that he was virtually bankrupt. The fellow is desperate, and may imagine that he is ruined, though if he had kept faith with Freddie he might have come out of it better than he has. Freddie would certainly not have done anything to harm him, but he may not have realised that the affair was over.'

'Good grief!' Tom was shocked. 'Then this is a personal vendetta against Freddie. I know that Nicolas discussed it with him, but they were not certain...' He frowned. 'This could mean that Caroline is even more at risk with him than she was before.'

'Yes, I fear that may be so,' George agreed. 'We have to warn him.'

'I shall set out at once,' Tom said and frowned. 'At least, as soon as I have told my mother that I shall not be able to attend her wedding...'

'Please do not disappoint Mrs Holbrook. It would only distress her more. I shall leave Bath in the morning. It is probable that Farringdon does not know they have left Bath, and that they are safe enough for the moment—but I think Freddie should be warned. Farringdon is the kind of petty individual who will do anything for spite—and at the moment he is like a wounded beast.'

Tom nodded his agreement and they parted, for there was little more to be done for the moment. They could only hope that Freddie was aware of his enemy and would take the proper steps to protect both Caroline and himself.

As he left George's house, Tom had come to a decision. He had been intending to wait until he returned from Jamaica to speak to Julia, but these attacks on Caroline had made Tom realise how precarious life could be. He would visit Mrs Fairchild in the morning and ask her permission to speak to her daughter. His visit to Jamaica could be put off for a few days longer, and, if Julia cared for him, as he hoped she did, they might be engaged before he left.

Caroline looked out of the upper window of Lady Stroud's country house. It was a very pretty establishment, and her hostess had made her welcome the previous evening. She had slept very well in a comfortable bed and was feeling happy and relaxed as she came downstairs that morning.

'Good morning, Miss Holbrook.' A woman that Caroline knew to be her hostess's housekeeper came to greet her as she entered the breakfast parlour, where food had been prepared and awaited her under silver covers. 'I trust you found your room comfortable?'

'Yes, thank you,' Caroline said and smiled at her. 'And thank you for the roses on the dressing table; they smelled lovely.'

'Lady Stroud wanted everything to be nice for you, miss,' the housekeeper said. 'She asks if you will attend her in her bedchamber—in about half an hour perhaps, when you have eaten your breakfast.'

'Yes, of course,' Caroline replied.

The housekeeper smiled and went away, leaving Caroline to help herself to the selection of tasty dishes on the sideboard.

She selected a little scrambled egg and bacon, and poured herself a cup of hot chocolate before sitting down to enjoy her meal. She had almost finished when the ring of boots on polished wood alerted her and she looked up with a smile as Freddie walked in.

He came to her, dropping a kiss on her cheek as she turned to greet him. 'I thought you would still be upstairs,' he said. 'I went for a ride as I usually do, but another morning we might ride together if you care for it?'

'Yes, I should like that very much,' Caroline said, sparkling up at him. 'But I should like to drive your horses even more, Freddie. Now that we are here at Lady Stroud's estate, do you think you might teach me?'

'Minx!' Freddie said and went to examine the contents of the silver chafing-dishes. 'I dare say I might be persuaded since you ask so nicely, my love. It will do no harm on the estate—and perhaps we may find you something of your own in good time.'

'Oh, Freddie,' Caroline said and got up to go to him. 'I think you mean to spoil me—do you?'

'Perhaps,' he said, giving her an enigmatic look. 'You are a temptress, Caroline, and you look beautiful this morning. Our wedding seems a very long time off at this moment.'

She gave a gurgle of laughter, reaching up to kiss him briefly on the lips. 'I think I shall enjoy being your wife very much, sir,' she said and drew back before he could prevent her. 'And now I have promised to visit your godmother. I must not keep her waiting.'

'Wicked one!' Freddie threw at her as she blew him a kiss and walked away. 'Have I met my match at last, I wonder?' He smiled at the thought, for he was feeling pleased with himself and the world that morning.

Caroline was feeling equally pleased with life as she went upstairs to Lady Stroud's private apartments. She knocked and a few moments later was invited to enter. Her hostess was sitting in bed, a pink shawl over her shoulders and a frilly cap on her head. She smiled and held out her hand, inviting Caroline to sit on the edge of her bed.

'You are up early, Caroline. I wake early myself, though I do not venture downstairs before noon these days.'

'I have always been used to rising early,' Caroline told her. 'I used to ride with my brother Nicolas when he was at home, and sometimes with Tom. If I did not ride, I went for long walks. Even in the winter I like to be outdoors as much as I can.'

'I approve of a girl with healthy habits,' Lady Stroud said. 'The moment I set eyes on you, I was sure you would make my godson a good wife. He has an old and valued name, you know, and he will inherit his uncle's estate in good time. Mine too when I am gone. It is right and proper that he should marry and marry well. We do not want any ramshackle filly in the family. No, you will make Freddie a good wife and give him several strapping sons, I have no doubt.'

'Yes…' Caroline stared at her a little uncertainly. 'I know it is important to provide sons for the family name to continue.'

'I believe in the family,' Lady Stroud said, her eyes narrowing as she saw Caroline's expression. 'Not frightened of that side of things, are you? Nothing to worry about, believe me. Freddie will look after you. He may have had his fling, but he won't let you down, child.'

'No, I did not think he would,' Caroline said, realising that she had almost betrayed herself. 'He is everything I could wish for in a husband.'

'And so I should think,' Lady Stroud said with a little frown. 'Get off and find yourself something to do then, girl. No sense in sitting here all day!'

'I shall see you later, ma'am. It is very good of you to have me here as your guest.'

'Stuff and nonsense! It was the most sensible thing in the circumstances—though why your mama would not permit your wedding immediately I do not know!'

Caroline smiled, but said nothing. She was thoughtful as she went downstairs. Freddie had assured her that she was more important to him than an heir, but she was sure Lady Stroud would be disappointed if Caroline did not produce the sons she expected.

'Ah, there you are.' Freddie came out of the parlour as he reached the bottom of the stairs. He looked at her for a moment. 'Is something wrong, Caroline? Did my godmother say anything to distress you?'

'No, of course not,' Caroline said and gave him a radiant smile. 'Lady Stroud has been everything that is kind and generous. I was merely thoughtful.'

'I have asked for the greys to be brought round,' Freddie said. 'Go up and change into something suitable, Caroline— and we shall begin your lessons at once.'

'You have done very well for a first lesson,' Freddie said as she brought the curricle to a halt in front of the house. 'You have good, natural hands, Caroline. I think we shall make a whip of you yet. I do not know that you will outshine Letty Lade at her best, but you will rival her once I have finished with you.'

'Freddie…' Caroline laughed up at him as he helped her

down. They stood for a moment in the sunshine, his hands about her waist, smiling at each other, both aware of a strong pull of sensuality. 'You are such a tease—but you do mean it? You really think that I shall be good enough to drive myself one day?'

'Yes, of course—' He broke off as a curricle came up the drive at a spanking pace. 'Now what the devil does George want here?'

Caroline turned in surprise as George Bellingham got down and came towards them. She was conscious of Freddie's hands about her waist, and moved away, a little flush in her cheeks to be seen in such an open embrace.

'George, my dear chap, what on earth are you doing here?'

'Forgive me for intruding…' George smiled at Caroline. 'How delightful to see you, Miss Holbrook. I had to see you, Freddie—just a small matter of business, you know.'

A small matter of business that had brought him here hotfoot from Bath! Freddie frowned, his eyes narrowing. Clearly George had something important to tell him. He turned to Caroline, a little smile of regret on his lips.

'We must postpone our conversation until another time, my love. I shall see you later.'

'Yes, of course, Freddie.'

She walked into the house, leaving the two gentlemen together.

'What is it, George?' Freddie asked. 'Why come all the way here, my friend? You have some news, I gather?'

'I am certain that Farringdon is behind those attempts on Caroline,' George said. 'I dare say he probably meant to harm you in that accident with the balloon, but after that he directed his malice at Caroline…to cause you more grief,

Freddie. I thought you should be warned of something I have learned…'

'Yes, that is much as I had thought,' Freddie agreed. 'It was good of you to come, my friend, but, as I told Caroline's brother, I have made certain arrangements. Even now, you are being watched—just as I have been all morning.'

'Then I need not have bothered,' George said ruefully. 'I was not perfectly sure…'

'No need to apologise,' Freddie said and grinned at him. 'Now that you are here, you must stay to nuncheon.'

'Congratulations, sir.' Tom shook his stepfather's hand. 'Mama, I wish you happy, but I know that you will be.'

'Oh, yes, very happy,' Marianne said and embraced her son. 'I am sorry that you must leave us so soon, Tom—but I know that you have much to do. You will write to me as often as you can?'

'Yes, Mama, of course,' Tom replied. 'When do you leave for Italy?'

'We have decided to postpone our trip for a week or two,' Marianne said. 'I wish to know that Caroline is safe, and I have something to say to Bollingbrook. We shall call there first and then go on to Holbrook, where I must supervise the packing of some things I wish sent down to Mr Milbank's estate—and then I intend to call on Lady Stroud to make sure that Caroline is all right.'

'Yes, well, I am sure that Caroline will be pleased to see you,' Tom said. 'I must leave now, Mama. I have much to do…'

Tom smiled as he put his other problems to the back of his mind for a moment. Before he left Bath there was one more call he must make.

* * *

'Come to gloat over me, have you?' Bollingbrook glanced askance at the new Mrs Milbank. 'Well, I cannot say that I blame you. I have not behaved well to you or your children.'

'There was a time when you might have done much to help me,' Marianne said, retaining her dignity. She had thought that she would exact revenge for past slights but, seeing him looking wretched, the desire had left her. 'However, that is past and I need nothing you can give me, sir. I have come to tell you that you have endangered the lives of my children and to ask if you will make it plain to whomever it concerns that you are no longer intending Tom, Nicolas and Caroline to be your heirs.'

'Well, I ain't able to oblige you,' Bollingbrook said, 'for I have signed most of the money over to Tom, though Caroline will have her dowry and Nicolas has something substantial. I've arranged for the funds to be available from my bank and that is that. Besides, I have news this morning that means it would make no difference if they were to die.'

'I assure you that it makes a great deal of difference to me!' Marianne looked at him indignantly.

'Oh, stop your mithering, woman,' Bollingbrook said. 'You know very well that I did not mean it that way.' He gave her a scathing look. 'Do you think I want anything to happen to that girl?'

'No, I do not,' Marianne said, 'and I suppose I must thank you for what you have done for them—though it might have been done sooner.'

'For once in your life you have said something that I agree with,' the Marquis said. 'And if you will listen, I shall tell you why you need not fear the Jamaican connection. I have received a letter just now telling me that the boy was killed in an accident some two months ago.'

'Then who is trying to harm my daughter?' Marianne was shocked. 'This changes things. Someone must speak to Sir Frederick about this, for he should be warned. It must be him who has an enemy…'

'If anyone had asked me, I would have said that that seemed the most likely in the first place.' The Marquis cleared his throat. 'We have all been damned fools! Will you forgive the past, ma'am—and will you and your husband stay to dine with me?'

'Thank you.' Marianne inclined her head. 'I think we can agree not to be enemies, sir—if only for the sake of my children. However, we wish to be at Holbrook by nightfall. I do not expect that I shall see you for a while, sir—but I wish you good health.'

Holding her head high, she walked from the room, leaving the Marquis to stare after her. He muttered beneath his breath, ringing the bell for Jenkins with some vigour. His valet, who had been hovering in the next room, came immediately.

'You rang, sir?'

'Of course I damned well rang, Jenkins,' the Marquis growled. 'Don't give me that injured look, man! I've had enough of it from that woman—though she isn't quite the milksop I thought her. At least she had the decency to tell me what was going on. That rogue has taken my gel off to stay with his godmother—and intends to marry her, I dare say.'

'Yes, sir.' Jenkins looked at a spot just above his head. 'I expect he does intend it. He loves her as she loves him.'

'Yes, I know I've only myself to blame that they've gone off without a word to me,' the Marquis said. 'Well, I can't do much about it now, but I think it's time to mend fences if we can, Jenkins.'

'Yes, sir.' Jenkins tried not to look pleased, but failed miserably. 'Your writing slope, sir?'

'No, damn you! What do I want with letters? Put up enough clothes for two days, Jenkins. We are off to Lady Stroud's estate to see how the land lies!'

'Ah…' Jenkins said, a gleam in his eyes. His master had hardly left his room in the past year. 'Are we certain about that, sir?'

'Damn your eyes, man! I'll get there if you have to carry me.'

'Yes, certainly, sir,' Jenkins said. 'And when do you wish to leave?'

'As soon as you can be ready, of course. You may give my instructions to the rest of the household and then come back and help me. And I shall want my knee breeches. Lady Stroud is a stickler for dress, as I recall…' He smiled as his valet went off to do his bidding. It might be the last thing he did, but he was going to see what could be done about this wretched business.

'Ah, there you both are,' Lady Stroud said, coming into the parlour where Freddie and Caroline were sitting together that afternoon. 'What are you doing indoors on a day like this? You should be out enjoying the fresh air, my dears.'

'Yes, you are perfectly right, Godmother,' Freddie agreed and looked at Caroline. 'I was just about to ask if you would like to take a turn about the gardens, my love?'

'I should enjoy it very much,' Caroline said, and gave him her hand. He pulled her to her feet and into his arms, looking down at her for a moment before he kissed her forehead. 'It is so warm that I do not think I need to put on my pelisse and I shall not bother with a bonnet.'

'Then let us go,' Freddie said, offering her his arm.

Caroline took it and they went out into the hall and through the door that an obliging footman opened for them. The garden was a riot of colour and perfume, for Lady Stroud was very fond of her borders, which were beautifully kept. A gardener was busy taking the dead heads from the rose bushes, and, seeing Caroline, he broke off a perfect pink rose bud and handed it to her with a little bow.

Caroline thanked him, and they strolled off. Birds were singing their hearts out because it was such a lovely day, and, as they walked towards the woods that lay beyond the wall at the end of the long garden, they were both aware of a feeling of perfect peace. It was a little cooler in the woods, but that was only to be welcomed on such a warm day.

'It is lovely here, isn't it?' Caroline said, looking up at him. They had been walking for a few minutes in perfect harmony. 'I was only thinking last night that I should like to walk in these woods…' She frowned as she remembered something. 'I forgot…I meant to tell you that I saw someone lurking out here last night when I glanced from the window—twice, actually.'

'Indeed?' Freddie arched his brows at her. 'I shall have to reprimand them, Caroline. My men are supposed to be guarding us, not frightening you.'

'Oh, no, I wasn't frightened,' she said. 'I remembered that you said you had set someone to watch over me in London— and I thought perhaps it was them.'

'Does nothing frighten you?' Freddie asked with a smile. 'Most young ladies would be near fainting if they thought that their lives might be in danger. But hopefully it will all be over soon, and you must not be distressed whatever happens, my love.' Something in his eyes seemed to carry a warning, and a little chill started at the nape of her neck.

'What do you mean?' she asked, gazing up at him in surprise. 'I thought…' The rest of her sentence was lost as she saw something in the trees just ahead of them, and then a man stepped out, and instinctively she knew what was happening. 'Freddie…be careful…'

'Yes, I know,' Freddie told her in a low voice. 'He has been following us since we entered the woods.' He let go of her, his hand moving slowly towards the deep pocket of his coat. Only when his fingers had closed over the pistol he sought did he turn his head to look at the man, noting the pistol in his hand, and the desperate look on his face. Freddie smiled slightly. 'Good morning, Farringdon. I have been expecting you. Your rogues have not served you well, I think? I thought you might feel it time to step out of the shadows and do the business yourself.' He took a step forwards, standing just in front of Caroline, shielding her from the line of fire. 'I hope you mean to be sensible? This business may all be settled without need for bloodshed. If you feel yourself ill used, I am sure we can come to some arrangement.'

'Damn you, Rathbone!' Farringdon snarled. 'It is always so easy for you, isn't it? You made it easy for me, but you humiliated me…stripped me of my pride and my pleasure in life by taking my horses. If I have nothing left, I may as well be hanged—but I'll see you and her dead first…'

He raised his arm, pointing his pistol at Freddie's chest. Caroline saw what he meant to do and launched herself at Freddie's back, pushing him so hard that he stumbled. As Farringdon fired, the shot went over his head and Caroline gave a cry as she felt his ball strike her arm. And then another shot rang out…

* * *

Moments after Freddie and Caroline had entered the woods, the noise of thundering hooves and clattering wheels announced the arrival of an old-fashioned coach at the front of the house. Grooms came running to attend it, for it bore the arms of a marquis. One of the grooms jumped down, and rapped at the doorknocker with some urgency. He was admitted into the hall, and asked for Sir Frederick.

'Sir Frederick has just gone out, but my mistress is at home,' the footman told him. 'May I ask who is calling, sir?'

'You may say that the Marquis of Bollingbrook has arrived and asks if Lady Stroud will see him.'

'Certainly,' the footman said. 'Be so good as to ask the Marquis to step inside, sir. I shall inform her ladyship that he has arrived.'

'What is it, Blake?' Lady Stroud had heard the voices and came out into the hall just as the Marquis had stepped out of his carriage. She went to the open doorway to look at her visitor and frowned. 'Damn my eyes, if it ain't Bollingbrook,' she said. 'All it wants now is for Southmoor to turn up and I shall think myself twenty years old again!'

'Harriet,' Lord Bollingbrook said and doffed his hat to her, with a creaky attempt at gallantry. 'I hope you won't refuse to put me up. I've travelled a deuced long way in too short a time and I'm done up. If you turn me away, I must go to an inn and it will probably be the end of me.'

'Burned your boats, have you?' She gave a cackle of laughter. 'Serves you right, you old rascal. Very well, I'll give you a bed, but if you upset Caroline I'll have my servants throw you out without the blink of an eyelid! I've become very fond of that gel, and that's the truth of it.'

'And you would,' Bollingbrook said, a glint of laughter in his eyes. She had swept him back to the old days when he had wanted to make her his mistress and she had shown him the way home. 'Like her, do you? She's a grand girl, ain't she?'

'Come about, have you, you old fool?' Lady Stroud eyed him severely. 'Well, you had best be prepared to grovel, for she will be back soon—' She broke off, for she had seen them advancing across the lawn, and she sensed that something was wrong. Freddie was supporting Caroline, and, even as she watched, he suddenly bent down and swept her up in his arms.

Bollingbrook turned and saw them. 'Something has happened,' he muttered and would have gone to them had his valet not forestalled him, hurrying to reach them and confer with Sir Frederick. He returned almost immediately.

'Miss Holbrook has been winged, sir. It is just a flesh wound and Sir Frederick has sent for the doctor—but I've told him that I'll see to her for the moment. It wouldn't be the first time I've patched up a similar wound.'

'Damn it!' Bollingbrook said wrathfully. 'What has that idiot been up to with my gel? If she takes harm from this, I'll have his hide!'

'Stop your mithering, you old fool,' Lady Stroud said. 'Whatever happened, it will not have been Freddie's fault.'

The Marquis glared at her, but Freddie had reached them now. He paused for a moment to glance at the Marquis, and then down at the girl he carried in his arms.

'Your grandfather is here, dearest.'

'Put me down for a moment, Freddie.'

He set her gently on her feet, keeping an iron grip about her waist, supporting her as she smiled at her grandfather. 'Do not worry, sir, it is merely a little scratch,' she told him, though her face was deathly pale. 'I shall be better in a moment, but please do not quarrel with Freddie, for I cannot bear it. Besides, it was entirely my fault that I was shot.'

'Well, I shan't quarrel with him,' the Marquis said, 'for you've set your heart on him and I don't want to be at odds with you, Caroline. I've come here to tell you that I'm sorry and ask you to forgive me.'

'Of course I forgive you,' she said, and then looked at Freddie. 'Do you think you could carry me upstairs? I am feeling a little odd…' She was swooning as Freddie lifted her into his arms. He nodded curtly to the others and went on into the house, swiftly followed by Jenkins.

Lady Stroud turned her fearsome gaze on the Marquis. 'You had better come in, Bollingbrook. You can tell me why you saw fit to forbid that gel to marry my godson in the first place!'

Caroline was barely conscious as Freddie gently deposited her on the bed. However, she revived under the gentle ministrations of the Marquis' valet, her eyelids fluttering open as he finished binding her arm.

'Thank you, Mr Jenkins,' she said, giving him a brave smile. 'You were very gentle and did not hurt me at all.'

'You are a brave young lady,' Jenkins said. 'You'll be as right as ninepence in a day or so, don't you worry. And don't worry about the Marquis, Miss Caroline. His bark is worse than his bite and he thinks the world of you.'

'Thank you.' Caroline looked beyond him to where Freddie still hovered, his expression grim. 'Please do not be cross with me, Freddie. I knew he meant to shoot whatever you said and I couldn't bear it if he had killed you.'

Freddie came to the bed as the valet moved away, discreetly leaving the room. He stood looking at Caroline for a moment, and then he smiled.

'How do you think I should have felt if he had killed you instead? You were very foolish, Caroline…reckless…but I know that you did it because you love me, and that makes me feel humble. I did not expect to be loved that much, my dearest. I have never truly known love before this.'

'Have you not, Freddie?' Caroline asked. The look in his eyes made her want to hold him and never let go. 'I do not see why you should not be loved that much. I think you are everything that is good, honest and decent—and I am very lucky that you love me.' She drew a shaky breath. 'If only we were sure that we could have a child…it would be my dearest wish…'

'Did I not tell you to forget this nonsense, my love? Believe me, you are perfectly healthy, and should have no trouble in bearing a child. There is no hereditary weakness, my love.'

'What makes you so sure?'

'Because my uncle Southmoor told me. He knew Angelica as a child—they were neighbours—and he remembers what happened. She caught scarlet fever as a child and almost died. In the end she recovered, but it left her with a weak heart. He did try to tell your grandfather once, but they had quarrelled years before and Bollingbrook would not listen.'

'Then it could not have been passed down to me through Papa?'

'No, definitely not,' Freddie said. 'My uncle tried to tell Bollingbrook. Angelica's brother lied to him because he wanted to prevent the marriage. It was a cruel lie, my darling, nothing more. Bollingbrook was too proud to listen.'

'So you knew all the time…'

'I wish I had mentioned it the last time we spoke of this,' Freddie said. 'But I thought I had set your mind at rest.' He smiled and leaned forward to kiss her. 'Remember, you are more important to me than anything else. Rest for a while now, my love. The doctor will be here soon, though I believe Jenkins has done all that need be. Your arm will be sore for a while, but no lasting harm has been done.'

'Your men killed Farringdon after he shot me,' Caroline said, remembering the second shot that had felled their enemy. 'So there will be no more attempts on either my life or yours.'

'It is over now,' he said with a grim look of satisfaction. 'But I must talk to your grandfather. It is time that we settled our differences.'

'You won't quarrel with him?'

Freddie smiled. 'I promise not to quarrel with him, Caroline—but I cannot promise that he will not quarrel with me…'

Caroline lay back against her pillows with a smile. Her arm was very sore and she thought that she might like to sleep for a while.

Caroline was feeling much recovered when she went downstairs at just after noon the following day. Lady Stroud was concerned and asked if she felt well enough to be up, but Caroline smiled and told her that there was no need to worry.

'My arm is a little sore,' she said, 'but the medicine the doctor gave me ensured that I slept and I do not care to lie abed too long.'

'I dare say my gel is as strong as an ox,' Bollingbrook said, looking at her with pride. It was obvious that Freddie had passed on the good news and he was now able to face the idea of her marriage with equanimity.

'Grandfather—' she began when the sound of a door-knocker and voices in the hall was heard. The next moment the parlour door opened and Mrs Milbank came in, shortly to be followed by her husband.

'Mama…' Caroline was astonished as she saw her, for she had imagined her on board a ship bound for Italy. 'Why are you here? I don't understand…'

Mrs Milbank was looking decidedly young and fashionable in her green silk gown. 'Caroline, my love,' she cried and opened her arms as Caroline went to embrace her. 'I could not rest for thinking of you, and so Mr Milbank said we should come and see if you were all right for ourselves before we leave for our honeymoon.' She suddenly realised that Caroline's arm was in a sling and gasped. 'But you are hurt! What has happened to you?'

'Stop fussing, woman,' Bollingbrook said, glaring at her. 'She is quite able to take care of herself without you mewing over her like a broody tabby. If you must know, my girl is a heroine and saved Sir Frederick's life!'

'I think I know my own daughter, sir. And I shall thank you to keep your opinions to yourself!' Mrs Milbank gave him a furious look, which startled him and then made him chuckle with laughter. 'I do not see what is so funny, sir, when my poor daughter is injured…'

'Damn me, Mrs Milbank, but it seems you suddenly acquired the spirit of a lion. I shall have to revise my opinion of you.'

'Caroline?' Marianne ignored Bollingbrook's sally, her anxious eyes on her daughter.

'It is nothing much, Mama,' Caroline said. 'Please, come up to my room where we can be private and I shall explain everything to you.'

Mrs Milbank stared at her in silence for a moment, and then sighed. 'It seems that I was wrong to delay your wedding, Caroline. You are not a little girl any longer, and I dare say you know your own mind. Yes, I shall come with you and you may tell me everything…'

'I was beginning to despair of ever having you to myself,' Freddie said to Caroline as they walked in the garden that evening. 'But perhaps it is as well that Bollingbrook and your mama are both here. They have finally settled it between them that we are to be married without more delay.'

'Now they are falling out over who is to pay for the reception,' Caroline said and gurgled with laughter. 'But Mama is no longer afraid of him and I think that they are secretly enjoying the battle. Indeed, they may even end up liking each other!'

'I am sure they already do,' Freddie said. 'I have invited my uncle to come for the wedding. I dare say there may be fireworks when he and Bollingbrook meet, but I believe we shall weather it.'

'Oh, I do not fear any of them,' Caroline said, gazing up into his eyes. 'I have nothing to fear now, dearest Freddie.'

Freddie reached out for her, gathering her into his arms, careful to avoid touching her right arm, which he knew to be a little sore. 'I love you so much, my darling girl. You do know that I would have married you even if you had inherited a weakness that prevented us having children, don't you?' he said, a growl of passion in his voice. 'You mean everything to me, Caroline. I want your children, but more than anything

I want you…' He kissed her hungrily, the desire flaring between them. 'Oh, God, I want you so much…'

Caroline melted into him, her body seeming to dissolve in the heat of their desire. She let herself drift on the pleasure of his caress, which was more intimate and passionate than anything that had passed between them before that night, his fingers lightly brushing her breasts.

'I love you…' she whispered, knowing that if he asked she would give herself to him now this night. Indeed, her body was clamouring for his touch.

With a groan of resignation, Freddie moved away. He had been swept to the brink, but drew back at the last. 'You are a sweet, wicked minx,' he muttered hoarsely. 'But torment me as you will, I shall wait for our wedding night.'

The sun was showering its blessing on them as they came out of church that morning. The bells rang out and a small crowd had gathered to wish the bride well, throwing handfuls of rose petals at her and Freddie as they walked to the carriage waiting to take them back to Lady Stroud's house, where it had been decided the wedding would be held to save more delay.

Freddie leaned forward to kiss Caroline on the mouth as the horses started forwards. 'Did it please you to have most of your family there for the wedding?'

'Oh, yes, very much,' Caroline said, smiling up at him. He looked so very handsome and she was so much in love. 'I was glad to hear that Tom doesn't have to go to Jamaica just yet after all—and the news that he is to marry Julia is wonderful! It has all worked out very well, has it not?'

'Yes, very well,' Freddie said. 'Now, tell me, my love—

do you wish to give a ball for our friends or travel abroad immediately?'

'I think perhaps I should like to spend a little time alone with you at your estate, Freddie,' Caroline said. 'And then we may give a ball before we go travelling—if it pleases you?'

He reached out to touch her cheek, trailing one finger down to her throat and sending little shivers of delight down her spine. 'You must know, my beloved, that for the rest of my life I want only to please you. I told you that I should probably never say no to you again, Caroline, and I meant it.'

'Oh, no, you will spoil me,' she said. 'Besides, you have said many things to me, Freddie. I seem to recall that you have several times promised to spank me.'

His eyes danced with amusement, for she was teasing him more often these days, and he liked it. 'Ah, yes, so I did,' he said, 'but do you know, my love, I think that must wait for a while. Our guests are expecting us at the reception my godmother has given for us, and, much as I shall look forward to the prospect, I do not think that we should keep them waiting—do you?'

Caroline smiled. They had reached the house now and all their guests were waiting to greet them. They had invited only their closest friends, most of whom had been in Bath and not forced to travel too far.

Caroline passed from one to the other, receiving congratulations and gifts. It was not until just before she was about to go up and change into her travelling gown that Julia asked to speak to her.

'You look so happy,' Julia said and there were shadows in her eyes that made Caroline reach out to take her hand. 'I am so happy for you, dearest Caroline.'

Caroline leaned forward to kiss her cheek. 'I am so glad that we are to be sisters, Julia.'

Julia blushed. 'I had almost given up hope. I could not believe it when Mama told me he had asked for me.'

'I knew he loved you, but he had such a hard struggle with the estate after Papa died. I suppose he needed to be sure he could support a wife before he dared think of approaching you.'

'I would have married him even had your grandfather not given him such a generous gift,' Julia said. 'I love him.'

'I know.' Caroline embraced her. 'I am so pleased for you both.' She kissed her cheek again and then saw her mother coming towards her. 'I must go and change, Julia. It will be your wedding soon…'

Caroline woke and yawned, a smile forming on her lips as she realised how good she felt. Freddie's passionate love-making had kept them both awake for much of the previous night. She stretched, remembering the sweetness of being loved by a man who had taken every care to please her. She had never realised how delightful the pleasures of loving could be.

The bed was cold beside her, and, glancing at the small enamelled clock on the chest beside the bed, she realised that she had slept long after her normal hour. Freddie must have left her to sleep on, which was very considerate of him in the circumstances.

Looking about her, Caroline saw that her maid had been in earlier and left a tray on the table near the window, but when she got up to investigate, she discovered that the choco-late pot had gone cold. She was about to ring for someone to come when she glanced out of the window, and what she saw there sent all thoughts of breakfast from her mind. Freddie was talking to some men on the lawn and they were preparing a balloon for flight.

She gave a shout of glee, flinging off her nightgown and hurrying behind the dressing screen to wash and dress in one of her simplest gowns, for which she needed no help from her maid. Within a few minutes she was running down the stairs and out of the front door, which the footman opened for his popular young mistress with a smile. Her hair was flying about her face, for she had not bothered to tie it up. She looked much younger than her years, the glow of excitement in her eyes as she ran across the smooth lawns towards the small group of men. And then Freddie turned and saw her.

'Ah, there you are, my love,' he said, smiling at her, a gleam of amusement in his dark eyes as he recognised that she had dressed hurriedly. 'I was about to come in search of you. We are almost ready for flight. I take it that you wish to go up?'

'Oh yes, please,' she said, her eyes bright with pleasure. 'You know that I do. It is so good of you to arrange this for me.'

'You were disappointed the last time,' Freddie said, 'which was possibly my fault for arranging such a public display. But you know this is a hobby of mine, and you will be able to go up quite often should you wish it. We are always trying new things—are we not, Mr Jackson?'

'Yes, sir,' the balloon master said and smiled at his sponsor's lady. Sir Frederick had some ideas for flight, which had not yet been thought of, and one day they would no doubt put the theory to the test. 'We have a fine day for it, Lady Rathbone. The wind is in the right quarter and we should be able to stay up for some time—if you wish it?'

'Oh, yes, please,' Caroline said, giving him her hand as he helped her to climb into the basket. Freddie hopped in beside her, and the other men on the ground began to cast off the ropes that were anchoring the balloon to the earth. As it started to lift, Caroline felt a little strange. She watched the people on the ground become smaller as the balloon started to drift across the sky, rising higher and higher until they looked down on the treetops. 'Oh, Freddie,' she breathed as he came to put his arm about her waist, 'isn't it wonderful? I never dreamed anything could be this exciting.'

'No,' Freddie agreed, but he was looking at her, at her lovely, expressive face and her glorious hair tumbling about her shoulders. He was remembering the previous night when he had seemed as though he could never have his fill of her, thinking of the pleasure she gave him with every word, every smile. Had he been bored with his life only a few short months ago? He certainly wasn't now, for every day seemed fresh and new. 'Do you know, my darling, neither have I…'

* * * * *

Special Offers

Every month we put together collections and
longer reads written by your favourite authors.

Here are some of next month's highlights—
and don't miss our fabulous discount online!

On sale 15th February   On sale 15th February   On sale 1st March

Save 20%
on all Special Releases

Find out more at
www.millsandboon.co.uk/specialreleases

*Visit us
Online*

0313/ST/MB407

The World of Mills & Boon®

There's a Mills & Boon® series that's perfect for you. We publish ten series and, with new titles every month, you never have to wait long for your favourite to come along.

Blaze.
Scorching hot, sexy reads
4 new stories every month

By Request
Relive the romance with the best of the best
9 new stories every month

Cherish™
Romance to melt the heart every time
12 new stories every month

Desire™
Passionate and dramatic love stories
8 new stories every month